PRAISE FOR
THE HOUSE ON FORTUNE STREET

"The most durable structure here, in fact, is not a house but the novel itself, whose design unites so seamlessly with its intentions that one wants to admire it from every angle.... [The narrative] keeps turning and turning, like an architectural model on a revolving pedestal, revealing something new with every spin.... It leaves readers with a surprising hopefulness. Some of this arises from the pleasures of its style: Livesey has chosen every detail here with precision.... But the book's hopefulness has an even-deeper source: the continuity of the English literary tradition.... Again, Livesey's skill keeps these relationships perfectly organic and never forced. By situating her novel firmly within the house of literature, she honors its history while adding on some elegantly appointed rooms of her own."
—Donna Rifkind, *Washington Post Book World*

"It's possible to imagine that this book is exactly what Murdoch meant by the notion that we profit from fiction—even the saddest, gravest works—by our pleasure in it.... Livesey's work—six novels, including this one, and a collection of short stories—displays the marvelous control of a writer who conjures equally well the tangible, sensory world (weather, furniture, kettles on the boil) and the mysteries, stranger and wilder, that flicker at the border of that world.... Even in paragraphs in which nothing actually happens, Livesey can make the blood race.... Beautiful, engaging."
—Carrie Brown, *Boston Globe*

"Splendid.... Like a psychotherapist, Livesey deftly unwinds their stories, exposing the ways in which each [character] learned to live with betrayal early on. Watching her work is mesmerizing; smart and suspenseful, this is a novel that will keep you in its thrall."
—Michelle Green, *People*

"With empathy and deftness, Margot Livesey brings to life a vivid circle of characters whose lives twist and turn upon each other in a Möbius strip of emotional entanglements. Structurally daring and compulsively readable, *The House on Fortune Street* illuminates the complexities of love in some of its most difficult guises and of loss in all of its immensity."

—Geraldine Brooks, author of *People of the Book* and *March*

"Livesey [is] a shrewd diagnostician of Western mini-maladies. . . . Ms. Livesey's writing is acutely observant; her psychological algebra is admirable and sometimes astonishing."

—Richard Eder, *New York Times*

"Resonant, heartbreaking. . . . A spectacularly compassionate work, brimming with sharp insight into why we do the things we do even when we know we shouldn't. . . . Livesey . . . gets everything right."

—Connie Ogle, *Miami Herald*

"I loved this book. *The House on Fortune Street* pulled me in and kept me rapt from start to finish. Margot Livesey is writing at her very best."   —Ann Patchett, author of *Run* and *Bel Canto*

"Engrossing. . . .While the psychological mystery that spurs the novel forward is gripping, it's her clarity, of both writing and understanding, that elevates the novel."

—Yvonne Zipp, *Christian Science Monitor*

"This intertwining novel about four Londoners references *Jane Eyre* and *Great Expectations*. It's fitting because *House* might become a classic all its own."   —*Entertainment Weekly* (The Must List)

"Fascinating."   —*MORE* magazine

"Beautifully crafted . . . . Breathtaking."   —*Newark Star-Ledger*

"Glorious. . . . Longtime readers of Livesey's fiction will recognize her signature attributes: enticing, elusive characters; bright lives that come to reveal dark, even sinister mysteries; a ravishing prose style. . . . Extraordinarily rewarding. . . . *The House on Fortune Street* is stunningly ambitious. In its exploration of these lives, intricately entangled and richly imagined, in its deep and wise comprehension of human possibility, and in the gorgeousness of its vision, it is not just a superb book and not just a transporting one. It is luminous."
—Erin McGraw, *Raleigh News & Observer*

"Absorbing. . . . The pieces cross-reference and fit together seamlessly. . . . Livesey's use of the classics enriches the narrative."
—*Publishers Weekly*

"Another probing, satisfying novel from Livesey. . . . Moving, gruffly tender, and piercingly truthful. Livesey has plenty of critical respect already, but her talents merit a broad popular audience as well."
—*Kirkus Reviews* (starred review)

"Intricately weaving the cause and effect of each character's circumstances into four self-contained but essentially linked episodes, Livesey—polished and intriguing as ever—incisively explores the sinuous themes of regret and responsibility, truth and trust with an understated yet tenacious certainty."   —*Booklist*

"Keeps readers brooding over the power of secrets in this dark and disturbing psychological tale."   —*Library Journal*

THE HOUSE ON FORTUNE STREET

ALSO BY MARGOT LIVESEY

Fiction

Learning by Heart

Homework

Criminals

The Missing World

Eva Moves the Furniture

Banishing Verona

THE HOUSE ON FORTUNE STREET

A Novel

MARGOT LIVESEY

HARPER PERENNIAL

NEW YORK • LONDON • TORONTO • SYDNEY • NEW DELHI • AUCKLAND

HARPER ● PERENNIAL

A hardcover edition of this book was published in 2008 by HarperCollins Publishers.

P.S.™ is a trademark of HarperCollins Publishers.

FIRST HARPER PERENNIAL EDITION PUBLISHED 2009.

The Library of Congress has catalogued the hardcover edition as follows:

The house on Fortune Street : a novel / Margot Livesey.—1st ed.
p. cm.
ISBN 978-0-06-145152-2
1. Luck—Fiction. 2. Psychological fiction. 3. Love stories. I. Title
PR9199.3L563 C47   2008
813'.54—dc22   2007029611

ISBN 978-0-06-145154-6 (pbk.)

10   11   12   13   ID/RRD   10   9   8   7   6   5   4

For Andrea Barrett

1

A SOFT NEST

THE LETTER CAME, DECEPTIVELY, IN THE KIND OF ENVELOPE A businesslike friend, or his supervisor, might use. It was typed on rather heavy white paper and signed with the pleasing name of Beth Giardini. Sean read the brief paragraphs twice, admiring the mixture of courtesy and menace. Perhaps it had escaped his notice that he was overdrawn by one hundred and twenty-eight pounds? As he doubtless recalled, the bank had waived the penalty last time; this time, regretfully, they must impose their normal fee. Would he kindly telephone to discuss the matter at his earliest convenience?

Sitting in the empty kitchen, surrounded by the evidence of Abigail's hasty departure, Sean understood that he was suffering from what his beloved Keats had called bill pestilence. When he was still living in Oxford, still married, most people he knew, including himself and his wife, were poor but their poverty hadn't seemed to matter. Of course he had yearned after expensive books and sometimes, walking at night, he and Judy had stopped to gaze enviously through the windows of the large lit-up houses, but for the most part his needs had fitted his income. In London, however, living with Abigail, the two had rapidly fallen out of joint, as Sean was only too well aware. This letter was not the result of any reckless extravagance. For six months he had been trying to cut back on photocopying and refusing invitations to the pub.

Now gazing at Abigail's plate, rimmed with crumbs and one glistening fragment of marmalade, he did his best not to dwell on all the steps, large and small, that had brought this letter to his door. Instead he concentrated on the hundred and twenty-eight pounds, not a huge sum but a serious amount to borrow and, realistically, he would need more, at least two hundred, to remain solvent. On the back of the envelope he jotted down dates and numbers: when he might receive his small salary from the theater, when various bills were due. The figures were undeniable, and irreconcilable.

He tried to think of people from whom he might borrow: his brother, one or two Oxford friends, his old friend Tyler. Much longer and more immediately available was the list of those whom he could not ask; his thrifty parents and Abigail jostled for first place. But then his second slice of toast popped up, and so did a name: Valentine. Sean had vowed, after their last book together, not to take on anything else until he had finished his dissertation, but such a vow, made only to the four walls of his study, was clearly irrelevant in the light of this current emergency. At once the figures on the envelope grew a little less daunting. With luck Valentine's agent would be able to find them another project soon. And if he knew he had money coming in, Sean thought, he could phone the bank and arrange a sensible overdraft.

He was reaching for the marmalade when he heard a sound at the front door. Thinking Abigail had forgotten something, he seized the letter, thrust it into the pocket of his jeans, and tried to impersonate a man having a leisurely breakfast. But it was only someone delivering a leaflet, one of the dozens advertising pizza or estate agents that arrived at the house each day. In the silent aftermath Sean couldn't help noticing that his familiar surroundings had taken on a new intensity; the sage-colored walls were more vivid, the stove shone more brightly, the refrigerator purred more insistently, the glasses gleamed. His home here was in danger.

FOUR DAYS LATER SEAN WAS SITTING ON VALENTINE'S SOFA, SCAN-ning the theater reviews in the newspaper, while across the room Valentine talked to his agent on the phone.

"So, it'll be the usual three payments?" The response elicited brisk note taking. Then Sean heard his name. "Yes, Sean and I are doing this together. He'll keep my nose to the grindstone."

Giving up all pretense of reading, he set aside the paper and studied his friend. In his gray linen shirt and expensive jeans, Valentine looked ready to hold forth, at a moment's notice, on some television arts program. His canary yellow hair had darkened in the last few years, and his features, which when he was an undergraduate used to crowd the middle of his face, had now taken up their proper places between his square chin and his high forehead. Even in June, Sean noticed, he was already mysteriously tanned.

"Excellent," said Valentine. Glancing up from the notebook, he twitched the corners of his mouth. After several more superlatives he hung up. "Well," he said, rubbing his hands, "I think this calls for an early drink."

He refused to say more until he had fetched a beer for Sean, and a gin and tonic for himself. Then he raised his glass and broke the news. His agent, Jane, had called to say that the Belladonna Society, a small but well-funded organization founded soon after the First World War, was commissioning a handbook for euthanasia. "They want to make the case for legalizing euthanasia and to give an overview of the medical stuff. They'll provide most of the material but there'll be some research and we'll have to do interviews with medical personnel, relatives."

As Valentine described the society's proposal, the number of pages, and the pay, Sean felt a cold finger run down his spine. "But isn't this like telling people how to kill themselves?" he said. "Isn't it better not to know certain things?"

"I don't think so." Valentine swirled his gin and tonic. "As I understand it the information is out there anyway. Our job is to present it in the sanest, most lucid form. Just because you give someone a gun," he added, his chin rising fractionally to meet Sean's objections, "doesn't mean they have to use it."

"I think people usually do feel they have to use guns," Sean said. "And I think whoever gave them the gun is partly responsible. Couldn't Jane find us something else?"

Feigning exasperation, or perhaps genuinely annoyed, Valentine popped his eyes, a trick that Sean had been observing for over a decade without being able to decide whether his friend could actually move his eyeballs, or if they bulged anyway and he merely flexed the lids. "Not immediately," he said. "And I don't see how I could ask her to. She worked hard to put this deal together. The society is paying surprisingly well."

Faced with the compelling argument of his finances, not to mention Valentine's, Sean was at a loss. How could he explain that any major decision had always felt to him like a kind of death, an irrevocable closing down of certain possibilities; he had no desire to spend his days in the company of people who really were making a fatal choice. Besides, Valentine had already changed the topic. Had Sean heard that one of their former tutors was doing a television series on utopian communities, beginning with medieval clerics and going all the way to Findhorn?

B Y THE TIME SEAN PRIED HIMSELF FREE, AFTER ONE MORE BEER, the book was a foregone conclusion. Outside, the gloom of the June evening mirrored his feelings. It was nearly midsummer, but the sky was overcast, and at the underground station a chill wind sliced across the platform. He paced restlessly from one vending machine to another, trying to resist the memories that Valentine's remarks about Oxford had aroused. Eventually the train faltered into the station and, after several minutes, departed in the same uncertain fashion. They limped south to Brixton. Above ground again Sean discovered the pavement speckled with rain. When he turned into Fortune Street the sycamore trees on either side were fluttering light and dark in the wind. Underfoot, dead leaves crackled, creating the momentary illusion that, during the hours he had spent with Valentine, the entire summer had passed by.

The house came into view. As so often these days, the upstairs windows, behind which he and Abigail lived, were dark; she was, he recalled, at one of her endless meetings. Downstairs, however, in Dara's flat, a window glowed. Briefly he considered knocking at her door. Dara was Abigail's oldest friend—they had met, like him and Valentine, at university—and she now worked as a counselor at a women's center in Peckham. A few weeks ago, when he'd run into her on the way home, she had invited him in for coffee. He had found himself sitting in her pleasant living room, complaining about Abigail's busyness: ever since she started the theater, she never seemed to have a moment; there was always a patron to be wooed, an actor to be coaxed or coached. Dara had been reassuring: Abigail was such a perfectionist, the theater would be on a better footing soon. Nonetheless he had returned upstairs with the sense that he had opened a book that ought to be kept tightly closed. Now he could feel that, given the chance, he would once again reveal to Dara's solicitous gaze what should remain hidden. He took out his keys and continued to his part of the house.

Inside he turned on lights, debated another beer, settled for tea, and sat down with a stack of plays. He had started reading scripts for Abigail's theater a little over a year ago—his official title was literary manager—and at first he had longed to write to each author, personally and at length, about how his or her work might be improved. But he had soon realized that the vast majority of the plays that flooded into the theater office were mediocre, or worse. His job was not so much to succor talent, as the soul-deadening one of saying no, no, no. He had learned to read quickly and savagely. Often weeks passed without his encountering a single submission that merited even a complete reading, let alone a second one. Still Abigail insisted that he was doing vital work. Finding new playwrights was one of the ways the Roustabout Theater would create an identity, which, given that the company had no actual theater, only a name, an office, and half a dozen underpaid employees, was particularly important.

The first couple of scripts he dismissed after a few pages. A look at the cast list of the third—eleven Girl Guides and a monster—was enough to place it in the reject pile. He reached for the fourth. At the sight of the title, *Half in Love*, the line rose to his lips: "'Oft-times I have been half in love with easeful death.'" And when he turned to the cast list, there were the familiar names: John Keats, Fanny Brawne, Benjamin Bailey, Joseph Severn, Fanny Keats. Sean felt a surge of indignation. If anyone was going to write a bad play about his favorite poet, it ought to be he. He had memorized "To Autumn" when he was sixteen to impress a reluctant girlfriend; almost a decade later Keats had played a crucial role in his meeting with his future wife; and for the last six years, nearly seven, he had gone over and over the poet's brief life as he struggled with his dissertation. Now, alone in the empty flat, he gave in to the memories that had, since he left Valentine's, been begging for attention.

A few weeks into the first term of his doctorate, Sean had attended a lecture on the Romantics. He had carefully chosen a seat between two empty chairs in the back row where, if the don failed to live up to his reputation, he could read unobserved. But just as the lecture was about to begin, a woman hurried in and sank into the chair on his left.

"The Romantics," proclaimed the don, "have the distinction of being not only the first coherent movement in British poetry but also the first self-conscious movement. That self-consciousness, however, had severe limitations."

Sean glanced over to see that his companion, whose head barely reached his shoulder, had her notebook open and was writing down the don's remarks interspersed with exclamations: *Rubbish! Balderdash! Crap! Bollocks!* . . .

The don moved on to Keats and she turned to a new page. "In the first fifteen years of his life Keats lost both parents, his grandfather, and a younger brother. His beloved brother Tom died when the poet was twenty-three, shortly before he started the 'Eve of St. Agnes.' When he wrote, 'The death or sickness of someone has always spoilt my hours,' he was being absolutely literal. No wonder the question of immortality seemed so pressing, even before his own illness. He believed, intellectually and viscerally, as he asserts in the magisterial opening of *Endymion*, that 'A Thing of Beauty is a joy forever.'

"As for women—" The don sighed. "Sometimes I think he would have given all his great odes to be four inches taller." He began to quote from a letter Keats had written in 1818 to his friend Benjamin Bailey: "'When I was a Schoolboy I thought a fair Woman a pure Goddess, my mind was a soft nest in which some one of them slept though she knew it not . . .'"

When the lecture ended the woman turned to Sean. "Excuse me," she said—she had a dimple in one cheek and a long, graceful neck—"but wasn't that awfully predictable?"

Sean had agreed that it was, and suggested a drink. Later he learned that arriving at the last minute and having strong opinions were two of Judy's more consistent traits. Like Sean, she claimed Keats as her favorite poet; she felt a special closeness with him, she joked, because she was the same height. "You'd have towered over him," she said. She had given up a promising career in data analysis to return to university and was writing a dissertation on Mary Elizabeth Braddon and her masterpiece *Lady Audley's Secret*. Sean described his own similar trajectory; he had spent five years working in insurance before deciding to do a Ph.D. He was studying the connection between Keats's medical training and his poetry. "I don't remember any medical references," Judy had said, "but that sounds fascinating." They had moved in together by Christmas, married by midsummer. For several happy years they had bicycled to the library, read and photocopied, eaten with friends, struggled with supervisors and teaching, flirted with the Socialist Worker, explored the Cotswolds. And then . . .

Quickly Sean retreated from these dangerous reefs and returned his attention to the play. In the opening scene, the twenty-two-year-old Keats and his fourteen-year-old sister, Fanny, were strolling on Hampstead Heath. Fanny begged her brother to let her come and live with him, and Keats urged the virtues of her continuing with her guardian. "I lead a muddled life, Fanny. I cannot offer you the constancy you need." As Sean set it aside to read later—he had the unnerving feeling that it might be quite good—the clock on the nearby church chimed eight. Three more plays, he thought, and then he would order a takeaway. He was reaching for the next one when he heard the front door open. Before he could move, Abigail was in the room, cheeks pink, hair flying, arms around him.

"You're here," she said, kissing him on each cheek and, wetly, on the mouth. "My meeting finished early."

From one second to the next everything changed. The dark mood that Sean had carried to Valentine's and brought home again in a slightly altered form was dispelled. Abigail had stopped at the supermarket. She piled groceries on the table, put on water for pasta, and began to chop sun-dried tomatoes. He opened a bottle of wine, washed a lettuce, and lit candles. While they cooked, he listened to Abigail talk about the theater and waited for the right moment to divulge his own news. The tour she had been trying to arrange for that autumn was coming together. They had bookings in three towns and two more looked promising. "I think this could be our breakthrough, Sean," she said. "A way to stay afloat and pay everyone a living wage. The arts council is very keen on the provinces, especially if you visit schools and nursing homes."

"Excellent," said Sean heartily. The theater already took so much of Abigail's time—did this mean she would be still busier?—but he knew better than to query her enthusiasm. Instead he watched the little curlicues of Parmesan emerge from the grater and agreed that outreach workshops were essential.

Soon the pasta was steaming in a bowl, the salad, freshly tossed, in another. They sat at their usual places and clinked glasses. "Here's to us," said Sean. "I have a new project too." He described his visit to Valentine and the euthanasia book.

"I bet you'll hear some amazing stories," said Abigail.

"Certainly some sad ones. Would you have killed your father? I mean, of course, if he'd asked you to?" Abigail's father had died of a brain tumor four years before she met Sean; she had nursed him in his final months.

"I don't know. He never did." She pursed her lips and thrust out her chin, a pouting expression he found particularly endearing because it contradicted her habitual prettiness. "But if he had," she continued, "if he'd been in pain, I'd have done my best. What about you? Have you ever wanted to put someone out of their misery?"

"Besides myself? No. Touch wood"—he rapped the table—"I've never known anyone with a terminal illness. It's a bit like being a virgin, or never having seen the ocean. There's a whole area of experience out there which I know will track me down. I just hope it's later rather than sooner. I have to confess"—he almost rapped the table a second time—"that the idea of this book makes me nervous."

"Why?" Abigail reached for the pasta. The first few times they had eaten together she had barely touched her food, but that, he soon learned, was an anomaly. She often ate more than he did, and joked about her birdlike metabolism. Watching her refill her plate, he thought she was the picture of health and certainty.

"I worry I might find it depressing," he ventured, "all these people with terrible illnesses, hoarding pills and plastic bags, stories with only one ending. Suddenly being an agnostic doesn't seem so simple. I really don't know what to think about that stuff. Death," he elaborated in response to her raised eyebrows, "the afterlife."

"More?" said Abigail, setting down her plate and reaching for his. "Isn't it better, though, to give people a choice, rather than forcing them to endure until modern medicine decides to release them?"

"Thanks. But what if you change your mind? What if you discover after it's too late that you did want one more day, even if all you do is watch the light move across the bedroom ceiling, and you die hating yourself? For most people the gap between thought and action is huge."

But not for you, he almost added. Abigail had already been talking about starting a theater when they met and in their early conversations had quizzed him about nineteenth-century dramatists. He had enjoyed their discussions, not recognizing them for what they were—another step in Abigail's courtship—and never expecting that the theater would become a reality. But soon after he moved in with her, a famous actor had agreed to star in her first production; people started returning her calls. "You brought me luck, Sean," she exclaimed. And suddenly she was gone from eight in the morning until midnight. "The house will be nice and quiet," she had said. "It'll be perfect for finishing your dissertation." The house had been perfect for many things—regret, loneliness, watching every single Arsenal match—but not for the sustained concentration that was necessary for Sean to bring into focus the mass of material he had gathered over several years as he changed the topic of his dissertation. Judy had been right; even the closest reading of the poems revealed few traces of Keats's medical studies.

Now Abigail wiped her plate with a slice of bread, and announced that she had to make some phone calls. Only as she stood up did she ask, muffling the crucial question in the scrape of her chair, how much he was getting paid for the book.

"I'm not sure. Valentine's agent is the one who sorts all that out."

"Whatever they offer," she said, heading for the door, "ask for more."

Alone, loading the dishwasher, Sean recalled, not for the first time, the conversation he and Abigail had had at their third meeting, at the British Museum. Standing in front of the Elgin Marbles, she had told him about the unexpected windfall from an aunt that had enabled her, at the age of twenty-six, to buy a house on Fortune Street in Brixton. "There's a downstairs flat," she explained. "The rent more or less pays the mortgage." "What a good arrangement," Sean had said, and pointed out the athletic centaurs. Later, when they became lovers, she had assured him that life in London didn't need to be expensive; she had made his poverty, like his marriage, seem irrelevant. For six months after he moved in they had taken turns, amicably, paying for groceries and films. Then one evening, walking home from the pub through the misty streets, his arm around her shoulders, her hand in the pocket of his jeans, she had remarked, as casually as if she were commenting on the weather, that he must start paying rent.

"Rent?" Sean had said. "But I thought Dara's rent covered things."

"No," said Abigail, and for several steps it seemed that might be her entire answer. Then she began to list all the expenses: insurance, water, taxes, repairs. "You need to contribute," she said.

He wanted to remind her of her promise that his work on Keats, a thing of beauty, was more important than the contents of his wallet. Instead, staring at the halo around the nearest streetlight, he asked how much she had in mind.

"I don't know." Through the fabric of his jeans she squeezed thoughtfully. "A hundred?"

"A month?"

"A week."

"I don't think," he had managed, "I could afford that."

She had finally agreed to two hundred pounds a month. The next day Sean had phoned Valentine, and they had embarked on their second project, the biography of a minor film star. To his own surprise he had, when he told Abigail about it, reduced the amount of the advance by four thousand. Another piece of the idyll gone—the promise of a life without lies—but only this one, he had vowed. Now, as he closed the dishwasher and set it humming on its journey, he realized that he was already planning to reduce the new advance too, and he felt entirely justified in doing so.

O VER THE NEXT WEEK FAXES AND E-MAILS FLEW BACK AND FORTH between Valentine and Sean, the agent and the Belladonna Society. An agreement was reached and a meeting arranged between the two authors and the society's secretary. One hot June afternoon (the weather had turned summery again), he and Valentine made their way through the stuffy streets and up four flights of stairs to an office near Ludgate Circus. The ruddy-cheeked man who rose to greet them looked, Sean thought, in his crumpled white shirt and faded brown trousers, as if he ought to be striding across a field behind a herd of cows. The secretary thanked them enthusiastically for taking on the book, apologized for the heat, turned on a fan, and urged them to sit down. On the table was a thick stack of documents. As the top pages lifted in the fan's passing, Sean glimpsed the heading "Interviews with the Deceased." For a moment he pictured a group of well-dressed people, who happened to be dead, strolling back and forth on the terrace of a Tuscan villa, sipping the local Chianti, and congratulating themselves: "The best thing I ever did," "Wish I'd had the guts to do it five years earlier."

"The spearhead of our argument," said the secretary, "is the case histories and interviews. I'm sure I don't need to tell you that it's important to include a range of ages, classes, occupations, races. We want to show that euthanasia is not just some white, middle-class, elderly thing."

"Though it mostly is, isn't it?" said Valentine, smiling broadly as he often did when being contentious.

"Not at all." The secretary fanned himself with a folder; Sean caught the flash of a wedding ring. "Given their circumstances, surprisingly few elderly people choose to die. Committing euthanasia is a sign of mental vigor, not the reverse."

"What about the role of doctors?" said Sean, wanting both to change the subject and to assert himself.

"That's tricky and, of course, a key factor. As the law stands a doctor who publicly admits to euthanasia faces jail. Privately it's a different story. Quite a number of physicians have talked to me about assisting patients. And of course there's a controversial no-man's-land between active assistance and benign neglect. Forgive my asking: do either of you have any personal experience with these matters?"

"I'm afraid so," said Valentine, and launched into an account of an aunt who had had a stroke. The secretary stopped fanning and leaned forward. Watching the way his face changed as he followed Valentine's story, Sean revised his earlier impression; this man would be wasted on cows. "And how did you?" the secretary asked delicately.

"That's the trouble," said Valentine, "we didn't. She took an overdose of one of her medicines but it just made her sick. After that, all we could do was watch her suffer."

"Terrible." The secretary's ruddy cheeks crinkled and he reached out to pat Valentine's arm. "You have my condolences but it does make you the ideal author for this book."

They discussed a timetable—the manuscript must be ready by December—and how to organize additional interviews. If there was anything he could do, the secretary said, don't hesitate to get in touch. The three of them exchanged rather damp handshakes. As Sean followed Valentine down the stairs he started to offer his own condolences. He had uttered only a phrase when Valentine, from the flight below, gave him a sardonic upward glance. In the embrace of his own stupidity, Sean fell silent.

B ACK AT THE HOUSE HE LEFT HIS BICYCLE IN THE COOL HALLWAY and ascended to his study. Like the society's office it was on the top floor, and step by step the temperature rose until, when he at last pushed open the door, the caged heat leaped out. He set the folder of case histories and interviews the secretary had given him on the desk and went to raise the window. There was not a breath of wind. Standing with his hands on the sash, he could see the honeysuckle in Dara's garden four floors below, and the plum tree with its first green burden of fruit. Sometimes last summer, on warm evenings, she had invited him and Abigail to have a drink. The three of them had sat around her picnic table, discussing the virtues of organic wine and whether Sean and Abigail should do the Thames walk this year. Often while they talked Dara sketched, making quick, beautiful drawings of her two friends, her garden, the neighbor's cat.

He stepped back from the window, and the view of the garden was replaced by the rooftops, chimney pots, and aerials that, from many long hours at his desk, he knew in intimate detail. This small room was his sanctuary, the place where, for good and ill, he felt most like himself. When he moved in with Abigail, they had painted it together, and chosen a new carpet. After the fitters left, he had remarked that the color reminded him of the beach where he'd played as a child. "I'm glad," said Abigail. "I want you to feel that this is your home." He had reached for her jeans and pulled her to the floor.

Subsequently he had put up shelves on the long wall and alphabetized his books. On the wall opposite the window he had hung his familiars: portraits of Keats and Fanny Brawne, and a copy of the famous death mask, which he had positioned so that the poet's closed eyes were a little below five feet. More recently he had bought a bookcase for the plays he ferried to and from the theater office; he had placed it near the door to signal their lowly status.

Now, looking around the neat room, he wondered how he was going to manage this third task. He was responsible for six chapters of the euthanasia book, and, to meet the deadline, he would have to exchange them with Valentine by late November, which meant more than a chapter a month. He thought again of the secretary listening so empathetically to Valentine's shabby lies. Suddenly it occurred to him that the man had almost certainly come to his position at the society through loss and hardship. Perhaps a dead wife, he guessed, picturing the gold ring. He glanced down at his own hand, still surprised by its bareness.

ALMOST EVERYONE IN SEAN'S LIFE, INCLUDING HIS FRIENDS, HIS younger brother, and himself, had been baffled by the demise of his marriage. He and Judy had been kindred spirits, and the only real quarrel between them had concerned his dissertation. While Judy worked efficiently, piling up chapters and footnotes, he was stalled in his analysis of Keats's longer poems. His advisor, a pale, angular woman, seemed more interested in the view from her study window than in his theories. It was after one of their more dismal meetings—Georgina had disputed his interpretation of Keats's unfinished faerie tale, "The Cap and Bells"—that he had run into Valentine in the covered market.

The two had become friends as undergraduates and continued to meet occasionally when they both moved to London. Since Sean's return to Oxford they had fallen out of touch; now they greeted each other with enthusiasm. Valentine was in town to review *Mother Courage* at the Playhouse. He suggested a drink which turned into lunch. Over steak and kidney pie, he expressed admiration for Sean's scholarly choice, pursuing a Ph.D., and Sean hastened to reciprocate, praising Valentine's more worldly activities. "How many people"—he waved toward the bar—"give a toss about Keats?"

"In this room"—Valentine pretended a quick survey—"probably eight. The rest prefer Coleridge." Then he confessed that he'd been trying to sell a book proposal. He had heard this morning that it had been rejected, again. From his jacket pocket he produced a letter, and began to read it aloud. The first paragraph was indeed a refusal, but the second mentioned a different project: writing the family history of a well-known Labour peer.

"That sounds interesting," Sean had said. "And it would give you a foot in the door."

By the end of lunch he had talked Valentine into accepting the editor's suggestion and Valentine had talked him into helping with the book. "Join me in Grub Street," he had said, laughing. When Sean went home and told Judy, she too had laughed. A fortnight later, however, when the contract appeared, she had been less amused. He needed to bear down on his dissertation, she argued, not get distracted. He reminded her that he'd been wrestling with the second chapter for most of the last year. A few months more wouldn't make a difference, and the money would. She remained unconvinced, but he had signed the contract, and even she had to admit that their household was a happier place without his writer's block. He no longer spent a morning on a sentence, a week on a paragraph. He liked the comparatively minimal research, and he liked the prospect of seeing the book in stores, where people might buy it and even read it.

Only after they exchanged chapters did he understand that his work was no longer his own; it was inextricably yoked to Valentine's. Valentine had rung up brimming with compliments. "Hey, this is in terrific shape. There's just one or two places where you're being a little too fancy for our readers." Then he asked about his chapters and Sean faltered. They were a mess at every level. The sentences were awkward; the organization muddled; the research poorly integrated. "I'm doing some fine-tuning," he said. "Ironing out some contradictions."

"So when can we put the whole thing together? This weekend?"

"How about next Wednesday?"

He hadn't worked so hard since he was an undergraduate writing essays at the last moment. By the time he finished scarcely a sentence of Valentine's chapters was left untouched. On Tuesday night he was smugly pleased with the results. On Wednesday morning he woke to the complications of what he'd done. He spent the bus journey to London rehearsing conciliatory speeches: Valentine's work was fine, most of the changes were due to the way he, Sean, had written his chapters. As he waited on Valentine's doorstep, he pictured his advisor staring listlessly out of the window while he offered his latest insights. He had always assumed that she was bored. Now he wondered if she hated his prose, despised his research.

Valentine had greeted him exuberantly, poured coffee, and begun to show Sean the changes he'd made on his pages, mostly for the worse. They were on chapter four when the phone rang. "Absolutely," said Valentine into the receiver. "I'm free for the next few weeks."

When he hung up he announced that he'd been asked to do some television reviews; all the pleasures of home, and you could tape them if you fell asleep. Then he looked at the clock and said there was no need to scrutinize every page; they could catch things in copyediting. And so Sean had pointed out a couple of alterations. "I thought headings would help." "This seemed a stronger conclusion." Within no time the manuscript was disappearing into Valentine's briefcase to be delivered to the publisher that afternoon.

Initially Sean had been jubilant. He'd done it, he'd got away with it. The book would be readable, intelligent, unembarrassing. They went out for an excellent meal, the editor was happy, the agent was happy, and Valentine himself seemed oblivious to the transformation his prose had undergone. Only later did Sean grasp the unfortunate precedent he'd established.

He was even slower to realize how working with Valentine had changed his marriage. His harmonious routines with Judy—those long afternoons at the library when they always seemed to reach a good stopping point at the same moment, the predictable discussion about whether to go to the pub on the way home, the pleasant encounters with friends—had been disrupted and were not to be easily restored. Before the book they had always spent weekends together, but that autumn when Sean's old friend Tyler invited them to Sunday lunch and Judy had a cold, he had not thought twice about going to London alone.

And then this woman, with hair the color of corn and eyes that made him think of the flowers his mother grew, had sat down beside him and hung on his every word. A few weeks later she was in Oxford to see a play and had asked, quite casually, if he'd like to have a drink, and a few weeks after that she had accompanied him to the British Museum. Nothing like this had happened to Sean before. University had cured him of the notion that he was an outstanding scholar. As for his appearance, he knew he was tall and dark, but it had never occurred to him that the combination of his father's thick hair and elegant nose with his mother's fair skin and full lips could be counted handsome.

By the time he understood that Abigail was not merely interested in his literary expertise, or he in her lively conversation, it was too late. She made him feel vivid and fascinating, and she made the world feel that way too.

There were obstacles—her career with its uncertain demands, his marriage, the fact that she was in London, he in Oxford, the protests of friends, including Tyler—but he and Abigail had believed that something amazing had befallen them. Which was not to say that he had ever intended to leave Judy. Bewilderingly, excruciatingly, his passion for Abigail failed to cancel his feelings for Judy, and vice versa. The thought of choosing one, and renouncing the other, made him feel as if he were wandering in a library where every shelf was bare.

"If you love me," said Judy, repeatedly, "you'll stop hurting me." One bleak afternoon—they had been walking by the river—she even hinted that her despair might be fatal.

Abigail neither accused nor blamed him; this thing had happened; it was no one's fault. Instead, as surely as any Socrates, she led him to the knowledge that his marriage was a failure or, more kindly, a way of getting through his twenties. He and Judy were friends, they had interests in common, but how could they make each other happy when there was no passion? Sean would listen, and agree, but later, after he and Abigail had made love, he would lie beside her thinking about the spring he and Judy had borrowed a cottage near Lyme Regis and spent a whole, blustery day walking the cliff path, gathering little pencil-shaped fossils, and debating where they would go if they won the lottery. Or the evening they'd gone punting on the river and come across a choir of schoolchildren, standing on the bank, singing Brahms, and Judy, sitting at his feet, had joined in. She was his other self; the thought of a future without her was insupportable. He just needed one more day with Abigail, one more night. Then he would give her up, without regret, and resume his old life.

His vacillation intensified Abigail's ardor, or so it seemed. She had strewn their bed with rose petals; she had taken him to Keats's house, and, embarrassingly, stood beside the plum tree reciting "Ode to a Nightingale"; she had examined the bumps and hollows of his skull and praised his fillings. Then one day she left a message on his phone saying she had had enough, and disappeared. Her voice mail was full and, when he made the journey to London, her door remained closed. At the height of his anguish, Judy announced that she was moving in with a vet named Roger, who had two Labradors and a six-year-old son, and wanted to share his life with her. In a daze Sean had packed his suitcases and gone in search of Abigail. Newly back from Paris, she answered the door and, when he said he couldn't live without her, flung her arms around him. He knew the syllogisms of romance. He had broken his life apart for her; therefore she must be the love of his life. Endless promises were exchanged, including the promise of no promises. You can't legislate affection, Abigail had argued.

At the time he had agreed. More recently, though, he had found himself thinking that marriage was not merely an empty ritual. It was a plea for patience on the part of those involved, and for mercy on the part of bystanders. Abigail's relentless assault on his marriage was, he'd discovered, most unusual. All very well for his friends to take the moral high ground, but how many of them, faced with such temptation, such ingenuity, would have fared any better?

S INCE STARTING HIS JOB AT THE THEATER, SEAN HAD LEARNED TO divide his working day. The morning hours, when he felt freshest, went to Keats. In the afternoons he read scripts and worked on program notes. In the evenings he did research or, when she was available, enjoyed Abigail's company. Now, in this full schedule, a space must be made to dash off his chapters on euthanasia. He had to remind himself what a relief it had been to make cordial arrangements for an overdraft.

The morning after the meeting with the secretary, he carried his coffee upstairs and sat down at his desk. He was in the middle of explaining how the parts of *Endymion* written in Oxford owed a debt to the seventeenth-century poet Katherine Philips. As he tried to retrace his argument, he caught sight of the folder of case histories lying on the corner of the desk. What had he meant by *c.f. Canto IV*? He reached for the poem, hoping to find a marginal note or yellow flag. A fat, metallic fly buzzed in through the window, orbited his desk, and sauntered out again. Following its flight, Sean noticed that the sky was no longer a cloudless blue but had, in the last hour, turned to some molten noncolor. It was already very warm. He stood up. On his way to fetch a glass of water, he moved the folder to the bookcase by the door.

Back at his desk he switched on his computer and, refusing the lure of e-mail, opened his current chapter. Was it necessary, he pondered, to give much detail about the obscure Philips? The mere possibility was aggravating, but he had an appointment with his supervisor next week. At their last meeting, when he had expected her to dismiss him until late September, Georgina had suggested that they get together once a fortnight throughout the summer. Sean had not had the wit, or the wherewithal, to protest that he could barely produce enough material for their present monthly schedule. The last four or five days before each meeting found him at his desk until midnight, trying to grind out a few more paragraphs. And (surely it was just his imagination) Abigail often seemed, during these busy times, to have free tickets to a play, or to want to invite friends to dinner. Judy had sometimes been frustrated by his working methods, by his need to have each sentence perfect before he could proceed, but she had sympathized with his ambitions. Abigail, at first so full of admiration, had lately seemed bewildered by his lack of progress. Last week she had remarked that Dickens wrote *Great Expectations* in less than a year.

Even more than the anguish of producing pages, Sean hated going back to Oxford. He had first come to the city as an eighteen-year-old, thrilled to have got a place at Wadham College. He had loved wandering the busy streets and he had loved leaving the streets for the cloistered world of the colleges. After graduation he had left reluctantly to pursue his sensible job in London. When at last he returned, he had thought of himself as following, far behind but honorably, in Keats's footsteps, choosing this arcane world over more conventional ambitions: a career, a mortgage, children. In leaving Judy, he had not understood that he was also leaving Oxford. Although he still went to the college, and still worked at the Bodleian Library, he was now an outsider. On the bus from London his heart sank as the city came into view; the sight of each familiar landmark was like a hammer blow to his spirits. When he finally got off the bus, near St. Catherine's College, he would wear his sunglasses and keep his gaze on the pavement, in the hope of not meeting anyone he knew, or if he did, of passing unnoticed. On the rare occasions when people recognized him, he asked about their lives, their work, and, as soon as they began to reciprocate, claimed an urgent appointment. Now Georgina was telling him to subject himself to these torments even more frequently only to end up in her study, stammering out his meager insights, while she gazed at the college's exquisite gardens.

Slowly Sean found his way back into his argument; slowly he tracked down a crucial passage in Philips, then looked up a phrase in *Paradise Lost*, losing himself for nearly an hour in Milton's fluent verse. He consulted a letter Keats had written to Benjamin Bailey, and reviewed Bailey's comments on Book III of *Endymion*, at which point it was time for lunch.

The kitchen was a little cooler, and he decided he might as well glance at the case histories while he ate. Stupid to dread a pile of pages. He must try to take Valentine's robust attitude: this was just a job; it meant gin in the cupboard, money in the bank. He put together a ham sandwich, retrieved the folder from upstairs, and sat at the table.

Each history consisted of a brief description of the person's age, circumstances, and illness, as well as an account, in his or her own words, of the reasons for suicide. Here was Anne, aged seventy-three, a widow, comfortably off with two married daughters, diagnosed with Parkinson's. *I'm a prisoner,* she wrote, *condemned to endless solitary confinement. Why would anyone inflict this on another person?* She had hoarded her prescriptions, painfully, for months, paid her cleaner, had her hair permed, and chosen the dress she wanted to wear in her coffin. She had consumed her pills and died, as she had hoped, at home in her sleep.

Here was Ian, paralyzed since an accident at a building site when he was twenty-four. Now, at fifty-one, macular degeneration was destroying his last great pleasure: reading. Sean winced and added mustard to his sandwich. Using considerable ingenuity and a gas oven, Ian had killed himself. *A friend helped me figure out how to do it,* he wrote with his specially modified keypad, *but I made sure he was down at the pub all evening so he wouldn't get in trouble.*

Here was Frank, thirty-three (my age, thought Sean), a landscape gardener, in the grip of an aggressive brain tumor. He was already researching euthanasia when his father had a stroke. *It's too much for my mum,* he said, *looking after the two of us. My dad is sixty-one. He deserves his best shot at the next twenty years.* After the failure of his first attempt, he spoke with fury about his doctor who doled out his pills a week at a time. *She'd rather I traumatize some train driver than die peacefully in my own bed. If I could, I'd detonate myself in her waiting room.*

These and similar testimonials formed the heart of the society's campaign to legalize euthanasia and, even more crucial, the assisting thereof. That the case histories were baldly written and largely lacking in self-pity only made them more affecting. Standing at the sink, rinsing his plate, Sean felt as if the room were filled with the members of that determined tribe who had decided to end their tenure on the planet and who could contemplate that decision so calmly that they were able to weigh the pros and cons of pills over plastic bags, cliffs over cars, razors over ropes. He turned off the tap, retrieved his notebook, and headed to the library.

H IS TRIP TO OXFORD BEGAN BADLY. HE WAS UP UNTIL MIDNIGHT the night before and woke early, uncertain about one of his key points. As he reached the bus stop the rain started; umbrella-less, he did his best to protect his bag of books. The bus, when it came, was crowded, and the large man he sat next to fidgeted throughout the journey. Staring past him at the sodden fields, still wan from the recent heat wave, Sean struggled to decide whether the results of his late-night efforts were brilliant or specious. In town with almost an hour to spare, he decided to go to a café near the college. Perhaps coffee and a croissant would clarify his thoughts. He was sitting at a corner table, going over his notes, when someone said his name.

"How are you?" said Judy. "May I join you?" She was standing before him, an umbrella in one hand, a book in the other.

"I'm here to see Georgina," Sean said.

"Well, I promise not to make you late," she said, setting her book on the table and herself in a chair. "It must be my month for meeting the Wymans. I ran into your brother last week."

Sean stared at her incredulously. Her voice was warm; she was smiling. Was this the same woman who less than two years ago had called him a moral pygmy, hauled his suitcases out of the closet, and told him to pack? "How was Lochlan?" he said, trying to match her tone. "I haven't spoken to him in a while."

"He seemed fine." Judy's dimple made a brief appearance. "Very pleased about his promotion. How's Keats?"

Sean felt himself grimace. In an ideal world he would report that everything was going splendidly, but the habit of complaining to Judy was too strong. He described his struggles with tracing Keats's influences and asked about her work.

Judy confided that she had defended her thesis, received her doctorate, and best of all, Macmillan was going to publish her manuscript next year; she just had to make it more accessible. "At first I wanted to defend every footnote," she said. "Then I began to enjoy myself. It's nice to think that people like my mother will be able to read the book."

"That's great." He would have given ten years of his life to be able to announce the same three events.

"And"—she smiled—"I'm pregnant. Your coffee smells so good."

As if realizing that he was having trouble processing the information, she added that the baby was due in January. "Great," Sean said again. It seemed the key word for his side of this conversation. He and Judy had talked about babies as something to be considered only after their dissertations were done, which, of course, hers was. He glanced at his watch, too rapidly to take in the time, and said that he had to go.

"I'm so glad we ran into each other," she said. "Maybe it's the baby, but I've been thinking about you recently, wanting to let you know that I don't bear you a grudge any longer. People do change. Roger and I are very happy together. I hope you and Abigail are too." She stood up—now he could see the small bulge taking over her waistline—and bent to hug him. As her arms wrapped around him, Sean smelled her familiar perfume. For a shameful moment he felt the sting of tears.

Back out in the rainy street he no longer cared whom he encountered. He strode along oblivious to pedestrians, umbrellas, puddles, traffic. Soon after their wedding, he and Judy had spent a day exploring the Cotswolds. They were driving from one exquisite village to the next when, in the middle of a field of cows, they spotted a small stone church. They had pulled onto the verge and gone to investigate. The door was locked, a bird's nest wedged in one corner, but round the back they had found a couple of milk crates and climbed up to peer through the leaded windows. Sean had never forgotten the sight that met his eyes. The narrow nave was crammed not with pews but with statues of knights, maybe eight or nine of them, lying on their tombs, hands folded on their chests, dogs or swords or, in one case, a book, at their pointed feet. How peaceful they looked. He wished he'd asked Judy if she remembered them too. It would have been nice to be back together, even briefly, in that pool of memory where no one else would ever swim.

At the college, he barely nodded to the porter. He made his way through the archway, along the gloomy cloisters, and up the dark stairs that led to Georgina's door. Although he was ten minutes early, he knocked twice. Her voice, surprisingly deep for such a reed of a woman, said, "Come in."

Inside she was sitting in her usual chair. The first time Sean had entered this room, with its large desk and walls of books, he had thought it the perfect scholar's lair, a place of high wit and deep endeavor. Now, by the feeble light of the desk lamp, the books looked dusty, the furnishings soiled; it seemed a fitting home for fraudulent theories and secondhand thoughts. "Sean," said Georgina, "you're very prompt. I worried the rain might slow you down."

"I caught an earlier bus."

Georgina stood up from behind her desk—she was wearing a smoke gray dress—and gesturing for him to sit in one of the two chairs by the window, left the room. Before he could speculate as to what she was doing, she returned with a white towel in her outstretched hand. Unthinkingly he buried his face in the fabric. It felt good to be surrounded, even momentarily, by warm darkness. If only he didn't have to emerge. But he did, and there was Georgina, staring out of the rainy window as usual.

"'In drear-nighted December,'" she said in a conversational voice, "'too happy, happy tree, thy branches ne'er remember their green felicity.'"

She was quoting, Sean knew, from the poem Keats had written when he finished *Endymion*; the promise of those lines had been one of the factors that persuaded him, after months of uncertainty, to give up his career in insurance.

"We're in the middle of Book III, aren't we?" she said.

"No." The towel lay in his lap, absurdly, like a napkin, and his hands, pink and raw, lay on top.

At last she turned to look at him. "I'm sorry," she said. "Am I misremembering?"

"No." All you needed for any conversation was one word. "You're correct about the book, wrong about the tense. We were in the middle of Book III, but no longer. I've decided to quit. I'm tired of being a burden to myself, and you, and everyone else. I'm tired of this endless quest."

In the silence that followed, he thought she might be about to start quoting again—something about the happy, happy brook—but instead she looked at him for a few more seconds, and turned back to the window.

"Of course it's your choice," she said, "but I do think it's a pity. Another six months and you would have made a really useful contribution to Keats scholarship."

So why did you always behave like I was boring you to death, thought

Sean. He was so angry he could hardly speak. "Thank you," he said. As he stood up, the towel fell to the floor. He left it lying there, a crumpled flag of surrender, and walked out.

O N THE NEXT BUS BACK TO LONDON, WITH TWO SEATS TO HIMSELF, he stared once again at the wan fields. He remembered how when he was ten he had smashed his entire collection of birds' eggs—three years' work gone in three minutes—because a boy at school had made a joke. Then there was the occasion he had stolen his brother's blazer and thrown it in a ditch. He had been a teenager before he learned, as his mother was always asking, to use his words, not his fists. And then, it was around the time he discovered girls, he began to realize that words were not just a substitute for fighting; they could persuade, seduce, get you things. Until then he had wanted to be a train driver, like his father, but suddenly he had started to study and do his home-work. He was only the third pupil from his small high school to get a place at Oxford.

Now, in an impulsive moment, he had turned his back on nearly seven years of work, and he desperately needed Abigail to tell him he had made the right choice. He got off the bus at Marble Arch and dodged his way through the crowds to the underground station. For once every train was punctual, every escalator working, and at the the-ater office his luck held. Abigail was at her desk; she smiled at the sight of him, and was happy to go to the pub on the corner. She had had a meeting at the bank that morning and, in her suit, with her hair pinned up, she looked disconcertingly like one of his former colleagues at the insurance company. Beneath her fuchsia umbrella her face glowed, from which he guessed that his own, beneath the black one he'd borrowed from the stage manager, must have a funereal tinge. "What is it?" she kept asking. But he refused to say anything until they were seated, her with a glass of wine, him with a scotch. The pub was nearly empty, save for a group of nurses—going off duty we hope, said Abigail—and four boys playing darts.

"Cheers," Sean said, raising his glass. The sharp fragrance of whiskey filled his head and was at once translated into the sharp taste. To his surprise his heart was racing, as if he were on the edge of something momentous, although surely he had stepped over that edge two hours before. He took a second, smaller sip and said, "I quit. I told Georgina I wasn't going to finish my dissertation."

As he spoke clapping broke out; the tallest of the boys had thrown a bull's-eye. On the bus Sean had pictured Abigail applauding when he told her what he'd done, giving him an exuberant kiss. Finally he was relinquishing this project that took so much time and brought him neither money nor delight. Finally he was rejoining the adult world, where people expected a proper return for their labor.

"But why?" She made her pouting expression. "You've worked on it for so long. You're nearly finished. Why would you give up now? I remember the first time we met you talked about Keats and Fanny. They're like members of our household."

Each sentence winged its way unerringly to the target, and each was more wounding because it was something he could also imagine Judy saying. And that, of course, their accidental meeting, was what he could not reveal to Abigail. "I thought you'd be pleased," he said. "You're always complaining about how slowly I work."

"Of course I complain. You do too. I never thought that meant you would give up." She put down her own drink and, moving their glasses aside, reached for his hands. "What happened? Did Georgina say something?"

"No." He struggled against the impulse to pull free of her grasp. "And please don't keep saying I gave up. This wasn't a search for the elixir of life; this was another book about a poet who's already been the subject of far too many books. I got tired of being overextended. I got tired of juggling the theater and Keats and the project with Valentine. It was too many words to read and write. And even when I finished the dissertation, nothing would have changed. You can't get an academic job without publications and you can't publish without an academic affiliation. You wouldn't keep putting on plays if no one came to see them."

"I suppose"—Abigail squeezed his hands—"but that's different. This just seems such a big decision. And you didn't mention it to me."

"I did drop a couple of hints. You've been so busy." He wasn't sure himself if this was true but, for the first time that day, a woman responded to him in the way he hoped. Abigail began to apologize for being so preoccupied. "I know sometimes things get away from me," she said.

Halfway through his second whiskey, he confided Georgina's parting remark. "It made me furious."

"But isn't it nice to know you were doing well?"

"It's so fucking Ox-bridge. I work like a dog for six years, nearly seven, without a glimmer of encouragement, and now out of the blue, when she's driven me to quit, she praises me."

"You don't have to be interested in everything you're good at. Besides"—Abigail smiled—"you've already been working on Keats's poems for longer than he took to write them."

Last week on the phone Valentine had made the same irritating comment. Now, while Abigail continued to mouth reassurances, he followed Georgina's example, staring through the window at the street outside. His heart had stopped racing; if anything it seemed to be going about its business even more slowly than usual. How could he say to Abigail that his failure as an academic had been one more item tipping the scales in her direction? If he had thought his dissertation was going well, he wouldn't have been lured into working with Valentine, spending time apart from Judy; he might never have met Abigail and surrendered to the barrage of her affection.

F OR SEVERAL DAYS HE DIDN'T TELL ANYONE ELSE ABOUT WHAT HE regarded as his second divorce. He talked to friends on the phone, he went to the theater office, he e-mailed with Valentine, and did not mention that his life had changed. Abigail, either sensing the fury that lay behind his decision or, more likely, busy and already consigning his failure to the unalterable past, asked no further questions. Almost a week after his trip to Oxford, on his way to buy groceries, he ran into Dara. She was kneeling beside the flower bed in the front garden. "Oh, Sean," she said, getting to her feet, "I was just trying to make more room. I overplanted, as usual."

Her reddish brown hair was falling around her face and her cheeks were flushed. She looked much more attractive, Sean thought, than Virginia Woolf, whose famous portrait adorned her T-shirt. The sleeves were rolled up, and he glimpsed the pale pock of a vaccination mark on one biceps. When he announced he was going to the supermarket—could he get her anything?—she set aside her trowel and said she'd come too. As they headed down the street, he asked if she had the day off; she often worked odd hours at the counseling center.

"I'm afraid not. I have to go in this afternoon to run support groups. Attendance is erratic in the summer, but the people who are around need the groups more than ever, so we decided to keep them going. You're off to Tuscany next week, aren't you?"

"Yes. I'm sure it'll be great once we get there, but right now we're both in a panic about how much we have to do before we go. What about you and Edward? When do you leave for Brittany?"

Dara's espadrilles scuffed the pavement. "Not this year, I'm afraid. His mother's got shingles again and he's going home to help out. I've decided to take a fortnight in Edinburgh. I can stay with my mother, see some shows at the Festival."

"That sounds fun. At least you won't be stuck in a traffic jam at Calais for days."

"I suppose."

Glancing over, he saw that her eyes were downcast and her lips tight. Belatedly it occurred to him that she was upset. He had met Edward, a professional violinist, a few times and enjoyed their conversations— they were both Arsenal fans—but he had little sense of how matters stood between him and Dara. Periodically Abigail reported broken plans and her anxiety that Edward might prove unreliable; he was still sharing a flat with his former partner. Now, before Sean could express his sympathy, Dara paused to smell the crimson roses in a neighbor's garden; her grandfather used to grow them, she said.

At the row of shops they separated to make their purchases and met up again to walk home. They were almost back at the roses when he told her—the words seemed to escape of their own volition—that he had given up on his dissertation. "Well, not given up," he corrected hastily, "but I decided to stop work on it, for now."

"I'm sorry." Dara turned to look at him, her brown eyes wide with sympathy. "That must have been a difficult decision, after all the work you've done."

He did not dare to speak for fear that he would voice the feelings he was trying so hard to ignore. Fortunately she kept talking, saying that maybe it would be nice to be able to enjoy his favorite poems without having to analyze every word. Sean studied the pavement, cracked stone by cracked stone; analyzing every word was one of his great pleasures.

"Oh, how sweet," Dara suddenly exclaimed.

Looking up, he saw a woman walking toward them, talking on the phone. On her back a baby, its head just visible over her shoulder, watched them with round blue eyes. As they passed, Dara waved and gave an exaggerated smile; the baby smiled back.

"So," she said, clearly having lost her train of thought.

Sean seized his chance. "Anyway," he said, "I've taken on this new project." He described the euthanasia book.

"That sounds interesting. And very timely. Would you like to come in? We could drink lemonade in the garden."

He pictured the two of them, sitting in the shade of her plum tree, and Dara asking thoughtful questions about the topics he wanted to ignore. "I'm sorry," he said. "I'm due at the theater." Before he could soften his refusal—add that they must get together soon—Dara had produced a neat little smile, quite different from the one she'd given the baby, and said, of course; she had to leave for the center in an hour anyway. She retrieved her trowel, and was gone.

F ROM THE MOMENT THEY STEPPED OUT OF THE AIRPORT IN FLOR-ence, Sean felt himself transported by the warm air, the mellifluous language, the vivid streets and blue skies, not only to this other country but to a younger, more joyful version of himself. And Abigail seemed to feel the same; for the first time in months she wasn't thinking about her theater, dashing to make phone calls. He was happily reminded of what life was like when she was fully present. From the flat they'd rented in Siena, they made outings to San Gimignano, Lake Como, Orvieto, and Lucca; they ate long lunches, stealing food from each other's plates, and meandered home for long afternoons of lovemaking. In the Etruscan necropolis below the town of Orvieto, she read to him from the guidebook. "'The Etruscans flourished between the ninth and sixth centuries B.C., shortly before the Romans rose to power, and most of what is known about them comes from their graves. Statues and paintings show the Etruscans greeting death with their arrowlike smiles. They seem to have regarded the afterlife as a halcyon place of feasting and dancing, fishing in well-stocked lakes and hunting plump, lazy boars.'

"Maybe you could put that in your book," she said. "Didn't you say there was a section on attitudes to death?" They were standing beside a marble sarcophagus; on the lid a lithe young couple, with long hair and graceful robes, reclined as if at a banqueting table.

"Good idea," he said, and told her about the vision he had had in the secretary's office of a Tuscan afterlife complete with Chianti. Abigail smiled appreciatively, looking, he thought, not unlike an Etruscan herself, and came to kiss him.

THEY FLEW BACK TO LONDON ON THE LAST DAY OF AUGUST AND, even as they traveled in from the airport, he could feel Abigail receding. The company was leaving for Hull in a few weeks and every hour had its task. When she wasn't rehearsing the two plays they were taking on tour, she was working on publicity and arranging accommodation. Over dinner their last night in Siena, she had remarked that the autumn would be hectic. "You'll have to cut me some slack, Sean, I know it won't be easy, but maybe you can get your book done and I can get the theater on a better footing and we can both emerge at Christmas into calmer times." He had said he understood; of course he'd be supportive. All night long, in her sleep, Abigail had held him fast.

Now he bought groceries, cleaned the house, did load after load of laundry, and dealt with the mail. Despite her warning he felt unprepared for how busy she was. During their hasty meals she kept getting up to make notes; at night she slept with fierce determination and woke with her alarm at six. Sometimes, when he couldn't bear being invisible, he went downstairs to Dara's flat. She was still in Edinburgh, and he had agreed to water her garden. While Abigail e-mailed and faxed and phoned—often all three simultaneously—he sat at the picnic table rereading the pages he had written that day. His apprehensions about the book had, so far, proved unfounded.

Before they went away he had been working on the chapter about preparations. The society's notes included, *Who finds you? Elaborate with interviews.* He had written several paragraphs urging those planning euthanasia to consider the trauma they might inflict on innocent bystanders. *Given Western society's attitudes to death, finding you may end up being the worst experience of someone else's life, resulting in nightmares, depression, and even psychosis. Try to ensure that the person who finds you is a professional: a doctor, a clergyman, a policeman. If two methods are equally appealing and available, then take the aftereffects into account.*

Soon, he knew, he must embark on the interviews, but for now, using a book from the library and various pamphlets from the Citizens' Advice Bureau, he drafted a section on wills. He was marking facts to check—were witnesses essential?—when Valentine telephoned. The secretary wanted to know whether they would be willing to do a short section on mental suffering.

"Quite a literate chap, that secretary," said Valentine. "He quoted Faust, 'The mind is its own place, can make a heaven of hell, etc.' which might make a good epigraph. Anyway I told him we'd write an appendix, which doesn't commit us to very much. Maybe you could talk to Abigail's friend Dara? She's a counselor, isn't she?"

"Why should I write it? The section on wills was a lot of work."

"Oh, come on, Sean. Mental suffering?" Valentine made a sound that could only be described as chortling. "Definitely your bailiwick."

Did Valentine really see him as an expert on angst, Sean wondered.

But already he was acquiescing. It was easier to take on more work than to confess how far behind he had fallen. As he put down the phone, he found himself thinking, once again, about Keats. During his final illness in Rome, the poet had asked his friend Severn, over and over, to give him the laudanum. He could not bear to open Fanny's last letter, for fear the emotion would destroy him, but throughout those feverish days and nights he kept tight hold of a carnelian she had given him, passing the smooth white stone from hand to hand. And then there was his bitter epigraph: *Here lies one* . . .

Oh, for Christ's sake, thought Sean. Resolutely he brought his attention back to his own affairs. He could not afford to return the advance, therefore he must write this book, and to write the book, he must behave as he had done when writing the last two books with Valentine: make a schedule and stick to it. On a new page of his notebook he wrote a list of dates and chapters. He adjusted it slightly to take account of Abigail's birthday and, buoyed up by his plan, picked up the phone.

"Mr. Wyman," said the secretary warmly. "How can I help?"

Sean explained that he was ready to start doing interviews and would like to talk to surviving relatives.

"Of course," said the secretary. "Broadly speaking there are two categories: those who find a body unexpectedly and those who are forewarned. The latter often absent themselves, most reluctantly, to avoid being implicated. If you want to know what it's like to spend a strange hour or two, you must talk to them. How do you pass the time when someone you love is dying? And, to make matters worse, you need to be in a public place so that you have an alibi. One man I know took a balloon ride while his wife was dying. He hoped to glimpse her soul flying upwards."

"And did he?" said Sean. He began to sketch a balloon in his notebook.

"I'm afraid not, but he did receive a consoling reminder of how small our lives are in the scheme of things. Then there was a woman who took her granddaughter to the zoo in Regent's Park while her son was dying." He described how the woman had broken down in the reptile house, pounding on the glass, and terrifying her granddaughter.

"I'd love to talk to the balloonist," said Sean, adding a basket to his sketch. He felt easily capable of imagining pain and panic; stoic calm was the mystery.

"That can be arranged," said the secretary. He promised to send a list of interview subjects by the end of the week.

THREE DAYS AFTER THIS CONVERSATION SEAN SPOTTED AN ENVElope lying on the doormat. The secretary's list, he thought, and opened it as he walked toward the fridge.

Dear Mr. Writer,

How is it that you don't see what's right in front of your face? Abigail was hanging out with Mr. Cupid in the pub last week and again yesterday, for all the world to see. Ask her who was with her in Manchester last March.

You deserve better, Sunshine. Open your bright blue eyes and wake up.

A well-wisher

Every part of the letter was typed, including the salutation and the address, and every part was spelled correctly, including the postal code; only the color of his eyes was wrong. Sean's first thought, staring at the neat lines, was not of their content but of their style. The partiality for nicknames reminded him of one of those American authors. And why Mr. Cupid? he wondered. Was that simply a witty reference to the clichés of love?

Then the content hit him.

He thought back to Manchester. Abigail had been gone for a week, teaching a drama workshop and, during the entire seven days, they'd talked twice. They were well past that lovely, absurd phase when it was imperative to talk every few hours; still he remembered being surprised at how hard she was to reach. Now these facts supported the letter writer's claims.

And who was the writer? It must, he thought, be someone who worked at the theater. All these weeks and months, when he had been going about his business there, someone had been watching him, him and Abigail, with a view to making trouble between them. That he should be the target of such scrutiny was another startling, and unwelcome, revelation.

He went upstairs, found a sheet of paper, wrote *Attention Abigail: 2 pages, inc. this one*, and faxed the letter to the theater. Then he sat waiting. In one of the case histories a man had described his first failed attempt: *I felt like a suicide bomber, wandering the market, buying a chicken, squeezing an orange, while I waited to explode.* Second by second, Sean's satisfaction in his gesture dwindled. All he had done was give Abigail a chance to prepare her response. Ten minutes after the pages slid through the machine the phone rang.

"Who the fuck wrote this?" she said. "Was there a return address?"

"You don't sign yourself a well-wisher and give a return address," he said in his most professorial tone. "Presumably someone who knows both of us and knows our address. My guess is someone connected with the theater. There must be a dozen candidates."

"We should report them to the police. This is a crime."

"I'm not sure about that. The letter doesn't threaten anything. Just gives advice."

"Advice," said Abigail contemptuously. She continued to fulminate until finally he interrupted. Was there any substance to the accusations?

"I did have a drink with Valentine last Monday."

A stinking yellow light broke through the darkness. Mr. Cupid. Suddenly he remembered that Valentine had been away around the time Abigail was in Manchester, visiting his parents in Bath, he claimed. Had it been the very same week? "What about Manchester?" he said. "You were hard to reach."

"I was teaching round the clock. Are you suggesting this crap might be true?"

"Not suggesting, asking. We did promise to make no promises." Trust Abigail, even in this situation, to seize the upper hand.

"Of course not. Someone just wants to make trouble between us or," she added thoughtfully, "between you and Valentine."

"Right." He believed her, and he didn't believe her. Each new piece of evidence seemed to weigh equally on both sides.

"I'll be home in an hour," she said, and hung up.

Wanting to keep busy, not knowing what else to do, Sean embarked on a long-overdue letter to his parents. Three years ago, when his father retired from train driving, they had moved from Dorset to the Isle of Wight, where they ran a busy bed-and-breakfast. This new enterprise seemed to have rendered them largely oblivious to their children's lives. Even the news of Sean's divorce had elicited only an understanding remark about modern life. His brother reported the same bewildering acceptance. Now, on the principle that the day could get no worse, he set out to tell them he had quit his Ph.D. Instead he found himself writing about Tuscany and the euthanasia book.

He was describing the latter when he heard the front door open and close, followed by footsteps mounting the stairs. Abigail embraced him where he sat. "Are you ready to take a break?"

"Five minutes," he said, and dashed off a last paragraph.

When he came downstairs she had set out beer and cheese. While he helped himself to both she told him that advance ticket sales for Hull were promising, and visits to two schools had been arranged. He nodded and ate and drank. He felt a keen determination not to bring up the letter.

"Have you ever been to Hull?" she asked, cutting a wedge of cheddar.

"No. I picture it as rather gray and gloomy. Maybe that's just the name: Hull, dull, skull."

"I was there with my parents when I was four or five. All I remember is a black dog in the park." She pushed her hair back purposefully. "Can I see the letter?"

Reluctantly he returned upstairs and retrieved it from between the pages of *Sir Gawain and the Green Knight*, a book he hadn't opened for nearly a decade and which he had hoped not to open for a decade more. In the kitchen he handed the envelope to Abigail. She looked closely at the blurred postmark and drew out the folded sheet. She read it a couple of times as if the original might yield a different meaning than the fax.

"Who do you think wrote this," she said, "a man or a woman?"

"Something about the phrasing—Mr. Cupid, Sunshine—seems more masculine."

"That's my guess too."

They began to debate between the stage manager, the accountant, and the wardrobe mistress. Sean was at his wittiest, proposing wild theories about who fancied whom. He made her laugh, he made himself laugh, with his increasingly outrageous suggestions. But later, in bed, levity failed him; only by dint of Abigail's efforts did they make love.

THE NEXT DAY WAS ONE OF HIS AFTERNOONS AT THE THEATER AND, even as he hung up his jacket, everyone seemed excessively friendly. In the middle of a conversation about props with the stage manager, or a joking exchange with the accountant, he would catch himself wondering, Did you write the letter? Did you? At his desk, ostensibly editing a grant application, he found himself parsing, in minute detail, the way the accountant had offered to buy him coffee—"You take it white," she had said—or the fund-raiser's praise of Abigail. Several times, he looked up from his computer, convinced he was being watched, only to find his colleagues absorbed in their tasks. Meanwhile Abigail was returning phone calls, making lists, pleading with people to take on one more thing. He could not detect the slightest sign of uneasiness.

Three days later she left for Hull. An hour after her taxi pulled away, the phone rang; it was Valentine. Before Sean could launch into his standard speech about how well his chapters were going, Valentine said, "So listen. Abigail told me someone wrote a stupid letter."

"A letter?"

"Of course you know the pub is on my way home," Valentine went on, very heartily. Once or twice he had stopped in for a drink and, no surprises, run into Abigail. Surely he had said something? But if he hadn't, if neither of them had, it was because it was such an everyday occurrence.

Everyday, Sean thought, or every day? "Of course," he repeated. "Did you ever hear back from that doctor the secretary recommended?"

They chatted about the book for what felt like fifteen minutes but was probably barely five. Without consulting him, or even mentioning it after the fact, she had told Valentine. Was that a sign of innocence or guilt? He couldn't decide, and there was no way he could ask; the natural channels of communication between him and Abigail, those glittering, lively streams that had begun to flow at their first meeting, were now clogged with doubt and disagreement, forced underground. Only after he hung up did he wonder whether the conversation might have taken place in person, rather than on the phone. Perhaps—he clenched his fists—she had even shown Valentine the letter. Once again he regretted the fax.

He paced the living room back and forth, back and forth, and at last flung himself down on the sofa. He had set aside the entire day for writing but now seemed doomed to squander it in hopeless speculation. His gaze fastened on the painting above the fireplace. Abigail had shown him the vivid oil the first time he came to the house and told him that the artist was her best friend. "That's Dara." She pointed. "And that's me. We were having a picnic on the beach at St. Andrews." Normally the sight of the two of them, sitting on a tartan rug, surrounded by food, cheered him, but today all he could see was Valentine popping his eyes. Had she? Hadn't she? Would she? Wouldn't she? That he had subjected Judy to similar torments only made him feel worse.

In an effort to distract himself he decided to read plays. He hadn't reviewed any since he sent back the one on Keats; after a promising start it had quickly lapsed into a lecture. Now a stack was sitting conveniently beside the sofa. He opened the first one. *Newcastle Baby* read the title page. A racehorse? A person? He didn't care. The cast list was acceptably short and he started reading. He reached the bottom of the first page with no idea of what he'd read, though he knew there was a typo in the third line. The next page yielded the same results. His eyes passed over the words, presumably they entered his brain, but he was unable to convert them into units of thought and sense. He closed *Newcastle Baby* and picked up the next script: *A Gift for Miss Honeyman*. Again the lines meant nothing. After a third attempt, he went to his study and fetched a pile of form rejections. Sitting on the floor, he went through the entire stack, plucking off the accompanying letters and neatly affixing rejections. He put them in the hall to await return to the theater, and decided to go to the one place he could think of that promised solace: the library.

Outside he almost collided with a familiar figure. As with the plays, he could not quite bring the man on Dara's doorstep into focus. Then the man said, "Hello, Sean," and he recognized her father. Cameron had helped Dara to move into the flat and Sean had lent him a hammer and assisted with the heavier boxes. Their conversations had been brief and mundane, and since then they had spoken only in passing, but now, seeing again his surprisingly unlined face and deep-set eyes, Sean remembered how, for no reason he could articulate, he had been struck by Cameron's faint, indecipherable air of melancholy.

"Your garden is looking lovely," said Cameron.

"All Dara's doing." In an effort at politeness, he added that he had the opposite of a green thumb. "My father used to make my brother and me mow the grass twice, first one way then at right angles. It's left me with a lifelong grudge against plants."

While he was speaking, Dara appeared. She was looking, he noticed, in a purple blouse and blue skirt, unusually pretty. "Hi, Dad," she said. "Come on, Sean. At a certain point we have to stop blaming our parents for everything. Besides, you like plants; you just don't like tending them." She linked her arm through her father's and added that they were going to Sissinghurst, the country house in Kent, to see the famous gardens.

"I've heard they're beautiful," Sean managed. The prospect of company, a destination, was so tempting that he almost asked if he could come too.

THE LIBRARY DID HELP, BUT ONLY WHILE HE WAS THERE. THE IDEAL distraction, he discovered in the next few days, was interviewing people. The secretary's list had arrived shortly after the anonymous letter and, at a particularly low ebb, he had picked a name at random— Mrs. Margaret Green—and phoned. He had worried that she might regard him as a kind of bailiff, come to collect emotional debts, but as soon as he introduced himself Mrs. Green was eager to describe how she had assisted her sister after a stroke. "She couldn't smile any longer, poor lamb, but when she felt herself going I could see her trying." The other people he contacted were equally eloquent and forthcoming. No one expressed regrets at having helped a loved one to die; indeed several claimed that doing so had eased their grief. Their quarrels were with a government that tried to make them feel like criminals and the occasional unsympathetic doctor. Much to Sean's relief no one expected him to give an account of himself; his job was simply to ask questions and listen while people volunteered deeply personal information. The process was almost addictive, he told Dara, when he ran into her at the bus stop.

ABIGAIL CAME BACK FROM HULL FOR FOUR BREATHLESS DAYS during which, although he thought of little else, he did not find a single opportunity to ask why she had told Valentine about the letter. She made love to him twice, and each time he pictured her ticking it off her list. Then she was gone again, to Bradford.

Two days later Sean went to interview Bridget Flanigan. A widow who lived in a small village near Cambridge, Mrs. Flanigan was in the unusual situation of having assisted first her mother, and then her husband. Her voice on the phone, however, gave no hint of these wrenching choices. She suggested he take the two o'clock train and gave directions to her cottage from the station. The walk, as she'd predicted, took ten minutes. When he reached the garden gate he saw a woman, wearing a man's shirt, jeans, and Wellingtons, kneeling on the grass, holding a blowtorch to a large metal sculpture: it looked like a tree flying apart. He would have liked to watch her unobserved, but two dogs, one large, one small, started to bark. The woman straightened and, still holding the flaring torch, turned toward him. She was at least a decade younger than he had expected, perhaps in her late thirties.

"Mr. Wyman, I presume," she said, turning off the torch and setting it down. "Wait a moment while I get Rollo under control." She whistled to the larger dog, and seized his collar. "Ignore Suzie."

He opened the gate and stepped around the smaller dog. "This is lovely," he said. "Am I interrupting? Please call me Sean."

"No, I was expecting you. I'm Bridget."

She released the dog and led the way indoors. In the hall she exchanged her Wellingtons for clogs and removed the shirt to reveal a white blouse. When they were seated on opposite sides of the kitchen table, each with a glass of water, he saw that her thick, straight hair was almost the same color as her lightly tanned arms.

"Do you mind if I record our conversation?" he asked.

"Of course not. So where do we start? I feel a little foolish."

"Start at the beginning, which I think means your mother. Do you have siblings?"

"No, and my father died when I was fifteen so it was just Mum and me. She was sixty-three, apparently in excellent health—working as an accountant, sailing at weekends—when she developed a cough that wouldn't go away. At first it seemed more irritating than serious. Then suddenly she had cancer."

She described the rapid advancement of her mother's illness; Sean asked her to spell a couple of the scientific terms. "Even when she didn't feel rotten, she was so scared that she couldn't enjoy anything. Over and over she begged us—Kingsley, my husband, and me—to kill her. Of course we said no, and then one day we were driving home from seeing her, and Kingsley said he thought we ought to listen to her. As soon as he spoke, I knew he was right. I'd been mouthing all these platitudes—you'll feel better soon—but if this was what she wanted, we had to help her.

"We were passing a small wood on the road back from Wisbech. Kingsley stopped the car and we got out. The sun had set, and there were one or two stars. We stood listening to the wind moving through the trees, and it was like a benediction on our conversation." She glanced toward the window as if the wood lay just outside. "The next time my mother said she wished she were dead, I said if that's really what you want, we can help. Once she understood what I was offering, she became her old self. If I'd ended up going to jail for five years it would have been worth it to see her have those last few weeks in control again, not scared."

Watching her face, Sean wondered was there any large choice in his life about which he felt such certainty, such a lack of regret.

Bridget insisted on making tea before she told him about her husband. While the kettle boiled they chatted about the village: the erratic train service to London, the newly reopened shop. Then he switched on the tape recorder again.

"This is harder," she said. "Kingsley was only forty-one when he was diagnosed, and it just seemed unacceptable that he wasn't going to have more time, that we weren't going to have more time. I wanted him to keep fighting, to keep looking for alternatives. Between conventional medicine and the acupuncture, the feng shui, the coffee enemas, the sleeping on electrical beds—well, there was always more to try. What I came to understand was that there is a level of pain that destroys a person. If you take enough medicine to avoid that pain, you don't become your old self; you become a drugged zombie. I finally realized that I couldn't ask Kingsley to endure that for a second longer than he had to."

She held out her hands, palms up, for inspection. A thin white scar bisected the mound of Venus on her left hand; a fresh cut nicked her right index finger. "They tell you to leave the pills in reach, not to actually give them to the person. Maybe that changes things legally but it doesn't change them morally. I look at my hands and I know I've killed two people. That's what the sculpture I'm working on is about."

"You must be lonely," said Sean.

"Yes."

She was looking at him across the table, her eyes deep and steady, and he knew that if he stretched out his hand she would lead him to her bedroom. He sat there, meeting her gaze, imagining the skin he could see leading to the skin he couldn't, imagining the pleasure of sex without history. At last, not sure if he was being courageous or cowardly, he looked away.

ALL THE WAY BACK TO LONDON HE KEPT THINKING NOT ABOUT that final moment but about the conversation. He and Valentine ought to be writing a much larger book, there was so much to say, and they ought to be talking to a commercial publisher. When he got back to the house, he phoned Valentine, first at home and then on his mobile. Valentine answered the latter on the fifth ring.

"I just did this amazing interview," said Sean. "I've been thinking we should try to take this book to another level. Or write another book."

"Sorry. I didn't catch that. I'm on the train to Leeds."

"Leeds?" His geography was poor but Leeds was no more than twenty miles from Bradford.

Valentine said something—the connection was bad—about a new museum. Then his voice came through, clear and strong. "The northern arts beat. By gum, lad, they do have culture north of Oxford. Listen, tell me your plan about the book when I get back. Or shoot me an e-mail. I'll be checking in."

"When do you get back?" said Sean, but the line was dead. He stood holding the empty phone in the empty house. He could call Abigail, he thought, but either he would get her voice mail, or she would talk at length about how well things were going. As he replaced the phone, he remembered a conversation he'd had with Georgina about Keats's attacks of jealousy. In May 1820 Fanny Brawne had gone to a party, unchaperoned, and Keats had written her a series of anguished letters: *You could not step or move an eyelid but it would shoot to my heart—I am greedy of you—Do not think of any thing but me. . . . If you could really what is call'd enjoy yourself at a Party—if you can smile in peoples faces, and wish them to admire you now, you never have nor ever will love me.* We have to understand this in the light of his illness, Georgina had argued; nothing else makes sense of his reaction. At the time Sean had agreed.

Now he wandered from room to room. In the living room another stack of plays was waiting. In the bedroom the neatly made bed seemed to mock him. In his study the chapters clamored. He ought to be work-ing, transcribing the interview, but he did not want to be alone with Bridget's voice. Why had he resisted her? Finally he went downstairs and knocked on Dara's door. A light shone in the window but there was no answer. He knocked again and, when he still heard nothing, retreated.

Back upstairs he telephoned his brother. For most of their adult lives, since he went to university and Lochlan decided to work in a men's clothing shop, the two of them had been on perfectly cordial, utterly different wavelengths. But Lochlan had liked Judy, and since the divorce they had spoken less often. Or so it had seemed to Sean. Now, as he heard Lochlan's voice, he wondered if he had simply imagined his brother's disapproval.

"How's it going?" said Lochlan. "Cleo and I were just saying we hadn't spoken to you in ages, our fault as much as yours."

Sean reported that he was working on a new book with Valentine. "About euthanasia. Not the most cheery topic."

"And what about your own book? Is there light at the end of the tunnel?"

"I'm afraid Keats is on the back burner." He couldn't deal with all that at the moment. "How are you and Cleo? Did you have a good summer? How's the job?"

"We did have a good summer. We had a terrific holiday in Corsica and my job is going well, touch wood. Sales for the last quarter are up. But the big news is that Cleo is pregnant, four months and growing. We told the parents last week."

"Great," said Sean. This time he managed to ask the right questions and exclaim appropriately. He couldn't wait to be an uncle, an Easter baby, fantastic.

Then Lochlan asked about Abigail, and he tried to sound just as pleased about his own life. That his brother had not, on the basis of a single awkward lunch, warmed to Abigail only made him more anxious to conceal his present difficulties. He described the tour and managed to bring the conversation round to their mother's birthday. Did Lochlan have any ideas for a gift?

ABIGAIL ARRIVED BACK FROM BRADFORD ON A SUNDAY AFTER-noon. When she had unpacked and dealt with the mail, she suggested they go to the local Italian restaurant for dinner. At their window table she plied him with wine, told amusing stories, reminisced about Tuscany, and asked about the interviews. Sean answered, drank the wine, and observed his own bifurcated reactions. One part of him blossomed in the warmth of her attention; the other was convinced that she was trying to pull the wool over his eyes. As she described a crisis with the sets, he remembered his father explaining how the train driver could stop and start the train but had no choice as to where he went. Whoever controlled the points controlled the route. Finally, from behind his raised glass, Sean mentioned Valentine: had she seen him up north?

"No. Was he planning to come to the show? This is almost as good as Siena, isn't it?" She gestured at her plate of ravioli.

"He was in Leeds, doing an article. I thought he might pop over to Bradford."

"If he does have any media connections in the north, I wish he'd use them. We keep getting great reviews that come out on our last day. Did I tell you that I met a young playwright, Sayid something? He's going to send us a play."

"I'll look out for it."

They were walking back to the house when Abigail asked if he had seen Dara, and he said not since that day he'd run into her and her father on their way to Sissinghurst. "Maybe we could invite her for supper tomorrow," he offered.

"I might have to work at the theater," Abigail said, her careless tone signaling that this was a plan set in stone.

She said the same thing when he proposed the next night, and he took some small comfort in the fact that she was too busy even to see her best friend. In the days that followed he studiously avoided any reference to Valentine and rearranged his schedule to work longer hours at the theater. Abigail was her usual whirlwind self but at least he always knew where she was. Then, the night before she was leaving for Coventry, she was late coming home. She had left the theater early to meet with a designer and told him she'd be back by six. After trying her mobile twice, he carried his bicycle into the kitchen and set about adjusting the gears. The designer lived miles away; perhaps the tube had broken down again. But why didn't she phone, or answer her phone? Every answer that came to mind was distressing. He was reaching for a spanner when at last the front door opened.

Abigail appeared with two bags of groceries. "Sorry I'm late. I ran into Dara. We went for a drink."

From below, he heard the sound of Dara's front door. "I wondered where you were," he said, tightening the spanner. He did not add that he also wondered why she hadn't phoned and why she had gone shopping, given her departure the next day. It was not like Abigail to stock the larder on his account.

"I haven't seen her in ages," she said. "We stopped at the Lord Nelson." As she put away the groceries, she told him that Edward was finally moving in with Dara, in the new year. "His daughter is settling down at kindergarten and he's got enough pupils to cover his expenses."

For the first time in several hours Sean forgot his own fears. "Oh great. I'm so glad."

At once he felt Abigail's mood shift. With a bag of coffee in one hand, a wedge of Brie in the other, she stood frowning at him. "But what if he doesn't do it?" she said. "He's been vacillating for so long. Dara will be crushed if this doesn't work out."

He didn't understand her anger—was it at Edward? At Dara? At him?—but all the feelings he was holding back kindled. "You're such an absolutist, Abigail," he said, glaring back at her defiantly. "You think a person decides to buy a red car and then hands over a check, but most people have to drive a black car and a blue one and talk to their friends, before they actually buy the red one. Vacillating is part of deciding. That's why the Belladonna Society insists on a waiting period. They don't want anyone killing themselves out of a single impulse of despair."

For a few seconds he continued to meet her gaze. Then, afraid of what he might say next—was she test driving Valentine?—he bent to lift the bike right side up. As he straightened, she came over and rested her hand on the handlebars. "Would you like to come to Coventry?" she asked, smiling at him appealingly. "You could visit the cathedral, work at the library."

Despite himself he smiled back. "I'd love to, but I'm afraid my chapters aren't very portable."

"Oh, your stupid book," said Abigail, pouting. She leaned over and kissed him.

Then she was gone again, this time for two weeks. In her absence Sean did his best to write his chapters. She invited me to go with her, he reminded himself, but that only quieted the beasts for so long. As for Dara, he forgot about her until one afternoon, while he was proofreading the transcript of an interview, a loud thud came from downstairs. What was the noise? Did she need help? In the ensuing silence he was struck by how quiet she had been recently, and that he couldn't remember the last time he had smelled her cooking. But there was no further sound, and he went back to checking his pages. He would knock on her door tomorrow.

Two days later his knock was again met by silence; he thought about leaving a note but didn't have a pen. Later he forgot. For one reason or another he did not try again. Ten days passed before, one rainy evening in late November, he ran into her, hurrying along the street.

"Won't you come in?" he urged as they reached the house.

"All right," she said in a muffled voice. "Just for a moment."

Inside he turned on the central heating, and went upstairs to change his sweater. When he came down again, he found the kitchen empty. Dara, still in her coat, was in the living room. She was standing in front of the fireplace, staring up at the painting. A pool of water circled her feet.

"Dara? I brought you a sweater. It's one of my favorites," he added, meaning the painting. "You both look so happy."

She turned to him, her usually expressive face blank. Perhaps he should have praised the composition, the handling of the paint? But before he could make amends, she was heading for the kitchen. There she exchanged her wet coat for Abigail's sweater. Although her hair clung darkly to her head, she insisted that she didn't need a towel. As he opened a bottle of red wine, he asked how she was. "We haven't seen you for weeks."

"Yes." She wrapped her hands around her glass. He was wondering if he ought, in spite of her protests, to fetch a towel, or even a blanket when, almost as if a switch had turned, she began to speak. There had been a review at the women's center, everything was in an uproar, and several of her colleagues had been ill. "I'm leading so many groups," she said brightly, "I sometimes can't remember if I'm doing substance abuse or taking control of your life. I have to wait for the introductions to give me a clue. And we've had a wave of dotty clients. One woman I work with has an obsession with fire extinguishers, another buys lottery tickets all the time. How are things with you and the euthanasia book?"

He described the interviews and how powerfully people spoke. As always Dara asked just the right questions, the ones that made him want to tell her more. "And what about people who've attempted suicide and survived?" she said. "Are you interviewing anybody in that situation? Anybody who regrets the attempt?"

She was watching him intently, and before he knew it he was holding forth again. The single biggest obstacle to euthanasia was the popular belief that most failed suicides were happy to discover their ineptitude. The society's position was that almost anyone who wanted to could commit suicide, from which it followed that failure was a sign of ambivalence, the famous cry for help. "Sorry," he said. "I don't mean to get on my soapbox. People seem to lose sight of the fact that the society is advocating euthanasia only for one particular group, those for whom the prognosis is nothing but pain."

He had coined the last phrase a few days ago and took particular pleasure in saying it. Dara seemed to appreciate it too.

"Nothing but pain," she repeated.

"The reports I've read by doctors are particularly convincing, and of course there are places—Oregon, Belgium—where euthanasia is already legal."

"You're an excellent advocate. I'm sure the book will be useful."

"It's nice to think it might actually do some good. So how are you and—"

Suddenly Dara's glass was on the table, and she was on her feet. "Time to go."

"Oh, can't you stay for supper? I'm sure we can rustle up something. It would be great to have company." In his disappointment he almost took hold of her sleeve.

"I have things to do," she said, not looking at him, reaching for her coat.

He was still saying that he hoped they would see her soon, that he knew Abigail missed her, as she left the room. He heard the sounds of first their front door, then hers, open and close.

Later that evening, when Abigail rang, he mentioned the encounter.

"How was she?" she said. "She left me a message the other day. I couldn't quite make it out, but I know she was upset. By the time I phoned back she was in a meeting."

"She seemed fine, a bit preoccupied. Or, I don't know, maybe tired. Things at the center sound even more chaotic than usual."

"I must call her. I just never have ten minutes free when we're touring." A rustling sound accompanied her words—was she sorting papers?—and then she began to talk about how well their school visit had gone.

ON THE FIRST DAY OF DECEMBER, SEAN WOKE ABRUPTLY TO THE knowledge that the euthanasia book was due in a week. For nearly a month he had been dodging Valentine's phone calls and writing optimistic replies to his e-mails, almost all of which reported finishing a section, or a chapter. Now he had to face the reality that his pursuit of the interviews, and his absorption with the subject matter, had led to many pages but not yet to the coherent chapters that represented his half of the book. The idea of discussing this, or indeed anything, with Valentine was out of the question. Instead, as he stepped into his jeans and pulled on a shirt, he decided to contact the secretary.

Three hours later he climbed the stairs to the attic office. He knocked at the half-open door and a voice called, "Enter."

The secretary was at his desk, on the phone. He smiled, and nodded toward a chair. "This is a matter for your doctor," he said into the receiver. "If you can't resolve it with him or her, then you should seek a second opinion, but it isn't grounds for a complaint to the BMA. People have to act according to their consciences. Forgive me, I have someone waiting."

After several more attempts, he managed to extricate himself. "Sorry about that," he said, approaching with outstretched hand. "Part of my job, as you've probably gathered, is to act as an informal counselor. It's hard for people to keep things in perspective when it's literally a matter of life and death."

He offered coffee, stepped out of the room, and returned a minute later with two blue mugs. "Please feel free to keep your coat on," he said, handing Sean a mug and seating himself opposite. "There's about ten days a year when this office is comfortable." He himself was wearing a dark green pullover and brown corduroy trousers that once again made Sean think of open fields and country lanes. "I'm fine," Sean said. "Thanks for seeing me at such short notice."

"It's nice to have a break from my normal duties. Besides, I'm eager to hear how things are going." He regarded Sean expectantly.

"That's what I want to talk to you about. I'm afraid I'm a little behind. It's not that I'm not working." He held up his file of pages. "But each person's story is so fascinating, and so heartrending." He trailed off, taking refuge in his coffee.

"I see," said the secretary. "The good news is that you've become a convert to our cause. The bad news is that everything is taking longer than you'd expected."

"Exactly," said Sean gratefully.

"I should tell you that Valentine phoned last week. He wanted me to know that his half of the book was virtually done but he was concerned that you might not make the deadline. He said you were a perfectionist."

Carefully Sean set the coffee down. Was there no end to Valentine's betrayals? His brain seethed with retorts and denunciations: Valentine's wretched prose, the way he cut every possible corner. He realized that the secretary was waiting. "That's one way to put it," he said lamely. "We're not ideal coauthors."

"But that is your present relationship. We have a contract and money has changed hands." The secretary was sitting straighter, his voice firm. "Let me take you into my confidence. Not all members of the society were happy that we were spending our limited funds in this way, but I was convinced that the right book could help people, and help to advance our cause. I very much need the book to be finished soon, and within the terms we agreed upon. Tell me what I can do to facilitate that."

The man's sudden briskness was even more jolting than Valentine's perfidy. How naive he had been in assuming that the secretary's sympathies would transcend his business interests. For a moment Sean felt like fleeing. Then, for some mysterious reason, he found himself picturing Bridget and her husband, standing beside the dark wood as the stars came out. The image was, as she had described the actuality, consoling. "I don't mean to suggest that things are dire," he said. "Basically I have drafts of everything except the last section, and the extra one you wanted on mental suffering. I'm sure I can have the manuscript on your desk by the end of the year. Meanwhile you could go ahead and give Valentine's chapters to a good copy editor. That way everything should be done by mid-January."

"Let me have a look at my diary," said the secretary. He stood up and retrieved it from his desk. "Suppose you bring me the manuscript the Wednesday after Christmas. And let's forget about the mental suffering. It's by no means certain that the board members would approve such a section, and we can always add it if we do a second edition. How does that sound?"

Sean said it sounded fine.

"Good. I'll send you an e-mail confirming these new dates. You may not have read your contract closely, but there is a clause that fifty percent of the advance is forfeit if the manuscript is late. I would hate to have to invoke that, but given the choice between doing so and losing my job, you'll understand which I'd choose."

"Yes, yes, of course," said Sean, getting out of his chair.

"So I'll see you here on the twenty-eighth," the secretary said.

Sean noted the small rudeness of his remaining seated. Somehow that made it easier to reply crisply that he would be here between ten-thirty and eleven that day. He was almost at the door when a thought stopped him. "I was wondering," he said, "if I could talk to the balloonist, the man who hoped to see his wife's soul take flight?"

The secretary looked up at him calmly. "That was me," he said.

In the weeks before Christmas Sean anesthetized himself with his chapters. He felt, as he had when working on Keats, a keen desire to make every sentence as good as possible but a greater ease in doing so without the poet's dazzling example. He sent an e-mail to Valentine announcing that he needed a small extension but that his chapters would require only light editing. Valentine wrote back in his usual cheery fashion: *Sounds good. The secy. has asked for some revisions on my pages. That'll teach me to give them in early.* Sean tried not to gloat; some revisions, he hoped, meant hours of strenuous rewriting. How fortunate, he thought, that Valentine had not grasped what he was trying to say during that phone call on the train, about writing another book together. To Abigail he offered the news of the extended deadline and asked if she could be very specific about her Christmas present.

"And vice versa," she said.

The previous year they had spent Christmas with Sean's parents on the Isle of Wight, but this year neither of them had time to make the journey. Happily Tyler had invited them to spend Christmas at his country house in Wiltshire. The house, like its owner, occupied a special place in Sean and Abigail's history—they had spent a weekend there right after he finally left Judy—and, as they drove down in their rental car on Christmas Eve, the mood between them lightened. Sean's chapters, save for the proofreading, were done and the company's Christmas show in Margate was going well; Abigail seemed more cheerful than in several weeks.

Two other couples were staying at Tyler's, and after a boisterous and delicious dinner Abigail suggested charades. She did an excellent *Harry Potter and the Goblet of Fire*, and everyone applauded Sean's *The Blind Assassin*. Together he and Tyler attempted *Endymion*, which Abigail guessed on the fourth syllable. When they at last retired to their room she turned to him even before the door was closed and kissed him, eagerly and solemnly. Then she led him to the armchair by the window, opened the curtains so that they could see the high white winter clouds, and sat in his lap.

"Tell me about the best Christmas you remember," she said.

"Besides this one? The one when it snowed and we all went tobogganing on the hill behind our house. My father made this fantastic run with red flags and taught me how to steer a sledge. We made this huge snowman at the bottom."

"I remember that Christmas," said Abigail. "I was with my grandparents. We didn't go sledging but we did make a snowman. My grandmother even let him wear a scarf she'd knitted."

When they went to bed, shortly after four, she made love with him as she used to do, in pursuit of pleasure rather than duty. Afterward, as he lay drowsily beside her, Sean allowed himself to hope that the glittering streams were flowing again. Perhaps she had had a few drinks with Valentine, but so what. All couples had tricky times. The important thing was not to allow them, as he and Judy had done, to overwhelm the relationship. As soon as he handed in his chapters, he would sit down with Abigail and talk about how they could have a better balance between work and play. How much money did he need to earn? Might they get married?

THEY ARRIVED BACK IN LONDON ON THE AFTERNOON OF BOXING Day to find the whole house dark—Dara was still away in Edinburgh—and, after two nights' absence, icy cold. They turned on the heat and went to buy groceries. While he printed out his pages, Abigail unpacked and repacked. Then they made moussaka together and, as they ate, discussed her schedule. She would be back on New Year's Eve, in time for the party the stage manager and his wife were throwing. For once Sean was almost impatient for her to be gone, so eager was he to check his chapters one more time and put them in the secretary's hands. The next day he reread them and found to his relief that they had not unraveled while his back was turned; the writing was clear and, at times, even eloquent. He was at the Belladonna Society's office by ten-thirty the following morning.

He and the secretary exchanged Christmas greetings. Then, he could scarcely wait, he handed over his pages.

"Thank you," said the secretary. "I'm sorry if I was a little heavy-handed during your last visit. I didn't mean to come on like the mob with threats and contracts." His face crinkled with the same look of concern he had worn as Valentine told the story of his fictional aunt.

Hastily Sean reassured him. "A kick up the backside was just what I needed. I'd got so carried away by the interviews, I couldn't see the wood for the trees. Thank you for your patience." He would have liked to have mentioned his idea for a more extensive book but now was not the time; first he must get free of Valentine. They parted in a wave of good wishes for the new year.

BACK AT THE HOUSE A LOUTISH BOY, SURELY A STUDENT DOING A holiday job, was ringing the doorbell. "It's for downstairs," he said, holding out a large brown parcel. "There's been no one home the last couple of times I've tried to deliver."

"Thanks," said Sean. "I'll make sure she gets it."

As he carried the package into the house, he recalled that Dara was coming home today. It would be a nice, neighborly gesture to turn on the heat in her flat, buy some provisions. He was so pleased with the idea that he turned around and headed at once to the corner shop. Then, with a bag full of groceries, he picked up the parcel, retrieved her keys from the hook in the hall, and let himself into the flat.

Inside it was cold and dark. He set the package on the table next to a stack of Christmas cards—perhaps Abigail had put them there?—and, trying to make the place more welcoming, went to open the curtains across the French doors. He adjusted the thermostat and put the groceries away, setting the apples in a bowl on the table with a note: *Welcome home, Dara. Milk in fridge. Love, Sean.* He was about to leave when he noticed that the bedroom door was closed and decided to check on the radiator in there too. Once again the curtains were drawn and he crossed the room to open them. Turning back to the radiator, he saw her.

Dara was lying under the covers, her face tilted toward the door, her hair spread across the pillow. When he knelt down beside her, he saw that she was very pale. He touched her cheek—there was no need to do so; he already knew—and found her skin as cold as the sheets.

He was moving toward the phone when he saw an envelope lying on top of the chest of drawers; *Mum and Dad*, read the inscription. It was unsealed. Without thinking, he looked inside and saw not a sheet of paper but many little pieces. He lifted one out. *And th*— Quickly he put the envelope in his pocket and continued to the phone.

L OCHLAN CAME AND FETCHED HIM SIX DAYS LATER, THE DAY AFTER the funeral. As they drove west out of London, over the ridge of the Chilterns, Sean sobbed until Lochlan pulled off the motorway and stopped beside a country road. "There, there," he kept saying. "Please don't cry." Sean could hear his words, but he felt helpless to obey. Blindly he got out of the car and started walking along the grassy verge. Through his thin-soled shoes he could feel the frozen ground. Then— he didn't know how far he'd walked—a van rattled by, much too fast and too close. He stopped next to a stand of rushes, took his first deep breath, and blew his nose.

"I can't talk," he managed to say when he got back to the car, "but I think I've finished crying."

"Good," said Lochlan. He put on Vivaldi and started driving again. They left the motorway for the busy country roads near Witney and, at last, turned onto the much smaller road that led to his and Cleo's village. Their house was at the bottom of the lane next to the village church. As soon as they stepped inside, Cleo appeared in the gloom of the hall. "We're glad you're here," she said, and hugged him.

Lochlan led him up the stairs to the guest room where he'd stayed on his previous visits. The windows looked out over the garden, past the swaybacked roof of the church, to stubbled fields. Between them stood a large desk.

"Here," Lochlan said. "You'll have plenty of space to work when you feel better."

"Thank you," said Sean. "I think I'll take a nap."

H E SPENT MUCH OF THE NEXT WEEK ASLEEP. HE ROSE LONG AFTER Lochlan had left for work, ate cereal, went for endless walks across the frozen fields, did whatever Cleo asked in the way of chores. The day after he arrived she told him that, although she was only six months' pregnant, she had taken leave from her job as a schools' inspector on the advice of her doctor. But there was nothing to worry about, she added quickly. Sean nodded, and allowed himself to be reassured. For a few seconds, concern for Cleo had distracted him from the images that were always right there, just behind his eyelids: Dara as he had last seen her alive, or as he had last seen her.

After he had called the police and her parents—she had left their numbers beside the phone—he had dialed Abigail's number. As usual he got her voice mail; she was doing two shows a day. He had left a message saying, Please call. It's important. Then he had taken a chair from the living room and sat down beside Dara. "I am so sorry," he had said. Being in her presence was not at all like the trauma he had described in the book; rather, what he had felt was an enormous calm. He did not know how long he sat there, watching her, before there came a knock at the door. He touched her cheek one more time, and went to let in the police.

An hour later he was back upstairs, sitting on the sofa, when the phone rang. He answered at once, hoping for Abigail. "Super that you got your chapters in," said Valentine. "The secretary's passed the whole thing on to the copy editor." He was in the neighborhood and wondered if Sean could meet for a drink at the Lord Nelson. As he walked there, Sean pictured himself telling Valentine about Dara; the two had met once, at one of Abigail's shows. Telling her parents, he had kept to the bare facts and got off the phone as quickly as possible. Now he imagined describing the solemn beauty of his brief vigil at her bedside, the shock of realizing, from the offhand remark of a policeman, that Dara—Abigail's friend, his neighbor—had taken her own life.

When he stepped into the pub, Valentine waved from a corner table. "I bought you a scotch," he said, which should have been a signal. His sleek leather jacket lay on the bench beside him. They raised their glasses, and Valentine said a few more complimentary things about Sean's share of the book, how his perspective had deepened the material; how fascinating his interviews were. Sean, to his abiding shame, felt a flash of pleasure. He drank some more scotch. He was setting down his glass, preparing to interrupt, when Valentine said, "I've got something to tell you," and popped his eyes. Then there were only the worst kinds of clichés. Sean had left him, mid-sentence, and gone back to the house to start packing. As he folded his shirts, he understood that Valentine had simply been waiting until he finished his half of the book to break the news. He had brought two suitcases and several boxes in Lochlan's car; everything else he had left, stacked in a corner of his former study.

WHEN HE DID EMERGE FROM HIS ROOM, LOCHLAN AND CLEO treated him like an invalid, lowering their voices and refraining from jokes. Lochlan set up his computer and offered to help him unpack; Cleo offered cups of tea and apologized for the odd Eastern music she listened to while doing yoga. Neither of them asked questions, which, mostly, he appreciated. He had not, since he left London, checked his e-mail or his voice mail. The one worldly task he managed, with Cleo's help, was to contact the secretary. He sat at the kitchen table while she introduced herself as Mr. Wyman's sister-in-law and explained that she was calling on his behalf to let the secretary know that Valentine would be responsible for any further work on the book. There was a pause while she cocked her head, listening. Sean noticed that her cheeks had grown plump with pregnancy.

"I'm not at liberty to say," she said, "but Mr. Wyman has had family difficulties. . . . Thank you. I will."

She hung up. "There, that's done."

"How did he sound?"

"Nice. He asked me to convey his sympathy. Would you like to go for a walk? It's a lovely day."

He had been about to retreat to his room, but something in Cleo's voice made him agree, and even the simple act of putting on his boots lifted him an inch or two from his slough of despond. Outside the weather was unusually mild. She led the way down the lane, past the village cricket pitch, and along the disused railway line. The rails had been removed and only the sleepers were left. Should he mention her condition, he wondered, ask how she was feeling, but she was in the midst of talking about the plans for a village museum. A grant from the lottery had come through and they were turning the old forge into an exhibition space.

"Great," said Sean. From beneath his right foot came a tiny crack. Looking down, he discovered a snail, irrevocably flattened.

"It's all due to Lochlan. He wrote the application. But he's probably going to have to resign from the committee. His boss seems to be getting ready to fire him."

"But that's outrageous. He told me sales were up for the last quarter."

"He doesn't want you to know," Cleo continued. "If worse comes to worst, I've said he can stay at home while I go back to work but he has some old-fashioned notion about being the breadwinner."

As she spoke, her voice grew scratchy. Sean hurried to offer consolation: maybe his boss would relent, and if he didn't Lochlan was sure to find a good job again soon; he had terrific qualifications. A few yards ahead a rabbit raised its head from the grass to give them a bright-eyed stare. As it hopped, in a leisurely fashion, across the tracks, he pictured Dara deftly sketching the neat paws and upright ears.

The next morning he woke to the sound of Lochlan driving away. Before he could think about what he was doing, he got out of bed and approached his computer. He turned it on, and went to make coffee. Back at his desk he checked his e-mail. The news of Lochlan's difficulties had made him realize that he couldn't keep hiding indefinitely. Among the rubbish and notes from friends were eight messages from Abigail, two from Valentine with the subject heading *The Book*, and one with the heading *Apologies*.

Abigail had finally phoned while he was packing his books, F through H. "I just got out of the evening show," she said. "We had three curtain calls. It was fantastic."

Earlier, before Valentine, while he sat on the sofa, he had tried to think how to tell her that her best friend had died, by her own hand, while they were playing charades. Or perhaps while they were driving back to London. Or while they were buying groceries. Or making moussaka. Or brushing their teeth. But now that the moment had arrived he uttered the simplest possible sentence, a noun and a verb. In the ensuing chaos he had eventually managed to convey two additional pieces of information: the manner of Dara's death and that Valentine had talked to him. What had Abigail done after he hung up? He didn't know, or care. He had seen her only once more, at the funeral; she had sat with Dara's parents while he sat in the back row.

Now he scrolled through the e-mails, forwarding them to her and then deleting them, the modern equivalent of sending letters back unopened. He did the same with Valentine's. He was about to log off when he noticed among the remaining messages one from Georgina, sent the day before. Still in his mood of brisk efficiency, he opened it.

Dear Sean,

I keep thinking about our last conversation and wish I'd tried harder to find out why you'd decided to give up on your dissertation. I can't help worrying that the fault may be partly mine for failing to convey sufficient enthusiasm. I am very poor at this sort of

*thing—I think it's called human relations!—but if you would care
to discuss the matter at any point, I am at your service.*

Belated seasonal greetings,
Georgina

Perhaps in some extreme way, Sean thought, he was finally learning
what Keats had meant when he claimed that soul making was the main
business of the world.

T HAT NIGHT HE FELL ASLEEP ONLY TO FIND HIMSELF, AN HOUR
later, open-eyed in the glimmering dark. It was the time he most
dreaded, the energy of the previous day gone and the next one still
impossibly far away. He tried to focus on the outline of the nearer
window, a dim rectangle, and count his breaths. At nineteen he glimpsed
a movement by the bookcase—Ian, the builder, figuring out how to
put his head in the oven—and at twenty-eight, here was Frank with
his brain tumor. He stopped counting when he saw Bridget's husband,
Kingsley, writhing in pain beside the other window. Then he spotted
Dara by the desk, her bicycle helmet in one hand, a gardening trowel in
the other. He seized his dressing gown, and fled.

Downstairs he was relieved to find a light on in the living room and
Cleo on the sofa, reading. "Hello," he said. "Couldn't you sleep?" He sat
down in an armchair.

"No, it's the baby. By nine at night I can scarcely keep my eyes open.
Then I wake up to pee and he starts kicking and I can't get back to sleep.
I find reading gardening books helps."

"Dara liked gardening," he said.

"She was Abigail's friend, wasn't she?" said Cleo.

And then he told the story the only way he could, zigzagging back and forth between what he knew of Dara's life and his own small role in it. "She was always ready to listen to me, always ready to help. I should have guessed something was wrong the last time I saw her when she wouldn't stay for supper. And then—it doesn't bear thinking about—I went on and on about the euthanasia book, and how no one regretted suicide."

He described Dara's questions and how he couldn't help feeling that the conversation, and his work in general, had in some way contributed to her death; how she had left a note for her parents, torn into many pieces. "I took the envelope before I phoned the police. I didn't think they could stand the disappointment."

"Do you still have it?"

He nodded.

Cleo was heaving herself off the sofa. "Please," she said.

Upstairs he retrieved the envelope from the bottom of his suitcase and, pushing his computer aside, carefully emptied the contents onto the desk. Cleo bent over the fragments and began to move the pieces of paper around: *Dear Mum an—*, *life tog—*, *little girl*. At last, with a sigh, she straightened. "Forgive me, Sean," she said, "but I think you ought to send this to her parents. It shows that their daughter was trying to reach them, that she thought about them during those last hours. Maybe"—she gazed up at him—"that's better than nothing."

He nodded again. Cleo was moving toward the door. On the threshold she turned, but whatever thought had waylaid her, she decided to keep to herself. She stepped out of the room and gently closed the door. He sat down at the desk and moved the lamp to shine on the fragments.

Dear Mum an—, *little girl*

Everything, he thought, he had got everything wrong. There he was with Abigail, claiming she was the love of his life, while she was screwing his old friend. There was Valentine betraying him on the page and between the sheets. There was Dara, seeming so cheerful with her useful job, her sketching and her gardening, as she walked further and further into the valley of shadow. There was the secretary, leaning out of the basket of a balloon, searching the horizon in all directions for his wife's soul.

Dear Cameron, he wrote, *I owe you . . .*

2

I MARK THIS DAY WITH A WHITE STONE

I ALWAYS INTENDED TO LIVE AS AN UPRIGHT MAN. I REMEMBER, when I was seventeen, telling my friend Davy that I thought it was wrong to eat anything I couldn't kill myself. "I don't mean that I have to kill everything I eat," I explained, "but I want to be sure that I can."

We were taking a break from doing our homework, leaning on the gate of one of his father's fields, smoking. It was our new, illicit hobby. Between us, when we put our minds to it, we managed to get through a pack a week. A couple of months before, Davy and I had followed the harvester across this field, stacking the bales of straw. Now, in early November, the drab stubble was nearly buried in mud. Rain had fallen every day for a week and, on the far side of the valley, coppery clouds promised more.

Davy had been to the barber that morning, and when he turned to look at me, all his features, his light blue eyes, his full red lips, seemed larger and more naked. "With your bare hands, Cameron?" he asked, mockingly.

I knew it was just an expression, the "bare" emphasizing the extremity of whatever the hands were doing, but I glanced down at my own hands—rather small for a boy of my age, with my father's short, flexible thumbs—and I couldn't imagine them clutching the neck of an animal or bringing a hammer down on a skull.

"Of course not," I said. "With a gun." I'd never held a gun of any kind, other than a toy pistol, but I'd seen enough films that I could picture myself squinting down the barrel, squeezing the trigger.

"How about one of Dad's pigs? If you kill it, I bet he'll let you have some of the bacon. Or there are the hens. But they're so easy, they don't count."

Davy himself killed hens on a regular basis, chopping off their heads with a little axe that the rest of the time was used for kindling. On the one occasion when I'd been present the head had fallen to the ground and the rest of the hen, a plump Rhode Island Red, had stood up, blood pulsing from its empty neck, and taken a few tipsy steps in my direction. I had come round to find myself staring at the sky, Davy's mother wiping my face with a towel, and the bird gone. I pretended I'd missed lunch but no one was fooled.

"Come on," Davy said, taking a last pull of his cigarette before flicking it into a puddle. "Let's go and choose your dinner."

I can't remember which came first—working on the farm during the summer or bicycling over on Saturday afternoons to do homework with Davy and talk endlessly—but for the last year I had felt more comfortable in his house than in my own. On Saturdays his parents were usually out doing their weekly shop and his older sister, if she was around, was either in her room with friends or absorbed in a book. That particular afternoon we'd been puzzling over a passage in Horace's *Odes* when Davy said, "Did you see the way Yardley was swinging his briefcase when he left school yesterday? I bet he and Stevenson had it off last night."

Mr. Yardley was our Latin teacher and Mr. Stevenson was our physics teacher, and Davy had some notion that the two men were a couple. I was equally adamant that they weren't. The argument could not be resolved, partly due to lack of evidence but mostly because the real subject of the dispute was something that neither of us was ready to mention; this was rural Scotland in the 1960s.

"Don't talk rubbish," I had said. "How are you translating *Nunc est bibendum, nunc pede libero pulsanda tellus?*"

"You always say that," said Davy. "You don't like to admit that anyone is doing anything. Freud would have said you're repressed."

"Of course I'm repressed. I live with my parents."

At that time I threw around words like "repressed" and "inhibited" with no notion of their true meaning. My ignorance about sex, both physically and emotionally, now seems unimaginable, but neither at school nor at home was the topic ever discussed openly. When we studied *Othello*, it was hinted that Othello's jealousy stemmed from his intimate relations with Desdemona. And one day while we were thinning the lettuces, my father said, "You'll be getting into the girls soon, Cameron. Just don't get carried away thinking that the first one is the love of your life. Not so close together," he added, pointing at the spindly green plants. So it never occurred to me to connect our playground words, "bugger," "fag," "queer," "poof," with the sense that had been growing in me for some time that Davy was different from most of our schoolfellows. The feeling had intensified that summer when, after an unusually hot day's harvesting, we'd gone swimming in the river. As I changed into my trunks, I had felt an odd pressure, as if a hundred people were watching me, not just Davy, also changing a few yards away, who'd seen me naked dozens of times. I had hurried into the water and kept my distance rather than indulging in our customary horseplay.

We finished the harvesting, school started again, and Davy had begun to harp on our teachers' private lives with tedious frequency. That afternoon, trying as usual to change the subject, I had said I wanted a smoke. We had set Horace aside and headed down the lane where I'd held forth about the ethics of eating meat. Now Davy led me to an adjacent field where the pigs held sway. We had last visited them while studying *Animal Farm*, and agreed that it was easy to see why Orwell made them his leaders. Their small, pale eyes were disquietingly human, as was their nakedness. Davy claimed that if you fell while feeding them they would try to eat you. After the rain their field was even more of a quagmire than usual. The teats of the sow nearest the gate grazed the mud.

"How about Mabel?" said Davy, pointing at a pig with a large black patch on one haunch. "She killed three of her last litter by rolling over on them. I'm sure she's ready for the great sty in the sky."

As Mabel rooted around searching for acorns, the poor pig's truffles Davy called them, I made one last effort to explain myself. "If I'm going to eat meat," I said, "then it seems immoral to be squeamish about killing animals but happy to benefit from someone else doing it."

"You eat carrots and you don't grow them. Come on."

The breeze was quickening and in the hedgerows the birds, as if at some secret signal, had fallen silent. Davy was already heading down the road, back to the house. I trailed a few steps behind. At the back door he told me to wait. I stood idly scraping my boots on the boot scraper, hoping that whatever prank he had in mind would restore our relationship to its former ease. When he reappeared, he was carrying a rifle.

"Are you allowed to have that thing?" I said.

The only answer came from above as the rain started to fall. Davy was already striding across the farmyard. Once again I followed, hands in pockets, head down, as if demonstrating my reluctance to him, and to myself. I could never have admitted that somewhere deep inside I was also excited, swept up by Davy's passion and wherever it was taking us. Back at the field, he balanced the rifle on the top rung of the metal gate and, just as I'd imagined, squinted down the barrel. Mabel had moved closer.

"Fifty feet," he said. "A tricky shot for a novice, but it's easier to aim when you have a support."

"No."

Davy lifted the rifle off the gate, and held it out to me. I backed away. "Do you want people to think you're a coward?" he said, looking me square in the face.

"What people? There's only you and the pigs."

Still looking at me, still holding out the gun, he took a step toward me. "Besides," I added, "I'm not."

Davy took another step. In the rain his hair had turned almost black, and his eyes had a flat, bright look. "Come on," he whispered, his face so close that I felt, rather than heard, his words. The barrel of the gun nudged my chest.

People sometimes claim that at moments of crisis everything was a blur or, alternatively, crystal clear. For me that afternoon in the pig field was both. Davy's eyes never left mine; the gun pressed against my chest; the pigs grunted and scuffled. I took the gun and I imitated Davy. I rested the barrel on the gate, peered along it until it seemed to be pointing, roughly, in the direction of Mabel's patchwork rump, and pulled the trigger. I had no intention of hurting her. This was all about Davy and me and a certain heat between us. The gun kicked; my head filled with noise and the sharp smell made my nostrils prickle. Mabel screamed and the other pigs plunged into confusion.

"Damn," said Davy. "What have you done?"

He scrambled over the gate. He had covered only a few yards—the mud slowed him down—when, still clutching the gun, I mounted the slippery metal bars and followed. The other pigs had stampeded to a far corner. If I fell, I thought, they could eat me in a minute.

Davy came to a stop a few yards from Mabel. "Damn," he said again. "I never thought you'd do it."

Close up she was much larger than she had appeared from the gate. Her eyes were the palest blue. She lay on her side, squealing, trotters churning the air. I hoped vainly that I had only grazed her. Then I caught sight of the blood, welling up through the mud on her belly.

We both stood watching, transfixed. "My dad's going to kill us," Davy said above her screams.

"I thought you said it was okay."

"What sort of idiot are you? Pigs are worth money. You don't go round killing them. Give me the gun."

I was about to do his bidding when suddenly I grasped his intention. Instead I threw the gun, clumsily, as far as I could. Davy started toward it; so did I. And then we were wrestling over it, struggling to keep our footing. Within seconds we were dragging each other down. I was underneath, my clothes instantly soaked. Davy was on top, red-faced, panting. I could feel, through his jeans, that he was excited and I knew he could feel that I wasn't. He pushed my head back into the mud—he was much stronger than me—and, quite suddenly, he leaned forward and bit my neck.

F OR THE REST OF THAT YEAR I WORKED TO PAY DAVY'S FATHER BACK for Mabel, and during all those months, while I mucked out the byre and fed the hens and watered the cows, Davy didn't speak to me. Several times I tried to explain that I'd never, in a million years, thought I would hit Mabel, but he cut me dead. I soon gave up and followed his example, keeping my head down when our paths crossed. At school we changed our desks to sit on opposite sides of the room, and when classes ended in June we went our separate ways—he to study French at Aberdeen University, me to do chemistry at Glasgow—without even saying good-bye.

After I graduated, I worked in a laboratory in Glasgow for five years before moving to London. A few friends lived there, and I'd been offered a well-paid job, developing new colors of paint, that promised to be more interesting than my current one. Fiona had started work at the company as a secretary the month before, and she was kind about showing me where to keep my lunch, how to request supplies. She was tall and ungainly, with a mobile, expressive face and a light, girlish voice. Her short, fair hair framed her face in little wisps. One afternoon when I found her having lunch at her desk, folding an origami crane, she told me that she'd gone to art school and had thought a job with a paint company might somehow benefit her work. "What an idiot," she said, holding up a blue crane. That evening we went for a drink, and from then on every few weeks one or the other of us would suggest a trip to the pub. Once we went to the cinema; afterward we caught our separate buses home with a casual wave. Then one day, when I had been in London for six or seven months, she asked if I'd like to join her and some friends that weekend for a picnic in the rose garden at Regent's Park.

Sunday, 15 June 1969, was a perfect summer day, warm with a light breeze, everything still fresh and green and not yet soiled by the heat. People smiled as they passed me, walking along in my white trousers and blue T-shirt, carrying a plate of cucumber sandwiches; I was taking part in some recognizable English ritual. I was almost at the garden when I caught sight of Fiona kneeling beside a dark-haired child, a girl of about eight or nine, who was wearing red trousers and a white blouse patterned with butterflies.

"Annabel," said Fiona, "this is Cameron."

"Hi," said Annabel. She had the kind of face we call heart-shaped: wide across the eyes, narrow at the chin. Her teeth were slightly too big for her mouth. "Please," she said to Fiona. "One more go."

"I'm sorry," said Fiona. "I have to help with the picnic. Annabel wants another shot on the swings," she added to me.

Unhesitatingly I held out my plate of sandwiches to Fiona and bent down. "I'd be happy to give you a go."

"Cameron," said Annabel. She gave my name all three syllables, and reached up a hot, sticky hand.

Years later Fiona told me that that was the moment when she began to fall in love with me, when she saw me walking off hand in hand with Annabel toward the swings. What did the two of us talk about on that first meeting? Her hamster, or school, or how her mother was teaching her chess, I have no recollection. I do recall Annabel's giddy delight as I pushed her higher and higher. A woman pushing a much smaller child on the next swing said, "Your daughter's very fearless."

"Just a friend," I said.

Annabel and I played until even she had had enough. As we started back to the picnic, she looked up at me from beneath her dark eyelashes and asked if I would carry her. Unthinkingly I hoisted her up. She wrapped her legs around me with practiced ease, and rested her flushed cheek on my shoulder; I felt she had delivered her entire self into my keeping. I would have carried her, happily, for hours, days. I was twenty-seven years old and, until that moment, I had no idea what my heart was capable of.

Since I left home I had had a number of girlfriends, several at university, more afterward. I had slept with them, taken holidays in Venice and the Dordogne, I had even lived with one for six months, but I had never been sorry when the relationship ended, had always been puzzled by the arguments, the vehemence. Things had worked for a while, now they didn't. What was the problem? Which was, of course, the problem. You're like a machine, one girl said. Another called me a cold fish.

The cucumber sandwiches were gone by the time Annabel and I reached the picnic, but plenty of cakes and scones remained. The hosts, Annabel's parents, offered me food as if I had returned from a long journey. They were old friends of Fiona's. She had grown up with Sheila in Lancashire and been on holiday several times with her and Giles. They were one of those couples I met frequently at that time where the woman did something virtuous and poorly paid—in Sheila's case social work—and the man did something businesslike and lucrative—in Giles's case, advertising. They had two other children besides Annabel, both younger.

Reunited with her parents, Annabel ignored me. She ate two slices of the lopsided chocolate cake Fiona had brought and played with the son of another couple, a quiet boy with a purple birthmark on his left ear. At one point, chasing him round the edge of the rug, she knocked over my tea. It spilled harmlessly onto the grass but Sheila grabbed her arm. "Calm down, Annabel. You spilled Cameron's tea. Say you're sorry."

"That's okay," I said. "I was finished."

"Sorry," said Annabel, not even looking at me.

Giles took a photograph of the group and I followed suit. As a boy, I'd had an old Brownie that I seldom used: the developing was so expensive and the results frequently disappointing. Soon after I moved to London, though, I had bought a 35-millimeter camera that I was gradually learning to use. Now I photographed our picnic from different angles before turning to take a picture of the children, who were searching the grass for four-leaf clovers. I took half a dozen. In the last shot Annabel is looking up at me, smiling; every eyelash is distinct. Later I gave a framed copy of that photograph to Sheila and Giles.

I put the camera away. Giles produced a bottle of gin, someone else had brought tonic, and we segued into cocktail hour. I drank two strong ones and listened idly to a conversation about Crete: the beaches, the labyrinth. Fiona sat beside me, contributing anecdotes from her visit there the previous spring. Then one of the children fell asleep and people stood up and began to reclaim their possessions. Without discussion, Fiona caught the bus home with me and we slept together. I liked her body, her small breasts, her narrow hips, more than I expected, and she seemed to like mine, which is five foot ten, reasonably fit, ordinary, save for the sickle-shaped scar where I had my appendix out when I was eleven.

The wedding took place a year later. I remember being relieved when Fiona agreed that a registry office made sense—we would use our small savings toward buying a flat—and then a little disturbed by my relief. Although I hadn't been to church in years, it had been a regular part of my childhood, and the prospect of making these very public promises before the altar had given me pause. But I put aside my doubts and allowed myself to be carried along by that optimism which was one of Fiona's most endearing traits: of course we would find a parking space, the train would wait, the weather would improve. Her parents and her sister, Leslie, came down from Lancashire and my parents from Scotland. We had visited both families at Easter and they had all exclaimed with pleasure when we broke the news.

Fiona wore a blue dress. Annabel came also wearing a blue dress and carrying a bunch of white flowers—they had a rather cloying smell—which she presented to Fiona. After the ceremony, Fiona threw them into our small crowd of guests, and her sister caught them. Then we retired to Sheila and Giles's. They felt pleasantly implicated in our marriage and gave a party for us in their garden. My parents spent most of the evening talking to Davy. He too now lived in London, and he and I were reconciled. He had shown up at the registry office wearing a white suit, his new boyfriend, Joe, at his side. From time to time I glanced over at this odd quartet, wondering whether to intervene, but conversation never seemed to falter, and twice I saw my mother doubled over with laughter. She thinks they're just friends, I thought; she hasn't a clue. But when I telephoned a fortnight later—Fiona and I were newly back from our honeymoon in Greece—she remarked how glad she was to see Davy with a nice young man. I could not have said exactly why I put down the receiver in such a bad mood.

After Mabel's death, Davy and I had not spoken for nearly a decade.

Then one evening, the January after the picnic, I went swimming at the pool near Covent Garden. I was standing in the shallow end, adjusting my goggles, when a figure walking on the far side caught my eye. Without thinking, I swam over and called his name.

"Cameron," he said, squatting down so that I was level with his muscular, freckled legs. "I knew I'd run into you eventually."

From that one sentence it was clear we were friends again. We thrashed back and forth—we both still did the crude version of the crawl we'd learned at school—and went out for an Italian meal. Davy managed a posh furniture shop. He had meant to use his degree in French, perhaps work at the UN, but he'd taken a summer job at the shop and never left. "Of course it's a stereotype," he said, "the poofter with the matrons, but I enjoy it." He smiled.

"That's the main thing," I said, trying to convey unruffled approval. Except for his pristine shirt and perfectly styled hair he did not, to my eyes, look queer, but I saw the waiter shoot him a sly glance as he took our order.

"Funny," Davy said, "when we were growing up, I was sure you were too. I was always trying to drop hints that your secret was safe with me."

"And I didn't know how to tell you that I wasn't. Do you remember you used to bang on about those teachers: Yardley and Stevens?"

"Stevenson. Yes, they were a bright light for me. I had these feelings that no one between Edinburgh and John O'Groats seemed to share, but here were two adults who, at least in my imagination, were doing unspeakable things and they had jobs and people calling them 'sir.'"

Then he told me that a couple of years before he had been up north, visiting his parents, and bumped into Yardley in a gay pub in Edinburgh. "At first we both pretended we were just there for a drink. Then Yardley said, 'Well, it never occurred to me that you were.' 'I can't say the same,' I said, and he laughed. I couldn't help asking if it wasn't a kind of torture teaching in a boys' school, all that forbidden fruit. 'Forbidden fruit?' he said. 'Don't *you* fancy yourself. Happily, I'm no pederast.'

"I asked about Stevenson, and Yardley said he was one of those odd ducks who wants to take care of his mum. He kept a photograph on his desk of a girl he claimed was his dead fiancée. Yardley's theory was that he'd bought it in an antique shop. We chatted for a few more minutes and then his pal showed up, a thickset, burly fellow. He looked like a plumber, which was exactly what he was."

The waiter came to clear our plates. I was pondering the word "pederast." From the Greek, I knew, but not the same root as "pedestrian." And what was the exact meaning, I was wondering, when Davy asked if I remembered the day we'd butchered Mabel.

"God, that was awful. I still can't believe that I hit her. I'd never even held a gun before."

"It was all in aid of some daft idea, wasn't it? Some theory about being an ethical carnivore. But when I wanted to put her out of her misery, you behaved as if I were a murderer."

"Stupid sentimentality. As you can see"—I nodded after my departed osso bucco—"I still eat meat." I didn't want to mention the rest of what I remembered: our wrestling in the mud, his biting my neck. For nearly two weeks afterward I had worn a polo neck at home, but at school, where all was revealed by the regulation white shirt, I was teased mercilessly. Several boys speculated that Christine Patterson was responsible; she must have heard the rumors because she started blushing when we met.

"That was a hard time for me," Davy said. "I'd got it into my head that I was in love with you but you seemed oblivious. What I'd have done if you hadn't been, I've no idea. And then, when you shot Mabel, Dad was furious. He even called the police."

"The police? About Mabel?" Both the fact itself, and that I hadn't known, were startling.

Davy nodded. "I had to tell him it was partly my fault to stop him from pressing charges."

Which was true, I thought, but didn't say. After he bit me, Davy had staggered to his feet and grabbed the gun. I didn't see what happened next—he was between me and Mabel—but I heard a single shot followed by a low piteous grunt. When I got up, Mabel's snout was in the mud and Davy's face was wild. "Get out of here," he cried.

"But the pigs will eat her." Since Mabel stopped screaming, the other pigs had begun to gather, slowly moving closer from various parts of the field. There seemed no end to the horrifying possibilities of the day.

"For God's sake"—Davy lunged toward me—"go away."

Now, more than a decade later, I once again apologized. "I'm sorry. I was an idiot. I didn't know about your father and the police."

"How could you? Mabel made delicious bacon. So have you managed to kill anything else?"

He spoke lightly, with no thought that I might answer yes, and I managed to respond in the same vein. "Nothing edible. The odd mouse, a few wasps. Does your dad know you're a poofter?"

"Yes and no. He knows I'm not 'normal,' but I haven't shoved it in his face. It's hard for both of us. I'm not the son he wants, and sometimes I can't help wishing I were. My sister's been great about it. What about you?"

"Me?"

"What do you do for sex?" He sat back, watching me, widening his eyes, a parody of flirtation that was also, in its way, a flirtation.

Just for a moment I imagined telling him that I felt like he used to do—that no acceptable way of life matched my feelings—but the moment passed. Instead I told him about Fiona and that we were planning to get married. "I think you'll like her," I said, which turned out to be true.

S OON AFTER THE WEDDING I MOVED TO A DIFFERENT LABORATORY and Fiona began to assist a man who painted murals in restaurants and shops. In our new flat she had done a mural on the dining room wall, a picture of our first picnic, with bears and lions and monkeys in attendance. Her friend Philip, over for dinner, saw it and one thing led to another. There was a surprising amount of such work around, and she had a gift for luminous skies and cuddly animals.

Our lives settled into a pleasant routine. We took turns cooking, went out on weekends. Most Thursdays after work we went round to Sheila and Giles's for supper. Often I came straight from the laboratory and Sheila and I had an hour with the children before the others arrived. It became understood that I would help Annabel with her arithmetic homework and with anything vaguely scientific: a project on hedgehogs, where snow came from, why Rufus, the family dog, had such a long tongue. She was a willful, deeply curious girl who could ask questions for hours. It took me a while to realize that, beneath her voluble exterior, she took everything to heart. One evening I described how there had once been wolves and bears walking down her street but they had all been hunted to extinction. Two days later Sheila phoned to say that Annabel was having nightmares about Rufus being killed.

As I sat at the kitchen table, coaxing Annabel through her sums or identifying the different kinds of clouds, Sheila would come and go. I could almost hear the thought running through her head: what a good father he'll make. And mostly, I admit, I basked in her approval. So when Fiona got pregnant I didn't have a leg to stand on. I did remind her that we'd agreed to wait a few years, but she brushed my doubts aside. "We'll manage," she said. "I can always go back to work in an office." Our daughter, Dara, was born when I was thirty, Fiona was twenty-six, and Annabel was nearly eleven.

At first we continued our Thursday evenings with Sheila and Giles; Dara was an easygoing baby and could sleep anywhere. But as she grew bigger and Sheila and Giles busier, running their children to music lessons and the houses of friends, our get-togethers grew less frequent. Within six months I had lost my particular closeness with Annabel. She no longer ran to meet me, dragged me off to her bedroom to see her hamster's new trick. I began to find excuses not to visit. When Dara was three, I was offered a job in Edinburgh and, after lengthy discussions with Fiona about the virtues of living in Scotland, closer to her parents and mine, accepted.

A T THE TIME WE MOVED NORTH, MY PARENTS WERE IN THEIR LATE fifties and both, seemingly, in good health. They had grown up on the same street in Inverness and married in 1939, the week before my father enlisted in the engineering corps. He had spent the war safely in England. My mother often described the time she had visited him at a base near Manchester. After supper he had proposed a walk up a nearby hill. "I thought we were looking for privacy," she would say with a coy smile. But as they reached the top, a plane approached. Before she could run for cover my father said, "Watch this." A column of light sprang up from the base and fastened on the plane; no matter how the pilot looped and banked, the light never lost it. What they were watching, my father explained proudly, was a system called radar.

He was away for most of the war, but evidence of his visits home exists in the form of first my birth and two years later that of my brother. Even in his pram Lionel was on better terms with life than I was. When my mother took us shopping, people exclaimed over his curly hair and his broad smiles. I have no memory of being jealous. I too was under his spell, and I remember being happy not to have so much of my mother's attention; I liked being able to play my games unobserved. When my father finally came home from the war, he got a job in a brewery and we moved a hundred miles south to the town of Perth.

Now I can imagine that this must have been hard for my mother, leaving her parents and friends, but people didn't think like that then: you just got on with it, a job was a job. As for me, I was still too young to care. I started school, I learned to read and count, I played with my friends. When I came home there was Lionel, eager to do almost anything I wanted, though he got fed up if I made him the prisoner in our games too often. We lived in a council flat until I was ten and then moved into a modest house with a garden where my father grew vegetables and the red roses my mother loved.

When I was sixteen and Lionel was fourteen he made the school rugby team. It was an honor for a boy of his age, but my parents weren't pleased; they worried that the practices would interfere with his homework. For as long as I could remember they had made clear that there was no question of either of us leaving school at fifteen. We would go to university, we would have the advantages they'd fought for and missed. Lionel kept assuring them that he could do both; the exercise cleared his head and helped him to study. In the autumn the team played a match every Saturday afternoon, either at home or away. None of us ever went to see him play.

On Saturday, 16 November 1957, he announced to us at lunch that he'd been moved to the forwards for that afternoon. "It should be a good game," he said.

My mother said she was baking. My father needed to plant the winter vegetables. It was a bright autumn day, cold but not bitter, and there was a wistful note in Lionel's voice. "I'll come," I said.

When I cycled over to the playing fields an hour later, I found maybe three dozen spectators, mostly men in anoraks and younger brothers, straggling along the edge of the pitch, watching the teams warm up. Lionel spotted me and waved. He was number 14. After a few more minutes of milling around the game started and the players began to run up and down, following the ball and followed by our gym teacher acting as referee and blowing his whistle. Soon Lionel's cheeks were red and his legs were streaked with mud. I was standing next to the father of one of his teammates, number 10, and he took it upon himself to explain the game—scrums, penalties, etc.—breaking off periodically to shout encouragement. His enthusiasm was contagious and I echoed his shouts. Lionel was three inches shorter and probably twenty pounds lighter than the other forwards but he was bold and nimble; several times he got hold of the ball and nearly scored.

"For a wee lad," said my neighbor, "your brother's not bad."

With fifteen minutes to go, Lionel's team was two up when the referee called a scrum. Ten or twelve players, including Lionel, put their heads down and began to shove back and forth, slipping and sliding on the wet grass. The referee threw the ball into the middle and blew his whistle. The man beside me cheered; so did I. Presently the ball emerged and the knot of players separated, leaving a figure lying on the ground.

"Is that not your brother?" said the man.

I wasn't worried; several times in the game Lionel had tripped or fallen. It was only when the referee bent down and immediately jumped up, blowing his whistle repeatedly, that I began to run.

He was still alive when I reached him. I put my hand on his back and felt his faltering breath. The referee yelled at me not to move him. But he was facedown in the dirty grass. "He can't breathe," I said. I put my hands on either side of his head, over his ears, and carefully raised his face an inch above the ground. "Lionel," I said. "Lionel."

They let me ride with him in the ambulance to the hospital where one of the doctors phoned my parents to say that Lionel had broken his neck. The funeral was held four days later. That night, at supper, I said that I'd return Lionel's library books. I had barely uttered his name when my father raised his hand for silence. In the months that followed, Davy's farm became my refuge. Gradually I learned to act as if I'd never had a brother.

F OR SEVERAL YEARS AFTER WE MOVED NORTH I WAS HOPEFUL THAT what I had experienced with Annabel was an isolated occurrence. I had glimpsed some dark, aberrant corner of myself, but there was no need to spend more time there. We don't have to be defined by our worst impulses. Almost at once coming to Edinburgh seemed like a good decision. We had a four-bedroom house on a quiet street near the university. My job was tolerable; my coworkers pleasant. And Fergus, who was born a few months after we arrived, was, like his sister, a good-tempered baby. Fiona took care of the children and gradually began to find work painting murals, not as much as in London, but enough to keep her busy. We had a circle of friends, couples whom Fiona met through the nursery school, or at the park. Periodically I ran into an old school friend; none stuck, except for Davy.

One unexpected bonus of our move was that we saw more, rather than less, of him. His parents were still on the farm but increasingly frail, and his visits grew more frequent and often included a stop in Edinburgh. Eight months after Fergus was born, he came to stay the night. He arrived in a taxi, as usual bearing gifts: flowers for Fiona, a set of crayons and a sketch pad for Dara. She lay drawing on the living room floor while we had a drink before dinner. Davy, who had last seen

Fergus when he was a few weeks old, bounced him on his knee in a way that made him gurgle and hum.

"That's my boy," said Davy and, turning to me, added, "He looks a little like Lionel."

"Who's Lionel?" said Fiona.

Quickly, before Davy could respond, I answered. "My younger brother. He died when he was fourteen, in a rugby game."

"I thought you were an only child," she said.

"Oh, he's smiling," Davy exclaimed, hoisting Fergus higher. Tactfully he embarked on a story about one of his fellow passengers on the train.

In bed that night I tried to explain to Fiona. "I wasn't keeping it secret," I said. "It's something we never, ever talked about, my parents and me. If we'd mentioned that there used to be a fourth person in our house, we'd have had to admit that he was dead." I pulled the duvet higher. "As long as I was alive," I added, "I was like everyone else."

"As long as he was alive," Fiona corrected gently. "I'm so, so sorry. I don't know what I'd do if I lost Leslie." It was then that she told me she had fallen in love with me that afternoon in the park when she had seen me walking, hand in hand, with Annabel.

While she drifted off to sleep, I lay beside her, wondering about my slip. Did I think I had died with Lionel? Absolutely not. Already I was more than twice his age, had spent more years without him than with him, had seen and done so many things he had never had the chance to experience. But since I met Annabel, and even before that in some dim way, I had been negotiating between two contradictory theories: on the one hand that if Lionel had lived I would have been like everyone else; on the other that he had died to avoid the shame of knowing my true nature. Several times recently I had caught myself thinking that Fergus resembled Lionel. Now Davy's comment seemed to signal that my secret hope was true: my children, Dara and Fergus, would save me.

W E HAD BEEN LIVING IN EDINBURGH FOR ALMOST THREE YEARS when my father died of a heart attack. We had seen him only the week before when he came through to the city for a reunion of his engineering corps and insisted on tidying up our garden. "I'll just get rid of these dandelions," he had said.

Now when my mother phoned to break the news, I kept saying, "What do you mean dead?" He had no history of heart problems and had spent his last day in typically vigorous fashion: washing the car, doing the shopping, and, in the afternoon, going down to the bowling club. At the funeral his friend Hamish told me that he had had his fourth-highest score ever. He collapsed while returning his ball to the rack. I hope it was like the optimists claim—white light, a kindly figure waiting, arms outstretched—though I know that he himself, a firm agnostic, would have been surprised by such a welcome.

From then on I tried to visit my mother most weeks, with or without Fiona and the children. The first sign of her unraveling came a few months later when she served us tea in cups and saucers that didn't match. The following week I went to get a glass for Dara's juice and found a bag of onions in the cupboard. After we moved to Perth, my mother had seldom seen her own mother or her formidable aunts, but she lived her life as if they might drop in at any moment to run a finger along the tops of the picture frames or peer into her cutlery drawer. Once she even told me that a tidy cupboard was a sign of a tidy mind. Now the sugar bowl was in with the glasses, a tin of soup on top of the plates.

The neighbors began to meet her in the streets at odd hours. She always seemed so purposeful that at first they didn't give these encounters another thought, but soon everyone realized that she had no purpose, or at least none that could be articulated. When they looked out of their windows and spotted her hurrying down the pavement, heedless of rain or cold, they would head out to engage her in conversation and lead her home. The phone calls started. Her neighbor Agnes, who worked as a receptionist for a dentist, twice retrieved her from the bus station. But her most common destinations were our old flat, where we had lived until Lionel was eight, and the primary school where she had met Lionel and me every afternoon for six years.

In spite of all this I was slow to understand that she was not herself. When we visited we still arrived to find the table set for tea with freshly baked scones; she admired Dara's drawings and played with Fergus's cars. There seemed to be no connection between her sensible scone-making self and her disheveled, wandering self. Then one night when I was brushing my teeth the police rang. She had been picked up loitering on a bridge across the River Tay. "I was admiring the moonlight on the water," she claimed when I collected her from the station at midnight.

After this incident I had a long talk with Agnes, who insisted that all my mother needed was a wee holiday. "Couldn't you say you need help with the children," she urged, "so that she'd feel she was doing you a favor?"

My mother agreed to come and stay for a couple of months and, for the first few weeks, everything was remarkably pleasant. She walked Dara to school, she minded Fergus, she cooked and cleaned. Fiona and I no longer had to juggle our schedules. When we arrived home, the house was tidy, supper was in the oven, and the children were playing happily. Fiona got on well with my mother—they shared a sly sense of the ridiculous—and she was pleased that the children would know at least one grandparent; her own parents in Lancashire were too frail to travel. She took on more work, and we even went to the cinema a couple of times. Then one afternoon she came home to find Fergus alone, red-faced and screaming, rattling the front door. Dara, fortunately, was at a friend's house.

"I could hear him from the bottom of the street," Fiona said.

He was still whimpering half an hour later when I got home and started the search for my mother. Had she been in some kind of accident, hit by a car as she returned from a quick trip to the local shops? I called the police in Edinburgh and Perth; I called the hospitals. Then I set out to drive the nearby streets in ever widening circles, pausing whenever I spotted a woman of similar age and gait. After a couple of fruitless hours, I returned home to find that Agnes had phoned; my mother had shown up at the house and begun cleaning. By the time I reached Perth it was dusk and she was standing in the garden, polishing the windows.

"Cameron," she said, "what are you doing here? Would you like a cup of tea?"

Inside she put away her duster and filled the kettle. As it came to the boil, she commented that the swallows were back; it was time to plant the peas. But when she went to the fridge, her face crumpled. "There's no milk," she exclaimed.

"You've been staying with us, in Edinburgh. Don't you remember?"

"We'll have to have condensed."

Tea with condensed milk had been a Sunday treat in childhood. Now, as I sat there in the chilly kitchen drinking the hot, sweet liquid, I remembered how Lionel and I had used to beg my mother for "special tea" and how slowly we had sipped the milky beverage, trying to make it last. When I drove home an hour later, I still had no answer as to why she had abandoned Fergus.

This incident revealed a side of Fiona previously hidden. One aspect of her optimism had always been a readiness to forgive—everyone was just about to behave better—but now she was adamant: under no circumstances could my mother darken our door again. "I don't care if she's confused. No one leaves a four-year-old alone."

The children were in bed and we were in the kitchen, making supper. I was peeling carrots and she was rinsing a sieve in which she had washed lentils. "It makes me think," she went on, shaking the sieve fiercely, "that there's something wrong with her. I don't mean physically, I mean morally."

I slid the peeler, very carefully, the length of the carrot. "Did you turn on the oven?" I asked.

AFTER SEVERAL CONVERSATIONS WITH AGNES, AND A CONSULTAtion with my mother's doctor, I took an emergency leave from work and moved in with my mother until other arrangements could be made. Since going to university, I had barely spent a night beneath my parents' roof. Now, except for my father's absence, it was as if I had never left. I slept in the same narrow bed in my old room; I would not have been surprised to wake to find my school uniform lying on the chair. When I came downstairs in the morning, my mother had the table set for breakfast: cereal, toast, and marmalade, Nescafé. We read the newspaper and chatted while we ate. Afterward she went shopping. She seemed so much her old self that it did not occur to me to go with her.

While she was out I worked steadily on getting the house ready to sell. I began in my room, where the cupboard was filled with schoolboy clothes and the bookcase still held the books I had owned between the ages of ten and eighteen. The former I piled unceremoniously in the hall to go to the charity shop. The latter I started to go through, searching for evidence of my younger self. Who had I been before I became a husband and father? I leafed through *Swallows and Amazons* and set it aside for Dara, pondered a book about Byzantium. On the second or third morning I picked up *Alice in Wonderland* and read the opening chapter where Alice falls down the rabbit hole and drinks the potion—labeled "Drink Me"—which makes her ten inches high, then eats the cake which makes her grow again.

I was about to add the book to Dara's collection when a photograph at the back caught my eye; I found myself looking at an intensely composed little girl with a bold, innocent gaze and bare feet. The photograph accompanied an essay about Charles Dodgson, and the caption explained that this was Alice Liddell, for whom the story was first told and later written down. Glancing through the pages I discovered half a dozen other little girls, staring at the camera or acting out some scene, but never smiling. I turned to the beginning of the essay.

The main facts of Dodgson's life were unexceptionally Victorian. He was born in 1832, the third of eleven children, the son of a stern minister father and a gentle mother. He grew up entertaining his brothers and sisters with games, plays, and poems. He built a model railway in the garden and wrote an opera making fun of Bradshaw's railway guide. At the age of sixteen, he went to Christchurch College in Oxford, where he became a don in mathematics and never left. In the midst of his lectures and social duties he assiduously, and quite publicly, cultivated his many friendships with children and especially with young girls.

The winter after I met Annabel I had purchased and read *Lolita*. Never, even for a page, did I identify with Humbert, and if Annabel had demonstrated a mere fraction of Lolita's precocity I would have stopped my visits immediately. Like every parent, I was filled with disgust and fear by the news stories of kidnappings and child abuse. But now, as I read about Dodgson and his passionate relationships—relationships that seemed to have no destination other than the giving and receiving of playful, rapt attention—I recognized myself. I put the book beside my bed to reread later.

IN THE AFTERNOONS, AFTER A MODEST LUNCH, MY MOTHER AND I usually again went our separate ways. I took walks up Kinnoul Hill, or along the river. Meanwhile she visited her neighbors or, following my example, continued what she thought of as spring cleaning. Her cupboards were again immaculate, and we took more than a dozen loads to the charity shop. A couple of times I caught myself thinking that if I moved back home, she would be fine; she was only fifty-nine. She might have twenty more good years, even remarry. And I would become like Mr. Stevenson, an odd duck who took care of my mum.

Although I had lived in Perth for my entire childhood, the places I walked were mostly new to me. I took my camera on these expeditions and amused myself by photographing the landscape. One day by the river I came across three girls; they must have been a little older than Dara, maybe nine or ten. The tallest of them had taken off her shoes and jeans and was wading out into the water in her underwear. Her dark hair was flying in the wind and her skin was winter white. The other two girls—one had similar coloring, the other was fair—were urging her on. In their absorption none of them noticed my approach. Before I knew what I was doing I had raised my camera and taken several photographs. Only then did I call out, "Hello. Can I help?"

For reasons that were not clear the smallest girl's shoes were in the water. I took off my own shoes, rolled up my jeans, and plunged in. When I returned to the bank, bearing the sodden shoes, the girls crowded around, thanking me. I asked if I could take their picture, and obediently they lined up with their arms around each other. The younger two offered toothy smiles but the oldest gazed at me with a sullen intensity worthy of one of Dodgson's subjects.

I HAD BEEN STAYING WITH MY MOTHER FOR NEARLY THREE WEEKS when the doctor rang to say they had secured a place for her in a nursing home that had facilities for coping with her condition. To my relief he suggested that I bring her in so that we could tell her together. At lunchtime, as we ate our scotch broth, I explained that we had to go to the doctor's that afternoon.

"Why?" she asked. "Are you ill?"

Since that first evening, when I had found her cleaning the windows in the garden, neither of us had mentioned the events that had brought me home. Now I said, "Mum, do you remember you were staying with us in Edinburgh?"

"Would you like some more soup?" She was blinking rapidly.

"You came to stay with us because you couldn't manage here on your own. The neighbors kept finding you wandering in the streets."

She blew on her broth and took another mouthful.

"The day you left Edinburgh," I persisted, "you were meant to be watching Fergus. You left him all alone."

She stood up abruptly. "I forgot the salt," she said.

The doctor was no older than I was, but he was more accustomed to breaking this kind of news, or at least trying to. Finally, even he was defeated by my mother's claims that she was fine; what was all this nonsense about moving into a home? He sent her out to wait with his nurse.

"Does she understand anything?" I said.

"Who can say? Terrible events are happening. Why would she want to acknowledge them?"

"She's only fifty-nine," I said. "Mightn't she get better?"

The doctor tapped his pen. "You're a scientist, aren't you, Mr. MacLeod? Let me be frank. Alzheimer's is destroying her brain; there is no cure. She's probably had it for a while and the shock of losing your father, their routines together, made it worse."

"But a lot of the time she *is* fine. I worry at the home they'll make her into an invalid." I remembered how the Victorians had insisted on being buried with a bell in their coffins so that if they woke up, they could ring for help. What if my mother rang and there was no one to hear?

The doctor stopped his tapping and looked me full in the face. "In an ideal world," he said, "your mother would be cared for by kind, thoughtful people who had known her before she was ill."

He paused, and I knew he was giving me the chance to say she could live with me. I pictured Fiona shaking the sieve and studied my dusty shoes. The doctor went on in brisker tones that the nurses would do their best and of course I would visit. Then he stood up and shook my hand. He was used to family members trying to make him feel bad about the things they ought to feel bad about themselves.

O N OUR LAST DAY IN THE HOUSE I FETCHED MY CAMERA AND, IN spite of my mother's mild protests, insisted on photographing her in her armchair, at the kitchen table, in the garden; I even took a shot of her sitting on the edge of the double bed she had shared with my father. I had taken photographs of her before, snapshots of her with my father and the children, and she had always proved disastrously self-conscious. Now, after her initial demurral, she seemed to forget about the camera. Even as I took the elegiac pictures, I knew they would be among my best.

That evening she made what had been my father's favorite meal: lamb chops with mint sauce, potatoes, and peas, followed by rhubarb crumble. I laid the table with proper napkins and the good cruet. Tomorrow at this time, I thought, she would be in a home and I would have my own life back; tomorrow this life would be gone. When we sat down to eat, I was suddenly choked with emotion, but she was in excellent spirits; the lamb had turned out well. As we ate she chatted about how the butcher had lost his lease.

"He and his wife are planning to move to Glasgow to be near their daughter. I thought I saw Lionel today outside the post office."

She held out the jug of mint sauce. I took it. To my knowledge she had not spoken his name in twenty years.

"I know he's dead," she went on, "but I'm always pleased when he visits me around the town. Your father used to say the same thing."

So that was why she had taken to wandering the streets. "Does he come here?" I said. "To this house?"

"Not yet." She looked over at the chair where Lionel had used to sit. "Do you ever see him?"

"No." I felt a pang of envy, like a stitch in my side.

"Maybe it's because you were there that day? You saw him then so you don't need to see him now."

"It's the other way round," I said. "I need him more because I was there." But, even as I argued, her suggestion made sense. That awful final image of Lionel, facedown in the grass, made it impossible for him to come to me.

"Well, he looks good," my mother said. "You know what a bright smile he has."

She cleared the plates and, when she returned with the crumble, broached a new topic. "Don't take this amiss, Cameron," she said, "but I worry about you. I know you have a lovely family, a good job, a nice home; still I worry there's something wrong. You often seem a little sad."

I looked at her high, unlined forehead, her eyes calm and kind behind her glasses. I could tell her, I thought, about that afternoon with Annabel. What safer confidante than someone who is losing her mind? If she said anything, people would just think she was mad. But I had no words. I was not a pederast, or a pedophile, or a child molester, but I was something close enough to dread the taint of those terms. "I'm a bit fed up at work," I said. "This crumble is lovely."

"It's a good year for the rhubarb," she said, and began to talk about her plans to make jam.

I N SPITE OF THE DOCTOR'S DIAGNOSIS, FIONA CONTINUED TO HOLD A grudge against my mother, and some of that spilled over onto me. It was our first major disagreement. Fergus could have been seriously hurt and she blamed me for being too forgiving. The fact that he wasn't, and that my mother was ill, seemed to make no difference. Finally we agreed not to discuss the matter, but not before I had glimpsed in her a steeliness that seemed utterly alien to the girl I had met folding origami cranes.

Dara at this time was, as far as I could judge, an average eight-year-old; she liked gym and running around and her schoolwork was good. She enjoyed spelling and arithmetic, things with right and wrong answers, but her best subject was art. Fiona worked on the preliminary sketches for her murals at home and, maybe from being around her, Dara had an unusual capacity for concentration; she could work on a single picture for an hour. In addition she had two traits that I envied: kindness and emotional transparency. If anyone in the family was ill, Dara would offer juice, handkerchiefs, books, hot water bottles. She would put her small hand on your forehead and say please get well. She was also quite without guile, and found mendacity bewildering. Fiona claimed that she was too volatile, but I was glad that my daughter was, as they say, in touch with her feelings. So often my own emotions were hidden not only from other people, but from myself. Or perhaps it was the other way round: I was hiding from them.

Dara had a gang of friends—Elspeth, Megan, Kim, Suzanne, Lucy, Evelyn—and they were constantly in and out of one another's houses: playing games, putting on shows, roller-skating in the park, swimming at the leisure center. As a parent, I did my share of chauffeuring and running after balls, helping with zips and shoelaces, pouring juice and making meals. I learned to remember who couldn't eat nuts and whose mother got upset if she stayed too long in the pool. Once again I heard the women murmuring approval.

But something had shaken loose. Since Fiona learned of Lionel's existence, since my father's death, my mother's illness, my encounter with Dodgson's photographs, I felt increasingly as if I were walking a tightrope: balancing between my good behavior and those occasional moments when I was aware of something else, persistent and persuasive, trying to get my attention. One of the girls would smile or bite her lip or gaze out from behind her hair and I would have to restrain myself, not from doing anything but from thinking, thinking, thinking. I started to second-guess my actions. Should I pick up Elspeth when she fell off her bike? Should I brush Lucy's hair back into a ponytail so it wouldn't keep getting in her way? Should I zip up Kim's jacket? Each time I did the proper, parental thing, but my feelings didn't always match. I comforted myself that there was an end in sight. In a few years I would be safe. Fergus's friends were mostly boys.

On Wednesday, 9 July 1980, at around three P.M., I walked home from work beneath cloudy skies and discovered a moving van in our street. A woman of about my age was watching four men struggle with an upright piano. I stopped and introduced myself.

"Iris Bailey," she said, offering her hand. She had thick, curly brown hair down to her shoulders and a warm, direct smile. "My daughters and I are moving into number eight."

I asked how old they were, and when she said nine and fifteen, told her that Dara had just turned nine. "If there's anything you need," I added, "we're at number twelve."

Over supper Fiona and I discussed our new neighbor. She too had run into Iris on the way home. "Did she mention a Mr. Bailey?" she asked.

"Not in our two minutes. She was worrying about the piano. She said she had two girls, the younger the same age as Dara. How's the bank going?"

A Victorian bank was being turned into a restaurant, and Fiona and her assistant were painting the ceiling with scenes from Robert Burns's poem "Tam O'Shanter." We had taken turns reading the poem aloud to each other and enjoyed the tale of Tam's drunken ride home, pursued by witches and warlocks. Not only was this Fiona's most ambitious project to date but it was also her last for the foreseeable future. That spring, after volunteering at Dara's school for months, she had decided she wanted to be a teacher; she would be starting her training course in August.

"I was working on the horse today," she said. "Tam's stout gray mare. I'm still learning how to paint stuff that high up so that it'll look okay from below."

"I'm sure it'll look fine," I said. "Anyway most of the clientele will be following Tam's example and getting smashed."

"Are you suggesting that people need to be drunk to appreciate my painting?" she said, but she was smiling. Then, to my surprise, she added that I'd seemed in low spirits recently. I used the excuse I'd given my mother: I was having a hard time at work. "Twice in the last month I've nearly made a serious mistake."

"Is there something else you'd like to do?"

I shook my head. "I don't have any particular talents. I make good minestrone soup. I like going for walks, playing with Dara and Fergus, pottering in the garden. Nothing I like doing would earn me tuppence ha'penny."

"What about photography?" She gestured to the wall behind me, where I'd hung some of my pictures. "People are always asking who did these. Maybe you could photograph children? Even if the parents didn't pay there'd be the pleasure of using your talents."

She gazed at me earnestly. "I'm glad we're talking about this," she said. "Sometimes with all the coming and going we forget to talk about ourselves. I want you to be happy. You've been so supportive of my work even when I was spending more on paint than I was getting paid. In a couple of years I should have a regular salary, even if it's not a very large one."

We made love that night, closing the door against interruptions and giving ourselves over to each other with abandon. I felt, once again, the good fortune that had guided me to this woman, and this life.

W E DIDN'T SEE OUR NEW NEIGHBORS UNTIL AFTER WE RETURNED from our summer holidays, a fortnight in the Lake District with Fiona's sister and her family. The following week I was at home with Dara and Fergus after school when the doorbell rang. I went to answer and found Iris. Beside her stood a slender girl, wearing a crimson top. Her dark blond hair was pulled back into a ponytail, and her skin, beneath our hall light, had a golden sheen. Her eyes, staring up at me, were a grayish green, like that stone called peridot, which means lost. Later I would see that they were flecked with brown. Her full lips were pale.

"I'm sorry to bother you," said Iris. "I was hoping your wife was home."

"She will be shortly. Would you like to come in and wait? The kettle's just boiled." I held out my hand to the girl. "Hello, I'm Cameron. I have a daughter about your age."

"I'm Ingrid," said the girl, still looking up at me gravely and ignoring my hand. "Is she home?"

I stepped back and opened the living room door. Dara and Fergus were lying on the floor watching television. "Dara, Fergus," I said, "this is our new neighbor, Ingrid. And her mother, Iris."

"Hello," said Iris.

"Are you watching *The Secret Seven*?" said Ingrid.

"Yes," said Dara. "They're about to go down to the cellar."

As she spoke, Ingrid crossed the room and lay down on the floor beside her. I stepped back, taking Iris with me, and closed the door on the three children.

"This is their favorite show," I said.

"Ingrid's too," said Iris. She seemed to forget about waiting for Fiona's return, and asked if I would mind watching Ingrid for an hour. She had to go to a meeting, and Carol, her older daughter, who normally babysat, had been delayed.

"Of course," I said. "I'm in the middle of making supper but it looks like they can entertain themselves."

In the kitchen the onion I peeled was suddenly a miracle of design, the potatoes more shapely, the parsley exquisitely curled. Sometimes Dara laid the table, but that evening I did it myself. I didn't dare to leave the kitchen until I heard the sound of a key in the front door. Then I went to greet Fiona, wearing my apron, holding a wooden spoon. "Ingrid Bailey is here," I said. "Her mother asked if we could watch her until her sister gets home."

"Did you invite her for supper?" said Fiona. She was already opening the living room door. The two girls were still sitting on the floor but now playing cards. Fergus was pushing a truck around them. "Hello, Ingrid. I'm Dara's mum, Fiona."

Ingrid scrambled to her feet. "Hi," she said brightly. "Thank you for having me."

"Fergus," said Fiona. "What are you doing up? It's way past your bedtime."

Like my mother, I had forgotten about my son.

WITHIN A MATTER OF WEEKS DARA AND INGRID WERE INSEParable. She still saw her other friends, but it was Ingrid with whom she would play for hours, giggling over private jokes and secrets. They both loved dressing up and inventing dramas. Sometimes Fergus tagged along—they found him useful in their games—but mostly it was just the two of them. We began to make joint arrangements with Iris about school, Brownies, ballet. The older daughter, Carol, became our main babysitter. Mr. Bailey never appeared and was never mentioned. Somehow the opportunity to ask about him came and went.

Since our conversation about my doldrums Fiona had been nudging me about photography, and it was with her blessing that I started taking pictures of the two girls. Of course I was careful to also photograph Fergus and his friends, but I had only one real subject. The camera loved Ingrid. In everyday life she often fell short of what I had seen that first evening. Her skin could look sallow and she was prone to spots. She had the habit of chewing on a strand of hair that hung limply in front of her face, her teeth pushed forward—she would probably need braces—and her lips were usually chapped. But through the lens these faults vanished or became part of some larger whole that they enhanced rather than marred.

As the girls grew more intimate our families became increasingly intertwined. Iris worked as an accountant for a large firm and was an energetic single parent. She volunteered at the primary school, she went swimming with Ingrid on Saturdays and attended Carol's hockey matches, she became involved with the drama club. She persuaded Fiona to help with this last. Often after the weekly meeting the two women brought the girls home and then went out again to have a drink. On such nights Ingrid would stay at our house, sharing Dara's room, and I would be responsible for getting the two excited girls into bed. There would be baths and much scampering back and forth before they settled down.

I didn't get careless but my confidence grew. Surely there was no harm in occasionally opening the bathroom door to tell them it was time to get out. Was I to blame if I lingered for a moment, waiting to be sure they did my bidding? One night, getting out of the bath, Ingrid dropped her towel. Both girls burst out laughing. I must have stood there for five seconds, staring at her slender shoulders, her whole smooth body, before I went to fetch another towel. As she wrapped it around herself, I thought of asking her and Dara not to tell anyone, but even as I framed the request I recognized the trap: the mere consciousness of guilt was evidence thereof. Innocence was my best protection. Later the girls came downstairs in their pajamas to sit in front of the fire. While Dara dried Ingrid's hair, I dried Dara's.

On special days, days when Dodgson had, for instance, gone for a glorious picnic, the sole adult with several children, he wrote in his diary, "I mark this day with a white stone." Over several decades he took thousands of beautiful, focused photographs, including the ones of girls "sans habillement" which were his favorites. But even in Victorian England his behavior did not pass without remark. He was always aware that what he most loved could be taken away. His book *Pillow Problems* was designed to ward off impious thoughts before sleep. No wonder he wanted to fall down a rabbit hole into a world where the natural laws were suspended and a ten-year-old girl could be ten forever. In his late forties, he stopped taking photographs, claiming to be too busy. His will requested that all his nude photographs be returned to the sitters or destroyed. Four survive.

A WEEK OR TWO AFTER THE MEMORABLE BATH, FIONA CAME HOME from the drama club and reported how grateful Iris was for my taking an interest in Ingrid. "She says it's so good for Ingrid to have a positive father figure."

I had finally got the girls off to bed half an hour earlier and was sitting in the living room, reading the newspaper. Now somehow the paper was on the floor and I was sitting tensely upright. "A father figure?"

"Also known," said Fiona, sinking onto the sofa, "as a man who isn't a complete wanker. You know how Iris talks."

Iris's commitment to counseling and self-help books was a joke between us, though recently I'd noticed that Fiona had begun to refer to Dara's self-esteem, Fergus's Oedipal phase. I realized from her raised eyebrows that I'd overreacted. "How was drama?" I said as I picked up the newspaper. "I didn't mean to sound so startled. I still have trouble thinking of myself as a father, let alone a father figure. My parents were always so certain about everything. Whereas I feel like I'm just bumbling along."

"So do I." Fiona smiled. "Hopefully it makes us better parents that we let our children see that we're not perfect."

"More fun," I suggested.

"Definitely more fun." She described that night's rehearsal of *The Wind in the Willows*. The boy who played Toad had fallen into the washtub and provoked much hilarity. Dara had taken a turn at being Rattie. "I thought she wouldn't like being the center of attention but she loved it. She's blossomed these last few months."

"And Ingrid?"

"She was the front of the motorcar that nearly runs over Toad and one of the weasels. The director was asking for someone to photograph the dress rehearsal. I volunteered you."

"If we can find someone to watch Fergus," I said.

CAROL AGREED TO BABYSIT DURING THE DRESS REHEARSAL, AND I took my camera and tripod down to the church hall. I had not done this kind of photography before and I enjoyed the challenge of trying to anticipate the movements of a group, catching the children at felicitous moments. Ingrid was an excellent weasel and Dara was an eager water rat. The following night I happily joined in the standing ovation. Everyone came back to our house, and the girls, still wearing their makeup, pranced around, giggling.

Only a week later they quarreled. Ingrid had copied one of Dara's drawings, and the unwitting teacher had praised it more than she praised Dara's. But what really vexed Dara was that Ingrid had lied. "She told Miss Hunt it was all her own work," she said, blinking in the way she did when she was upset; my mother had used to do the same thing. For four interminable days we didn't see Ingrid. By the third day my lungs ached as if I had inhaled one of the chemicals I was testing at the laboratory; I could barely lift a book. I told Fiona that I thought I was coming down with something, and on Friday she insisted that I stay at home. One of us had to be back by noon anyway because school finished at lunchtime. Fergus was going to play with his friend Paul.

After everyone had left and the house was quiet, I lay in bed trying to think what I would do if the two girls continued to be estranged. I did not want much from Ingrid—just more chances to watch her, more conversations about how electricity gets into houses or why cuckoos use the nests of other birds—but if she and Dara weren't friends, how was I to spend five minutes in her company? The prospect of living so close and seeing her so seldom was unbearable. Could I tutor her in maths? Or teach her to swim? Everything I could think of seemed like a red flag signaling my acute need, the opposite of Dodgson's cool white stone. I turned off the light and closed my eyes.

I woke to the sound of voices, not one but two, high-pitched, girlish voices. I was still listening intently when there came a soft knock at my door.

"Daddy?"

"Come in." I pulled myself into a sitting position and turned on the light.

Dara stood beside my bed in her school uniform, her hair pulled back into absurd bunches. "How are you feeling?" she said. "Can I take your temperature? Would you like a cup of tea?"

"I'd like some orange juice," I said. "Who were you talking to downstairs?"

"Ingrid. If you're feeling better, Daddy, would you mind coming downstairs so we can make grilled cheese sandwiches?"

I was already half out of bed. "I'll be down in five minutes," I said. In the bathroom I checked to make sure that I didn't look too unkempt. There was no time to shave but I splashed water on my face, combed my hair, and brushed my teeth. Back in the bedroom I flung open the curtains and put on clean clothes.

Downstairs Dara was searching the fridge. Beside her stood a familiar figure. "Are you feeling better, Cameron?" said Ingrid.

"Much," I said. "I just needed a lie-in. How are you?"

"Fine. We got to use the trampoline in gym. I almost did a somersault. So did Dara."

"Do you want a grilled cheese sandwich?" said Dara.

I'm sure our lunch was quite ordinary, but in my memory it stands out as a meal fit for kings: the tomato perfectly sliced, the cheese stretching right to the edge of the bread and lightly freckled, the glasses of orange squash perfectly mixed. The two girls regaled me with the details of their morning. Could Ingrid's hair have grown in four days? She told us that her sister, Carol, had a new boyfriend who walked like a cowboy; she and Dara both tried to imitate this and collapsed in laughter. "Mum doesn't like him," Ingrid added, "because he's so much older."

"How much?" I asked.

"Three years," said Ingrid, and the girls collapsed again.

After lunch the three of us went to the garden center and bought bedding plants. Dara chose pansies and petunias and lobelias; Ingrid preferred impatiens and geraniums and marigolds. We spent the afternoon planting them, first at our house, then at Ingrid's. We were kneeling in their front garden when Iris came home.

"What a great job you've done," she said. "This is lovely."

"Hi, Mum," said Ingrid. "Do we have a watering can?"

"I'll fetch it. Would you like some tea?"

It was when she brought the mugs of tea out to the garden that Iris suggested we go camping together at half-term.

A FEW WEEKS LATER DAVY PAID ONE OF HIS PERIODIC VISITS. His mother had broken her ankle at Christmas and he and his sister were trying, yet again, to persuade their parents to sell the farm and move to a sensible bungalow in town. Fiona, whose parents lived outside a small village in Lancashire, was having similar conversations. Over supper she and Davy discussed their difficulties.

"They're in total denial," Davy said. "When I ask what will happen the next time one of them falls, they say they'll cross that bridge when they come to it."

"My parents are the same," said Fiona. "There's very nice sheltered housing in the next town, but it has a huge waiting list and they won't even put their names down."

"At least you have parents to worry about," I said.

"You have your mother," said Davy. "How is she?"

"If you saw her, you'd know that I don't have her. She hasn't just lost her memory; she's turned into a different person. She makes spiteful remarks about the nurses and sometimes—I can't tell you how weird this is—she tells dirty jokes."

"My theory," said Fiona, "is that's she's always been this way. Now she's lost her inner censor and it's all out in the open."

As she spoke, the tendons in her neck grew taut. I got up to clear the table. Even after several years I found Fiona's hardheartedness about my mother upsetting. Davy, with his usual tact, began to talk about her teaching: had she enjoyed her most recent placement? Presently she went off to bed, leaving the two of us alone with our nightcaps. I asked after Robert.

Davy had been living with Robert for nearly five years, but last spring he had started an affair with a French boy. Everything had gone swimmingly until Robert, coming home early from a business trip, had caught them in flagrante. During the explosive row that followed Davy had promised to give up Jean-Paul. Now he confessed that he was seeing him again. "I didn't mean to. He came into the shop, we went for coffee and . . ." He spread his hands, smiling, inviting me to imagine the details.

"So what are you going to do?"

His smile vanished. "I have no idea. Every day I swear I'm going to give him up, and then I think I'll just see him one more time. It's madness."

"Maybe you want Robert to catch you again?"

"No. I want to grow old with Robert but unfortunately that doesn't seem to stop me from wanting Jean-Paul." His Adam's apple bobbed. "I wish I understood why I keep doing this. Maybe it's because our childhoods were so repressed."

"So can you keep it secret? Can you balance the two in a way that makes you happy rather than insane?" I leaned forward, waiting for Davy's answer.

"If Robert hadn't caught us, perhaps. But he's on his guard. Any slip-ups and—" He drew his hand across his throat. "You sound as if you know what I'm talking about."

I invoked a shadowy woman at work. "The children keep me on the straight and narrow," I said. Beguiled by the intimacy of the hour, I was thinking that our situations were not really so different when Davy remarked that what he'd like was to be able to be open with Robert. That he could even voice the fantasy reminded me, abruptly, of how alone I was. I stretched and yawned and said it was time for bed. Following my example, Davy rose to his feet.

In the hall he paused beside my photographs. "Who's this?"

He was pointing to one of my favorites: Ingrid and Dara had been roller-skating in the street and I had caught Ingrid gliding along, arms outstretched. "Ingrid," I said. "She lives three doors down. I like this one too," I added, drawing his attention to a photograph of Ingrid alone. She was sitting on the lawn making a daisy chain. "You can't see in this photograph but she has the most beautiful—" I was about to say "shoulders" when Davy's curious glance stopped me. "She and Dara," I went on, "remind me of us when we were young. The way they can spend hours together, doing homework and messing around."

"That's nice for Dara. I worry sometimes that she's like me, more sensitive than she looks. For some reason people tend to think you only have feelings if you're thin. Everyone assumes a certain level of stoicism for the well-built."

In bed that night, lying beside the sleeping Fiona, I wished I had one of Dodgson's pillow problems to distract me. For a few seconds I had almost confided, and for another few seconds Davy had almost guessed at, my inner life, perhaps not its exact nature but that I had something to hide. I wondered if I should follow Iris's example and find a therapist, but I could not imagine voicing my feelings to a professional any more than to my mother. Unspoken they were lovely, pure; spoken who knew what form they might take.

THE PLAN WAS FOR US ALL TO GO CAMPING DURING THE SCHOOL half-term in late May. Iris knew a place on the Fife coast, a little over an hour away and right by the sea. Fiona arranged to borrow a couple of tents from friends and we started to amass the necessary equipment. The children were excited and we invited Fergus's friend Paul to join us. I wasn't keen on having an extra child to take care of, but Fiona suggested that we offer to pay Carol to babysit. She had just lost her part-time job, and the bandy-legged boyfriend, after one outing to the cinema, had disappeared.

The campsite turned out to be a grassy field bounded on three sides by hawthorn hedges and on the fourth, beside the shore, a line of rushes. To the west was a small wood; the battlements of a castle were visible above the trees. The farmer charged a pound a night per tent for which he provided a toilet, a shower, an outside tap, and a dustbin. Rough camping, Iris called it. When we arrived at lunchtime the only other occupant of the site was a small blue tent pitched in the shelter of the hedge. With much hilarity we set up our encampment right behind the rushes: a tent for Dara and Ingrid, one for Iris and Carol, and the largest one, big enough to stand up in, for Fergus, Paul, Fiona, and me. As we made the sleeping arrangements, it dawned on me that I was the sole adult male in this company of women.

After lunch we went down to the beach: a broad swath of sand between two headlands. Occasional outcroppings of rock provided shelter and interesting pools. Between the brackish line of seaweed that marked high tide and the slowly receding water we set up a game of rounders. I volunteered to bowl. Lionel had taught me years ago, and, after a shaky start, my skills returned. Dara hit the ball almost into the water and scored a rounder. Fergus and Paul both missed and ran anyway. When it was Carol's turn she bent over, holding the bat quite professionally, but swung clumsily. The ball hit her thigh.

"Cameron," she cried, "that's much too hard." She pretended to limp to first base.

"Poor Carol," said Dara.

While we were playing the sun came out. Ingrid and Dara insisted on putting on their bathing suits and splashing around in the small waves. Fiona, Iris, and Carol lay on a blanket, reading their books. The boys and I made a sandcastle. I had been to the beach only once or twice as a child and I was soon absorbed in digging the moat, sculpting the turrets. We decorated the ramparts with shells and seaweed and a few gull feathers. The boys were fetching water to fill the moat when Carol came over. I had always thought her rather plain compared to Ingrid, but as she knelt beside me, with her flushed cheeks and bright eyes, I saw how pretty she could be.

"I used to build castles with my dad," she said. "I like the shells."

"That was Fergus's idea. We should have brought some smaller buckets to make another row of towers." I gestured at the turrets. "Are the girls still swimming?"

"No, now they're playing leapfrog." She bent down and straightened one of the feathers. "You need a flag. Maybe a piece of seaweed tied to a stick."

"Dad, Dad," said Fergus. "We've got water."

He and Paul emptied their buckets, gleefully, into the moat. In less than a minute the water was gone, but they were already running back to the sea for more. Meanwhile Carol had wandered off. Watching her walk across the sand, it occurred to me that this was a lonely holiday for her: no friends her own age, sharing a tent with her mother. We must give her a bonus when we paid her.

Before we went back to the campsite Iris organized us to gather wood. That evening after supper we took groundsheets and blankets down to the beach and made a fire. The tide was going out, the wind had dropped, and the evening star dominated the sky. The children toasted marshmallows, laughing when they caught fire. Ingrid gave me her first unburned marshmallow; my mouth filled with sweetness. Iris had brought her guitar and she led us in songs we all more or less knew: "Over the Sea to Skye," "Old MacDonald," and "Rambling Boy."

First Fergus and Paul, then the girls began to yawn. We took turns walking them back to the field, helping them get settled in their sleeping bags. Fiona got each of them to shout "Help," to make sure we could hear them. When only Carol remained Iris said, "Well, I think a nightcap is in order." She tramped up the beach and returned a few minutes later with four mugs and a bottle of scotch.

"I hate scotch," said Carol. "Don't you have any wine?"

"I did too at your age," offered Fiona. "I'm still not that keen on it but I like the jolt afterward."

"The jolt is nice," Carol agreed.

I looked over to see if Iris was shocked by this revelation of her daughter's proclivities, but she seemed absorbed in balancing the mugs in the sand and pouring measures. I got up to put more wood on the fire. For a few minutes the flames died down and our faces were in shadow.

"One of the few useful things I learned from Evan," remarked Iris, "was how to drink scotch."

"Until he overdid it," said Carol.

"Who's Evan?" I asked. Too late I saw Fiona's frown.

"My dad," said Carol nonchalantly.

"Before I met Cameron," said Fiona quickly, "I used to go out with a comedian."

While she launched into a Trevor story, I went to check on the children. The boys were lying curled up in their sleeping bags and so was Dara, but Ingrid lay on her back, her face in full view. I bent down, pretending to secure the flap of the tent. In the twilight I could make out the curve of her nose, the bow of her lips. I was bending closer when she gave a small cough. I jumped up and gave the flap a last tug.

Since the days when I worked for Davy's father, I had never been alone in the countryside at night. Now walking back to the beach, I was acutely aware of my own noisy progress—the crackle of grass and twigs underfoot, the rustle of clothing—mingling with the other night sounds: the wind in the rushes, the waves tumbling the pebbles on the beach, and, once or twice, the women's voices rising in conversation. I felt exhilarated and free in a way that I barely recognized. My affection for Ingrid was part of a larger feeling that included Iris and Carol and Fiona and Dara and Fergus.

THE NEXT MORNING, SATURDAY, 23 MAY, I WOKE TO FIND FIONA'S sleeping bag empty and Fergus sitting on my chest, holding out his small hands to show me a ladybird. "Pretty," I said. "Why don't you let her fly away home?" He darted off. The tent was full of light, and when I stepped outside, the sun was shining in an almost cloudless sky. Fiona and Iris were making bacon rolls; Carol was sitting with Ingrid and Dara, brushing and braiding their hair. I walked across the dewy grass to the toilets and, using the spotted mirror above the sink, shaved meticulously and brushed my teeth until they felt slick. I was putting my toothbrush away when a young man walked in, wearing a T-shirt and jeans. Beneath his short, fair hair, his ingenuous face seemed, even before he smiled, on the verge of smiling.

"How are you, mate?" he said in a soft Australian accent, and introduced himself as Mike, the owner of the blue tent in the corner of the field. I had noticed a motorbike parked beside it.

We chatted for a few minutes and I ceded my place at the basin. Back at our tents I asked if we had an extra bacon roll and, when Mike emerged, I waved him over. He shook hands with everyone, even Fergus and Paul, and accepted the roll with enthusiasm. As he ate, he explained that he had come over from Sydney last year and spent six months working in London and saving up. Now he was taking another six months to go round Britain, wherever the fancy took him. All his friends, he said, were doing Europe, but he liked the idea of learning about one place in depth. He had been on the road for three weeks, mainly on the west coast of Scotland. When Iris and Fiona began to make suggestions—what about Findhorn? Had he been to Inverness?—he said wait a minute, went over to his tent, and came back with a small notebook. As he took notes, Carol stood up and, leaving her two charges, came across to join the adults. I caught her studying Mike's muscular arms, his well-defined chest.

"You should go to the abbeys in the borders," she said. "Melrose, Jedburgh, Kelso. They're really old and pretty."

"How old?" he said. His handwriting, I could see, was very neat.

"I don't know," said Carol. "Middle Ages? There are guides and notices."

After breakfast Iris announced she was going into town to buy provisions—we needed more marshmallows, as well as several staples—and asked me to accompany her. "Sorry if we put you on the spot last night," she said as we drove out of the field, "suddenly mentioning Evan like that."

"No problem," I said. "Of course I've wondered about the girls' father, but I didn't like to ask."

"My fault," said Iris. "I used to worry about upsetting them by mentioning him—after all he lived with us until Ingrid was four—but my therapist keeps saying it's important to speak about him in a normal way."

"Do they ever see him?"

"Not anymore. He was so irascible. Once, when he got angry—Ingrid had spilled her juice—he locked her and Carol out of his flat. They had to wait on the landing until he thought they'd learned their lesson. It was winter. and by the time he let them back in, they were freezing, not to mention terrified. And he was always criticizing them, saying they were fat, or stupid, or lazy—all the things he worries are true about him. I was scared he was going to do something really violent."

"It sounds like a nightmare," I said.

"Which is maybe why I kept thinking I'd wake up. It was nearly two years before I realized that I couldn't expect the girls to say they didn't want to see their father; it was up to me to say enough. I've told them they're welcome to phone him or write to him but, until he gives real evidence of having changed, no visits. It's hard for Carol because she remembers him from before, when he was mostly okay."

We had reached the outskirts of the village with its stone houses. "She seems to have turned out remarkably well," I said. "Dara adores her and she's very mature for her age."

"I'm glad you think so," said Iris. "It's been great for her spending time with you and Fiona. Maybe you don't remember, but the first time she babysat for you, she spilled cocoa on the sofa. She was so upset she phoned to ask if she could come home. When you got back she showed you the stains and you said not to worry, accidents happen. She couldn't stop talking about it. She says you never raise your voice, though sometimes she can tell you're upset."

"How can she tell?"

"Apparently," said Iris, "you tug your ear. Oh, look, there's a parking space."

I had always assumed that I barely registered on Carol's teenage retina. Now, as I followed Iris into the shop, I wondered what else she might have noticed. It seemed like another small blessing when we got back from the shops to find that Mike had joined our party and was flirting with Carol.

We spent the morning at the beach. Fiona had brought a book about the seashore and she set the children to hunting for shells and seaweeds. They had a competition to find the most sea anemones. Carol and Mike joined in; their searches took them to distant rock pools and, briefly, out of sight into the next cove. A couple of times I saw Iris watching them. Perhaps it was with some thought of separating them that after lunch she suggested a walk to the castle whose battlements were visible above the trees, but Mike immediately said great; he was trying to visit as many castles as possible.

Tactfully on the walk there he took turns pushing Fergus and Paul on their tricycles, and chatted with Fiona. She was questioning him about Australian wildlife, kangaroos and koalas, and the four of them soon fell behind. I walked with Iris and the girls. I had brought my camera and I snapped a few shots of our straggling party; that way no one would notice when I took the pictures I most wanted.

The outer walls of the castle were in ruins, but the main hall with its huge fireplace and the stone keep were intact. A winding stair led up to the roof where a narrow walkway circled the battlements, offering a panoramic view of the sea and the surrounding countryside. Iris,

Ingrid, and Dara turned one way, I followed Carol in the other direction with the thought of photographing the girls against the battlements.

"Look." Carol pointed. "There's our field."

The wind was whipping her hair around her face and when she turned toward me, I pressed the button.

"Oh," she said, "I didn't think you photographed anyone over ten."

I stepped back, hoping I had misheard. Happily Iris, Ingrid, and Dara were out of earshot, leaning over the wall on the far side. "Fiona doesn't like having her photograph taken," I said. "Nor does your mother." Then, Carol was still eying me, I had a sudden inspiration. "Would you like me to take your photograph? I mean properly, like a portrait."

Her face lit up. "Would you? With Mike?"

He, the boys, and Fiona had just arrived, and the next thing I knew she was waving him over and the two were posing in the corner, his arm around her shoulders. By the third shot Iris had come over. "Pretending to be Lord Snowdon," she said.

Quickly Carol stepped away, ducking her mother's sarcasm. I lowered my camera. "Our tents look so small," I said, pointing toward the field.

For a few seconds Iris was silent and I thought she was still cross. Then she said, "My eyesight isn't what it used to be, but isn't there someone snooping around?"

We all turned to look. Two men were walking across the grass. I started to say something about fellow campers but, as I spoke, the men approached the large tent, where Fiona and I slept, and one of them bent down.

"Shit," said Mike, and headed for the stairs.

Carol was at his heels, and Iris, calling to her to wait, followed.

"You'd better go with them," said Fiona. "I'll stay with the children. All our valuables are in the car."

"I hope to God I locked it," I said and scrambled down the stairs.

Outside the castle Mike was already out of sight. Carol was running toward the track with Iris, who went jogging most Saturdays, in close pursuit. It was barely a mile to the campsite and by the time we reached it, I had closed the distance. The three of us arrived just in time to see a dirty white van pulling away. Mike was standing in the middle of the track, yelling.

"Are you all right?" said Carol.

"What happened?" Iris asked.

"I'm fine," said Mike. "When I got here one of them was pushing my bike across the grass and the other was rummaging in the big tent. As soon as he saw me, the guy dropped the bike and started shouting for his mate. They were out of here in no time flat. As far as I could see, they were empty-handed."

"Well done," said Iris.

"You were amazing." Carol smiled at him rapturously.

While Mike, Iris, and Carol went to talk to the farmer, I retraced our steps in search of Fiona and the children. I met them walking along the track, talking in excited voices. Cops and robbers was one of Fergus and Paul's favorite games, and now they had seen a scenario enacted before their very eyes. Ingrid and Dara too were thrilled.

Back at the campsite Mike reported that the farmer had recognized the thieves from his description—two hooligans from the nearby town—and had gone off to phone the police. Meanwhile Iris and Fiona, after a quick check of the tents, confirmed that nothing was missing. Iris made tea and Fiona poured juice for the children; we stood around, exclaiming. The excitement had put everyone in a spirited mood.

"We saw you from the castle," Ingrid told Mike. "You were very brave."

"You ran right up to them," said Dara.

"I was so mad that they were trying to take my bike. I worked for months to buy it and, even though it's insured, it would have been a hassle to replace. Usually I padlock it. But this place seemed so safe."

I don't remember which of us three adults said that nowadays nowhere was safe.

At Iris's suggestion, we went down to the beach and played football. Then the girls decided to go swimming, and went back to their tent to change. On impulse I decided to go in too. As I drew near the tents, I heard shrieks of laughter. The girls' tent was too small for them to stand and they were trying to change lying down. I listened for a moment. Then I leaned through the opening. Dara had her bathing suit up to her waist and was struggling to take off her sweatshirt and T-shirt. Ingrid was lying on her back, naked from the waist down, kicking her slender legs as she tried to aim her feet into her suit. Both girls were convulsed with laughter.

Ingrid saw me first. "We can't get our suits on," she gasped.

"Would you like to use our tent?" I said. I tried not to stare at Ingrid's smooth stomach, the delicate V where her legs met. If only I could have a photograph, one photograph, of her like this. I had the camera round my neck. I raised it to my face.

"We're fine, Dad. Are you coming swimming?"

"I'm just going to change." The flash went off. Quickly I stood up.

As I stepped back from their tent I saw Carol crossing the grass. She had been to the toilet and was going back to the beach. Now she swerved and headed toward the girls' tent. I was suddenly aware of how it would look if she found her sister as I had done. "Carol," I called. "Can I ask you something?"

I had no idea what I was going to say but, as she approached, I recalled our exchange at the castle. "Listen," I said. "Would you like me to take more photographs of you and Mike? After my swim, we could pick a quiet spot on the beach and I could shoot a couple of rolls of film. That's what professional photographers do. Take lots of pictures so they can be sure of getting some good ones."

"That would be brilliant."

"And maybe"—behind us the girls were still giggling in their tent—"you could wear that sweater you were wearing yesterday, the cream-colored one. This is nice"—I gestured at her striped top—"but something plain looks better in pictures."

"I'll change now." She ran off to her tent and I went to mine. Normally such a narrow escape would have made me anxious but today it simply increased my exhilaration. Everything was fine; everything was under control. While I was changing, Fiona came in with the boys. They wanted to go swimming too.

"Look, Daddy's here," she said to Fergus. "He'll help you." She gave me a quick kiss and retrieved her book.

Soon I was splashing in the freezing water with the four children. Iris and Fiona had settled down with their books. Carol and Mike were sitting by some rocks, deep in conversation. I took turns throwing the boys up and down in the water and then helping the girls to float. Dara kicked and struggled and soon began to sink but Ingrid lay back with her eyes open, smiling.

When I let go, she floundered to her feet. "What's that?" she said, pointing to my stomach.

I looked down uncertainly. The water came to just below my waist and my trunks were firmly in place.

"That's his appendix scar," said Dara. "He had it out when he was eleven." She paddled over and took my hand.

For almost a year I had been keeping my balance, being a good father to Dara and Fergus, being a good friend to Iris and her daughters, largely ignoring any other feelings. My restraint may have made me more virtuous but it did not make me more observant. Otherwise I would have understood sooner that Carol had fairly intense feelings about me.

By the time I ushered the children out of the water they were all four blue and shivering. Fiona came over with towels to dry the girls. I took care of Fergus and Paul. We played chase until we were warm. Then I fetched my camera from the car and, while the women and children gathered wood for that evening's fire, I photographed Mike and Carol. I was very professional, bossing them around, using a light meter. Through the lens Carol looked much older than fifteen and together they made a near perfect couple: smiling, starry-eyed, the energy sparking between them.

When I finished, they wandered off. I picked up a couple of pieces of driftwood and carried them over to the rocks where Iris was once again supervising the wood gathering. "I wish you hadn't done that," she said, as I added my logs to the pile.

"Done what?"

"Taken those pictures. Carol is head over heels about this boy, and I foresee nothing ahead but heartbreak. He's much too old for her, much too experienced, and is about to vanish like a ship in the night."

"I'm sorry," I said. "I shouldn't have invited him over this morning. It never occurred to me that anything would happen. I think of Carol as just a teenager."

"She is," said Iris. "With a thing for older men. I don't mean to bark at you. This would probably have happened without your raising a finger. We're in the presence of an irresistible force. But perhaps you could help to run intervention."

I was promising to do whatever I could when Dara and Ingrid came over, dragging a log between them. "Well done, girls," said Iris. "Put it here."

At the children's request we made supper on the beach, cooking over the fire. It took a dozen disorganized trips to bring down the food and utensils. Iris had taken Carol aside, and to my surprise the girl responded to whatever her mother had said with good grace, fetching and carry-ing uncomplainingly. Meanwhile Mike read to Fergus and Paul.

We ate baked potatoes and baked beans and sausages, charred over the flames. Then the children roasted marshmallows again and I made hot chocolate for everyone. The adults added rum to theirs. We sang songs. Mike led us in "Waltzing Matilda." Predictably, he turned out to have a nice tenor voice. The children went off, two by two, to sleep. When Iris announced, at a fairly early hour, that she was exhausted, I took the hint and said, "Me too. I'm not used to all this fresh air."

I expected Carol and Mike to object but Carol yawned and stretched, and Mike agreed it had been a long day. Fiona was the one who demurred. She was going to walk down to the water to see how many constella-tions she could identify with her star chart. But I had been in my sleep-ing bag for only ten minutes before she joined me. The sky had clouded over, she said, and she had barely been able to find the plough. She kissed my cheek and we fell asleep.

"Cameron," someone whispered. "Wake up."

My first thought was that the thieves had returned. I groped for my jacket and shoes and stepped through the flaps of the tent. Outside the wind filled my pajamas. Iris grabbed my arm and pulled me away. "What is it?" I whispered. "What's wrong?"

"Carol's disappeared. I woke up and she was gone. She's not in the toilets and when I went over to Mike's tent, it was empty. I think they must be on the beach." It was too dark to make out her expression but her voice was full of urgency.

"Perhaps they went for a walk," I said feebly.

"Come on."

She started toward the line of rushes. I followed, protesting. "Iris, I feel very strange about this. Carol is your daughter but I'm just a friend."

"Carol is underage," she said, still whispering. "If they're doing what I think they're doing, then Mike is committing statutory rape."

We had passed through the rushes and were walking across the sand. The darkness covered my eyes like a gloved hand. "Christ," said Iris. "We'll never find them." She turned on a flashlight and handed one to me. The narrow cones of light shone on the sand. "You go that way," she said.

I set off in the direction she had indicated. The tide was almost in, and along the water's edge I caught the glint of white foam and the occasional dark mound of seaweed. For the first time since that afternoon I was able to think about Ingrid in the tent: her laughing eyes watching me, her slender legs kicking. How happy she had looked, and how beautiful. I was nearly at the rocks that marked the headland when Iris cried out.

At the far end of the beach I saw the small glow of her flashlight. I ran toward it, slipping in the sand. As I drew close I made out Mike sitting up in what must be a sleeping bag; standing over him were Iris, clothed, and Carol, not.

I had always thought of Carol as modest and rather shy. Now she stood there naked in front of two men, yelling at her mother. "Just because you had a hard time with Dad you think all men are rotten. You think no one else should have a boyfriend. I'm fed up with your rules and curfews. I'm old enough to do what I want and I want to be with Mike. Mind your own business. Go away."

Suddenly she caught sight of me standing behind Iris. "And you," she said, "always ogling my little sister. Who the fuck do you think you are, trying to tell me how to behave?"

"Carol, I—"

I don't know how I would have finished the sentence if Iris hadn't lunged forward and grabbed her daughter's wrist. "Do you want to ruin yourself?" she asked. In a moment the two were struggling.

Mike had somehow got into his jeans. Now he stood up and begged them to stop. It was all I could do not to turn and run back to the tent, grab the car keys, and drive away. As I'd feared, words had transformed beauty into ugliness. "I don't think we're needed here," I said to Mike.

"You're not," he said, "but I'm not leaving Carol in the lurch." He stepped forward and seized each woman by the arm. "Stop," he shouted. "Please stop. Carol, put some clothes on. You'll freeze. Iris, listen to me."

Both women did what he said. While he protested that this was all his idea, he'd got carried away, I stepped back, trying to figure out my own situation. Even in the midst of my panic, I knew that the essential thing was to speak to Iris as soon as possible. It was true, I'd explain, that I'd taken a lot of photographs of Dara and Ingrid but only at Fiona's suggestion, as a way to hone my skills. There was nothing I couldn't display in St. Giles' Cathedral.

"I'm no Casanova," Mike was saying. "Carol was just as keen as I was."

"She's fifteen," said Iris. "However she behaves, she's legally a child. We should prosecute you."

"Let's talk about this in the morning," said Mike. "You and I both want the best for Carol but we're all worked up now. And I'm freezing."

Eventually Iris relented. Before I had a chance to talk to her she was marching Carol down the beach, leaving me to accompany Mike.

"Christ," he said. "What a battle-axe. Glad I'm not sharing a tent with her tonight."

I looked over, taken aback by the easy contempt in his voice. Where was the frank, cheerful young man I had met that morning? "She's worried," I said. "Her husband is completely out of the picture."

"From what Carol says, you're the one she should be worrying about, mate." He was shaking out the sleeping bag.

So much for my hope that, in the chaos, Carol's comment had gone unnoticed. "I don't know what got into her," I said, trying to match his tone. "I'm working on becoming a children's photographer—it was my wife's suggestion—but there's never been anything"—I hesitated— "weird about it."

"Still you want to watch yourself. A mate of mine, a great guy, worked in a nursery school in Sydney. He had to quit because someone saw him lifting a girl onto the slide and reported him. It was a real shame." He slung the sleeping bag over his shoulder and started walking.

I followed. "'There is nothing either good or bad,'" I said, "'but thinking makes it so.'" The quotation—I had no idea where it came from—sprang unbidden to my lips.

"Try telling that to Iris," Mike said.

I had turned off the flashlight, the beam was growing dim, but my eyes had adjusted to the point where I could distinguish the piles of seaweed and occasional rocks. I thought one or the other of us might say something—maybe Mike would tender an apology, or I might explain the purity of my feelings—but neither of us spoke until we passed through the rushes into the field.

"Good night, mate," said Mike.

I WOKE TO THE PLEASING PATTER OF RAIN ON THE TENT. FOR A FEW moments I lay there, listening, enjoying the snugness of my sleeping bag. Then Fiona was standing over me, fully dressed, telling me to get up. "We need to have breakfast in here," she said.

I pulled on the clothes I had worn the day before, shivering at the touch of the chill fabric. As soon as I was dressed, a disheveled group crowded into the tent. Carol's cheeks were red and her eyelids puffy. Iris looked tired. Paul and Fergus were grumbling loudly. Even Ingrid and Dara seemed subdued. Only Fiona was brisk and jolly as she filled cereal bowls and offered instant coffee.

"Why did he leave?" said Paul.

"He promised we could ride his bike today," Fergus said. "He promised."

A suspicion took shape in my head. I started to ask a question, thought better of it, and, on the pretext of fetching more orange juice, stepped outside. For a befuddled second I wondered if I was looking in the wrong direction, but no, the field was empty. The blue tent, the motorbike, every vestige of Mike was gone. Relief swept over me. I lifted my face to the rain, struggling to compose my expression, before I returned to the tent.

As soon as breakfast was done, we settled Fergus and Paul in the backseat of the car with their coloring books and began to pack. There ought, in all the coming and going, to have been several opportunities to talk to Iris privately, but either Fiona or one of the girls was always present. Nothing untoward about that, I thought, but when Iris spoke to me—had I seen the groundsheet? did we have the kettle?—her voice sounded different, almost as if I had been last night's perpetrator. I kept telling myself not to be paranoid; I hadn't done anything; there was nothing to be worried about except Carol's state of mind. She, unlike her mother, seemed desperate to talk to me and, after several attempts, cornered me by the dustbins.

"Cameron," she said hoarsely.

I paused, the lid of the bin in one hand, a bag of rubbish in the other. For a few vain seconds I hoped she was about to apologize for her remark of the night before.

"Did you see Mike before he left?" she said. "Did he leave a message for me?"

"No."

She screwed her eyes shut, and when she opened them tears spilled out. "Do you know his surname?" she said.

"No," I said again, and whether out of pity or an impulse to torture her further added, "Maybe the farmer can help?"

Before I could say more, she was hurrying toward the farmhouse. Judging by her face when she reappeared a few minutes later, the farmer knew no more than I did.

On the drive up Fiona and I had brought Fergus and Paul, and Iris had brought the girls. Without discussion we fell into the same arrangement going home. Soon both boys were asleep and I was alone with Fiona. "So what went on last night?" she said. "I woke up and it was as if I'd missed Armageddon. Iris said you'd explain."

I told her everything, everything except what Carol had said about me, and that, of course, was my mistake. An innocent person would have been outraged, or at least perplexed, and taken the first opportunity to confide in his wife. But that only occurred to me later. As we drove along, talking quietly while the windscreen wipers slid back and forth and one of the boys, Fergus I think, snored softly, our conversation was all about Iris and Carol.

"Poor Iris," said Fiona. "I bet Carol's going to blame her for this. It's much better to think Mike fled because her mother threatened to prosecute him than because he's a charming wastrel."

"Maybe we can lock Dara up until she's twenty-one? I couldn't answer for my behavior if someone treated her like that."

Fiona patted my knee. "Dara will have friends her own age. She won't yearn after unavailable men. According to Iris's therapist, it's girls who don't get enough attention from their fathers who are most vulnerable to the attentions of older men."

"What amazed me," I said, "was how Carol stood up to Iris. She didn't seem to feel ashamed or embarrassed for a second."

I was still describing the scene when, from the backseat, Fergus asked for a drink, or perhaps it was Paul.

I DIDN'T FORGET CAROL'S ACCUSATION, BUT IN THE BUSTLE OF OUR return I allowed myself to ignore it and to hope that she and her mother were doing the same. When Iris phoned two days later and said not to worry, she would take the girls to and from ballet that evening, I was mildly disappointed but such changes of plan were common. I settled down to play snap with Fergus and make his favorite supper: plain pasta with tuna. The next night Dara announced that she and Ingrid were going to a friend's house. On Friday I was working late and Fiona took care of the children.

That Saturday I went to visit my mother, and while I was gone Fiona did something so obvious and so clever that I realized I had always underestimated her. She collected the rolls of film from my camera bag, including the one that was in the camera, and took them to be developed. Five days later, on Thursday evening after the children were in bed, she closed the dining room door and spread the pictures out on the table.

They were fine, they were all fine, except for the last one: Ingrid lying on her back in the tent, kicking her bare legs in the air.

"Dara was there too. I must have pressed the button by mistake." I reached for the picture but she stayed my hand.

"Iris was so embarrassed when she told me what Carol had said about you, she barely managed to get the words out after three glasses of wine. I was dumbfounded. Then I couldn't say enough to defend you. You were a great father. Carol was just jealous that you didn't pay her more attention. Iris kept nodding. But why were you constantly photographing the girls, she asked. I told her that had been my idea and that clinched it; she apologized profusely.

"Afterward, though, I kept wondering why you hadn't mentioned Carol's comment. I decided to get the films developed. I was sure they would show that Ingrid was your daughter's best friend and nothing more." She exhaled with such force that her hair fluttered. "As soon as I saw this picture, I knew I'd been deceiving myself." She waved at the wall behind us. "Over and over Ingrid is at the center; Dara is off to the side. And it wasn't only when you were taking photographs. Suddenly I could recall dozens of occasions when you were a little too attentive to Ingrid, when you ought to have been focusing on Dara and instead you were chatting away with her best friend. I used to feel so smug when my friends talked about their husbands: you were such a good father, I was sure you'd never pay attention to another woman. Which was true but in the worst way. I just didn't want to see it. God knows what harm you've done."

I reached out my hand but I didn't dare to touch her. "Fiona, this is ridiculous. We're talking about a hysterical outburst by a teenage girl who's babysat for us a few times. Of course I was nice to Ingrid. She's Dara's friend. In my opinion that's part of being a good father." I was trying to muster a tone of outraged innocence.

"So why did you take this photograph? And why didn't you tell me what Carol said? We spent the whole drive home talking about what had happened and you never once mentioned it. When Iris asked if we'd discussed it, I hadn't a clue what she was talking about."

I started a dozen useless sentences but what could I say? Except for the moment in the bathroom when I had stared too long at Ingrid, the moment in the tent when I had raised my camera, half a dozen other moments in the course of nearly a year, I was blameless. And yet I was utterly to blame.

Fiona, however, knew exactly what she wanted to say: "I want a divorce."

With ferocious calmness she outlined her terms. "I get the house and the children and as much money as you can manage. You get my promise that I won't tell people as long as you leave Edinburgh and stay away from the children."

I begged, I protested my innocence, I promised to get professional help, I swore up and down that I had never done anything untoward, that I loved Dara and Fergus, that I would give my left hand to prevent harm coming to a hair on their heads. I said how much I loved her, how happy she made me. But Fiona was relentless. She didn't cry; she didn't shout. Her cheeks, her lips, her eyelids, even her eyelashes seemed to stiffen. Whatever I said she simply pointed to the photograph. She would have liked me to move out that very evening. I argued that we needed time to break the news to the children, to sort out arrangements. Fiona's promise of secrecy was worthless if we separated so suddenly; everyone would guess there was a sinister secret.

IN THE END SHE LET ME STAY FOR FOUR EXCRUCIATING WEEKS, SLEEPing in the guest room. My life in Edinburgh, which I had thought so firmly established, turned out to be surprisingly flimsy. I gave notice at work and applied for a job in London. When I came to pack I had only a few more possessions than the first time I went south, and our mutual friends, relationships of nearly a decade, were now all Fiona's. With colleagues I used the phrase "trial separation," and they offered condolences. As for my mother I tried several times to explain that I was moving and would be visiting less often. She nodded and continued to describe the night she'd first seen radar. "And then the beam leaped up," she said, clasping her hands, smiling. Fiona and I communicated mostly through notes. Before we had shared child care and household tasks. Now I did the shopping, cooking, and cleaning while she took care of the children, keeping them away from me as much as possible. Of course they sensed the tension and were difficult by day and restless at night. Together one Saturday morning she and I explained that I had a new job in London and would be living there for the foreseeable future.

"Where's London?" said Fergus, cheeks quivering. "Can I come?"

"Maybe when you're older," I said.

"London is where I was born," said Dara. "Why do you have to go, Daddy? Why can't you stay here?"

"Darling," I said. "I have to earn money to take care of us."

"You can talk to him on the phone," said Fiona. "Get your shoes on. We're going swimming."

I packed stealthily until the fatal Monday arrived. Then I announced at breakfast that I was going to London that day. Dara frowned and started to question me, but Fiona interrupted to ask what kind of sandwich she wanted. Fergus didn't seem to register my remark; he was too busy talking about his spelling words. I had got permission from Fiona to walk them to school one last time. As we made the familiar journey—the school was only a few streets away—Dara asked about Fiona's birthday. Would I take her shopping for a present? Could we bake a cake? I said yes to everything. At the school gates, I bent to kiss first her, then Fergus. As soon as I released them, they darted off to join their friends.

I was waiting to cross the road when, on the far side, I saw Iris and Ingrid. I had run into all three members of the family several times since our camping trip but, given that I was working overtime, leaving early and returning late, not as often as usual. Each occasion had been horribly awkward. In spite of her claim to believe in my innocence, Iris treated me with a breezy reserve. Carol seemed to simply hate me. As for Ingrid, that was worst of all. She ran toward me smiling and suddenly checked herself. What words, I wondered, had her mother used to warn her against me? Now I stood watching her and Iris. They still hadn't noticed me. Iris, on her way to work, wore a navy suit. Ingrid was dressed in the school uniform: a short-sleeved white shirt and black trousers. Her hair was pulled back into a tight ponytail. For a few seconds I saw her as my singular, golden beloved. Then that moment too passed and she looked just like all the other girls I had seen milling around in the playground. There was a pause in the traffic and, at the same instant, we stepped off the curb. As we passed each other in the middle of the road, I raised my hand in a little wave. So did Ingrid.

EXCEPT FOR MY MANNER OF EARNING A LIVING, MY LIFE CHANGED utterly. The dissolution of my marriage swept away my family and my friends. I rented a bedsit in North London which was as grim as it sounds. I got a job that was well paid and then—I was lucky—another job, even better paid. For a few months I did phone the children but it was too hard. I was no longer part of their daily lives; I no longer knew what questions to ask: Who were their teachers? Who were their friends? Instead I wrote weekly, trying to make my letters entertaining with stories and little jokes. I even attempted a few sketches as Dodgson had used to do in his letters to his many young friends.

The one person who survived this radical housecleaning was Davy, who was also now living on his own, although in a far pleasanter and more sociable fashion. He had moved to a different, even smarter furniture shop and become part owner. We started meeting regularly to swim or play squash. I told him that Fiona and I had separated because of irreconcilable differences and he said how sorry he was. The first few times we met I was braced for prying questions—if anyone had the right to ask surely it was my oldest friend—but he said nothing. So I was caught off-guard when, almost a year after I moved south, he said, "Are you ever going to tell me why Fiona threw you out?"

We were at his flat, nearing the end of a leisurely dinner and well into the second bottle of wine. "How do you know she threw me out?" I said.

"Why would you leave your lovely family for a crummy bedsit?" He reached across to refill my glass and topped up his own. The light hung low over the circular table, illuminating the remains of the stuffed trout, and when Davy sat back his face was in shadow. "Whatever you've done," he said, "I'm sure I've done something worse. I speak as someone who's buggered an underage boy in a public toilet. He charged me twenty quid."

"Don't bet on it."

For one minute, perhaps two, the silence expanded around us. "Remember Dara's friend Ingrid?" I said at last. "She was in several of the photographs in the hall."

"The roller-skater," he said.

Slowly, haltingly, I began to tell him what had happened since that day Annabel took my hand. Davy listened in silence. He expressed neither shock nor dismay. Finally I got to the camping expedition and my injudicious photograph. "I never touched her, I never said a word to her, I was never alone with her, but Fiona wouldn't listen."

"So if you were alone with Ingrid, if you could do whatever you wanted with no fear of the consequences, what would you do?" said Davy.

"Feast my eyes."

"Not a little fondling? A little"—he tilted his head—"squeezing?"

When his meaning reached me, I was so angry that I forgot to breathe. He hadn't understood anything, not a word, if he thought that I would do with Ingrid the smallest part of what I'd done with Fiona. "I would not," I said stiffly, "touch her in any way that a good father doesn't touch his daughter."

"But of course you're not her father. Calm down, Cameron. I'm not accusing you. I'm trying to understand." He stood up and left the room. I heard him cross the small hall and then the sounds of pissing, flushing, hand washing. When he came back, he was carrying a new bottle of wine. "So," he said, "I was right."

"Right about what?"

"When I thought you were different though not in the same way as me."

"You're not"—I hesitated—"repulsed?"

He shook his head. "I'm just sorry. Sorry that everything came crashing down, that Fiona freaked out, that you feel all alone with this. At least if you were gay you'd have company."

I asked if he thought there was any chance Fiona would allow me to see Dara and Fergus again. "That's what I feel worst about. It's as if I'd abandoned them and they've no idea why."

Davy promised to test the waters the next time he went north. "Maybe," he said, "if you talked to someone, a psychiatrist or therapist. If Fiona knew you regarded this as a problem and that you were trying to fix it, that might mollify her."

He stood up, swaying slightly, crossed the room, and bent to kiss me.

I DID WHAT DAVY SUGGESTED. WITH HIS HELP I FOUND A SYMPA-thetic therapist, a man of about my age. I went and talked to him every week for over a year, after which he wrote a letter saying that in his opinion the possibility of my harming any child, particularly my own, was remote. Meanwhile Davy talked to Fiona. He must have exercised all his diplomatic skills. Almost four years after I left Edinburgh, she allowed me to see the children again in meticulously regulated circumstances. It was probably no coincidence that her leniency coincided with her remarriage. Her new husband was a barrister, a long-faced Scot with a comfortable income and, I gathered, a keen wit. I appreciated his kindness to the children even though it gave me a pang.

As for the visits, they were, I imagine, what most divorced parents endure: better than nothing but painful. Gone was the easy flow of daily life. We had to have plans, and Dara and Fergus were at such different stages that it was not easy to find common activities. Then too they each grew busier with friends, and spending time with their father was not a priority. But at least I was present again in their lives; there was a relationship, however attenuated.

THERE ARE TWO MORE PARTS TO THIS STORY. LET ME BEGIN WITH the easy one. Shortly before my forty-seventh birthday I remarried. Louise is buoyant, energetic, sociable; she sings in a choral society and has two grown children from her first marriage to an Italian. After living in Rome for nearly twenty years, she now works at the Italian Embassy in London. Thanks to her I have another life: sunnier, simpler, full of good food and music. Every summer we spend a month in Italy with her sons and their families. I am always on hand at these gatherings as the photographer. Two granddaughters are fast approaching what for me is a difficult age. I have learned to take pleasure in their company, but not too much. Neither, happily, possesses Ingrid's charms.

The other, the harder part, concerns my children or, to be precise, my daughter. Fergus took a degree in engineering, got a job in Aberdeen, and married a fellow engineer with whom he has a son. He seems unscathed by his childhood, and our rare meetings are jolly occasions. As for Dara, she studied English at St. Andrews University and then trained as a counselor in Glasgow. I would see her when I went to visit my mother once or twice a year. Several times she pressed me about why I had left the family, and I seldom felt at ease in her company. Then, in her late twenties, she got a job in London, working at a women's center. I hoped proximity would at last allow us to be comfortable together. Louise and I made a point of having her over to dinner every few months, and periodically she and I would go to an exhibition or on an outing.

A year after she came south, she became involved with a violinist who made his living teaching and playing in various orchestras. She moved from the group house where she'd been living to the garden flat in her friend Abigail's house. Edward, she explained, lived with his former girlfriend, they had a daughter, and his erratic comings and goings required privacy. Once she'd realized that I wasn't shocked, she talked about him with increasing frequency. She still had her childhood openness, and when she spoke I could see in her face her longing for this man. As soon as his daughter got over measles, he would leave. As soon as he had more pupils. As soon as they'd sorted out the insurance claim on their roof.

At first I believed her confident pronouncements. But as six months passed, a year, nearly two years, I began to suspect that Edward's version of events might be rather different. Meanwhile Dara lived like a soothsayer, poring over signs and omens, always, apparently, convinced that he was about to make good on his promises. I was painfully aware that her skills as a counselor did not make her own life easier.

The autumn of her thirty-second year she suggested that we pay a visit to Sissinghurst. A couple of her friends had been and had enthused about the exquisite gardens. That September we had a spell of glorious weather, and I pictured us wandering among the flowers in brilliant sunshine. But when the chosen day arrived the sky was so overcast that I would have canceled if we hadn't each taken time off work.

I arrived at Dara's flat in Brixton soon after ten and had just knocked at her door when the other door opened and Abigail's partner, Sean, appeared. He'd been very helpful when Dara was moving in, and I'd thought him a pleasant young man. Today he seemed startled to see me; his pale face was haggard and unshaven. We exchanged greetings and I remarked on the dahlias in the front garden.

"All Dara's doing," he said. He was explaining how his boyhood chores had left him with a hatred of gardening when she appeared.

"Hi, Dad," she said. "Come on, Sean. At a certain point we have to stop blaming our parents for everything." She added that we were on our way to see the gardens at Sissinghurst.

"I've heard they're beautiful," he said, his voice suggesting the opposite, and headed down the street.

"Sean seems a little out of sorts," I said as we walked toward my car.

"He's just overworked," said Dara. "He has a contract for a book about euthanasia, and Abigail is away a lot, touring. I think he doesn't know whether he's coming or going."

As we drove out of London, she described our destination. Sissinghurst was famous because of its owners: Harold Nicholson and Vita Sackville-West. He was a diplomat and a writer; she was an aristocrat and a writer. They had bought the fifteenth-century manor house more or less as a ruin in 1930, and gradually restored it and made the famous gardens. Harold and Vita were also famous, she continued, for their open marriage. Vita had had several passionate relationships with women; Harold too had explored the pleasures of his own gender. One of the sons had written a wonderful book about his parents.

We swooped through a hilly village and the Kentish countryside spread out before us. A few miles later signs led us from the main road into the village of Sissinghurst and out again, down a narrow lane, to the grounds of the house. The gloomy weather had kept people away and the car park was virtually empty. We paid our admission and walked through the main building into the gardens. I was amazed by the orderly profusion. The different areas were divided by hedges and walls; many of the beds were organized by color. "How pretty," Dara kept exclaiming, bending down to touch or smell the flowers. Her skirt was almost the exact blue of the periwinkles. I took several photographs.

Only one part of the house was open to the public: the tower. At the bottom the name Vita was spelled out in tiles on a windowsill, and halfway up the winding wooden stair was the room that had been her study. We leaned against the grille that covered the doorway looking at the walls lined with books and the floor with its shabby Oriental rugs. Vases of fresh flowers on the desk and the mantelpiece made the room feel inhabited.

We continued climbing and stepped onto a flat roof surrounded by a four-foot-high brick wall. Above us fluttered a flag, the ropes rattling against the flagpole. The tower was only fifty, perhaps sixty feet high but we seemed significantly closer to the sky. As far as the eye could see dark clouds were massing. Beyond the garden a small lake ruffled in the wind.

"Do you remember," said Dara, she was staring out toward the orchards and the wild garden, "that time we went camping? We went up a tower then, didn't we?"

"Yes," I said. "There was a castle near the campsite and we climbed up to the battlements." Whenever Dara asked why Fiona and I separated I had taken refuge in vague generalizations about drifting apart. Years ago my therapist had said on no account should I try to tell her and Fergus my version of events. "Normally," he had added, "I'm in favor of honesty between parent and child. But this would demand too much of your son and daughter."

Now I looked at Dara where she stood leaning over the wall and wondered how much she remembered of that weekend. "We were on the battlements," I went on, "when we saw the men trying to steal stuff from our tents."

"And that Australian guy stopped them. Then he disappeared in the night and you left a few weeks later. It was our last family holiday. I used to go over and over those days in my mind, trying to cheer myself up."

"I'm sorry."

She turned around to face me, hands resting on the top of the wall. "Why did you leave?" she said, blinking rapidly. "I've never understood. You said we could bake Mum a cake for her birthday and then you disappeared. Of course I was only ten, but you and she seemed to get on pretty well."

"We did," I said helplessly. The top of the tower was the size of a small room.

"I talked about it with Ingrid," Dara went on. "She was one of the few girls I knew whose parents were divorced. But she just said her dad drank and couldn't hold down a job and I knew neither was true of you."

"Whatever happened to Ingrid? The two of you were inseparable." I had not had news of her in nearly a quarter of a century.

"I don't know. She started going to a different school and suddenly she was into makeup and boys whereas I was playing hockey and learning French. Then a couple of years later Iris got a job in Glasgow and they moved. At one point"—she waved away an insect—"I wondered if you might have had an affair with Iris."

"With Iris? Absolutely not." I was glad to hear the genuine surprise in my voice. "I took the job in London because it paid so much better, and then Fiona and I—"

My feeble words were interrupted by the clock, a few feet below us in the tower, striking the hour. When it finished, Dara said, "Yes, yes, you drifted apart but it didn't feel like that. After that holiday Mum was furious with you. Fergus and I learned never to mention you. Then for years we didn't see you. You even stopped phoning. We thought you must really hate us."

The last sentence was spoken in a voice so small that she could have been ten years old again. So this was the rock and the hard place: allow my daughter to think I didn't care for her or tell her why her mother had banished me. I ran my hand over the mossy stone. Later I thought how much might have been changed if I had crossed the few feet that separated us, put my arms around her, and told her that I loved her. Wasn't that all she was asking? But I was too worried about my own plight to register her pain. The sound of approaching footsteps, other visitors to the tower, rescued me. "Let's go down," I said.

Outside we followed a path to the white garden. Dara bent to examine a small, starry flower. "Obviously," she said, "the situation with Edward has made me think a lot about all this. I would never want to inflict on someone else what I suffered as a child. Part of what I love about Edward is that he would never walk out on his daughter. Anyway this summer when I was up in Edinburgh I asked Mum again what had happened between you two. She said I should ask you."

She left the flower and wandered over to a tree, some sort of willow, beneath which stood a statue of a woman. "Stand still," I said, raising the camera. "Move a little closer."

"For heaven's sake, Dad. That's another thing I remember from our last few months. You always had a camera between you and whatever was going on. Snap, snap, snap. It was infuriating."

"I'm sorry. You looked so pretty with the statue. I am listening."

"But not answering."

She had moved away from the tree and now stood no longer blinking but gazing at me sternly across a rose bush. I wondered if all along she had planned to bring me here and have this conversation. My temples were throbbing and for a few seconds I thought I might faint as I had, long ago, when the headless hen stepped toward me. Dara gasped and raised her hand to her mouth.

"What is it?"

"The rose," she said, "protecting itself." She held out her hand, displaying a few bright beads of blood on her index finger.

"Let's find somewhere to sit down."

We walked across the lawn, past several more flower beds to an avenue of trees. Beyond, the edge of the garden was marked by a beech hedge. Two benches, both empty, gave a view across a field and down to the lake. I chose the nearest bench and Dara, leaving a careful distance, sat beside me. We were entirely alone, or perhaps more accurately all our companions were absent or dead. In the silence I could hear the rustling sounds of Dara arranging her skirt; she didn't speak. She had asked her question. It was up to me to answer. A couple of sparrows hopped hopefully around our feet.

"Did you know," I said, "that I had a brother?"

"You do?"

"Did. Losing Lionel was the worst thing that ever happened to me, until the divorce. He was on the rugger team and his neck was broken in a scrum. It was the first time I had been to see him play. I held him as he died. He was fourteen and a half. But then afterward, after the funeral, we never spoke of him. It was how my parents dealt with disaster. You pulled yourself together and went on as if nothing had happened."

As I spoke the wind sighed in the trees. Lionel, I thought.

"What was he like?" said Dara gently.

"He was great. I mean he was only a boy, but he was so lively and thoughtful and funny. I don't think you could be with him for ten minutes without sensing that here was someone who liked people—not just other kids but Dad's bowling pals, Mum's friends, the neighbors—and people liked him. You knew that he was on your side."

"I wish I'd known him."

"I do too. It's hard to explain—I've never tried to put this into words before—but Lionel made everything easier for me. When he was around I could connect with other people. My whole life changed when he died." I stared down at the camera on my lap, the small birds at my feet. "What I've never told anyone is that I moved his head. I couldn't bear to see him lying with his face in the mud. Later, much later, I realized that maybe I'd killed him. People can survive a broken neck; he might have been one of them. When I met Fiona, I thought I'd put all that behind me. But then, and please don't take this the wrong way, something about you and Fergus began to bring it back. As a boy, Fergus was very like Lionel. I had these fears, irrational fears, that I inflicted on our family, especially on your mother. Not that I understood any of this at the time."

Beside me Dara stood up. Before I knew what was happening she was bending over, hugging me tightly. Then she began to talk. She said what a familiar story this was. How over and over in her work she saw people who had suffered some terrible event and never come to terms with it. Years later it would surface, destructively, in their lives. The only way to end the cycle, to stop passing the damage down to their children, was to face the event and endure the fear. "When we went to that exhibition in Whitechapel," she said, "I remember thinking that you had a secret, but I had no idea where to look."

As she spoke the sky darkened and the wind began to stir. A couple walked by, two women arm in arm, both white-haired, the taller one wearing plaid trousers, the smaller a colorful skirt. The one in the skirt smiled at us as they passed. In spite of the ominous weather they sat down on the next bench.

"Thank you," Dara was saying. "I always assumed that your departure had to do with us, with Fergus and me, that if you'd loved us you'd have stayed. You don't know how much it means to me to hear that it was the other way round. You left because you loved us, to save us from your limitations."

That wasn't what I'd been saying, not exactly, but maybe it wasn't so far from the truth. "Would you do something for me?" I said.

"What?"

"Would you allow me to ask one of those women to take a photograph of us? I'd like to have a souvenir of today."

"I'd like that too," she said.

As I approached the two women, I heard them talking in some language I didn't know, but as soon as I said, "Excuse me," they switched fluently to English. After a brief argument as to who was the better photographer, they both came to take our picture, one each. The first drops of rain fell as they handed back the camera.

Over lunch at a pub in the village Dara talked about Edward. They finally had a plan that made sense. He was going to see his daughter through her first term of kindergarten, keep everything together for Christmas, and then break the news to his partner as soon as school started again. Meanwhile he and Dara would find a flat to rent, or buy, ideally within walking distance of his present flat so that his daughter could go back and forth easily between the two households. And sometime soon, maybe even next year—she looked down shyly—they were going to try to have a baby.

"That's wonderful," I said. Her tone did not permit a shred of doubt.

WE SPOKE ON THE PHONE SEVERAL TIMES IN THE NEXT COUPLE of months, but I didn't see Dara again until she came to the drinks party Louise and I gave in mid-December. She arrived late, a number of guests had already gone home or on to other engagements, and, when I first caught sight of her in the hall, I thought that a bag lady had wandered into our house. It was not just that she was carrying several bulky bags—other guests had arrived similarly burdened—but that she was wearing such ill-assorted clothes: a threadbare Eastern jacket, several clashing scarves, a faded black skirt with a tear in one side and, in spite of the weather, red sandals. When I reached to hug her I smelled an odd, almost chemical odor.

"Is everything all right?" I said.

"Fine. Fine. Sorry to be late. Things are hectic at work. We had a review recently and several people are off with colds . . ."

Alarm bells should have rung at the way she delivered this speech, much too loudly and quickly, but I was thinking about my precious party. I poured her a glass of wine and said we hoped she'd stay to supper afterward. She'd met a number of our friends on previous occasions, and over the next hour I glimpsed her in conversation with various people; whoever she was talking to seemed to be backing away. Twice I was about to intervene when Louise asked me to pass the hors d'oeuvres or open more wine. And then I looked around our few remaining guests and discovered that Dara was gone. Every other year she had stayed to help us clear up and to eat scrambled eggs. I phoned but reached only her answering machine.

A week later a card came saying she was, as usual, going to Edinburgh for Christmas. I sent back a card and a check for art supplies. Louise and I were visiting Rome, I wrote. We hoped to see her early in the new year.

Louise's Italian family Christmases were always a pleasure, but that year everyone seemed in especially good health and spirits. As I sat at the candlelit table, my daughter-in-law on one side teasing me about my Italian, my oldest granddaughter on the other asking me about a magic trick I'd shown her, I felt blessed. I smiled across the table at Louise and she, in the midst of talking to our other granddaughter, smiled back.

Two days later I had just returned from a solitary stroll around the Piazza Navona when my daughter-in-law called me to the phone.

"I don't know how to tell you this," said Sean.

THE ESSAYS I READ ABOUT DODGSON DID NOT SAY IF HE HAD A counterpart to the days he marked with a white stone, days to be marked with blood and thorns. Certainly he suffered such days. On 27 June 1863, or shortly thereafter, he did something that caused a difficult break with his beloved Alice. The crucial page is missing from his diary.

I left for London within an hour of hearing the news of Dara's death. I met Fiona at the hospital. Together we saw our daughter. A soft-spoken woman told us that there would be an autopsy but that an empty container of sleeping pills had been found in her bathroom. Then we took a taxi to her flat. We searched everywhere, hoping to find a note. Fiona remarked on how tidy everything was, how clean. The Christmas cards Dara had received were stacked on the dining room table, unopened. She had told Fiona that she would be spending Christmas with Louise and me.

I have no memory of her funeral other than the women, the many women, coming up to me one by one, mostly in tears, to say how Dara had helped them, had rescued them, had understood their shortcomings. "She never made you feel bad about yourself," said one. "However often I messed up," said another, "she was there." Her coworkers offered the same story. The director of the center, I recognized her from a photograph Dara and I had seen in an exhibition, told me that Dara was one of the most lovely and selfless people she had ever met. "But we failed her," she said, her eyes brimming. "Somehow we failed her." A couple of people remarked that Christmas was a tricky time. I kept searching the congregation for a man who might be Edward. Finally I asked Sean, who told me that he hadn't been able to get away.

DURING THE WEEKS THAT FOLLOWED I WORKED, I ATE, I SLEPT, I did whatever I was meant to do, but all the time it was as if I were standing in front of a huge black wall. Sometimes, for a few seconds, I would become absorbed in a task, but when I looked up the wall was still there, blocking my view of everything and everyone. A fortnight after the funeral a letter arrived from Sean. It turned out that Dara had written a note and torn it up. In the confusion of finding her, Sean had taken the envelope. "Forgive my presumption," he wrote. "I thought it would make things worse." Now he enclosed the fragments. I put them in the drawer where I kept the photographs from Sissinghurst. Dara had not wanted us to read her letter; surely there must be a good reason for that?

One Saturday afternoon in early March when Louise was out with a friend—she found it hard to be around my despair day after day—Davy phoned and suggested a walk. We met at the British Museum and, with no destination, wandered through Bloomsbury toward the City of London. It was a misty day, not quite raining. Most of the shops were closed for the weekend, and the streets were deserted. Presently we found ourselves in the shadow of St. Paul's; the front facade was half covered in scaffolding. We crossed the road and headed down the flight of shallow steps to the footbridge across the Thames. Halfway across, Davy stopped to lean on the railing; I joined him. We were facing upstream toward the painted arches of Blackfriars Bridge. The river, swollen with spring rain, flowed swiftly beneath us.

I don't know how long passed before Davy began to speak. "A few days before my father died," he said, "he asked if he was to blame for my being the way I am. I said no, I'd been this way for as long as I could remember. I also told him that I knew my being gay was hard for him but that I felt lucky to have been born at a time when I could live according to my affections without fear, or shame. He didn't speak but he smiled."

On the last phrase his voice cracked. I knew, if I turned to look at him, I would see his eyes watering. It's not the same, I wanted to say—my affections could never have found a place in the world—but I held my peace. The therapist I had consulted years before was dead; Fiona and I, even in our grief, never ventured beyond polite necessities. Davy was the only one now who knew, and spoke, about that hidden part of my life.

"Dara was the way she was," he continued. "Someone else might have had more ballast, might have coped better with your leaving, with whatever drove her to despair. Of course you're to blame, but you mustn't be greedy. You have to share the blame with Dara's friends and colleagues, with her mother and her boyfriend, with her own fragility."

A branch floated past, a beer bottle wedged in one fork. Behind us a group of heavy-footed tourists marched by.

"The day we went to Sissinghurst," I said, "she said two things I can't get out of my head. We were chatting on the doorstep with her neighbor Sean, and she told him that at a certain point you have to stop blaming your parents for everything. Then later, in the gardens, she talked about damage and how it surfaces if we don't deal with it." I clutched the metal railing of the bridge in my bare hands.

"You didn't tell her?" said Davy sharply.

"No. She did ask again why Fiona and I split up. I finally told her about Lionel and how his death separated me from other people."

Almost but not quite, I told Davy the true lie I had told Dara—my fear that I had been Lionel's unwitting executioner—but even as the words formed I offered them to the river and the wind. Davy already carried enough on my behalf. At last I did turn to look at him. On his face I saw the same marks of age that I saw in the mirror. He was already sixty-three; I would be in a few months. How unimaginable that would have seemed to the two boys who shot Mabel. And how unimaginable the alternative of never being sixty-three.

Eyes still watering, Davy returned my gaze. "Poor Lionel," he said, "always coming to your rescue."

THE DAY AFTER I CAME BACK FROM ITALY THAT SUMMER, I WAS finally able to put up the photographs the two women had taken at Sissinghurst. They are almost identical. In neither is Dara or I smiling. We are sitting side by side on the bench, the leafy hedge behind us, our hands clasped in our laps, our ankles crossed. But in one photograph we aren't quite ready and the camera has captured on her face an expression of despair and on mine a bewildered frown. In the other, a few seconds earlier or later, we are facing the camera intently, resolutely, ardently. You can see that Dara has my mother's widow's peak and Lionel's eyebrows, which are also mine.

3

THE FEAST OF EPIPHANY

E VEN AS DARA STOOD WATCHING, THE MIST BEGAN TO STEAL AWAY, thinning and dissipating from one minute to the next, revealing the lawn, gray with dew. Standing on the terrace in front of the quiet house, holding a cup of coffee, she looked down and tried to decide whether she minded getting her new shoes, red sandals, wet in a way that would make them irrevocably less new. She had risen early unnerved by the silence of the countryside and the way it rendered the occasional noises—the whine of a power tool, the cry of a bird—so much more intrusive than the endless roar of London. In the strange kitchen she had made coffee and, eager to escape her hosts, decided to go for a walk. As soon as she got off the train the evening before and saw Sean and Abigail waiting on the platform of the little country station, she had worried that this weekend was a mistake; their incandescent happiness would only cast her own solitude into relief.

A tawny shape emerged from behind a clump of tall grass. A handsome male pheasant glanced at her with red-rimmed eyes and continued, stiff-legged, across the lawn. Dara set her coffee cup on a windowsill and followed. Her momentary concern for her shoes was compensated for by the satisfying chain of dark footprints that appeared behind her in the wet grass. At the gate into the lane she looked in both directions, hoping for something to determine her choice and, seeing nothing, turned left. She found herself walking between two rows of tall, evenly spaced chestnut trees; someone who believed in the future, she thought, must have planted them a century ago. The leaves were fringed with brown and the branches thick with nuts; many had already fallen. By the time Dara reached the road she had gathered a pocketful, choosing not those lying loose but the ones still in their cases that shone so brightly when she released them.

Again she hesitated, uncertain which way to turn. Then, on the far side of the road, she spotted a small stone church surrounded by trees and beyond it the canal Abigail had mentioned the previous evening. She crossed the road, skirted the verdant graveyard, and climbed down a short flight of steps to the towpath. While the mist was fleeing in other places, here it almost entirely concealed the dark green waters. Three narrow boats floated in the vaporous clouds, each looking—with chairs, a wineglass half full, a doll in a pink dress, even a book lying on their respective decks—as if the Rapture had occurred in the night. Dara walked by, gazing curiously at the curtained windows.

Her friendship with Abigail was one of the more unlikely and persistent facts of her life. They had met at university in the laundry room. One day they didn't know each other; the next they were best friends. At least that was Abigail's version. Dara's first memories dated from a few weeks earlier. One rainy afternoon she had seen a girl standing outside the library, wearing a duffle coat, a long red skirt, and Wellington boots, and talking to two men. As Dara approached, the girl burst out laughing with such gaiety, such a seeming lack of reserve, that everyone nearby had smiled. Then the following week in an English seminar she had heard Abigail read a page of *Mrs. Dalloway* and somehow, although she didn't appear to be acting, the whole scene was magically present in her voice. When she finished there was a rare moment of silence. "Thank you, Ms. Taylor," said the lecturer.

The mist thinned and two ducks with subtle brown plumage swam by. Now that she was past the narrow boats the towpath was bordered by fields; on the other side of the canal willow trees hung low over the water. Dara would have liked to draw the ducks and the trees—before leaving the house she had slipped a sketchbook into her pocket—but there was nowhere to sit. Then, at the end of the second field, she came to a stile. She took off her jacket, spread it on the top step, and sat down.

After university Abigail had gone to America to study theater and come back to nurse her father. Then she had moved to London and, for several years, with Dara in Glasgow, they had been in touch only intermittently until Dara had got her present job, and moved south. Gradually they had renegotiated their relationship as adults living in the same city, rather than students living side by side. She had helped Abigail to write a one-woman show based on interviews with some of her clients at the women's center. And Abigail had helped her to feel at home in London.

Now Dara drew the willow tree on the far side of the canal with its long, flowing branches; she added a narrow boat, the ducks, and, in the distance, a church spire. She was shading the spire when she heard a soft tearing sound. Two cows, one black and white, one brown, had approached and were grazing nearby. "Hello," said Dara, but neither raised its head: all those stomachs to feed. Turning back to the canal, she was in time to see a large black dog, like something out of a fairy tale, bounding along the towpath. It passed her without a glance. As the dog disappeared she heard pounding footsteps. Someone in pursuit? No, the man who came into view, wearing dark shorts and a white T-shirt, was just running. From the stile, Dara had an excellent view of his approach, arms and legs pumping steadily. And then, quite suddenly, he was sprawled on the ground at her feet.

She jumped down to help. "Are you all right?"

"What the hell?" He struggled into a sitting position, his shirt grazed with dirt. "Where did you come from?"

"I was sitting on the stile. I didn't mean to startle you."

"You didn't. I must have caught my foot on a root, or a stone. That's the trouble with running in the country. You never know what you'll find."

He uttered this last remark as if, Dara thought, rural irritations might include her. "Is your leg all right?" she said. "Let me help you up."

On the second attempt, leaning heavily on her, swearing, he managed to stand and hobble to the stile. As he sat on the bottom stair, the black dog reappeared, still running at top speed. Before it could reach them, the man called out, "Boris, sit," and it dropped to its haunches. Tongue lolling, the dog watched the man alertly. So did Dara as he bent forward to probe his ankle and flex his foot. His dark hair, which from a distance had looked short, turned out to be tied back in a ponytail. His well-muscled legs and arms were covered with fine dark hair, though not, Dara thought, too much. "Are you all right?" she repeated.

"Fine," he said brusquely. But when he pushed himself up off the stile, he gasped and swayed. Involuntarily she moved toward him. For the first time his eyes—they were almost the same shade as the chestnuts that filled her pocket—registered her presence. "Sorry," he said. "I'm staying a few hundred yards away. Do you have time to give me a hand?" His Welsh accent was less pronounced when he wasn't swearing.

With Boris trotting ahead, the man—he was six inches taller than Dara—leaning on her shoulder, they made their way slowly down the towpath.

"It's going to be a nice day when the mist burns off," offered Dara.

After four steps he said, "Yes."

"I'm never normally up this early," she tried again. "I'm visiting some friends who've borrowed a house and the quiet woke me."

After six more lurching steps he said, "It can do that."

No more, thought Dara, but as they continued their unsteady progress the silence began to feel companionable rather than adversarial, and when a pair of swans slid by, scarcely stirring the water, she sensed them both watching appreciatively.

BACK AT THE HOUSE ABIGAIL WAS WANDERING THE KITCHEN IN her nightgown, a confection of white cotton she had bought in a vintage clothing shop. Dara remembered her holding up the gown in front of a mirror and claiming that it was waiting to be stained with the blood of a virgin. Now she saw that the gown was indeed stained; brown splotches, probably coffee, patterned one sleeve.

"Where were you?" Abigail asked, holding a cafetiere. "I thought you were still in bed."

"I went for a walk by the canal. A tall, dark stranger fell at my feet." She described the encounter, mentioning her sketching and the house where she had left the man but not his good looks or taciturnity.

"Like Jane Eyre," said Abigail. "Remember how she's sitting on a stile when she hears a horse clattering over the ice and Rochester falls at her feet."

"That's right. He even had a dog like Rochester."

Dara was delighted by the comparison but, before she could reflect on it further, Abigail was asking if she wanted porridge or scrambled eggs. Knowing that the day would hold several substantial meals, she chose the former. One of Abigail's more annoying attributes was her ability to eat astonishing amounts with no visible result. "I have the metabolism of a bird," she claimed. Whereas Dara, to her chagrin and against her principles, often found herself making complicated calculations of food versus exercise versus happiness.

When the porridge and coffee were on the table, Abigail volunteered that Sean was finally moving his possessions to London the following week. They had borrowed a van to bring them down from Oxford.

"And what about his wife?" said Dara.

"She's got herself a boyfriend. A vet with dogs, kids, well, one kid, the works. So now he can stop worrying that she'll put her head in the oven if he leaves."

"Was that ever a possibility?" Dara paused, coffee cup suspended. The picture she had formed of Sean's wife, via Abigail, was of some desiccated academic too involved in literature to pay attention to human passions.

"Who knows?" said Abigail between bites of porridge. "I don't mean to sound heartless. I mean, who does ever know that sort of thing about another person. Or even oneself. Sometimes people say they want to kill themselves to make sure you understand they're unhappy. Sometimes they mean it." She licked her spoon thoughtfully. "Of course I was worried but it wasn't easy to know what was going on. Sean was all over the place those last few weeks."

Dara had been nodding—at the center she and her colleagues often debated the threats of their more despairing clients—but still she bristled a little at Abigail's last comment. "It's not easy to end a marriage," she said. "Poor Sean."

"Poor me," said Abigail, putting her hand on her chest in melodramatic fashion. "I've passionately wanted this since the first night we spent together, and I've done everything I could to make him want it too. Toward the end I felt like I did when I was looking after my father. Because he had a terminal illness, I couldn't even have a cold." She spread her arms, as if to seize the space that had for so long been denied her; the nightdress slipped briefly off one shoulder. "So do you have any interesting clients at the moment?"

"There is one woman." Dara had been saving the story. "She's in her early thirties, has a fancy job in advertising, a devoted husband, and she's just remembered, with the help of a therapist, that her father molested her when she was fourteen."

"Does she have that syndrome: repressed memories, buried memories?"

"I don't know if it's a syndrome, but she certainly buried the memory for many years. She went to a therapist because she started having panic attacks after making love with her husband. At first all she could remember was a happy childhood, she's the middle of three sisters, a good time at university, a couple of nice boyfriends, working up to her present job which she loves, getting married to her husband whom she loves. But the more she saw the therapist the worse the attacks became. She reached the point she couldn't even share a bed with her husband. She was talking about divorce when suddenly, in the middle of a session, she remembered her father coming into her room at night."

"How awful," said Abigail. "And did he molest her sisters too?"

"They were away that summer. Once they returned the visits stopped. She never dared to tell them, or her mother, and the only way not to tell them was to forget." Dara was describing how Claire and her husband had confronted the parents to no avail when footsteps sounded on the stairs.

Sean entered, dark hair damp, freshly shaved, wearing a faded green T-shirt and jeans. "Good morning, girls," he said, bending to kiss first Dara, then Abigail. "You both look radiant. What a perfect day."

Standing at the foot of the table, he declaimed:

"Season of mists and mellow fruitfulness,

Close-bosom friend of the maturing sun;

Conspiring with him how to load—"

"And bless with fruit," Dara joined in.

Occasionally prompting each other, they recited the rest of "To Autumn." Abigail listened, smiling. "Gorgeous," she said when they had spoken the last line in unison. Then she was on her feet, urging Sean to sit down. While he and Dara reminisced about the circumstances under which they had learned the poem—for him an attempt to impress a teenage girlfriend; for her a primary school teacher—Abigail fetched him coffee and porridge and refilled Dara's cup. In her nightgown, with her hair hanging down her back, her feet bare, she looked like a handmaiden or a servant. To his credit Sean protested and tried to help. Dara, however, just sat there, saying please and thank you. She spent so much time taking care of other people; it was nice, even for a day, to have the roles reversed.

WHEN BREAKFAST WAS FINALLY OVER THEY DROVE TO THE nearby town and toured the modest art museum. Then they went to the farmers' market and bought too much food because everything looked so fresh. As she followed Sean and Abigail from stall to stall, Dara's good mood slipped away. Contrary to her fears at the station, she had enjoyed dinner the night before and later she had overheard their lovemaking with only mild curiosity—Abigail made less noise than she used to—but when she saw Sean holding a sample of local cheese to Abigail's parted lips, she was suddenly so keenly aware of the shared pleasures of domestic life, from which she was currently excluded, that she had to step over to an adjacent stall and pretend to admire a basket.

Lunch, both the preparation of it and the eating, helped to restore her equanimity. Afterward they went for a walk along a bridleway and visited the local stately home; it had belonged to a well-known eighteenth-century naturalist. Back at the house they segued from cups of tea to glasses of wine and cooking. Abigail talked about her idea of adapting *The Faerie Queene* to the stage.

"An Italian company did this amazing production of *Orlando Furioso* in an ice rink in Edinburgh," she said. "When you strip away the folderol these epics tell wonderful stories. That's why they're still around."

"Folderol." Sean paused over the pear he was peeling. "I can't remember when I last heard someone use that word. It would be a good name for, I don't know, an umbrella. Or maybe flimsy underwear."

He described a friend whose job was naming new products; she had recently christened a dessert and was working on a brand of garden furniture. Dara listened, intrigued. She had met Sean several times during the past year but always in the midst of a crisis. Now, as he expounded on the associations of various words—anything rural was positive; blue was good but yellow was risky—she began to understand why Abigail had courted him so relentlessly.

After dinner Abigail suggested an outing to the local pub. Dara tried to beg off—she was tired, and surely Abigail and Sean wanted to be alone—but Abigail made short work of both excuses. "You can't be tired," she said. "All we've done is walk and eat. And we wouldn't have asked you this weekend if we hadn't wanted your company."

When they stepped outside a surprise was waiting. A huge moon hung low over the chestnut trees, so bright that their shadows followed them across the grass. Wasn't it Gustav Mahler, said Sean, who had painted the moonlight on his lover's bedroom floor and said we will always have moonlight. Neither Dara nor Abigail had a clue but they ran back and forth doing pretend Isadora Duncan dances, twirling and swooping on the moonlit grass. In the lane they turned in the opposite direction from the one Dara had chosen that morning and were soon at the Waterman's Arms.

Dara was at the bar, buying a brandy for Abigail, a pint for Sean, and she wasn't sure what for herself, when a voice said, "If it isn't my savior."

Standing over her, not quite smiling, was the man who had fallen at her feet. "Edward Davies," he said, holding out his hand. "Sorry I was so foul-tempered this morning. I definitely owe you a drink."

"Dara MacLeod. I'm getting a round for my friends." She pointed out Abigail and Sean. "How's the ankle?"

"Ice, elevation, and an Ace bandage have made it bearable. May I join you?"

In spite of his limp, he helped carry over the drinks, and Dara performed introductions. As Edward explained the circumstances of their meeting, she saw Abigail's eyes widen. Dara experienced the antithesis of that morning's pain at the cheese stall: she was single, anything could happen. Seeing Edward and Sean side by side, she guessed that the two were of an age, but Edward, with his emphatic eyebrows, his bony forehead, and his forceful nose, had an aura of adult gravitas that made him seem appealingly older. Within minutes they had established that they all four lived in London, that they were all four interested in the arts, and that Abigail and Edward were each borrowing houses from friends. "Boris's owners," Edward added with a glance at Dara. Then it emerged that he and Abigail had actually crossed paths before. Edward had been a violinist in the orchestra of a musical in which she had had a very minor role. A ghastly show, they agreed. Just as Dara began to be afraid that he too would be unable to resist Abigail, he turned to ask where she was from. When she said Edinburgh, he said he thought he'd caught a Scottish accent. He had been to the Festival, first as a teenager, with his youth orchestra, and then a few years ago, playing for an opera. "I couldn't get enough of it," he said. "The city itself, and all the music and theater."

The sense that they could have met, walking down the Royal Mile or jostling for drinks at the Traverse bar, seemed to please them both. Abigail chimed in with how the Festival had given her her start in theater and Dara said how brilliant she'd been in that play about the oil rigs. For a while she felt herself to be in excellent form, uttering witty, compound sentences, making a good team with Abigail and even with Sean, but after two more rounds—foolishly she had followed Abigail's example and was drinking brandy—she lost her footing. Both the conversation and the room started to slide. She pushed aside her glass and made her way to the ladies'. In the stall nearest the window she sat down and put her cold hands to her hot cheeks. How peaceful, she thought. No voices, no demands.

Someone else came in, did the normal things, and left. Then the door opened again. "Dara, are you all right?"

She forced herself to emerge from the safe little room and discovered Abigail leaning toward the mirror, applying mascara. After three brandies, her hand was entirely steady; perhaps her birdlike metabolism burned up alcohol as well as food.

"He seems nice," she said, running the wand over her lashes. "Did you notice he has the same first name as Mr. Rochester? I almost said something when you introduced him."

"So he does," said Dara, smiling.

Then Abigail said it was time to go home, and suddenly she worried that she'd ruined everything. What if Edward had gone back into the night as suddenly as he had appeared? But no, he was waiting with Sean, the two of them discussing football; they both approved of Arsenal's new goalie. "I drove," he said. "Would you like a very slow lift?"

"We'll walk, thank you," said Abigail, "but maybe you could take Dara? She's a little tired." She gave directions to the house, put her arm around Sean, and headed off down the lane.

Alone with Edward, Dara placed one foot in front of the other, matching her careful gait to his limp as they crossed the car park. "What a lovely night," he remarked in a tone that did not require an answer. In the car he pressed a button, and music—a piano, violins—flowed out of the speakers. The moon was higher now, smaller and more silvery, gilding the fields on either side of the road. Dara had a sudden image of what the canal must look like. "Too bad we can't see the swans," she said.

"What swans?" He sounded amused. Did he think she was so drunk she was hallucinating? Before she could explain, he was saying he liked her friends, an interesting couple.

"Finally," said Dara. "They've been seeing each other for a year and Sean's just decided to leave his wife."

"One of those stories," said Edward. He was driving, as he'd promised, very slowly. "Do you know this piece? Brahms's First Piano Trio."

While the moonlit fields crept by, he asked if she spoke Gaelic and was she a member of the Scottish National Party. Dara said no to both. She liked the idea of speaking Gaelic, but the only word she knew was "bhideo," meaning video, which surely didn't count. When they pulled up outside the house, the music was building toward what even she recognized as a crescendo. She sat there until the last notes. Then, as she turned to thank him, Edward leaned over and kissed her. "I'm too drunk to be much use now," he said, "but I'm not too drunk to know I'd like to see you in London." He scrawled his number on a piece of paper and handed it to her.

O N MONDAY MORNING DARA COULD TELL, EVEN AS SHE STEPPED into the women's center, that something was amiss. With a staff of seven, the center was a volatile institution given to dramas and crises, mostly revolving around Halley, the director, who had started the organization six years ago, and who remained very much in charge. Halley had come to London from St. Kitts at the age of three and was tall, bisexual, and a keen amateur fencer. Now, as Dara hung up her jacket, she wondered if some controversial memo was making the rounds. Before she could go and investigate, Frank appeared in the doorway of her office. "Have you got a minute?" he said.

The only man at the center, the cherubic Frank played the role of both peacemaker and gossipmonger. In his spare time he studied ballet, and while he spoke he often adopted flamingo-like poses. This morning Dara knew, by the way he simply sat down, that matters were serious. "You'll never guess," he said. "Halley's applied for a job at City Hall."

"A job?" said Dara.

"Managerial and"—Frank grimaced—"well paid." The news, he went on, came not from Halley but from Joyce, another counselor, who had learned from a mutual acquaintance that Halley was on the short list. "Joyce is furious. She says for Halley to do this, without consulting us, is a complete betrayal of what the center stands for. She's drawing up a list of complaints about Halley so that she won't be able to leave. Your name came up." He eyed her alertly. "Have you been keeping something from me, darling?"

"How do you mean 'my name came up'?"

"As someone with a complaint. Joyce didn't give details." He stood up and twirled neatly around. "Off to my anxiety group."

"Wait. Is Halley here? Is Joyce?"

"That's what's so weird," he said over his shoulder. "They both are."

Alone, Dara gazed at the painting above the filing cabinet, one of her mother's, which depicted a tiger, a bear, a lion, a sheep, and other ill-assorted animals convened amid lush vegetation beside a river. On good days she often thought of the center as a Peaceable Kingdom where the seven of them, each so different, came together to make a place of calm and safety. And no two were more different than the stocky Joyce, whose main asset as a counselor was her gift for languages—she spoke Bangladeshi and Hindi—and the statuesque Halley. Frank claimed that back in the mists of time they had once been lovers, but no one seemed to know for sure. Dara had met Halley with several supposed amoretti—a tall Brazilian woman who also fenced, a man with an aquiline profile who studied pond life, a waiflike woman who made stained glass—and none of them was remotely like Joyce. One thing for the lamb and the lion to lie down together, quite another for them to copulate. Now the idea of Halley wanting to leave filled Dara with emotions too murky to grasp, but she did have a clear reaction to Joyce enlisting her as a fellow complainant: outrage. She was about to go and confront her when the phone rang.

ALL DAY THE SCHEDULE AND VARIOUS INTERRUPTIONS MADE IT impossible for Dara to speak to Joyce alone. Finally she caught her at six o'clock, maneuvering her bicycle down the front steps. "Joyce," she said breathlessly, "I need to talk to you."

Halfway down the stairs Joyce, already wearing her helmet, paused. "What about?"

"This business. With Halley."

Joyce carried her bike down the remaining steps and glanced, ostentatiously, at her watch. "Okay. The Duke of York?"

She began to push her bicycle along the pavement, and Dara, not daring to suggest that she retrieve her own bike, followed. At the pub, she bought two halves of lager and joined Joyce at the table outside where, in spite of the cool evening, she insisted on sitting. The other tables were being used by young men in suits, standing around in a comradely fashion, drinking pints and smoking.

"What's up?" said Joyce. To make clear how limited her time was, she did not remove her helmet. After months of surreptitious study, Dara had, at last, figured out why she found Joyce hard to talk to. It was not her low forehead, nor her smallish eyes, nor her thin lips, but rather that these features revealed so little of her thoughts or feelings. Now, beneath the shadow of her helmet, Dara detected a faint frown.

"Frank told me," she said cautiously, "that there's some question about Halley."

"Question," Joyce snorted. "She's planning to leave us in the lurch." She raised her glass and Dara noted, with surprise, that her nails were painted a deep cinnamon.

"There's no rule against applying for a job."

"There is against applying under false pretenses and keeping it secret. Halley has great gifts but she's one of the worst administrators I've ever met." Joyce enumerated various occasions on which Halley had muddled the schedule and once failed to get a grant application in on time. When she fell silent, Dara asked whether, if Halley was so inept, they wouldn't be better off without her. Unfazed by this childish maneuver, Joyce said Halley was a brilliant fund-raiser and good with the center's various support groups.

"She's fantastic with the groups," said Dara. "Frank said you thought I had a complaint against Halley?"

At last Joyce removed her helmet and set it on the table between them. Her fair curly hair sprang back as if it had never known confinement. "Remember," she said, "when we had a drink last April, after running that session for volunteers? You told me that Halley had made inappropriate remarks about the Bangladeshi women."

Dara seldom blushed but she could feel the blood surging behind her eyes as she recalled the conversation. She and Joyce had been the only ones working that evening and had gone for a drink together at this very pub. And then, it was coming back to her, she had repeated a conversation she had had with Halley a few days earlier. She had been letting Joyce know how close she was to Halley. And look where her boasting had landed her. "Halley and I were just letting off steam," she said. "We've all commented that counseling is culturally specific. It is uphill work with some of our Bangladeshi clients."

"Which is no excuse for denigrating them. Just because Halley's black doesn't mean she can't be racist." Joyce's nostrils flared as she explained that several of her clients—she was the sole Bangladeshi speaker among the counselors—had been made to feel unwelcome.

The cause of her fury might be obscure but there was no mistaking its intensity. "Well," said Dara, "with luck she'll be leaving soon."

"A woman in the midst of a racial harassment suit is unlikely to get a job at City Hall," Joyce replied tartly.

Dara had a sudden flash of sympathy for the men some of her clients described who ended discussions with a blow to the head, a kick to the stomach. "Joyce, surely this doesn't need to come to court. Can't you and Halley sit down with a mediator?" In the urgency of her plea, she reached for Joyce's hand.

Joyce shook her off. "This is what I'm up against. Everyone wants me to keep quiet and not do anything to upset the wonderful Halley. But I'm not going to keep quiet. I'm going to work to make things better."

Without waiting for Dara's response to this speech, which she had delivered so loudly as to draw the attention of two or three of the cheerful men at nearby tables, Joyce put on her helmet, seized her bike, and pedaled vehemently into the traffic. A bus swerved to avoid her.

For nearly a week Dara refrained from dialing Edward's number. This luxurious period of almost infinite possibilities ended abruptly when she left a message on his phone and began to wait in an entirely different way. Four days later, she had already rehearsed an excuse for a second call—a friend wanting advice about music teachers—when he phoned to ask if she was free for a drink that evening.

"I'm afraid not," said Dara. "It's my turn to cook."

"Oh"—she heard music in the background—"how about tomorrow?"

Reluctantly she explained she was working until nine, but it turned out that Edward was too; they settled on nine-thirty at a pub near Waterloo Station. Dara pretended to study case notes for five more minutes. Then she headed for Frank's office.

"Very romantic," said Frank after she recounted her two fated meetings with Edward, "but remember Pavarotti." At last month's staff meeting Halley had described how the famous tenor, when asked if he thought a particular audience would like him, had replied: the question is will I like them. Dara promised to keep Pavarotti in mind. Was there still space in Frank's anxiety group? One of her clients, a single mother in her forties, would benefit from attending.

A T THE END OF A LONG DAY OF COUNSELING, SHE BRUSHED HER hair, put on the silver earrings she had bought in Ireland the previous summer, and bicycled to the pub. She succeeded in arriving a satisfactory ten minutes late, but among the half-dozen groups of young people and scattering of solitary older men there was no sign of Edward. She ordered a glass of white wine, sat down at a corner table, and took out her sketch pad.

While her pencil moved over the page, Dara imagined car accidents, terrorist bombs, falling objects, violent crimes. Growing up she had assumed this behavior was unique, a result of her father's sudden disappearance. She had been both relieved and a little disappointed to discover how many people used this strategy to fend off disaster.

The door opened and a dark-haired man came in. Dara half rose before she saw that he was with a woman. Two more men appeared, each of whom, fleetingly, looked like Edward. She began to wonder if she would recognize him. Soon after moving to London, she had arranged to meet a friend at the National Gallery. She hadn't seen Toby for four years but, as she came into the building, she had spotted him, waiting at the foot of the stairs. She had almost reached him, was smiling, holding out a hand, when the man's blank stare signaled her mistake. The incident would have been merely a small embarrassment, soon forgotten, if the man hadn't, as she turned away, given a savage smirk. The real Toby had appeared a few minutes later, full of apologies, but throughout their pleasant afternoon, the stranger's hostile behavior had stayed with Dara.

Now she decided to wait five more minutes, long enough to finish her sketch of the elderly man playing solitaire in the corner. She was shading the folds in his jacket when Edward appeared, instantly recognizable despite his evening dress. "I'm so sorry," he said, bending to kiss her cheek. "I had no idea we'd be doing three encores."

The car crashes and the bombs vanished. She was having a drink with a man she barely knew; they might not even like each other. As he returned to their table, carrying two glasses of wine, she noticed that he was still favoring his left leg and that several people in the room were watching him, perhaps trying to decide if his smart clothes meant he was famous.

"Cheers," he said. His eyes beneath his thick brows appeared darker than they had by the canal; otherwise he looked as she remembered, his features not exactly handsome but full of passion and intelligence. She would like to draw him someday.

"The new conductor is such a ham," he was saying. "I should have guessed he'd milk the applause for all it was worth. He had the audience cheering. I kept wondering what they'd think if they knew he had a tracking device in his little toe."

"A tracking device?"

"He has a taste for young boys. Rumor has it that the device is part of his contract, so he can't stray."

She was about to say that she had encountered men like that in her work but instead asked what they'd played. She did not want Edward to have the opportunity to offend her by displaying the kind of prurient curiosity such topics sometimes elicited.

"Mozart, Dvořák, Shostakovich—something for everyone."

Dara confessed she was hopelessly unmusical. "My mother is an art teacher and my father is a keen photographer but it never occurred to either of them that I should have music lessons."

"You draw, though, don't you?" He gestured at the pad on the table. "I remember you had a sketchbook by the canal."

"I did." She had not thought he had noticed in the midst of his accident. "I take classes occasionally but I'm strictly an amateur. When I was young, my mother painted murals in restaurants. That cured me of any romantic notion of making a living as a painter."

She showed him the sketch she had done while waiting and the still unfinished drawing of the canal. He exclaimed at how well she had captured both scenes; she could tell that her skill surprised him. "So," he said, "you don't think photography has rendered drawing obsolete?"

"That's what my father would say, but I think photography is the opposite of seeing. When I was little he always had a camera round his neck, so he didn't have to engage with us."

They exchanged the details of their families. Edward had grown up in Cardiff, the older of two sons; his father had worked his way up from being a bricklayer to running his own building company; his parents were still happily married. Dara told him about her parents and that she had moved to London partly for her job, partly to get to know her father.

"I hope he appreciates your efforts," said Edward. Before she could respond he added that he hadn't yet eaten. Nor had she, and they decided to try the Thai restaurant on the corner. As they headed down the street, he asked what she'd meant on the phone when she said it was her turn to cook. She explained that she shared a house with three other people; they had dinner together once a week, and took turns cooking. She described her housemates—a journalist, an accountant, and a graphic designer—trying to make them sound interesting. In fact the house had proved a minor disappointment, providing neither close friends nor a larger social world. Edward said that sounded like a good arrangement. His own flat, near Kennington, had been chosen solely because it was on the top floor; he didn't have to worry that he was torturing his neighbors every time he practiced.

In the restaurant they ordered pad Thai and curry. Edward reminisced about a trip to Thailand with a girlfriend who was studying Eastern music; one day they had visited a temple in a village. "The whole of the inner courtyard was a mass of yellow flowers. Half a dozen children were watering them."

"It sounds beautiful," said Dara. She recognized with pleasure a familiar milestone on the road to romance: the discussion of previous relationships. She contributed Ian, her halfhearted boyfriend of two years ago, and their trip to Amsterdam. For her the highlight had been visiting the Van Gogh Museum.

"Did you see the field with the crows?" said Edward. "I love the way the wheat and the birds and the sky are all in motion." He had lived in Amsterdam for six months, helping a friend start a recording studio.

Suddenly it was late, nearly midnight, and he had to hurry to catch the tube. "Let's do this again," he said. He kissed her on the mouth, but decorously.

Bicycling home through the dark streets, Dara pictured them living together in the top-floor flat, making trips to Paris and Amsterdam; perhaps she might even take music lessons. Stop it, she thought. She did like him, but so what? Forget Pavarotti. She had learned, early and often, that her feelings had little effect on the world. All that fuss about the tree in the forest, watched or unwatched, was mere wishful thinking. If a passionately concerned participant made no difference, why on earth should a detached observer?

I N THE DAYS THAT FOLLOWED SHE CONTINUED TO OSCILLATE between idyllic daydreams and precautionary disasters. Meanwhile at the center Joyce remained rigidly aloof. My cause is righteous, her posture signaled as she made a cup of tea, walked down the corridor, used the photocopier. As for Halley, she was unfailingly cheerful and even more colorfully dressed than usual. The general opinion was that Joyce had misunderstood one of Halley's offhand comments. At an ad hoc meeting the other counselors decided that Frank would offer to take over Joyce's addiction group in exchange for her doing his shift at reception. "She's too angry," said Frank. "We can't expose our clients to that."

But the clients seemed to sense the turmoil anyway. For Dara the actual counseling had always been the most rewarding part of her job, the part where she felt most confident and competent. She knew how to put people at ease, how to mirror back their emotions, how to help them identify and resolve their rage and shame. Now client after client was hostile, cagey, rude, ungrateful. "What do you know about it?" demanded one woman, after half a dozen friendly sessions. The rest of the staff reported similar experiences. Some worm of discontent had wound its way into the core of the organization.

Only Claire Frazer, the woman she had described to Abigail, appeared immune. She phoned Dara to say how helpful her survivors' group was. "I used to feel so alone, but two of the women have had terrible battles with their families. They know what it's like to have a person you love do something awful, then deny it and call you a liar."

"How are the panic attacks?"

"Better. I still have them but not as often, and now that Ben knows they're not about him, he can cope. Thanks to you, we're managing."

Which hopefully, thought Dara, was code for making love.

Still basking in Claire's thanks, she went to meet her next client, who was in fact one of Frank's; he had an appointment with the chiroprac-tor. "Millie is a handful," he had warned, and as soon as Dara saw the sixteen-year-old slouched in the waiting room, her blue skirt barely reaching her thighs, her red T-shirt embossed with a diamond heart tight across her chest, she knew he wasn't exaggerating. Millie had gone to the police with a torn dress and a lurid story about her virginity and her mother's boyfriend. The subsequent lab report had shown evidence of two partners.

"Where's the poof?" Millie said when Dara introduced herself.

"If you mean Frank, he had a doctor's appointment. He passed your file on to me."

Dara stepped back, holding the door open. After a few seconds Millie stood up and followed. In the meeting room she flung herself down in a chair and gave the box of Kleenex on the nearby table a contemptu-ous shove. Dara asked her to repeat whatever she regarded as essential from the last meeting.

"I don't regard nothing as essential."

"So how are you doing?"

"My mum won't speak to me, Larry's moved out, and everything's a drag. They want me to shut up and not make a fuss. But I've been raped. I know my rights."

"Of course you have rights," Dara said. "It is a little more compli-cated, though, since the lab report."

The girl exploded out of her chair. "You're not my fucking mother."

"No, I'm not. And no one is making you talk to me. If coming here is helpful, that's great. If it isn't, you're free to go." Usually this speech had a calming effect, reminding clients that, unlike almost every other aspect of their lives, sitting in this comfortable room, talking to a sym-pathetic listener, was their choice.

"Christ," said Millie. She seized the arms of Dara's chair and leaned so close that Dara could see the dark pinpricks left by plucked hairs beside her eyebrows. "You're the kind of stuck-up bitch who doesn't know her twat from a hole in the wall. Free to do this, free to do that. You don't have a clue what my life is like."

"So tell me"—Dara tried not to edge back—"if you want to."

"If you want to," Millie repeated mockingly. "You should fucking hear yourself."

It was what Dara had been trained to say, what she believed, but suddenly the words struck her in the way they struck Millie: empty and fatuous. And then Millie reached out and grabbed her left breast. "The trouble with you is you're not getting any."

She gave a brisk squeeze, let go, and sauntered out of the room.

For a few seconds Dara was completely undone. Even while her body recoiled from Millie's behavior, her mind was agreeing with the girl's brash assessment of her situation. She was thirty years old and, since university, she had never, even for a few months, had a relationship that seemed likely to lead to what she most wanted: a partner and a family. And she had no idea why. She was modestly pretty, kind, intelligent, loyal, and gainfully employed. Day after day she saw women who were plain, bad-tempered, dull, in debt, and yet had accomplished this thing that eluded her. Before she moved to London she had gone to see a counselor, hoping to discover some obstacle in herself that was keeping her single. After two sessions the woman had urged her to get out more. "Join a church," she had said. "Or get involved in a sport: football, or squash. You can't expect life to hand you everything on a plate." Dara had not gone back.

A knock interrupted her misery. Had Mille returned? Before she could do more than hide her handkerchief, Halley appeared. "I met a girl—" she started to say, and hurried across the room. "Are you okay?" She bent to take Dara's hands. "What happened?"

Dara blinked several times; Halley's clasp was warm and steady. Presently she managed to explain that Millie was really Frank's client. "I said something that upset her and she stormed out. I should have gone after her but I just needed a minute to pull myself together."

"No harm done. I showed her the door. If she rings for another appointment, let's transfer her to me. That girl's out of control." She gave Dara a final pat and stood up. "We must get together soon. It's ages since we've had a chat."

"I'd like that." Eager for Halley's company but not her attention, Dara asked how she was.

"I've been better. Thank you for asking. One of the odd things about this brouhaha is that no one says anything. Some days I come in and I want to shout. It's so bloody English, no one mentioning the elephant in the room."

"People don't know what to say," said Dara. "And you're not very forthcoming."

"Of course." Halley flicked back her braids. "I want concerned sympathy, but on my own terms."

"Aren't you angry? All this fuss Joyce is causing in the midst of your trying to get a new job."

Halley pressed her lips together and her eyes darkened. She looked, as she hardly ever did, Dara thought, sad. "The job is the least of my worries," she said. "I'll get it, or I won't. In the meantime there's Joyce, the grief, the bad vibes. I've spent six years making this place and now I'm smashing it to bits as hard as I can."

In her vivid scarlet dress Halley seemed to droop. Dara reached to embrace her. "Don't worry," she said. "This will get sorted out soon."

"You don't know what you're talking about," said Halley. "But thanks."

T HE SHRILL OF MILLIE'S VOICE, THE TOUCH OF HER HAND RECEDED, but Dara was left with the fear that her longings were visible, even to a self-centered teenager. She redoubled her efforts to pretend that all was well. This was another kind of magical thinking she had learned was common. When she wasn't keeping ill fortune at bay by imagining crises, she was doing her best to attract good fortune by pretending it was already present. The following week, as she bicycled over to have supper with Abigail—Sean was in Oxford—she resolved on no account to mention Millie; Abigail's sympathy would only bring back the painful encounter. Instead, once they were settled, each with a glass of wine, at opposite ends of the sofa, she described the feud at the center. Abigail, who had met Halley and knew about Joyce, was the ideal audience.

"The nerve of her," she exclaimed when Dara revealed that Joyce had tried to persuade her too to bring a complaint against Halley.

"I said something she misconstrued and now she simply won't hear my explanation. She's determined to hold on to the wrong end of the stick."

Without answering, Abigail stood up and began to prowl the room, straightening a book here, rotating a plant there. She was wearing baggy white trousers and a dark blue pullover, the sleeves rolled up to reveal cream-colored streaks on her forearms. "Joyce must have a crush on Halley," she said, bending to snap a dead frond off a fern. "It's the only thing that makes sense of how contrary this is."

"Maybe," said Dara doubtfully. "There is a rumor that she and Halley had a fling, but ages ago."

"So who's in charge when it comes to complaints?"

"The borough liaison officer. She seems pleasant enough."

"Phone her," said Abigail decisively. "At least you can explain that you've no axe to grind. Now come and watch me cook and tell me about your love life."

At the kitchen table Dara confided the details of her three dates with Edward. "We always have a good time. Then he disappears and I never know if I'll hear from him again."

"I remember that stage with Sean." Abigail stirred the risotto. "What made it faintly bearable was that we both knew Tyler."

"But Edward and I don't have any mutual friends."

"You could make some," said Abigail. "You could invite him to your house. That way he'd be in your world. And having a bedroom nearby might help. Sean and I would still be groping each other like teenagers if I hadn't brought him here and fed him gin and tonics."

This was a new version of his insatiable passion, thought Dara. Dutifully she asked how he was. Was he settling down to life in London?

"I think so. We're painting the top bedroom, making it into a study for him. I want him to feel that this really is his home."

"Nice color." Dara pointed to the streaks.

Abigail glanced carelessly at her arm and added mushrooms to the rice. It wasn't easy, she said, after the months of drama, adjusting to daily life. Suddenly they had time for stupid arguments about recycling, and money. She hadn't realized that Sean was quite so broke. And her tenant was planning to give notice. "If you hear of anyone who's looking for a place, do let me know."

"But"—Dara clutched her glass—"this is what you wanted, isn't it?"

For nearly a year she had listened to Abigail strategize, with boundless optimism, about her campaign to conquer Sean. On the one occasion when she had asked if he was worth so much trouble, Abigail had stared in amazement. "You don't understand," she had said solemnly, "I've never felt this way before. Nor has Sean." And Dara had glimpsed that she was in the presence of something extraordinary. Now the possibility that true love had triumphed, only to be proved as mutable as any other emotion, seemed, like Joyce's fury, Millie's lunge, to call into doubt all that she was aiming for with Edward.

Perhaps Abigail didn't notice her dismay, or perhaps, in the midst of grinding pepper, she didn't hear the question. "Did I tell you that it looks as if the play is going ahead?" she said. She spooned risotto onto plates and began to talk about her fledgling theater company.

D ARA FOLLOWED ABIGAIL'S ADVICE TO THE LETTER. SHE INVITED Edward over to the house when Glen, the journalist, was cooking. The meal went well, everyone joking about Glen's stir-fry—was it slightly better, or slightly worse, than the last one?—and gossiping about their eccentric neighbors. Afterward her housemates drifted off to watch TV or make phone calls. Dara led Edward to the living room and kept refilling their glasses until he put his hand on her thigh and suggested they go upstairs. In her room she closed the door and turned on the bedside light. She had given him a tour of the house when he first arrived and he had admired her room with its blue and apricot walls and many pictures, mostly by her, some by her mother. Now she stood there, not knowing what to do with her eyes or her hands or her feet, not wanting to sit on the bed, which sent one kind of message, or to choose a chair, which sent another. She was staring at the pictures, trying to think of something to say, when he stepped across the room, gazed down at her for a few seconds, and kissed her.

From then on it was all haste and confusion. He undid a few buttons on her blouse and left her to manage the rest while he wrestled with his own clothes. She undressed quickly, eager to be hidden between the sheets. Edward, clumsy with his underwear, took a few seconds longer. Then he was beside her, the whole shocking length of him, and they were clinging to each other. It seemed to Dara that they were struggling to surmount some huge barrier—the barrier between not being and being lovers—and they must do whatever was necessary to get over it. There was one more fierce kiss, the awkwardness of protection, and then Edward was fumbling with her, on top of her, inside her.

It was not pleasurable, not at all, but something even more powerful than pleasure: a painful, naked intimacy. Repeatedly both work and life had taught Dara that the act they were committing was well-nigh meaningless, or at least quite unreliable in its meaning, yet the feeling swept over her. Now we are lovers, she thought jubilantly.

When he was finished Edward turned to her. "What can I do to please you?" he said, his chestnut eyes fixed on hers.

"I was pleased," she protested. "I am."

"No. I was rushing. Show me what to do."

She was embarrassed, fearful. What if he did everything and she still couldn't climb over that other barrier, the one inside herself that often at such moments kept her slightly apart, observing her own experiences rather than experiencing them? Then he reached out and the barrier began to fall away.

Perhaps twenty minutes later, perhaps half an hour, Edward got out of bed and started to dress. She assumed he was going to the bathroom, one of the inconveniences of a shared house, but he was bending down, kissing her, and wishing her sweet dreams. Alone, Dara rolled over to the place where he had lain. In her last waking moments, she summoned a series of comforting disasters: Edward struck by lightning on his way home, the house bursting into flames, herself penniless, lost, wandering in some barren landscape. And her dark imaginings worked. In the morning, before she had time to get anxious, Edward phoned to ask if she was free next Tuesday. There was a film he wanted to see.

T HAT WEEKEND DARA ACCOMPANIED HER FATHER TO A PHOTOGRA-phy exhibition. For reasons she didn't care to examine she was usually late for their meetings, so it was not the sight of him, waiting patiently at a corner table in a café near Bond Street, that startled her, but his hair. For as long as she could remember he had worn it falling over his forehead, parted on the left. Now, barely half an inch long, it bristled salt and pepper, leaving his face oddly exposed. Beneath the pale expanse of his forehead his eyes were an almost watery blue.

"Dad, you've cut your hair."

With an awkward shrug, he rose to greet her. "Louise claimed I was getting shaggy," he said. "What a lovely scarf."

"You gave it to me last Christmas," Dara said, kissing his cheek. That too, she was sure, had been Louise's choice. Her hopes of getting to know her father were constantly colliding with his second marriage. For years he had said that she was always welcome at their house, but when she had phoned to tell him about her new job in London, his first words had been not "Come and stay," but "Where will you live?" She had said not to worry; she'd stay with Abigail until she found her own place. The truth was, as she had come to understand over months of awkward meetings, she was welcome in her father's life when she was in a good mood and could take an intelligent interest in Louise's projects and had a home of her own. She was not welcome in need, or disarray, or pain.

Now he insisted that the scarf suited her. "Would you like some coffee? Or a cake?" He waved his hand toward the counter with its trays of baked goods and, taking in their sparse contents, frowned.

Watching his furrowed brow, Dara remembered those awkward outings in Edinburgh when he had plied her and Fergus with food as if this were the only way to prove his affection; any small problem, a restaurant running out of Fergus's favorite pudding, a dearth of chocolate ice cream, had threatened disaster. "Let's go to the gallery first," she said, "and have coffee afterward."

"Good idea," he said, sounding disproportionately relieved.

In the street, walking past the sleek, expensive shops, he told her that his friend Davy hoped to open a second branch of his furniture shop in the neighborhood. "The rents are astronomical but he thinks it'll put the seal of approval on the business."

That her father had a best friend from childhood was one of the things that made Dara feel more optimistic about her own relationship with him. "I finally went to his shop," she volunteered. "Everyone who works there looks as if they belong in a fashion magazine. They were ignoring me until Davy came out of his office."

"I know. I'm always telling him how rude his staff are but he says people won't pay his prices unless they're abused."

They passed a shop with a single black dress hanging in the window. As they waited to cross the street Dara asked whose work they were going to see.

"It's an exhibition of Charles Dodgson's photographs, the man who wrote *Alice in Wonderland*. They're meant to be exquisite."

The walls of the gallery were hung with large black-and-white photographs simply framed. Several couples and a very tall gray-haired man were looking at them. Her father stopped at the first photograph. A girl of perhaps eight or nine, wearing an odd, ragged costume, stood barefoot beside a wall. Her dark hair was bobbed and she gazed at the viewer with great intensity. "This is Alice Liddell," he said. "Apparently her mother didn't like this photograph. She thought it made Alice look like a beggar."

"I think she looks like a fairy in *A Midsummer Night's Dream*," Dara offered. "Cobweb or Pease Blossom." In fact the girl, with her knowing stare, resembled no fairy Dara could imagine, but she was glad to see her father smile.

The next photograph showed a young girl, Alice again, pretending to be asleep. And the next showed two girls in Oriental costume, one holding a large parasol. A quick survey of the room confirmed Dara's growing suspicion. All the pictures were of girls—the youngest maybe four or five, the oldest perhaps ten—each carefully posed, never smiling. Her father was talking about how complicated photography was in Dodgson's day, what astonishing results he had been able to obtain using the wet collodion plates. "Look at the depth of focus," he said, gesturing to a girl lying amid a mass of drapery.

"Did he only take pictures of girls?" Dara said. Beside her the tall man leaned forward to examine the girl's face.

"No, he photographed many famous people, including Tennyson and Queen Victoria's younger son. And he did landscapes as well. But this exhibition is his photographs of children. Don't you like them?" In a gesture she remembered from childhood he tugged his earlobe.

"Yes and no. The first one was beautiful, but when there are more and more girls, it gets a bit creepy. I wish they'd included some of the adult portraits."

"He never harmed them," said her father. "He was a great friend to children. He taught them riddles, made up stories, wrote them letters. But he never harmed them."

"How do you know?" Quickly she pushed her hands into her pockets. "I don't mean what is the documentary evidence, but how can we be sure what harms a child? Some therapists claim that you can molest someone without touching them, without even saying anything. Just the inappropriate desire can be harmful." Claire had never said what happened after her father came into her bedroom.

Her own father gave a small cough and stepped back from the pictures.

"Sorry, Dad. I don't mean to preach. I can see these are gorgeous but I can't rise above the content. In my book men who like young girls are bad news."

"Let's go and get that coffee."

In the street she saw that his eyes, clear when they met half an hour ago, were bloodshot. If only she hadn't been so strident in her disapproval. He had been offering her a part of himself—his enthusiasm for the photographs—and she had spurned it. Why was she so quick to fly off the handle? As they again passed the black dress in the window, she tried to make amends by telling him that she'd met someone. "A tall, dark Welshman and he's a violinist. Maybe we can go to one of his concerts."

"That would be nice," said her father. "How did you meet?"

Dara regaled him with the story as they made their way through the crowds of Oxford Street to a café in St. Christopher's Court. They each ordered cappuccino and cannoli. Reaching for the sugar, her father remarked how much he admired her work at the center, dealing with women from such diverse backgrounds. Dara listened and watched the sugar sinking, crystal by crystal, beneath the foam. All these compliments, she thought. He too was trying to make amends.

When he paused to sip his coffee she said, "On my training course we figured out that, of the eighteen of us, sixteen had parents whose jobs didn't involve people."

"Science involves people, but I know what you mean. So you were all reacting against your parents when you went into social work?"

She shook her head. "I can't speak for the others but I don't think you had much influence either way. A friend asked me to do a shift at the Samaritans and I realized I was more interested in the clients' stories than the ones I read in books. There is a theory that people go into counseling because they need help themselves—the wounded caregiver—but I think that's because society distrusts the notion of altruism. At the same time"—she reached for her cannoli—"no one likes the idea that counseling is just a job."

"So either you're neurotic or coldly calculating? That's not fair. But it does seem the ideal job for you. Even when you were little, you were so good with people."

Dara allowed herself a moment to enjoy the sweetness of the pastry. Then she gave a theatrical sigh. "I'm not sure how good I am these days. Counseling is meant to work irrespective of the practitioner, but recently I've begun to wonder."

Anyone else would have asked what she meant; her father simply nodded. "When I first came to London," he said, "I saw a therapist. Most of the time I didn't have a clue what he was thinking."

He continued to talk about the process—the one-sided conversation, the strict time limit—while Dara grappled with this amazing revelation. Her father, her stuffy, reserved father, had been to a therapist. Did this mean he actually regretted abandoning his family? As if he sensed that she might be about to ask untoward questions, he changed the topic. Fergus was coming down from Aberdeen at the end of the month and hoped to have dinner with them. "And guess what," he said. "Pauline has enrolled them in a ballroom dancing class."

"Brilliant," said Dara, and allowed herself to be distracted by one of the few subjects on which she and her father consistently saw eye to eye: her brother. They both found him, and his marriage, utterly mysterious. He doesn't know the nature of subtext, her father had said once, and she had agreed. Fergus was always fine.

A T THE CENTER HER DESCRIPTION OF THE EXHIBITION CAUSED A heated debate. Why should a hundred and fifty years make exploitation into art, said Reina. But what if Dodgson was just an adult who paid an unusual amount of attention to children at a time when they were largely ignored, asked Frank. Think of the lovely stories he invented for them. That's no excuse, said Joyce. He sexualized the children for his own pleasure. Even if all he did was take photographs, it's still wrong. To her surprise Dara, now that other people were voicing her reservations, sided with Frank and her father. The photographs were beautiful. Something can't be beautiful when people have been hurt to make it, said Reina. People like Dodgson ought to be carefully supervised. This last reminded Dara of Edward's story of the conductor with the tracking device in his toe; she repeated it.

"Poor guy," said Frank. "That sounds a bit gruesome. I don't approve of molesting children, but I do have some sympathy for people with inappropriate desires. Until recently I'd have been regarded as one of them."

While they were talking, Halley had come into the kitchen. "That is the big question, isn't it?" She reached for the kettle. "What to do with inappropriate desires?"

"These days," said Joyce, "there are quite a lot of alternatives: drugs, aversion therapy, electronic monitoring, self-control."

"Good, old-fashioned self-control," said Halley quietly.

Joyce set down her cup—they all heard it hit the counter—and left the room.

"I think that's my phone," said Frank, cupping a hand to his ear, and followed, with Reina at his heels.

Still holding the steaming kettle, Halley stared after them. "Well"—she turned to Dara, smiling brightly—"I wanted to ask if you could switch with Reina tomorrow and run the four o'clock group."

"Let me check my diary," said Dara, also eager to get away.

A S THE LIGHTS IN THE CINEMA DIMMED EDWARD PUT HIS UM-brella on the floor and reached for her hand. Dara had been with men who held her hand as if it were a dull but useful book, and she had been with those whose touch was so careless as to seem irrelevant.

But she had never been with anyone who held her hand like Edward, tenderly, firmly, as if they were having a secret conversation. She barely registered the opening scenes of the film. Now she understood why her relationships with other men had broken down. Although she had pretended to be, wanted to be, she hadn't really been in love with them. Her deepest self had always been hanging back, reluctant to fully engage, and that in turn had engendered reluctance. Her feelings did make a difference. But with Edward . . . Quickly she summoned precautionary disasters: the flautist, with whom he'd gone to Thailand, reappeared, the center went bankrupt, her bicycle was stolen.

The film, when at last she focused on the screen, was about a musical prodigy, a pianist of dazzling virtuosity who swept all before him only to give up playing at the height of his career. At his farewell concert women threw flowers and hotel room keys on the stage and the conductor had tears in his eyes but the pianist was adamant. The final scene showed him five years later, living in a secluded cottage in Cornwall. As he poured tea, his hand trembled with Parkinson's. Then the camera took in the rest of the room; a small child was playing in front of the fire and a woman held a plump-cheeked baby.

"So he got the things that mattered," said Edward. While he leaned forward, studying the credits, Dara tried to hide her elation. He did like children; how wonderful; it had seemed too soon to ask.

Outside they discovered that the rain, falling when they arrived, had stopped. Edward suggested they walk in the direction of Blackfriars Bridge and look for a restaurant. As they passed the National Theater, he began to reminisce about his first music teacher: the angelic Miss Luke. "She was the one who persuaded my parents to let me have lessons. Of course they regret it now. Playing a wooden box with strings is an absurd job for a man. They're still hoping I'll move back to Wales and work for my father's company."

"Why can't your brother do that?" said Dara. "He already lives there."

"Because he has zero interest in the building trade, and, more importantly, he's their golden boy. If he wants to work in a bookshop and make sculptures out of bric-a-brac, that's fine."

For a moment, Dara thought, he sounded ten years old. Wasn't it strange, she remarked, that he and his brother had both become artists, given the lack of either nature or nurture. Edward said that actually his paternal grandparents had been very musical. Maybe the artistic genes had skipped a generation. She was saying that made sense, when he stopped, mid-stride.

"You're doing your counseling stuff, aren't you?" He gazed down at her. "All these understanding questions. I should be on a sofa, paying you fifty pounds an hour."

"We don't use sofas but I suppose I am. It's an occupational hazard. You should tell me to get lost."

"Or retaliate."

"Or make up wild stories. Some of my clients do that."

As they started walking again, past the brimming restaurants and empty offices, the sound of a trumpet, playing nearby, grew louder. "How do you know?" he said. "About the wild stories?"

"Usually people slip up." She stepped around a puddle. "Or they volunteer that the situation is a bit different than they'd led me to believe."

"Aren't you upset, though," said Edward, "when you discover people have been stringing you along? Getting your sympathy under false pretenses?"

His voice rose and, for a few seconds, as they passed the trumpeter, she imagined herself saying yes, she found it deeply upsetting. She and her tutor on the counseling course had talked at length about Dara's difficulty in accepting mendacities, large and small. She remembered the outburst she had had about two friends: one, after years of saying she'd never get married, was engaged; the other, who'd claimed she didn't want children, was pregnant. Why do people say these things if they aren't true, she had demanded. Dara, her tutor had said gently, your friends weren't swearing an oath; they were describing how they felt at the time. Which of course Dara already knew.

But she was not yet ready to reveal this childish part of herself to Edward. Instead, as the music receded, she quoted one of Halley's maxims. "If someone tells you a lie, they're not telling you the truth, but they are telling you something. It just takes longer to figure out what."

"Look at St. Paul's," said Edward, pointing to the glowing dome of the cathedral that had, all along, been in view.

D ARA WAS STILL THINKING ABOUT THIS CONVERSATION TWO DAYS later when she met with Ms. Banks, the borough liaison officer. Reluctant to commit herself to e-mail, or the phone, she had made an appointment. Now, in a small office full of straggly plants, she explained her concern that Joyce might have implicated her in complaints about Halley. And then, because Ms. Banks was listening attentively, she added that she couldn't help wondering whether Joyce's own complaints were occasioned by Halley's applying for a job at City Hall.

"Are you suggesting," said Ms. Banks, "that Joyce has strong feelings about Halley?"

"I suppose I am," said Dara, taken aback by her acumen.

"I hate situations like this." Ms. Banks shook her head so that her earrings flew. "One person's word against another's. Of course you must be used to it."

Useless to say that as a counselor she seldom heard both sides of the story. "Is there anything to be done? Hally is an amazing organizer. She'd be great at City Hall."

"Actually"—Ms. Banks stood up—"she withdrew her application last week."

"She withdrew?" said Dara. "What do you mean withdrew?" But even as she spoke there was a knock at the door and Ms. Banks was apologetically ushering her out.

Back in the busy street Dara stood staring at the traffic, trying to gather her scattered thoughts. Amid the cars and buses two hearses were rolling slowly by, each carrying a coffin surrounded by flowers. Watching them, she briefly forgot the startling news and remembered an afternoon in Edinburgh, when she and her grandmother, on their way to the shops, had passed a funeral. Her grandmother had said it was bad luck, they must try to find three black cats to cancel it out. Within a few minutes, amazingly, they had seen the cats and both become delighted, much happier, Dara thought, than if they had never met the funeral in the first place. As the second hearse disappeared she stepped into an empty doorway to phone the one person with whom she could discuss Ms. Banks's revelation.

"Halley's withdrawn from the job," repeated Abigail. "Does that mean she did whatever Joyce claims?"

"I've no idea. I just want things to be back to normal." For a moment she felt like crying. Work was meant to be the place where everything was calm and orderly. Meanwhile on the phone Abigail was saying she had done what she could.

THE FOLLOWING WEEK EDWARD AGAIN CAME TO DINNER AT THE house. He brought cheese and wine and Dara made a fish stew which everyone praised. Looking around at the candlelit guests, she thought she had finally arrived in her life. Here she was with her lover, her friends, sitting around her table. She offered more stew, lobbed a new topic into the conversation. At eleven o'clock, though, when they were still debating public funding for opera, she began to long for the evening to be over. She stood up, reaching for the cheese plate; immediately Edward pushed back his chair. Within fifteen minutes the table was cleared, she had carried the candles upstairs, and they were safely in bed. Fifteen minutes after that—their bodies with practice had grown more fluent—he slid away.

"Where are you going?" she said drowsily. "You don't have to go."

"I do if I don't want to queue for the bathroom in the morning and struggle with the rush hour. For me, that's the antithesis of romance."

For me, Dara wanted to say, the antithesis is our making love and your calling a mini cab ten minutes later. Instead she reached for her underwear. "I'll come with you. I'm not due at work until eleven."

Edward had not shaved that day, and as he stood over her, turning the sleeves of his white shirt right side out, his face, lit from below by the candles and framed by his long dark hair, looked almost savage.

"Darling," he said, "I'd love to have your company, but my friend Max is sleeping on the sofa, the heating is kaput, and I have to be at a rehearsal at nine sharp." He slipped on the shirt, quickly buttoned it, and bent to kiss her. As his mouth touched hers, the room went dark and the smell of candle snuff filled the air.

The next morning she telephoned Abigail to ask if she still needed a new tenant.

A T THE CENTER DARA DISCOVERED THAT SHE WAS SCHEDULED TO meet with a Mr. and Mrs. Lyall that afternoon. A clients' parents, she assumed, and thought no more about it until she came into the waiting room and a woman, dressed in an elegant navy blue suit, rose to greet her. Dara introduced herself and led the way to a meeting room.

"Thank you for talking to me," said Mrs. Lyall. "You probably don't realize who I am."

Close up, her shining hair was more white than blond and her blue eyes were fanned with lines. She was older than Dara had thought, but no less beautiful. "I'm sorry," she said. "I have so many clients."

"I'm Claire's mother, Claire Frazer."

At once Dara could see the younger face still visible in the older. So this was the woman who had turned a blind eye while her husband did unspeakable things with their fourteen-year-old daughter.

"Claire told her sisters she'd talked to you," Mrs. Lyall went on, "and how helpful you'd been. I know that means she told you that Bill molested her, and that we deny it. I was hoping"—she gazed at Dara—"that you'd let me tell you our side of the story."

"I'd be happy to listen but I can't reveal what Claire told me, or pass anything on to her."

"I understand. Thank you, thank you so much."

Mrs. Lyall's voice wavered, then steadied as she began her story. Of course, she said, they weren't a perfect family, but she could honestly say that, until this happened, they had enjoyed each other's company. Their last normal contact with Claire had been the previous Easter when she and her sisters had come to lunch in Suffolk and they had gone for a walk by the sea. Claire had looked tired and confessed to sleeping badly. She blamed it on work.

"The following week I phoned to ask if she was sleeping better and recommend lavender. I didn't hear back. The next thing we knew she begged off her sister's birthday party and then, a few weeks later, she announced that she and Ben were coming to see us. From the moment she stepped out of the car it was obvious she was very upset. We sat in the garden and she talked in this childish voice. She said she'd remembered something important. She described how one night, the summer her sisters were away, she couldn't get to sleep. Suddenly the door of her room opened and Bill was there in his pajamas. He sat down on the edge of the bed."

Mrs. Lyall folded her arms tightly. "I can't tell you the horrible story she'd concocted. She claimed he'd visited her several times, maybe half a dozen, and stopped when her sisters came home. Then she said she wasn't planning to prosecute. All we had to do was admit what had happened and apologize and that would be the end of the matter. Bill was superb. He said, very quietly and firmly, that he was sorry she'd had these awful thoughts but he had never done anything like that.

"Claire jumped up; so did Ben. She said her therapist had warned her this might happen. They got into their car and drove away. A few days later a letter came from Ben saying there would be no more communication until we confessed. Since then our letters are returned, our phone calls are ignored. We can't bear not to have news of her so we persuaded her sisters not to argue with her. Now Bill has heart problems, and last week we learned that he needs a bypass. He's terrified he'll die without speaking to her. He's almost ready to admit to anything to hear her voice again."

Mrs. Lyall fell silent. Dara gazed at her, confounded. In theory, as she'd told Edward, she knew that her clients might be lying, but in practice she had believed Claire's story unhesitatingly. Now it was impossible not to believe her mother's. Where was the common ground of truth? And where, she suddenly wondered, was the husband? She asked and Mrs. Lyall explained that they'd thought it would be better if she talked to Dara first. "He tires easily but he should be in the waiting room. I'll fetch him."

She left the room and presently returned with a small, gaunt man swaying between two canes: the demon father.

"I won't sit down," he said when Dara offered him a chair. "I might not get up. Thank you for listening to Valerie. It means a lot to us just to be heard, though I'm afraid it's useless to say we're not trying to pressure you."

"I'm sorry," said Dara. "This must be terrible for you but I don't know how I can help. Claire would be furious if she knew I'd met with you."

"What we were hoping," said Bill, "is that you might talk to her therapist, ask her to meet with us. Perhaps as a colleague she'd listen to you. And perhaps Claire would listen to her. We can't help thinking that she'd never have reached this point without that woman urging her on." His body swayed as he spoke but his voice never lost the quiet firmness his wife had described.

"Do you have any idea," Dara said cautiously, "what might have started Claire's panic attacks? You're saying you were a close family and none of this ever happened, but there must have been some incident that made Claire accuse you."

"We've asked that question over and over," said Valerie. "So have her sisters. The only thing we've come up with is that last autumn she told Paula, her younger sister, that she had a crush on her boss. She made it sound like a joke, but for a couple of months she talked about him all the time. Even we noticed that she was always singing Nick's praises. Then, quite suddenly, she stopped. Paula's theory is that something happened between them, something that Claire is ashamed of and blames herself for, and so she came up with this story where she's utterly blameless."

Dara nodded. "I don't remember her talking about Nick but she did say—" She silenced herself just in time.

"Please," said Bill, "don't feel you have to respond. Valerie, have you given her the phone numbers?"

Mrs. Lyall held out an envelope. "Call any time, day or night. Bill's operation is scheduled for January. We can't thank you enough."

They shook hands, Bill swaying perilously, and Dara showed them out. Her next appointment was already waiting but for a few seconds she remained standing in the hall, holding the envelope, feeling nothing but envy. What had Claire done to deserve these loving, forgiving parents?

FOR ALL HER MANY VISITS TO ABIGAIL'S HOUSE, DARA HAD NEVER seen the ground-floor flat. As she bicycled over, she pictured it as similar to the upstairs: light, beautifully proportioned, tastefully decorated. When Abigail unlocked the door and showed her inside she felt a thud of disappointment: the door of that imaginary flat slamming shut.

"Simon is so untidy," said Abigail, stooping to pick up a newspaper. "The sofa is a little shabby but it's very comfortable, and the garden used to be gorgeous. There's a plum tree."

Who would paint a low-ceilinged room this shade of muddy red? Who would put down a filthy, garish carpet and line the walls with makeshift bookcases? Who would use bare bulbs for lighting?

"This is what made me buy the house," Abigail continued. "If I was broke I knew I could always rent out the upstairs and live here. The kitchen is great, lots of counter space, and the fridge is almost new."

Continuing to point out the virtues, she guided Dara through the flat. It consisted of a long double room with a kitchen and dining area at one end, a sitting area at the other, with French doors opening onto the garden. In addition there was a modest bedroom, now strewn with clothing, and a bathroom that they didn't attempt to enter. Dara didn't say a word. Forgetting that this was her idea, she raged inwardly. Here was yet more evidence that her best friend regarded her as inferior. Of course these low, dingy rooms were good enough for Dara. And, to add insult to injury, her rent would support Abigail and Sean, swanning around in luxury above her head.

When a few minutes later Abigail led the way upstairs, the contrast confirmed her anger. Passing the living room, she glimpsed a book and a red cardigan lying on the sofa; a vase of lilies decorated the mantelpiece. The kitchen was warm and smelled of the peppers Abigail was roasting. "Wine? Tea? Gin?" she offered as Dara sat at the table.

"No, thanks."

Abigail bent over the oven and stood up, cheeks flushed, the dish of peppers in her hands. "Forgive my asking," she said, setting the dish on a trivet, "but do you really want to do this? What about Edward? Wouldn't it be better to see which way the wind is blowing before you do something radical, like move?"

"He's the reason I want to. He never spends the night." Beneath Abigail's curious gaze, she explained about his early rehearsals, and how he couldn't deal with queuing for the bathroom. "Which I can understand. It is the major drawback of communal living."

"So why don't you stay at his place?" Abigail shrugged the skin off a pepper.

It was the question Dara herself kept asking. Now she said that his flat was too far from work. "And," she hurried on, "I need to live somewhere he can come and go without worrying about other people. But I hadn't expected—"

"The flat to be such a tip," finished Abigail. "I should have warned you. Because I know how nice it can be, I tend to forget the state it's actually in." Knife in hand, she studied Dara. "Suppose you don't pay rent in January in exchange for painting the place. And maybe you could sand the floors. That would make a huge difference. I'll try to get Simon to move out by Christmas so you can decorate over the holidays."

"That would be terrific." Then she caught herself. "Are you sure?" For reasons that made perfect sense, given her history, Abigail had always been a complicated mixture of stinginess and generosity. She would show up on the doorstep with a spectacular bunch of flowers, only to insist on meticulously dividing the bill for dinner.

"Absolutely." Abigail raised the knife for emphasis. "I hate to see the place getting so squalid, and it'll be brilliant to have you as a neighbor again. You know what you should do? Get your dad to help. I'm sure he'd be glad to."

"As long as it's all right with Louise. But that is a good plan." Already the dinginess of the downstairs rooms was receding, being replaced by gleaming possibilities, one of which was that this move would lead to a new intimacy not just with Edward but with her father. Living in a communal house had made her seem like a child. Now with her own front door, her own bathroom, she would become an adult.

"Did I tell you," said Abigail, "that I ran into him—your dad—last week at the National Theater? I'd stopped in for coffee and he was there for a matinee. It was so strange. I was looking at this man across the lobby, thinking how solitary he looked. Then I realized it was Cameron. We had a nice conversation." She spread her hands. "'There's no art to find the mind's conception in the face.'"

"What's that from?" said Dara, startled.

"The Scottish play." Abigail reached for the blender. "One of Shakespeare's more chilling insights. After all, we have to judge by appearances, anything else is too complicated, and yet they're so often misleading. Did you ever find out why he and Fiona split up?"

At university she and Abigail had speculated endlessly about their respective parents. Now, between bursts of the blender, she said she had asked him, more than once, and he always said, unhelpfully, that he and her mother had run out of steam.

"So maybe the secret is that there is no secret?"

"Maybe," she said reluctantly. "I still think that there's something he isn't saying, but most children want to believe that there's a good reason for their parents' divorce. It's just too hard to accept that we're not at the center of their lives."

"Not if you had my parents," said Abigail, pouting.

T HAT FRIDAY DARA WAS WORKING THE LATE SHIFT WITH JOYCE. Throughout the afternoon the temperature fell and by dusk rain was banging against the windows; twice the lights flickered ominously. Her five o'clock appointment spent most of the hour talking about what to buy her son for Christmas. Then her six o'clock appointment phoned, sounding close to tears, to say she couldn't make it. Dara urged her to go round to a neighbor's. "You don't want to be on your own on a night like this." As she hung up, the wind moaned in the street outside as if a wolf had escaped from her mother's Peaceable Kingdom.

She tried to focus on the report she was writing, but after a few sentences she was again staring out of the window. It was pointless to work in this distracted state, yet what would she do if she were free to leave? She too didn't want to be alone on such a night; Edward was playing, and Abigail, now that Sean was in residence, was no longer available at short notice. Frank was busy. Other friends seemed to require too much effort. Might she call her father? She could already hear his voice falter at the prospect of her disrupting his cozy evening with Louise. The only thing she could imagine doing with pleasure was sitting in the cinema, her own life suspended in favor of those on the screen. But she couldn't leave Joyce alone at the center.

As she walked down the corridor she could see the light spilling out of Joyce's office door. Joyce herself was seated on the desk, her sweater pulled tentlike over her knees, staring at the window where her dark reflection, and now Dara's, appeared. "Hi," she said without turning around. "My six o'clock canceled."

"So did mine. I was wondering when you might be ready to go?"

"Now." Joyce slid off the desk. "It gives me the willies being here on a night like this. Do you feel like doing something?"

Arrangements fell into place with unexpected ease. They bought a newspaper, agreed that they wanted to see the French film at the nearby cinema, and were in their seats for the early show. Joyce was an excellent companion, watching the screen attentively. They both gasped when the older daughter revealed her affair at a family dinner. Afterward, in the Middle Eastern restaurant next door, they ordered meze plates and couscous and debated the film. Dara thought it had been too extreme: the daughters so eager for attention, the father so selfish.

"Actually," said Joyce, "he reminded me of my dad." In the candlelight her small eyes gleamed. "He wasn't rich and handsome but he had the same knack for tyrannizing his family. Even now, when I haven't seen him in nearly two decades, I often get depressed around five. He used to come home at five-thirty."

"What does he do?" said Dara, abashed to realize that she didn't know.

"He checks the filters at a sewage plant. You can imagine the jokes at school, but that was nothing compared to the jokes at home. Savage humor was his specialty, and"—Joyce smiled ruefully—"making kids feel bad."

"That must have been hard," said Dara. Joyce's confidences made it easier to offer her own. After the waiter had refilled their water glasses, she described the Lyalls: how she had believed Claire's story, then the parents had been so convincing and now, from day to day, she was failing to make good on her promise to talk to the therapist. "Half a dozen times I've gone to pick up the phone and ended up watering the plants or checking e-mail instead."

"But it was the therapist who recommended her to us, wasn't it?"

"Yes, but I'm worried she'll think I'm interfering."

"This is a medical emergency," said Joyce. "You're going to hate yourself if you don't try to help. Come on, let's rehearse. Pretend I'm the therapist." They went over the dialogue several times. "All you want," she reminded Dara, "is for her to see the parents."

As she allowed herself to be coached and comforted, Dara felt a prickle of remorse; a few weeks ago she had as good as called Joyce a liar. She was still searching for words to thank her, when Joyce announced she must be going and signaled the waiter. They lapsed back into pleasantries until the bill was paid.

"I hope I didn't steal you from your beau," Joyce said as she zipped up her jacket.

"Beau?"

"Stupid French word for fellow. I saw him waiting for you one night. He looked nice."

"He is," said Dara. "Edward's lovely."

"Good for you and good luck tomorrow. I'll be around if you need me."

In the back of a mini cab Dara checked her phone and found a message from Glen: was it all right to show her room tomorrow? He and her other housemates had greeted the news of her move with an equanimity that might, in different circumstances, have been disconcerting. As for Edward, he had remarked what fun it would be to have Abigail and Sean for neighbors and begun to talk about one of his pupils. Dara had just enough self-control not to tell him of the role he'd played in her decision. No matter how wonderful what happened between them at night and how it made her feel—and him too, she was certain—as if they had known each other from time immemorial, by daylight, by the calendar, they had met barely three months ago. There were still moments when Edward withdrew to some secret place in himself—some childhood trauma, she guessed—and failed to respond. Privately she called these withdrawals his nonreactions.

I N THE REMAINING WEEKS BEFORE CHRISTMAS, LIFE AT THE CENTER returned to normal. The day after the storm Dara reached Claire's therapist. When she explained about Mr. Lyall's imminent surgery, the therapist said that, in the circumstances, she would talk to him and Valerie. A few days later Halley let slip that she'd withdrawn her application for the job. Joyce said her Bangladeshi group more or less ran itself and volunteered to take back the addiction group. Meanwhile Dara's clients became their former, grateful selves. The one shadow was Edward's busyness. They talked on the phone almost daily but his many seasonal engagements—*Messiahs*, carol concerts, *Nutcrackers*—made it hard to meet. "January will be quiet as a mausoleum," he promised. He was going back to Cardiff for Christmas and seemed pleased when Dara announced that she was visiting her mother in Edinburgh. She would stay north for the New Year, he urged, nothing like a Scottish Hogmanay. When she said no, she was coming back to paint the flat, his nonreaction was clearly audible. "Not to worry," she said. "My father has promised to lend a hand."

So it was not until the evening of the sixth of January, Twelfth Night, as Edward remarked on the phone, that they met. They had not discussed gifts and, after some hesitation, she had bought a book about Van Gogh that she set inconspicuously on the dining table; if he didn't have anything for her, then she would hand it over casually. She spent the day buying groceries, cleaning, running out to buy the extravagant bunches of tulips and daffodils that suddenly were essential. She pictured that moment when he would walk down Fortune Street, knock on her door, and step into her flat. Surely when he saw how nice she'd made it, a bright, harmonious space, he would turn to her with new passion. Only as she made the mulled wine, slicing oranges and counting cloves, did she remember to summon disasters: Edward had had an accident; Edward had met his childhood sweetheart in Cardiff; Edward had realized how plain and ordinary and unmusical she, Dara, was.

When he knocked, she took one last look at the living room, the candles burning tall and steady, the white tulips beginning to open, and went to answer. There was his dark, familiar figure. Then he was in her living room, his cheeks red with cold, and his hands, she couldn't help noticing, empty, save for a bandage on one finger. Oddly, he wore a suit.

"I smell paint," he declared, smiling. "And mulled wine."

"The latter was meant to conceal the former. You're looking very smart." She could hear the curtness in her compliment. Here he was standing in her flat, just as she had imagined for the last ten days as she painted and cleaned and hung pictures and arranged furniture, and he had scarcely glanced at its irresistible beauty. Where were the exclamations of praise? Where were the wine, the flowers, not to mention a Christmas present?

But Edward still seemed oblivious. He talked about the lunchtime audition he'd had. The room was so cold it made everyone sound out of tune. At last, as she ladled out the wine, he finally seemed to take in his surroundings. "This is lovely," he said.

Too little, too late, but showing him around, Dara was once again delighted by the transformation she'd accomplished. She started with the bedroom: the white bed surrounded by soft blues and greens. "The colors are meant to make you feel as if the garden continues inside, or at least they should in summer."

In the living room, she had chosen a deep yellow for the kitchen area and, after several experiments, a lavender blue for the wall around the French doors into the garden. The rest of the room was painted a soft white. "The bathroom is where I went wild."

"This is amazing." He stepped into the small room to study the mural that covered two of the walls.

"Do you recognize it?"

"Should I?" He leaned closer to the painting.

"It's the canal where we met. Here are the narrow boats and the willow trees. This is me sitting on the stile. This is you running, and your friends' dog."

"Oh"—his voice lifted—"you've made me so athletic. And look at your lovely hair. You even put in the swans and the church spire."

"I had that sketch I did to work from. Do you like it?"

"You should charge admission," he said.

Back in the living room, he settled on the sofa and began to describe the production of *Twelfth Night* he'd been in at school. "We set it during the sixties, which we thought was the height of sophistication. I played Malvolio wearing a tie-dye T-shirt and strumming a guitar."

Dara scarcely heard him. She was holding up her glass so that the light shone dimly through the mulled wine. Her hand, she was pleased to see, was quite steady. In Edinburgh her mother had greeted the news of Edward with enthusiasm. "He sounds very nice," she had said. But as she asked more questions, urged Dara to phone him on Christmas Eve, Dara had found herself increasingly evasive. "It's still early days," she had cautioned. "We're taking things one step at a time." Now the lack of a gift, the inappropriate clothes, brought back the doubts her mother's questions had prompted. When Edward finished his reminiscences, she said, "I sometimes get this feeling that you have something to hide. Or that you want to hide me. You seem happy enough to meet my friends, but after nearly four months I still haven't been to your flat or met any of your friends. When I come to hear you play, you always whisk me away afterward. In Edinburgh I wanted to send you a card and I realized I didn't have your address."

"We have a modern relationship. Here's to the mobile." His smile was so tight she could have reached over and lifted it off.

"So what I'd like to do," she went on, with no idea of where her words were coming from, "is to get in a taxi, right now, and go to your flat. I don't care about heating or plumbing or guests or mess. I just want to see where you live. Afterward we can come back here and make supper." She drained her glass, set it on the coffee table, and rose to her feet.

"Dara."

She held out her hand and looked at him steadily, willing herself, as she often did with clients, not to break the silence.

His eyes spun toward her, and away again. He set his own glass on the table. "Please," he said. "Sit down."

She did, choosing an armchair rather than returning to the sofa. She slid her hands under her thighs, to keep herself from doing, or saying, something untoward.

"I don't know how to tell you this. I live with someone."

In her scenarios of disaster she had imagined, over and over, old girlfriends reappearing, fellow musicians beckoning. Now she understood how flimsy those imaginings had been compared to the reality. Every night he left her bed and went home to share a bed with someone else, perhaps even to do—with that someone else—the very things he had done with her. So this, not some childhood trauma, was the source of his nonreactions.

"Aren't you going to shout?" Edward said. "Or hit me?"

She wanted to do both. Instead she stood up, went over to the French windows, drew back the curtains, and flung them open. The cold night air rushed in. Instantly the candles went out.

"What's her name?" She stared at the plum tree, trying to decipher its crooked branches. "How long have you been together?"

"Cordelia. Six years, nearly seven."

Cordelia, thought Dara. Perhaps it was fear of saying the wrong name that made him call her "Darling" in bed. "I don't want to hit you," she said, "but I do want to know the obvious things. Why would you hurt Cordelia, and hurt me? I was just getting on with my life."

"When I fell at your feet."

She turned at last, arms tightly folded, wanting him to see her refusal of their oldest joke. Under her stony gaze, he embarked on a story of which she had heard many similar versions from friends and clients. Cordelia was a pianist. They had fallen in love while working together; he had moved in with her. Now the relationship had run its course— they were no longer lovers—but convenience and professional ties made it hard for either to leave. "I meant to tell you that first evening, but I was swept away by the moonlight, Brahms"—he risked a quick glance at her face—"you."

"Are you married?" Now that she had discovered the deception she wanted every detail.

"No. I swear we're not. Please, shut the door. It's freezing."

His relief at being able to deny the charge was palpable, but there was something, she thought, as she went to latch the doors, something that he was still trying to hide. "I can't ask the right questions," she said, returning to the armchair. "I need you to tell me the truth."

"Promise not to hate me."

"I promise," she said meaninglessly.

"We have a daughter. Rachel is nearly two."

A tide of bitterness swept over Dara so powerful that she thought it might carry her out of the armchair, across her beautiful, useless room, past the neatly wrapped present and the kitchen brimming with food, through the front door and into the street. In all her imaginings of disaster this had never occurred to her: not only a woman in the attic but a woman and a child. Of course it had been too good to be true that Edward, a man like Edward, loved her and was available. How stupid she had been, how presumptuous, how willfully myopic.

"I know I should have told you," he said. "At first I thought you knew, that you must have seen the car seat and the toys when I gave you a lift. But then we had that conversation by the river about your clients lying to you and I realized that you didn't."

"Christ, Edward, it was dark, I was drunk, how was I going to see a car seat?"

"I know, I know. I'm not trying to defend myself, just explain. I did try to tell you a few weeks ago."

"You tried?"

He shrank back into the sofa. "That day," he said, "when we had lunch together."

A couple of weeks before Christmas he had phoned one morning to say he was near the center; they had met at a busy café. What Dara remembered about the occasion was the shock of seeing Edward by daylight and discovering that his brown hair was threaded with gray and his front teeth faintly stained. Gradually, as they discussed the center's nondenominational party and the toy, plastic and garish, that Dara had bought her nephew, he had turned back into his good-looking self. There had been nothing that resembled confession, but now she understood that the lunch had been occasioned not by proximity but by her suggesting, yet again, that she come to Edward's flat.

"You tried?" she repeated furiously.

"You were in such a good mood I didn't have the heart."

"Don't try to pretend that your cowardice was kindness. I think you'd better leave." She was still sitting on her hands, not now to silence herself but to stop from tipping over the flowers, knocking the candles to the floor.

"Wait, please. There is an explanation."

"Other than that you're a liar and a coward?"

This final volley of scorn seemed to revive him. He sat up straighter. "Haven't you ever done something you bitterly regret? Or failed to do something you bitterly regret?"

While he described his good intentions, his inability to act on them, Dara felt her head clear. She was still enraged but there was no harm in listening. When he paused she said, "It doesn't matter how it happened. The fact is you have a partner and a child. I can't go on seeing you." She looked at her watch. "Where's Rachel now? Who's taking care of her?"

Edward glanced at his own watch. "She's with Cordelia's mother."

Dara's despair quickened: a mother too. In some distant corner of her brain she registered this reaction as a sign of secret hope. "And where do they think you are?"

"*The Nutcracker.*" He plucked his trousers. "Hence the suit. Please, Dara. Cordelia and I have a platonic relationship, but we both thought it was better for Rachel if we went on living together. We didn't want her shuttling back and forth as a baby. The question isn't whether we split up, but when."

"So what's stopping you?"

He brought his hands together in an attitude of prayer, which was, she knew, one of the several exercises he did every day. "I never had an incentive to leave before. Now I think about it all the time: trying to figure out what I need to do. I'll have to keep paying half the rent, plus child support, and I'll have to rent a place nearby so that I can see Rachel regularly. At the moment it's easy for Cordelia and me to trade child care when last-minute jobs come up. And then"—he folded and unfolded his fingers—"there's Rachel herself."

"What do you mean?"

Question by question, Dara knew, she was ceding the high ground of righteous anger. And Edward, sensing the shift, was sounding less crushed. He described his daughter's temper. "Some nights she simply won't go to sleep. She keeps crying and calling out until two in the morning. And she has terrible tantrums." He held up his bandaged finger. "Yesterday she bit me. That's why Cordelia's mother is so crucial. Most babysitters can't cope."

Dara stood up and walked over to the French windows, meaning to draw the curtains. Instead she stared out into the tangled darkness.

"Tell me what you're thinking," said Edward. "What you're feeling."

"I feel stupid. I feel taken for granted. I feel miserable. I feel betrayed."

She heard him stand up and take a step toward her. "I made a terrible mistake," he said.

"I can't begin to count how many lies you must have told me."

"Because I wanted you."

He took another step. Even as the distance between them disappeared, Dara struggled against the feeling, small but robust, that there was something wonderful about having inspired such bad behavior. "You should leave," she said. "This is your problem. Come back when you're free and we can see what's possible between us. I can't be the other woman, the one who breaks up the family."

"No, because the family is already broken. I need you, Dara. Perhaps I shouldn't but I do. Sometimes I think Rachel senses that Cordelia and I don't love each other; that's why she's so volatile."

Dara knew what she ought to do. She ought to step away, she ought to open the door and push him out into the street and forget his face and his phone number, every syllable and every gesture that had passed between them. "So you don't sleep together?" she said.

"Not since Christmas a year ago." He was still uttering protestations and denials as he pressed his lips against her neck. After a few seconds—perhaps as many as ten, certainly no more than fifteen—she turned to meet his embrace.

B Y THE TIME EDWARD LEFT THEY HAD A PLAN: A SERIES OF STEPS that needed to be accomplished in order for the two of them to live together. "That's what I want," he had said, "more than anything." And Dara, in the exhilaration of being needed, was the one to look at the clock and say he must go home. In spite of his forceful looks and square shoulders, Edward was more like her than she had previously understood; he would not cope well if Cordelia ambushed him. Before he left, she gave him the Van Gogh book. Together they looked at several of the illustrations and she added it to her bookshelf. Then he asked for a piece of paper and wrote down his address.

After the door closed behind him, Dara returned to the sofa and poured one last glass of wine. It was nearly midnight but she felt ready to climb the dome of St. Paul's, walk to Scotland. Edward's revelation had unleashed others; she had talked to him in more detail about her father leaving, her dread that intimacy would lead to loss; he had talked about his own insecurities, the pain of being belittled by his parents, how important it had been when he first met Cordelia, who was older and more established, that she admired his musicianship. Later, as they sat up in bed, ravenously eating the smoked salmon that Dara had bought, he had turned to her and said, "This is exactly how I want to feel about another person." Now she drank the wine and wondered if she had, in some way, known all along that Edward was not free. On the surface it seemed absurd that a person who feared abandonment would seek a person with other commitments, but maybe the fact that the worst had already happened had allowed her to discover her feelings.

She set aside her glass and fetched her sketchbook and pencils. She drew a picture of the two of them, sitting up in bed, giving herself a decorous nightgown. Underneath she wrote Edward's words and the date: *The Feast of Epiphany, January 2003*. She laid it on the table beside the piece of paper with his address. Edward Davies, 79 Thornfield Road, London SE 11. The name of the street was dimly familiar. Perhaps a client lived there. Or perhaps it was the contradiction between the two halves of the name—the sharp thorns barring the way to the gentle field—that was familiar.

T HE NEXT MORNING AT THE CENTER, AS SOON AS SHE HAD GREETED her colleagues, Dara sought out Frank. At the sight of her, he stood up and closed his door. "Tell me everything," he said, reaching for the back of a chair.

While he bent and stretched, Dara did, including her theory about her own ignorance. "There were so many signs: he always went home at night, he never used his car, we never went to his flat. Surely part of me must have known what was going on?"

"Maybe, but some people are odd about these things. Vic and I dated for a year, we stayed with his family, we went on holiday together, and he never let me past the threshold of his flat. My theory is that we only suspect people of our own faults, which is to say you're too honest to suspect Edward of deceit. Don't scowl. It's one of your strengths, Dara, that you think the best of everyone." He reached forward to place his palms on the floor.

"Not if it makes me stupid. What do you think I should do?"

Frank asked the standard counseling question: where would you like to be a year from now? She answered unhesitatingly: living with Edward, being a stepmother to Rachel, planning to have a child together.

"And what do you need to do to bring that about?"

She described the steps she and Edward had discussed: his finding more pupils, looking for a flat near his present one, talking to Rachel's doctor. "I know it seems sleazy," she said, "but he isn't the kind of person who can extricate himself from this situation alone. Even though living with Cordelia isn't great, he'd stay indefinitely."

"So you're going to help him?" Frank raised one leg behind him. "I must say I admire you. I don't have the patience for this kind of crap. Or maybe I've never met someone I like enough."

"It's something you can't imagine until it happens."

Frank nodded. "The one piece of advice I'd offer, and you know this already, is that you're the latecomer to a complicated situation. Despite his best intentions, Edward won't be able to tell you everything you need to know."

I N THE OLD DAYS DARA WOULD AT ONCE HAVE TELEPHONED ABIGAIL to recount these developments, but she was still learning the rules of their new proximity. The evening she moved in, after her father left, she had knocked at Abigail's door on the pretext of returning a hammer and, as she'd hoped, been invited to supper. The meal had been pleasant—Sean, carefully supervised, had made spaghetti—but she couldn't help realizing that she was more in need of their company than they of hers. And afterward Abigail had immediately gone back to work; it was Sean who had come downstairs to admire the flat and help her unpack her books.

It was the first time Dara had been alone with him for any length of time and she was glad to find that they were on easy terms. He had teased her about still having a copy of *Sir Gawain and the Green Knight*, like everyone else who studied English. In the next box he came across *Jane Eyre*. "This was one of my wife's favorite books," he remarked, holding it up so that Dara could see the famous portrait of Charlotte Brontë on the cover. "She wrote an excellent essay about why readers are so willing to believe in Rochester's unlikely passion for Jane. Her theory was that it had to do with Brontë's cunning use of autobiographical elements." As he put the book away an expression had passed over his face so rapidly that Dara wondered if she had imagined it. For a few seconds Sean had looked utterly despairing.

Since then she had come home most evenings to see the lights on upstairs, to hear music, either Brazilian or classical, and to smell the fragrance of cooking. Meanwhile in her own flat everything was as she had left it, only a little colder and staler. She had never lived alone before, and she missed the humdrum conversations with her old housemates, their weekly dinners. That missing, combined with Abigail's busyness—she hadn't knocked on Dara's door once—and Sean's presence, made it hard to get in touch. So she was delighted when, a week after Twelfth Night, Abigail phoned to ask if she was free for supper. At the news that Sean was out, she insisted on playing host.

Abigail had not been downstairs since the floor was sanded, and she couldn't stop exclaiming how lovely the flat looked. "You've got such good taste," she said, surveying the living room. "Did Edward put up those shelves?"

"No, my father. He must have made a dozen trips to the DIY shop and the supermarket. And look what he gave me." She pointed to the rug at their feet.

She had opened the door to find him standing there, the rolled-up rug like a sentinel beside him. He had tied a red ribbon around it. "Surprise," he had said. "You have ten days to change it so please don't pretend to like it." But Dara had liked it from the moment they unrolled it to reveal the cream-colored background, patterned with blues and greens, reds and golds. "It's beautiful," she had said. Only as she saw his smile did she understand how nervous he had been about her reaction.

Now Abigail said the rug was perfect. "Here," she added, "I brought a bottle, and some nuts." When they were seated on either side of the coffee table, she asked how things were at work.

"Weirdly peaceful. A month ago Halley was leaving, Joyce was furious, everything was fraught. Now it's as if none of it ever happened. But there's something I want to tell you." Sipping wine, in the company of her oldest friend, she went into far more detail than she had with Frank: her realization that she had made it harder for Edward by putting him on a pedestal, his insecurities about his parents.

"You know," said Abigail when she finished, "I do remember thinking it was odd for him to be at the pub alone if he was visiting friends. But if he was there with his family, that makes sense. Cordelia stayed with the baby, and he came out for a drink."

Dara kept her gaze on the rug, trying not to show her dismay. It had not occurred to her that, even at their first meeting, Edward had been accompanied.

"So, what are you going to do?" said Abigail.

"Follow your excellent example. Help him to leave Cordelia."

"Does he know this?"

"It's his idea. The relationship has been over for years, but there are various practical problems."

"Like a child."

Quickly, seeing her expression, Abigail continued. "I don't mean to sound negative. Plenty of people with children split up, but it is more complicated. Sean and his wife ended up at daggers drawn, which was awful for them but no one else. Whereas Edward and Cordelia need to stay on good terms if at all possible."

"I know that."

She stood up and walked over to the kitchen. She had pictured Abigail greeting her as a comrade in arms, offering to strategize. Instead here she was pointing out problems of which Dara was already only too well aware, and once again confirming her suspicion that Abigail saw her as a poor relation rather than an equal. Of course Sean would leave his wife for Abigail, but who would ever leave his partner for Dara?

But as she opened the fridge, Abigail was standing beside her. "Don't be cross," she said. "I'm just surprised. I knew from the beginning that Sean was married. I was duly warned, and I pursued him anyway. You've been going out with Edward for four months and none of us had a clue about his family. You didn't have a chance to decide whether you were up for this before you fell for him."

"He fell for me," said Dara. "Literally and metaphorically."

"Okay, but you can't expect me to be thrilled that he's been deceiving you."

"Not thrilled." Dara set a saucepan on the cooker and turned to face Abigail. "But you could try to understand. I hate that he lied to me but I'm not like you. If he had told me immediately, I wouldn't have gone out with him; I'd never have known what it was like to feel this way. However much I wish he'd move in tomorrow, I couldn't care for a man who would walk out on his daughter." In all their years of friendship she had never spoken to Abigail so forcefully. "I need you to understand," she repeated.

The next thing she knew Abigail was hugging her. "I do understand. Really, I do."

As they cooked, they had the kind of conversation they had had so often at university, and seldom since. For the first time Dara realized how painful it had been for her friend to endure Sean's indecision. "We'd have these amazing days together," Abigail said, slicing garlic to almost transparent thinness, "days when I felt that here was the person I knew best in the world. Then he'd go back to Judy and I wouldn't hear from him for a week."

"You never thought of giving up on him?"

"Hundreds of times." She slid the garlic into a frying pan. "Remember when I went to Paris? Beforehand I'd told him it was over. I don't think I've felt so wretched since my grandparents died. I kept walking to get away from the pain. I walked from Notre Dame to Sacre Coeur, from the Arc de Triomphe to the Place des Vosges. When I got back, he'd filled the answering machine, there were so many letters I could barely get through the door. And suddenly there he was."

"I had no idea," said Dara. "From the outside you always seemed so sure you were destined to be together."

"One of us had to be." She gave the frying pan a shake. "I know this sounds arrogant but I used to think there were special cases, and that I was one of them. I'm attractive and I have an interesting life. Sean changed that. Over and over he said one thing and did another. People may make extravagant claims when they first start fucking, but once the novelty wears off, they pretty much revert to type."

"But you do still love him," said Dara, "don't you?" She was startled by the bitterness in Abigail's voice, and by how much she sounded like her old, pre-Sean self.

"Yes, but not in an 'I will go to the ends of the earth, die without you' way. I was right when I thought that was all an illusion, a nice, big middle-class illusion. For a year I woke up most mornings with a quote from Keats running through my head: 'Life must be undergone.' According to Sean"—she stepped back from the stove—"he believed that suffering is what gives us souls."

"I believe suffering makes us stupid," said Dara.

When they were seated at the table, with plates of roast chicken, potatoes, and spinach, she asked if Abigail remembered the woman she had told her about last autumn, the one who had been molested by her father. She described her encounter with the Lyalls. "It was so confusing. I completely believed each of them."

"So somebody's a good actor," said Abigail. "Or completely deluded. I take it that now you're siding with the parents?"

"Yes, but I worry I'm being unduly swayed by the father's frailty."

"Who wouldn't be swayed by the sight of him wobbling on his walking sticks? It doesn't necessarily mean that he didn't do everything he's accused of. And more."

"That's what gives me a headache. I suddenly understood the value of lie detector tests. I wanted so badly to know who was speaking the truth."

"Although if Claire really believes her story she'd pass the test with flying colors. Some people can't tell the truth, even if they want to."

When Frank had made almost the same comment, Dara had nodded sagely. Now Abigail's words seemed to hover over the table. She felt a stab of pain in her forehead. The metaphorical headache was suddenly piercingly literal. Was she having a stroke? A seizure? She felt a curtain of darkness slowly falling between her and everything else. If she moved, she knew, even the table, even her plate, would vanish. She pressed her hands to her forehead, trying to push the pain back through the bone, back into some hidden crevice of her brain from which it had emerged and where it belonged.

"What is it? Is something wrong?"

Abigail was on her feet, squeezing Dara's shoulders, but Dara couldn't speak, or move. Abigail's hands disappeared. There came sounds: a drawer opening, the fridge door. "I'm going to hold ice to the back of your neck," Abigail said. "If you're having a migraine, that will help. And I've put the kettle on for coffee."

The ice shocked, then burned, but at least she felt something besides the pain. Abigail moved away; the smell of coffee filled the air.

Dara lifted her head a few millimeters; she ventured a few more. The curtain was rising, the pain slipping away, leaving in its place a memory of pain that was almost as frightening. Abigail was sitting beside her, gazing at her anxiously. "Are you all right? What happened?"

"I don't know." Even this simple sentence was an effort. "I felt as if my head was going to break open."

"Your lips turned white. If you hadn't started talking, I was going to phone for an ambulance."

"Thank goodness you didn't. I'd have felt like an idiot."

"Promise you'll go and see your doctor tomorrow. I'll come with you, if you like."

Dara protested that she had no other symptoms, but Abigail was determined; the first sign of her father's fatal illness had been headaches. Finally Dara promised she would go. Abigail tucked her into bed, loaded the dishwasher, fetched a hot water bottle from upstairs, and exhorted her to phone immediately if the pain returned.

Alone in bed Dara lay staring at the ceiling, both exhausted and preternaturally alert. Sometimes she asked her clients to imagine themselves in a significant landscape. Now she saw herself walking in a wood at dusk. Leaves and twigs crackled underfoot. In the distance she could make out the lights of the house she was trying to reach, glowing and welcoming. But as she wound her way toward them through the trees, she began to realize she was not alone. Someone was following her, stalking her. If she wasn't careful, she would catch sight of this dark figure. It took all her energy, all her vigilance, not to turn around.

THE DOCTOR, A YOUNG INDIAN WOMAN CLOSE TO DARA'S AGE, listened to her account of the previous evening, checked her blood pressure and advised rest and exercise. Perhaps you've been under stress recently, she suggested. A multivitamin with iron is a good idea. Dara nodded, and confessed to sleeping badly. "Which of course can make you dizzy," said the doctor. She scribbled a prescription. "This should do the trick," she said. "Good luck."

While Dara waited, she had been telling herself stories about brain tumors and strokes, not so much to ward off these dark possibilities but to keep at bay the more immediate threat that the doctor might ask awkward questions: Do you have a partner? Are you in a monogamous relationship? Now, once again, her strategy was vindicated. She filled the prescription and treated herself to a taxi home. Back at the flat, she retrieved *Jane Eyre* from the bookshelf and returned to bed. Remembering Sean's comments, she started with the brief biography of Brontë. She knew the main facts about the grim parsonage and the mother's death, but she had forgotten that the dreadful school, Lowood, was based on the one Charlotte and her sisters had attended. Later, in Belgium, Charlotte had developed an attachment to a married man. In writing *Jane Eyre* she had combined this passion with several accounts of madwomen kept in attics, and one in particular about a man revealed on the eve of his marriage to already have such a wife. Brontë herself, the biography concluded, had married when she was nearly forty, and died a few months later.

Quickly Dara turned to chapter one. Almost as soon as she read the opening sentence—*There was no possibility of taking a walk that day*—these disagreeable facts melted away. She became absorbed in the struggle of Jane's childhood, first with her aunt, then at school. At last, after a typhus epidemic, the latter improved. The eighteen-year-old Jane advertised for a job as a governess and received a single reply, from a Mrs. Fairfax of Thornfield Hall. Dara got out of bed and went to the desk in the living room. In the top drawer was the sheet of paper on which Edward had written his address: *Edward Davies, 79 Thornfield Road, London SE 11.* So that was why the name had seemed familiar. She was still staring at his neat printing, unnerved by the coincidence, when the phone rang and there was Edward. At the news that she was in bed, he at once said he would come round. "Can I bring you anything?"

"Orange juice would be great." She hung up and went to hide the carton she had bought that morning.

By the time he arrived, she was sitting up in bed working on reports for the center. She had stopped reading soon after Rochester's arrival; she had no interest in the vicissitudes that Brontë seemed to need to inflict on her lovers. Still, at the sight of Edward, his hair spilling over his collar, his shoulders broad in his heavy coat, her first thought was that he could have stepped out of Thornfield Hall; his carriage would be waiting outside, ready to bear them away to some extravagant ball. While she told him about her headache and how Abigail had made her see the doctor, he took off his coat and sat on the edge of the bed.

"Maybe you should stop bicycling until it gets warmer," he said, gazing at her earnestly. Then he told her that two new pupils had signed up and a third was coming for a trial lesson. "I probably need six or seven more, given that people quit and cancel for all kinds of reasons."

"That's wonderful. Have you a chance to talk to Cordelia?"

"Not yet, but I did talk to our friend Gordon. He said I should wait until I'm ready to move out to tell her about us."

Dara clasped her knees, trying to conceal her happiness. At last she was no longer a secret. "What else did he say?" she asked greedily.

"He's happy for me." Edward bent to take off his shoes. "Very. He's known for ages that things were difficult. And he thinks it's good you're not a musician." Before she could question him further, he stepped out of his trousers and climbed into bed.

For several weeks Dara waited for the headache to return. Once or twice she felt the smallest twinge, enough to make her pause in whatever she was doing, but it vanished as quickly as it came, and by the time she met her father in late February her wariness was gone. He had suggested they go to a photography exhibit and she had invited him to lunch beforehand. It was the first time he had been to the flat since he helped her move in, and he was the ideal guest, praising all the improvements she'd made, commenting on the possibilities of the garden, where snowdrops and crocuses were already blooming beneath the plum tree.

When they were seated at the table, each with a bowl of carrot soup, she told him about Edward. "Do you remember," she said, hearing her voice, despite her best intentions, grow awkwardly stiff, "that I've been seeing a violinist?"

"Of course." He smiled; with his new short hair, the smile spread right up to his forehead. "We're looking forward to meeting him. Louise was saying this morning that she hasn't seen you in ages. The Christmas party was so crowded it doesn't count."

Dara refrained from saying that she had spent over an hour helping Louise clean up after the guests left. She was determined to tell her father everything, not to be guilty of Edward's evasions. "I want you to meet him," she said, "and he's eager to meet you, but life is a little tricky at the moment. He's still sharing a flat with his ex-girlfriend, and their daughter."

Her father took a mouthful of soup. "Delicious. How old is their daughter?"

Searching for signs of disapproval, Dara found none. If only her mother were this sanguine. "Rachel," she said. "She's two and a half. We haven't met yet but I'm eager to get to know her."

"Patrizia, Louise's younger granddaughter, was two when I met her and we've become very good friends. Well, the four of us must get together soon."

"Would you like to see the picture I did of him?" She led the way to the bathroom.

"This is fabulous," her father said. "Your mother would be proud of you. I love the swans and the cows." He remarked other details of the landscape, the willow trees, the sky, the canal, before leaning closer to the running figure and saying how handsome Edward was.

"And do you know who that is?" said Dara, pointing to the figure on the stile.

"It's you, isn't it?" said her father. "I remember those red shoes."

THE EXHIBITION WAS TITLED "LOVERS IN BLACK AND WHITE," AND the gallery consisted of one large room and two smaller ones. The photographs showed amorous adults of all ages. In the large room her father pointed out the work of his friend Harvey: an elderly man and woman sitting on a bench at the seaside, eating fish and chips. Next to them was a portrait of a much younger couple on a motorcycle, the man glowering, the woman, with her arms around him, smiling.

Dara moved from picture to picture, happily absorbed. A few months ago the exhibition would have struck her as yet more evidence of her father's persistent failure to understand her, but now romantic love was a subject about which she had many proprietary opinions.

The photograph was in one of the side rooms. Halley was standing behind Joyce with her arms around her. They each appeared to be naked from the waist up, though Halley was largely hidden by Joyce and Joyce's breasts were hidden by Halley's embrace. Halley was looking at the camera, wide-eyed, joyful, the light gleaming off her dark skin. Joyce was gazing down at her own pale hands resting on Halley's arms.

Did Dara gasp or utter some sound? All she could think, for those first few seconds, was that the two women looked as if they belonged together. Then, as she stepped over to read the placard, came the second shock. The photograph was dated not back in the mists of time, as Frank had claimed, but last year.

She was still standing there when her father came over. "Beautiful," he said. "I like how the photographer has lit the black woman and

included some of their possessions, like a sixteenth-century painter."
He pointed to the left of the photograph, where, on a table, lay a fencing
foil, a bicycle helmet, a book, and an egg whisk.

"They work at the center. Remember I told you there was this furor
because our director, Halley, might be leaving? That's her, and Joyce is
our Bangladeshi expert."

"Her plainness is part of what makes the picture so affecting. I must
keep an eye out for this photographer."

He took out a notebook, wrote something down, and was moving
toward the next photograph, when Dara heard herself saying, "I didn't
know they were having an affair."

Her father stopped. "But most of the women you work with are les-
bians," he said, "aren't they?"

He was standing twenty feet away, looking at her across the empty
space with that expression which suggested simultaneously surprise,
helplessness, and detachment, and which he had worn that last morning
when he said good-bye to her and Fergus at the school gates and during
every major quarrel they had had since then. Yes, his raised eyebrows
and barely parted lips signaled, this was upsetting, but what could he
do about it? At the sight, Dara's anger leaped the always-narrow divide
between the present aggravation and the enraging past.

"Who cares," she exclaimed, "who the fuck cares, whether people like
men or women or poodles? I don't. What hurts is that they lied to us;
they pretended to have one kind of relationship, to be friends, and, all
the time, they had another."

Her father's still raised eyebrows drove her on.

"Do you remember Kevin?" she said. "My boyfriend at university.
Once he asked me what was the happiest day of my life. I told him
about an afternoon at Granny and Grandpa's. I was maybe five or six
and we were having tea in the garden. Granny was bustling around,
laying the table. Grandpa was showing me the upside-down flowerpots

he used to lure the earwigs away from his dahlias. You'd been cutting the lawn and your feet were covered with bits of grass. You and Mum were trying to get Fergus to walk and he kept sitting down, which made you laugh.

"A few years later it was all gone: Grandpa dead, Granny confused, you and Mum mortal enemies, Fergus and me too different to be friends."

While she was speaking two women and a man had come in and stopped before a photograph of a Jamaican couple. The women were deep in discussion but the man glanced over at Dara and her father.

Her father didn't seem to notice their audience. "Maybe," he said, "they couldn't help it, Joyce and Halley. Maybe, in spite of themselves, they fell in love, and they couldn't speak about it without changing everything. Secrecy isn't always a lie. People talk nowadays as if there are no taboos, as if everyone should act on their feelings, but what if you have the wrong feelings, what are you meant to do then?"

As he spoke his voice rose until Dara saw the two women look up, but her father's eyes never left her; he was waiting for her answer. And her head was full of answers, too many to speak aloud. If the photograph was true then Joyce and Halley's behavior at the center was a lie. If her father loved her and Fergus and their mother, then his leaving was a lie. Or if his leaving was true, then the first ten years of Dara's life had been a lie.

She blinked, shutting him out, letting him in again. But it's not all lies, she reminded herself. Feelings change; change can be for the good. If I hadn't stopped imagining I was in love with Kevin, and Edward hadn't realized his mistake with Cordelia, he and I couldn't be together. Not everyone can be like Jane Eyre and meet the love of their life at eighteen.

The man and the two women moved on to the next photograph. Dara took a step toward her father, then another. As her feet carried her across the wooden floor, she remembered that first drive with Edward through the moonlit fields while the exquisite music played; if she had turned around, she would have seen Rachel's car seat. She stopped a yard away and fixed her gaze not on her father's face—no need to see that earnest expression—but on the second button of his blue shirt.

"I don't know," she said, "who gets to say what's right and what's wrong but I do know that I used to be furious with you and that now I can enjoy an afternoon in your company. Some feelings change, and some"—she turned to wave at the couples on the wall—"don't."

But just as she was about to say that that was how she felt about Edward, her gaze snagged on Halley's joyful smile, Joyce's downcast gaze, and at the same moment, her father reached out to touch her upraised arm.

"Never mind," he said softly. "Never mind."

4

THE MARSHES

WHEN ABIGAIL WAS ASKED ABOUT HER FIRST MEMORY, WHAT SHE most often recounted was the afternoon she and her grandfather had gone for a walk and found a Roman plate buried in the muddy foreshore of the River Medway. She would describe herself in her T-shirt and shorts, skipping along beside her grandfather. He was wearing a white shirt, faded gray trousers, and a straw hat that was almost the same color as his mustache. The tide was out, and he had said they should dig for Roman remains, or Saxon as a second best, but only for twenty minutes.

"We can't excavate the entire shore," he said, "so we depend on luck. Without it, we could dig all day and find nothing but stones and worms."

"I like worms," Abigail said, thrusting her trowel into the mud. What she did not like was her grandfather mentioning that mysterious phenomenon which played such a large and aggravating role in the lives of her parents. Great luck, her father would say at any piece of good news. This is my lucky day, her mother frequently announced, opening her blue eyes wide as if to trap every particle of good fortune. One reason Abigail loved spending the summers with her grandparents was that their household did not depend on such random interventions: they got up at seven-thirty every day, they went to the library on Thursday afternoon, and on Saturday, if it wasn't pouring, they bicycled or took the bus to the nearby town of Rochester. When she went shopping with her grandmother, they met the same neighbors who made the same remarks: how much Abigail had grown, what beautiful hair she had.

Her grandfather marked out a square in the mud. "You start in this corner," he said. "I'll take that one."

They had been digging for eighteen minutes; she had asked how much longer twice, when he held up a thin gray disc with one small shard missing. "Who do you think ate dinner off this?" he said.

"You," said Abigail, coming to look. "Granny."

"No." He shook his head so that his straw hat rocked from side to side. "This is very old. You can tell by the kind of pottery. Julius Caesar could have used this plate, or Maximinus I. We'll take it home to show Mama, then we'll ask the museum if they want it." One case at the local museum already contained several fragments labeled as the finds of Hans Taylor.

The memory grew less exact at this point, but probably they had done what they did most Sundays: headed to the large oak tree at the bend in the river. While they walked her grandfather would have talked about a writer called Charles Dickens who had lived in Chatham when he was a boy. The marshes of the Medway and the convict ships moored in the River Thames had inspired his novel *Great Expectations*, which Abigail would enjoy when she was older. Charles was the second of six children and sometimes, on afternoons like this, he had walked with his father in the woods near Higham. On one such outing they had come across a house known as Gad's Hill Place; his father had told Charles that the name appeared in Shakespeare and added that if he, Charles, was persevering and worked very hard he might someday live in such a house.

"Thirty years later," said her grandfather, "he discovered Gad's Hill for sale and he bought it and came to live here with his children; he had nine or ten. But the happiest days of his life were when he was your age, before the boyslaughter."

"Boyslaughter?" The strange word filled her mouth in a satisfying way.

"It's a made-up expression. When a part of his childhood was destroyed, a place or a memory he loved, Charles called it boyslaughter."

Her grandfather knew all this because, when he first arrived in England from Hamburg, he had started reading Dickens to improve his English; the great writer had been his guide to his new country. More than most people, he told Abigail, Dickens understood how suddenly life can change: one day you can be respectable, the next in debtors' prison. And the next back again, in your top hat and gloves.

"I want a top hat," said Abigail.

At the tree they turned and walked home to where her grandmother would have tea waiting. Later the three of them would play snap or pellmanism, and later still one of her grandparents might read a story by Hans Christian Andersen. The Danish writer had idolized Dickens and paid him an interminable visit. Abigail listened, enthralled, although the stories made her eyes water; the children had such hard lives.

Week followed blissful week. But in late August she would notice, at first doubtfully, soon with awful certainty, that the sun was no longer shining when she went to bed. She would attempt to bargain the calendar to a standstill, try to keep her eyes open all night to prevent the arrival of a new day. Please let me stay, she would say to her grandparents, over and over. I can go to school here. Over and over they would say that they would like nothing better but that she belonged with her parents.

"They don't want me," said Abigail. "Sometimes they don't even have a bedroom for me."

During that period her parents were moving among various towns north of London: Chigwell, Enfield, Watford, Barnet, Cheshunt, Potters Bar. When, at the end of the summer, her father came to collect her, she never knew where he would be taking her, what shabby dwelling she would be told to call home. You won't believe the amazing place we've found, Abby, he would say. In one flat she slept in the living room on a mattress behind the sofa. A few months later her bedroom was all by itself in the attic of a large, dusty house. Her grandparents would listen to her father's accounts of his latest venture and politely decline his invitations to visit.

Dickens had cherished his years in Chatham not just because he had been so happy there but because after he left everything was so terrible. His father, a navy clerk, lived constantly beyond his means, and when he was transferred back to London his finances rapidly unraveled. The twelve-year-old Charles was forced to leave school and work in a shoe-polish factory. As he pasted labels onto jars of black polish, he could hear the river rats scrabbling beneath the floor. And despite his small earnings his father was soon in debtors' prison. The rest of the family joined him in jail, leaving poor Charles living alone, sticking on endless labels.

"Never forget," said her grandfather, "school is the gateway to life."

She didn't, not least because he said it so often. And then, the winter she was ten, came the awful, singular events that were also unforget-table. Her grandmother fell, broke her hip, and caught pneumonia. A month later her grandfather had a heart attack. With their deaths, she lost her refuge and her parents lost their last constraint. Later she understood that they had also inherited some money, though not enough. Her father gave up his current job, in an estate agent's, and they moved to the Channel Islands to start a daffodil farm and a guest house. Both failed. They returned to Cornwall and her father worked in a boatyard while her mother did the afternoon shift at a fish shop. That winter they moved to Exeter. With neither qualifications nor con-tacts, her mother decided to open a kindergarten: See your wee ones flourish in Mrs. Taylor's Garden. When no pupils enrolled, she offered cookery classes instead. The two women who signed up soon became her friends and stopped paying. Meanwhile her father led walking tours and gave canoeing lessons. Then they went to Cardiff.

The year Abigail was fourteen they moved so often that she couldn't go to school. She would find the library in whatever town they happened to be living and study as best she could, reading about the Corn Laws and the periodic table, but the prospect of missing crucial exams put her in a frenzy. The day after they unpacked their suitcases in a flat on the outskirts of Reading, she told her parents that they couldn't move again for three years. "I need to go to school," she explained. "The same school, every day."

"Of course, darling," they said. "No more moving, cross our hearts."

And her mother, who had grown up in foster care and run away when she was sixteen, had said she would tutor Abigail. "I'll get to learn the things I skipped the first time around. Amo, amas, amat."

Stupidly, as if the tutorials were really going to happen, Abigail had said she wasn't studying Latin.

Six weeks later, in mid-October, they were evicted for not paying rent. Her parents moved to Blackpool and Abigail found herself, at fifteen, renting a room above a launderette, going to school, and working every evening at a supermarket. For two years all she did was study, work, and occasionally fuck one of the boys who stocked the shelves. An English teacher took her under her wing and helped her to apply to university. Abigail secretly dreamed of going to Oxford or Cambridge and ended up applying to Sheffield, York, and St. Andrews. She got into all three and chose the Scottish town where her parents were unlikely to set foot.

That summer she worked furiously. The teacher had said she shouldn't have a job during term time; after all, this was her chance to explore ideas. So Abigail worked at the supermarket from eight until four, then changed into black trousers and a white shirt and waitressed at an Italian restaurant. She had not seen her parents since they'd passed through town in the spring, but they sent a postcard with each new address. Now she wrote to them, asking for money. Her father sent another postcard, announcing that he and her mother were getting divorced, and saying nothing about money. Her mother sent the news that she was remarrying—*If you're ever in Newcastle, do come and see us*—and a check for a hundred pounds that, amazingly, cleared. Abigail spent it on clothes at the charity shop and secondhand copies of books she needed.

S HE ARRIVED IN ST. ANDREWS ON A SEPTEMBER DAY SO PERFECT that it was enough to make one believe in the pathetic fallacy; the iridescent sea, the wide beaches, the famous golf course, the ruined cathedral and castle. Abigail had never seen anything so beautiful, and the main buildings of the university were satisfyingly old, like Oxford and Cambridge. Her first weeks passed in a swirl of happiness; she adored her classes, she met such interesting people, she couldn't get over how many hours there were in the day to study, or to drink coffee and talk. More often than she cared to acknowledge, however, there were these jolts, moments when she was suddenly aware of how different her childhood had been from those of her peers. She would miss a reference to a TV show and, just when she figured it out, the topic would change and she would fail to recognize the name of the home secretary. For three years she had seen almost no television, read no newspapers, and listened only to the radio station they played in the supermarket. It was almost as if she had grown up in a foreign country. At first she did her best to conceal her past; then she discovered that people were interested in her odd life story; her parents—her athletic, mercurial father, her charming, sylphlike mother—became characters whom she acted out for her friends, guyed and caricatured.

Only more gradually did she discover that she was different from the other students in ways that went far beyond culture and politics. In theory they were, like her, independent, living on their own, but in fact they still had rooms in their parents' houses, endless "loans" available. By the middle of the term they were talking about going home for the holidays. For the last three years Abigail had worked in the supermarket on Christmas Eve and then spent Christmas Day with the English teacher's family, showing up at noon with a box of chocolates. Now she realized she would be alone in St. Andrews for four weeks, and she needed to get a job; her savings were shrinking with alarming speed. She mentioned her holiday plans to one or two of her interesting new acquaintances. "Lucky you," they said, "not having to deal with chores and curfews." Abigail quickly grasped that this was a difference to which she shouldn't draw attention. Then in late November she found a note in her mailbox. College rooms had to be vacated by noon on 10 December. The college would reopen on 12 January.

"What does this mean?" she asked the porter.

"The college closes for Christmas, love. We all go home."

She went to see her supervisor, a stringy, disheveled man, who often brought his golden Labrador to his office and, sometimes, his infant son. He nodded as she talked and promised to see whether the university could provide alternative housing. But as she rose to leave he said, "Are you sure there isn't anyone you can stay with? An aunt? A family friend?"

"I am absolutely positive," said Abigail, and slammed out of the office. Did he think she'd ask this humiliating favor if it weren't a last resort?

The next day in the laundry room a girl, whom Abigail recognized from her seminar on modernism, said hello. "I'm Dara MacLeod. I enjoyed hearing you read from *Mrs. Dalloway*."

Abigail introduced herself and explained that she had had a teacher who thought reading aloud was one of the best ways to understand what an author was doing.

"I wish I'd had someone like that," said Dara. As they loaded their clothes into adjacent machines, she admitted that she had been struggling with the novel. "I know that Woolf is a feminist hero but I didn't understand how the war and the party fitted together. Then, after you read that page, suddenly it began to make sense."

Abigail said that she didn't see how Woolf could count as a hero when everything had been handed to her on a plate. Including being abused by her father and brother, said Dara. They debated, cordially, the effect of Woolf's childhood difficulties, which Dara saw as mitigating, Abigail as irrelevant. "Look at Dickens," she offered. "He went to work at the age of twelve and he still managed to write brilliant novels."

When their laundry was finished, they went upstairs to leave their clothes in Abigail's room. Dara remarked on the tidiness. Abigail said she liked to know where things were; her parents' chaos had made her neat. In the cafeteria she told Dara first about her nonexistent family, and then—Dara had asked about Christmas—she confided her housing problem, and her money problem. Something about Dara's steady gaze, the crease of her lower eyelid, suggested that she might understand.

"So," said Dara, "you need a place to stay and a good job. I'm sure you could get a room in town, but I bet holiday jobs here are badly paid. Let me ask my mother if she has any ideas. She and my stepfather live in Edinburgh. There are lots of big shops and restaurants."

Abigail started to say that she didn't know Edinburgh and how could she look for a job there when she was here, but Dara told her not to worry. "I'll let you know as soon as I hear from my mother," she said. She leaned over and gently moved a strand of Abigail's hair that was dangling perilously close to her coffee cup.

THREE DAYS LATER ABIGAIL WAS CIRCLING HELP WANTED ADVER-tisements in the local newspaper when there came a knock at the door. "Here's the deal," Dara said, coming in and sitting down on the bed. Her mother, stepfather, and younger brother were going to South Africa for Christmas to visit her stepfather's brother. "I asked them if you could stay in the house with me and they've said yes, subject to meeting you. They weren't keen on leaving me on my own, especially over Christmas. You can have the spare room and the house is handy for the buses. Would that suit you?"

"That would be perfect." Pleasure and relief propelled Abigail out of her chair; she stood there, beaming uselessly.

"I was going to ask you." Dara paused, one hand smoothing the already smooth bedspread.

Abigail felt her heart drop. Here came the pound of flesh. "Yes," she said, trying not to sound too grudging.

Still fidgeting with the spread, Dara confided that she too would like to get a holiday job: how would Abigail feel about them applying together? They could visit the city next weekend. That way her mother and Alastair could meet Abigail and they could fill out applications at some of the big stores. For a moment, she raised her eyes to Abigail's as if she were asking an enormous favor. Hastily Abigail set about reassuring her—it would be great to work together; she was good at getting jobs—at the same time wondering why reassurance was necessary.

O N THE TRAIN THE FOLLOWING FRIDAY, WHILE DARA MADE A LIST of stores, Abigail watched the dingy landscape and worried that Dara's parents would take one look at her and change their minds. She had braided her hair and settled, after several changes, on a dark brown sweater and black trousers; still the possible faux pas seemed endless. But as soon as she saw the tall woman at the station, wearing a red jacket and jeans, waving and walking toward them, her anxiety began to fade. Fiona's fair hair stood up in little tufts and she wore bright blue earrings that Abigail might have chosen. She shook Abigail's hand, hugged Dara, and turned back to compliment Abigail on her minimal luggage. In the car she asked if Dara had finished her essay on Woolf. Then she asked if Abigail knew Edinburgh and pointed out the Castle.

For the first time since her grandmother died Abigail was a guest in a well-run home. There was nice furniture, central heating, hot water, clean sheets, ample towels, a brimming refrigerator. It made her want to weep with self-pity as all her long hours in the supermarket never had. When Fiona showed her the spare room and asked if there was anything else she needed, Abigail almost hugged her. On the way downstairs she paused to look at various paintings: a landscape with sleek lions and fluffy sheep, a portrait of a girl who looked like Dara, a seaside scene.

"Who did the paintings?" she asked as she came into the kitchen.

"Mum or me," said Dara. "She does the animals."

"They're beautiful. I didn't know you could paint."

"I can't. Mum's the painter in the family. She teaches art in a high school."

"Nonsense. You're very gifted," said Fiona. "You just have more sense than to want to be a starving artist. Would you mind slicing the mushrooms?"

The three of them were in the kitchen, chatting and chopping vegetables, when Dara's brother, Fergus, a lanky fifteen-year-old, came home. He hugged Dara, greeted Abigail, and went off to do his homework. He had barely left the room when the front door opened again and Dara's stepfather, Alastair, appeared. All Abigail knew about him was that he was a barrister, and it was easy, she thought, taking in his long, bony face and thick gray hair, to picture him in a black robe, settling someone's fate.

"We're glad you could come and stay," he said, shaking Abigail's hand.

"Thank you," she said. She found herself looking into oddly youthful gray eyes.

Later, over dinner, Alastair was generous with the wine and she allowed herself a rare second glass. Fiona asked where she had grown up and Abigail explained about her parents and her peripatetic childhood. Her father was over in Ireland at the moment, last heard from in Donegal. As for her mother and her new husband, they had made it clear that Abigail was welcome for lunch, but nothing more.

"So you're an orphan," said Fergus, sounding pleased.

"I'm so sorry," said Fiona, her eyes rounding like Dara's.

"No, really," Abigail protested. "They've always been like this. If my mother had gone on the pill a month sooner, I'd never have been born."

She stopped, dismayed at the direction in which she'd taken the conversation, but Alastair said he knew what she meant. Every year he dealt with cases involving women like that, who didn't know the meaning of the word "maternal." Even though the court hated to separate parent and child, sometimes it was for the best. While he described a recent case, Fiona offered more chicken, more rice; Abigail accepted both.

THE FOLLOWING DAY SHE AND DARA FOUND JOBS IN A DEPARTMENT store on Princes Street. Dara had never worked in a store before, but Alastair provided a character reference on his firm's ivory-colored stationery; at the brief interview Abigail answered all the questions. When they started work a few weeks later, they turned out to be a surprisingly good team. Abigail could dazzle and charm, but Dara was better with the more indecisive customers. She listened carefully and made suggestions: the blue pullover, not the green one, a scarf was safer than gloves. She and Abigail grew adept at knowing who would be best for whom. "My colleague can help you," they would say, trying not to giggle. Meanwhile Abigail got a second job working four nights a week in a restaurant. She needed to earn as much money as possible before the January lull.

After the first hectic Saturday at the restaurant, when she was still buzzing from running around, she asked Luke, the bartender, if he wanted to get a drink. Earlier that evening, he'd made a good joke about Bloody Marys, and she liked the way he bit his lip when the orders piled up.

"I'm not sure if anywhere's still open," he said.

"I was thinking of your place."

"Oh," he said and, for a moment, she thought he was going to turn her down. "That's a brilliant idea."

His flat was ten minutes' walk away and they spent a pleasant hour in bed. Then Abigail reached for her clothes. Sleepily Luke asked her to stay, but she was not tempted, even for a second, to exchange the clean comfort of Dara's house for his dingy room, similar to so many she had known. "I'll come by tomorrow," she promised, and wrote down his phone number. Back at the house she let herself in quietly. Dara had left on the hall light; a note lay on the stairs:

Hope you made a ton of money. See you tomorrow. xox D.

The next morning at breakfast Abigail told Dara about Luke. Dara said she wondered if she knew him. What was his surname?

"I don't know. It's just a holiday thing. I don't want you to feel you have to take care of me all the time."

"You're the one taking care of me," said Dara earnestly. Then she announced that her friend Sarah's parents had asked them to supper that evening.

"How nice," said Abigail. As soon as Dara went to take a shower, she telephoned Luke to say she couldn't make it.

IN THE NEW YEAR BUSINESS DID SLACKEN BUT NOT FATALLY. THE restaurant, thanks to Luke—he turned out to be the owner's nephew—kept her on for Fridays and Saturdays, and the store had her and Dara doing inventory. One evening, at Dara's suggestion, the two of them went to the theater, something that Abigail had done only twice in her life. When she was eight, her grandparents had taken her to *Cinderella*. Abigail had been intrigued—poor Cinderella doing endless housework and the ball scene was so pretty—but she hadn't fallen in love. Nor had she a decade later when her English class went to *Othello* and the stage swarmed with men in baggy tights, brandishing swords and making speeches.

But Edinburgh was different. Even before the play began, she noticed that there was no curtain and that she was much closer to the stage. Presently the lights dimmed on the audience, and a couple of people, wearing jeans and scruffy jackets, were standing on the stage talking as if they had wandered in off the street. The play was set partly on a Glasgow housing estate and partly on the island of Arran; changes of scene were indicated by a few props or by a shift in the lighting. When the interval came Abigail had to remind herself who she was, where she was. "Are there other plays like this?" she said, meaning this wonderful.

Dara consulted the program. "It says here that the playwright is twenty-nine and this is his third play. Do you like it?"

"It's fantastic," said Abigail. "It's brilliant."

Dara smiled and went to buy ice creams.

Afterward they were having a drink in the theater bar when several of the actors came in, including the hero. "Look," said Abigail, "there's Donald. Let's go and congratulate him."

"You go," said Dara. "I'm going to the loo."

Abigail carried over her beer. "Excuse me," she said, reaching toward Donald's elbow. "I wanted to tell you, you were fantastic."

Donald turned to her with a vivid smile. "Thanks," he said in a voice quite different from the one he'd used on stage. "I'm Stewart Henderson."

Abigail introduced herself and asked if he'd had to work at his accent. What she really wanted to know was what he had done that made you feel as if you had to look at him every second he was on stage, even when he wasn't talking, or moving. But Stewart was already saying that he had grown up near Aberdeen; his character spoke like the people in his village.

When Dara came back, she offered her congratulations and surprised Abigail by saying she'd seen Stewart last year, in a play about a factory. "You were great in that too."

"What were you thinking when you tipped over your mother's wheelchair?" Abigail asked.

"Truthfully?" Stewart smiled. "I was thinking about my bike. I'd only had it six months and I'd bought a super expensive lock. Last week it was nicked from outside the theater."

"How did you become an actor?"

"What is this, an interview?"

"No. I need to know."

Something in her voice or her face must have convinced him. "Okay," he said. "You can ask me questions for fifteen minutes, then I'm going for supper."

Dara moved to leave them alone but Abigail said she had to help her listen. The three of them sat down. She got out a notebook and Stewart talked.

WHEN THEY RETURNED TO UNIVERSITY THE FOLLOWING WEEK, Abigail arranged to swap rooms so that she would be across the hall from Dara. It was as they were carrying over her boxes of books that she spotted a poster for the Drama Society. She went to the next meeting and found fifteen students debating the spring production. She listened carefully as they threw out titles, trying to figure out where the power lay. Was it with the boy in the black sweater who kept mentioning Beckett? Or with the slightly heavy girl with the intellectual glasses whom everyone deferred to? Or the bearded boy, who simply sat at the table, greeting each suggestion with a little smile or, once, a slow shrug?

Finally, in the lull following a heated argument about an Irish play, Abigail raised her hand. "I wanted to say that I saw a wonderful play in the holidays by a Scottish playwright. I don't know the rest of his work but I liked that it was set in Scotland, nowadays."

"That's right," said the bearded boy, speaking for the first time. "In case some of you haven't noticed, we are in Scotland. If we're going to do a contemporary play there's a lot to be said for acknowledging that rather than trying to fake Irish accents."

The evening ended with no clear resolution, but several people, including Abigail, volunteered to research contemporary Scottish plays and bring suggestions to the next meeting. In the bar afterward Abigail managed to insinuate herself between the heavy woman and the bearded boy. She asked Phoebe and Axel the same question she'd asked Stewart: how did people learn to act.

"God," said Axel, "mostly in front of their wardrobe mirrors."

"The Byre Theater runs workshops," Phoebe added. "You should look out for those."

"I'll probably be hopeless," Abigail said, "but I'd like to try." Axel, she noticed, was smiling sardonically: another starstruck idiot. Phoebe, however, gave her an appraising look as if, dimly, she sensed that Abigail had possibilities.

O VER THE NEXT SIX MONTHS, EXCEPT FOR THE EASTER VACATION when Abigail took a job at a hotel near the university, she and Dara were inseparable. Night after night they started off working in their separate rooms. Then one of them would appear in the other's doorway, ostensibly to offer a cup of tea or ask a question about an essay, and soon they would be sitting on the bed, talking. Each of them, they discovered, had had a version of Eden from which she had been expelled, abruptly and irrevocably, at the age of ten. Dara described the summer her father left home, the last camping holiday, how the whole atmosphere of the house changed. Cautiously Abigail asked if he might be gay, but Dara said he'd remarried last year, a woman his own age. "When he says his family now, he means Louise and her children. He never means us."

Abigail talked about her parents, how her father loved anything outdoors, boats, climbing, horses, but couldn't find a way to make a living, and how her mother was a person of a hundred enthusiasms—baking, jewelry making, running a kindergarten, batik, pottery, beekeeping— none of which ever lasted. "They were both always convinced that something wonderful would happen in the next town."

"But what you did was incredible," said Dara. "Moving out when you were fifteen and supporting yourself. I couldn't have done that."

"I had no choice," said Abigail. "I knew if I ever wanted to have a normal life, I had to leave home." For the first time since her grandparents died she felt recognized and understood. Later, after they had reluctantly agreed to call it a night, she would lie in bed replaying the back-and-forth of their conversations: Dara advising, listening, consoling, teasing.

I N February the Drama Society held auditions—Axel had decided on a play by a young Glasgow writer—and Abigail was chosen for the lead's sister. From then on her sessions with Dara included going over her lines. Night after night Dara corrected her, asked questions: "Should you sound angry here?" "Why do you shrug when he asks about the baby?"

On opening night Dara, her mother, and her stepfather were in the third row. "I can shout out your lines if you forget," she said. "Not that I'll need to." Waiting in the wings, Abigail could just make out her rapt face. Then she heard her cue. She stepped into the lights, she said her first line and felt it reach the back of the theater. At last she had entered her proper element.

Afterward at dinner Fiona, Alastair, and Dara raised their glasses to her. "Well done," said Fiona. "You had us on the edge of our seats."

"Magnificent," said Alastair.

Abigail feigned modesty—she couldn't have done it without Dara—but she knew she had been good, almost too good for the rest of the cast.

The conversation turned to summer plans. Abigail was again applying for jobs at hotels in St. Andrews. "The place I worked at Easter was okay, but waitressing is how you make money. I need to work in a fancy restaurant where Americans give you huge tips after a game of golf."

"That sounds a bit grim," said Alastair.

"I bet it'll be fun," said Fiona. "There'll be lots of other students working, and St. Andrews is so pretty in the summer. Dara said you might be coming to the Festival."

"Touch wood," said Abigail. "If I get a part, and if I can afford to take time off."

"We'll keep our fingers crossed." Fiona smiled. Turning to Dara, she said she'd enrolled in a printmaking course at the art college. Maybe Dara would be interested in taking the second session.

Back at the hall of residence, Abigail said good night first to Alastair and Fiona, then, after a brief, exuberant postmortem, to Dara. Twenty minutes later, unable to sleep, she slipped out of her room and down the stairs. She made her way through the quiet streets to the old stone pier. As she stepped onto the wall the wind tugged at her hair and stung her cheeks; the farther out she walked, the stronger and saltier the air grew. Dickens had been two years older than she was when he had published his first sketch, and described his eyes *so dimmed with joy and pride, that they could not bear the street, and were not fit to be seen there.* Her own eyesight was as keen as ever—she could distinguish the stark ruin of the cathedral and beyond it the headland—but she understood about hiding joy. She stared into the darkness which was not quite darkness and wished that her grandparents could have seen her triumph.

SOON AFTER ABIGAIL'S DEBUT, DARA TOO FOUND HER VOCATION. A friend had asked her to do a shift at the local Samaritans—no one ever calls, she claimed—but just as Dara sat down the phone rang. In a high, breathless voice, a girl declared that she could see no reason to go on living. "She was ranting away," Dara told Abigail. "She was plain, she was stupid, her friends were all busy and in love. Her parents had their own lives. No one would even notice if she committed suicide."

"Did you ask her if she had a place to live? If she had any money?"

"I asked if there was anything that cheered her up. Of course she said no, so I started making suggestions: hot buttered toast? The smell of lilacs? A song? A friend who makes you laugh?" After forty minutes the girl had promised to get counseling.

As Dara spoke, an expression appeared on her face that Abigail had seen when she helped a customer to find the right gift, or when she herself finally mastered a difficult speech. The next week Dara signed up to take the training course at the counseling center. "I'm much better at this than writing essays," she said. "I love George Eliot but I've nothing new to say about her moral sensibility."

"I don't know how you have the patience," said Abigail. Her own secret belief was that most of the people who came to talk to Dara had money, education, families; they simply needed to pull themselves together.

"Counseling is short-term," said Dara. "You seldom see anyone more than a dozen times. Besides each client is different." She described one of her cases. A first-year girl had briefly dated a local boy who worked in a garage. When he broke up with her, she started stalking him. "She knows she shouldn't, but she can't stop hanging around the garage. She's missing lectures and she's been late on two essays."

"I don't get it," said Abigail. "He's not interested in her, she scarcely knows him, and now she's messing up her courses to spy on him."

"But she thinks he's the love of her life," said Dara, as if that phrase answered all objections.

Abigail shook her head. Romance was another topic about which she often felt hopelessly out of step with her peers, even with Dara.

When she'd told her that sleeping with Luke was convenient—"We can go to his flat right after work"—Dara's lips had tightened in a way that made Abigail wish she'd kept quiet. Sex was about love, as far as Dara was concerned. She wanted Abigail to be in love; she wanted to be in love herself. In their late-night conversations she had talked about her boyfriend, Peter, with whom she'd broken up before coming to St. Andrews. "We weren't really in love," she had said as if this were an insurmountable problem. Abigail didn't understand this complicated way of going about things—What about pleasure? What about being in the present?—but she did understand that her bringing boys back to her room so often upset Dara. "Everything's easy for you," Dara had said. "You just look at someone and they want you." Abigail began to insist on going to their rooms instead.

Two of the hotels she'd applied to offered her a job for the summer and she was debating between them—one had better hours, the other a more expensive restaurant—when she received a letter on ivory-colored paper. It came from Alastair's office; indeed it came from Alastair.

Dear Abigail,

I have some surprising and, I trust, welcome news. One of my clients is eager to offer support to a young artist at an early stage of his or her career. This would consist of a very modest stipend, to be paid during the university summer vacation, and of free accommodation in a small flat in Edinburgh. Certain duties and conditions would pertain, none I think too onerous. After some discussion with the client, I have been authorized to offer you the

*situation. Please get in touch at your earliest convenience to let me
know if this appeals to you.*

Kind regards,
Alastair

In a daze Abigail wandered out into the street. A light rain was falling
and overhead the seagulls were crying. Heedless of both, with neither
jacket nor umbrella, she made her way to the hall where she knew Dara
was attending a lecture and sat waiting outside. Only Alastair's dry
prose suggested that there was any chance that this was real. As soon
as Dara emerged, she drew her over to the window and handed her the
letter. Dara read it and looked up with a smile.

"Brilliant," she said. "You'll be spending the summer in Edinburgh
rather than slaving in a hotel."

"But I'm not a young artist. Why would this happen?"

"Yes, you are. You're an actress. I've heard Alastair talking about this
kind of arrangement. He has wealthy clients who want to do good
works but not go through an organization. Last year he got one of
them to pay for art courses for a couple of Mum's pupils. Let's go and
phone him."

The stipend turned out to be a hundred pounds a month and the
conditions were two: Abigail would use the money to study acting and
she would refrain from having overnight guests at the flat. "My client is
rather old-fashioned," said Alastair. "Is this acceptable?"

"Yes, yes, of course. How do I thank this person, my benefactor?"
The pompous, Victorian word seemed suddenly appropriate.

No thanks were necessary, Alastair declared. His client, Mr. MacPherson, was glad to provide assistance to such a deserving young person.
Her only duty was to write him a letter at the end of the summer detail-
ing how the money had fostered her art.

Abigail sat through her afternoon seminar in a daze. So this was what it was like to be lucky, to experience random, undeserved good fortune. But as the discussion rose and fell around her, one thought took firm shape. This event was not entirely random: Alastair barely knew who she was; it was Fiona who had given him the idea, who had made this happen. When the seminar ended, she went to find a phone.

"Oh, Abigail. Alastair told me about the summer grant. I'm glad he put your name forward. Did Dara manage to change her shift at the counseling center?"

"I can't thank you enough," said Abigail, putting all the emotion she could into the "you."

Two boys were passing, talking loudly, and she didn't quite catch Fiona's reply—"It was nothing"? "It was nothing to do with me"?—but she didn't like to ask. She said that Dara had changed her shift, and asked about the printmaking course. Fiona described the series she was doing based on a medieval tapestry. Then she had to go and make supper for Fergus. Abigail could feel herself smiling as she put down the phone. How typical that Fiona would not want to be thanked.

A HUNDRED POUNDS A MONTH WAS NOT ENOUGH TO LIVE ON, AND both the store on Princes Street and the restaurant welcomed her back. Luke had a new girlfriend, but once or twice they got together for old times' sake; she didn't have a moment to look for anyone else. On her rare evenings off she went round to Dara's. She would sit at the kitchen table with Fiona and Dara, drinking wine, cooking, and talking. It didn't matter the topic—bleaching one's teeth, the neighbors' greenhouse, a new film—what mattered was Fiona's lively interest and concern, the way she remembered about the difficult customer, asked what Abigail's boss had said. Sometimes Fergus joined them, pretending to study his maths book, smiling at their jokes. When Alastair came home the two of them would head off for a session on the computer.

In August the Edinburgh Festival started. Abigail had been hearing about this phenomenon for months but she had had no notion of the scope and scale. The city was transformed. Wherever she looked there were actors, performers, artists, musicians. She slept only three or four hours a night and spent the rest of her time either performing or advertising their show by doing impromptu scenes on the Royal Mile. She walked around in a minuscule skirt and high-heeled boots with a martini shaker, offering thimble-sized portions to passersby. She loved the uncertainty of no one being quite sure whether she was acting or making martinis as a public service.

Dara meanwhile was employed in a summer program for what she called nonattenders: girls and boys who one day simply refused to go to school and, despite their parents' pleas and threats, went on refusing.

"But what do they think will happen to them?" said Abigail. The whole idea made her furious.

"They're not thinking about the future. They're trying to make the present bearable. Maybe they've had a hard time with bullying. Sometimes they just want attention. Most of them are middle-class kids with busy parents. Suddenly they discover that by not going to school they can get their parents to focus on them."

She persuaded Abigail and the rest of the Drama Society to come and do a workshop for the nonattenders. "It'll be good publicity," she said, "and the program will pay for them to come to one of your matinees."

The workshop was a huge success, and at the end of the afternoon Abigail found herself standing on the stage, making an impromptu speech. "I want to tell you," she said, "about what happened to me." She described how for nearly a year she hadn't been able to go to school, and how that had made her feel that all the doors were closing. "I left home and worked at a supermarket to pay my rent so that I could attend school and I'm glad I did because now I'm here, talking to you."

At the back of the room Dara began to clap; other people joined in. Abigail stood there, smiling and bewildered. She was used to applause when she acted but not for her true self.

THE LAST NIGHT OF THE SHOW ABIGAIL NOTICED A MAN IN THE second row of the audience. He was middle-aged and not particularly good-looking but he watched the stage with unusual intensity and, she soon realized, watched her. Might he be a reviewer for a major newspaper, or a talent scout? Superstitiously she didn't mention his presence to anyone else. When the play ended, he rose to his feet, applauding loudly. Abigail could feel his eyes on her as she bowed. A few minutes later she emerged from the dressing room to find him still sitting among the empty seats. He stood up, smiling, and moved toward her with outstretched hand. For a moment she was radiant with possibility.

"I wanted to introduce myself. I'm Dara's father, Cameron MacLeod. You were terrific."

"Oh," said Abigail stupidly. Here was the subject of so many late-night conversations, so much speculation: an ordinary, rather slender man in a navy blue sweater and black trousers. She pulled herself together and gave him one of her best smiles. "Thank you. And thanks for coming tonight. It's nice to meet you." To see what would happen, she held his hand a little too long.

Cameron's expression didn't change. He explained that he'd come up from London just for the weekend; he and Dara had gone to a photography show that afternoon.

She introduced him to the rest of the cast, including the gorgeous

Antonio, who also flirted to no effect. Cameron praised everyone. Then with a wave of the hand, he was gone. The next day she phoned Dara and thanked her for sending him to the play. "He seemed nice."

"Nice?" said Dara.

Abigail could hear the disappointment in her voice but what else could she offer. That she'd thought he was somebody important? That he hadn't responded to either her or Antonio? "He was very complimentary about the play," she said.

"That's the main thing."

"I'm sorry, Dara. We only spoke for a minute and everyone was milling around."

"I know. It's stupid to think you'd have an amazing insight in sixty seconds. I keep hoping that someday I'll understand what made him leave us."

"You will. Now you've left home you'll get to know each other in a different way, as equals."

"I don't want to be his equal. I want to be his daughter."

"At least he stays in touch, at least he sends money."

Then it was Dara's turn to apologize. "You're right. Lots of parents behave worse than him," she said. "Far, far worse."

THAT AUTUMN DARA STARTED SEEING KEVIN, A THIRD-YEAR POLItics student whom she had met at a meeting about proposed renovations to the halls of residence. "He's a union steward," she reported. "He thinks students should have a say in whatever plans the university adopts. After all, we're the ones who use the buildings." For several days after the meeting she mentioned Kevin frequently; that Thursday she didn't show up to study for their tutorial. The following morning Abigail found a note under her door.

Sorry about last night. Ran into Kevin. xox Dara.

When Abigail finally met him she was startled to discover that the fount of all happiness and wisdom was a rather stolid young man with muscular forearms and untidy hair. The three of them went out for a drink. Conversation was already faltering when Abigail confused the deputy prime minister with the treasurer and Kevin said something savage about ill-informed citizens, and where did she think the grants for her precious theater came from.

"I know more about the working classes than you ever will," Abigail said. She downed her beer and left.

Later Dara made excuses for him but Abigail didn't care about Kevin, or what he thought of her. What she cared about was the way Dara had disappeared into the relationship. She was seldom in her room; she forgot arrangements or changed them at the last moment. And when they did spend time together she talked endlessly about Kevin. Abigail was at first puzzled, then hurt. In the course of their friendship she had slept with many more people than Dara, but she had never once changed their plans to meet a lover.

D URING THEIR LAST SUMMER AS STUDENTS, KEVIN GRADUATED and moved to London. Dara went with him and got a job in a holiday program for under-twelves. Abigail returned to Edinburgh and stayed in the flat. She had still not met Mr. MacPherson, her mysterious benefactor, but at the end of each visit, she wrote him a heartfelt letter and, at Fiona's suggestion, left a bottle of wine. In Dara's absence, she continued to go round to the house most weeks. Fiona was teaching her to cook. Her own mother, although capable of producing elaborate feasts, had barely taught her to use a toaster. Now Abigail enjoyed the measuring and slicing, the stirring and blending, and the way in which, amid such mundane activities, conversation occurred. She and Fiona talked at length about Dara—neither of them cared for Kevin—and about Abigail's parents. I had such a boring, stable childhood, said Fiona. In spite of Abigail's veiled questions she never mentioned her first husband.

One evening Abigail's knock at the door was answered by Alastair. She guessed, seeing his suit, that he was newly back from the office, but he greeted her warmly. "Come in. What a pretty dress."

Inside he explained that Fiona wasn't back yet and Fergus was at the cinema. He hung up his jacket and, without consulting Abigail, opened a bottle of wine and poured them each a glass. In the living room she sat in the chair by the window while he settled himself on the sofa. As they exchanged news of Dara, he meticulously rolled up his shirtsleeves, first one, then the other, each fold exact. Abigail watched, amused by his fastidiousness. Suddenly aware of her scrutiny, he looked up with a smile. "What happened to your young man?" he said.

"Which one?"

"The one at the restaurant."

"Luke. That was ages ago. He's going out with the pastry chef. She makes the most delicious éclairs."

"Don't you ever fall in love?" Satisfied with his sleeves, he leaned back, his youthful eyes fixed on her.

"Not yet." She had used the word once or twice but only out of politeness, when somebody said it to her and the pause grew embarrassingly long. Now, to avoid Alastair's gaze, she drank her wine and looked out of the window. The houses across the street were ablaze in the evening sun.

"When I was your age," he said, "I was in love with a friend of my mother's. Rosalind played the flute and had a little black dog she carried around in her bicycle basket. I was tongue-tied every time I saw her. Later I settled for more earthly delights, but I still sometimes think that was the purest feeling I've ever known. I would have done any-thing for her."

"I felt like that about my grandparents," said Abigail. Coaxed on by his questions, she told him about the summers in Chatham, the walks by the River Medway, and the visits to the town of Rochester with its ancient cathedral, and its many reminders of Dickens. "My grandfather thought he could learn everything he needed to know about England by studying Dickens. He said everyone had a book, or a writer, that was the key to their life."

"That's an appealing idea," said Alastair, getting up to refill their glasses. "Does the person have to have read the book? Or is the connection there anyway, and some people figure it out and others don't?"

"I don't know." She was abruptly dismayed. "He died before I could ask him. I do know that he thought of my father as being like Mr. Micawber, overly optimistic about practical matters."

"To put it kindly. There aren't a lot of great choices in Dickens for girls. I don't see you as Little Nell. Maybe Estella, though she's a cold bitch. Better to give up on gender and be poor, blundering Pip. That scene when he meets Magwitch again makes my hair stand on end every time."

She was still registering the word "bitch," as he continued. "There are three great novels about romantic love and they all have great in the title." He ticked them off on his fingers. "*Great Expectations, Le Grand Meaulnes,* and *The Great Gatsby.*"

"I haven't heard of *Le Grand Meaulnes,*" she said, hoping to keep the conversation on literary topics.

"It's by a French writer, Alain-Fournier, who died in the First World War. The same story as the other two: boy loves inaccessible, mysterious girl. Boy loses out. You're probably already too old to read it."

"I'm only twenty-one."

"Oh, Abigail, you've never been twenty-one."

To disguise her discomfort she reached for her glass and, finding it empty, got up to go to the bathroom. When she came out into the hall, it took her a few seconds to realize that she was not alone. Alastair was leaning against the wall, holding another bottle of wine.

"You're a hot little thing, aren't you?" he said in a low, thick voice.

For a few seconds Abigail was torn between running out of the house and kicking him, hard, on the shins. Then she did the only thing that seemed feasible: pretended he hadn't spoken. "I'm going to start supper," she said.

In the kitchen her hands trembled as she opened cupboards and began blindly taking out pasta, onions, olives, tomatoes, basil, pine nuts. Why was she wearing this flimsy dress? She put on the biggest, dirtiest apron she could find, pulled her hair back into a rubber band, and set to chopping onions as if their odor could keep him at bay.

Ten minutes later she heard the sound of the front door. Fiona came into the kitchen. "What a treat," she said. "You're making supper."

"Yes." Abigail could feel herself smiling breathlessly. "I was wondering whether to put in anchovies as well as olives."

"Why not? They'll give everything a little more zip."

At the table the three of them talked and laughed as they had done on half a dozen occasions that summer, but later Abigail walked home with a heavy heart. The safe, well-run house was no longer quite so safe. Why did this have to happen, she thought fiercely. She had never flirted with Alastair, not for a second. He was Dara's stepfather, Fiona's husband, and besides, with his gray hair, his abstruse conversation, it had never occurred to her that he was like the men who eyed her in the street, or cornered her at the restaurant behind the kitchen door.

T HAT YEAR SHE WAS STARRING IN ONE OF THE DRAMA SOCIETY plays, but instead of giving out martinis she went, at Axel's urging, to see as many other plays as possible. Day after day she leaned forward in her seat, studying the actors, trying to figure out what worked and what didn't. Later she would scribble notes and discuss her observations with Axel in person, and with Dara on the phone. Why was Masha's grief in *The Three Sisters* so powerful? How was it possible for a brief shrug to resonate across a theater? What made a one-person show absorbing? Was physical theater still possible?

In return Dara told her about life with Kevin; they had visited Marx's grave, they were giving out leaflets for a local Labour candidate. After they said good-bye, Abigail would wander around the flat, restless and out of sorts. However long they talked, she didn't have the feeling of being understood that she almost always did in Dara's presence. "I miss you," she would say, and Dara would say the same, but Abigail knew that her missing didn't have the same weight.

Dara had planned to spend the last week of the vacation at home, but she kept postponing her return; she couldn't bear to leave Kevin. Finally she came north the day before classes began, stopping in Edinburgh only to repack her suitcases. Abigail had returned to St. Andrews the previous day and had put up a sign on the door of Dara's room— *Welcome back, Dara*—with a red balloon bobbing above. "You idiot," Dara said and threw her arms around Abigail. They went to the local fish and chip shop and sat there for three hours. Abigail acted out highlights of the plays she'd seen and Dara listened and asked exactly the right questions and then answered all of Abigail's. Most of her answers involved Kevin—he would be coming up for a weekend in November; they would see each other at Christmas—but Abigail smiled and nodded. She and Dara were here, together, and he was more than four hundred miles away. As they parted outside their rooms, Dara said, "I forgot to tell you Alastair sent his love. He said how nice it was having you around this summer."

"Wait until I make you the chicken puttanesca your mother taught me."

Maybe when they were older, twenty-five or, unimaginably, thirty, she could tell Dara what had happened with Alastair. For now she must wrap it up tightly, tightly, and hide it away.

D URING THE NEXT FEW WEEKS ABIGAIL DISCOVERED, OVER AND over, that she was wrong about Kevin. He might be physically in London but in every other respect it was as if he were still here. Dara talked about him incessantly. She canceled plans in order to phone him or write letters; she insisted on seeing the films he'd seen, reading the books he'd read. She was too busy to help Abigail rehearse her lines, too busy to discuss arrangements for December. Abigail had spent the last three Christmases in Edinburgh, staying at Dara's house, working at the store and the restaurant, but now Dara was planning to visit Kevin and seemed to forget that Abigail had nowhere else to go. Not knowing how to raise the topic without mentioning Alastair, Abigail reluctantly contacted the last hotel she'd worked. At first the manager said he didn't need anyone but when she agreed to waitress both Christmas Day and New Year's Eve he hired her.

Two days later Abigail was just getting into bed—it was almost midnight—when she heard an odd scraping sound at her door. She opened it to find Dara huddled on the floor, her face red and swollen, her hair tangled, sobbing. Abigail pulled her inside and guided her over to the bed. Her first thought was that something terrible had happened: Fiona had been in a car crash, or was deadly ill. Or Dara herself had discovered a lump, or a virus. When she pieced together that Kevin was the cause of this distress—he'd met someone else—she was so relieved, she almost laughed. "I hope someone else treats him like dirt."

"You don't understand. I can't live without him."

"Of course you can." She knew she oughtn't to scold but she couldn't bear such hyperbole. People couldn't live without food and air and shelter and money. Romantic love was an extra, nice if it came along, but definitely superfluous to the main requirements of existence. Trying to be more tactful, she added that perhaps Kevin hadn't meant it. But Dara had disappeared again into a storm of weeping. She was coughing and gasping for breath, and nothing Abigail said seemed to reach her. At last, at her wits' end, Abigail recalled what Dara had said the students at the counseling center were told to do in emergencies. She got dressed, went out into the hall, and phoned the porter.

"Stay right there," he said. "I'll have someone with you in five minutes to take her to the medical center."

She went to Dara's room and hastily chose a jacket and a pair of shoes. In her own room Dara was still lying on the bed, moaning. She managed to get the shoes on and wrapped her in the jacket. Then the porter appeared and together they maneuvered Dara into the lift, and out to the waiting car. At the center while Dara wept, Abigail told the doctor what had happened. "She won't stop crying. I didn't know what else to do."

"You did just the right thing," said the doctor. With his crumpled shirt and bitten nails he looked disturbingly like a student. "Has she taken anything?"

"Taken anything?"

"You know, pills, booze."

"No, of course not," said Abigail, appalled.

"Do me a favor," he said. "When you go back to her room, have a look. Phone me if you find any empty bottles."

Walking back to the hall of residence, Abigail was torn between fury and worry. How could Kevin have done this? Didn't he know Dara was fragile? And how could Dara be so fragile when Fiona and Alastair were always there? Love was about the people who loved you, which in Abigail's world meant only her grandparents and Dara. Men were strictly for pleasure and for experimenting with versions of the self. What had made Dara give such a large piece of herself into Kevin's careless hands? I never want to feel this way, thought Abigail.

She let herself into Dara's room and checked the wastepaper basket and the desk. In the former were tissues and an empty coffee cup. On the latter was a crumpled piece of paper: Kevin's last words. She picked it up, suddenly hopeful. Perhaps this was merely a lovers' quarrel; she could phone him, get him to phone Dara. But as she read his feeble sentences, any fantasy of reconciliation fled. Dara was wonderful; he'd always think of her as a friend but this was the real thing. Liza worked at the House of Commons, she'd grown up in London and shared his politics and his ambitions. *I hope you find someone who suits you as well,* he concluded. *You deserve it.*

She nearly tore the letter to shreds but it was not hers to destroy. She returned it to the envelope and slipped it into Dara's copy of *Mrs. Dalloway.*

T HE NEXT DAY AT THE MEDICAL CENTER SHE FOUND DARA LYING in bed, her face no longer red but rather pale. Her eyes were closed and, standing in the doorway, Abigail noticed, as she had the first day they spoke, the delicate crease of Dara's lower eyelids, which was part of what made her appreciation of the world seem so wholehearted. She stepped forward and Dara opened her eyes. "Thank you for coming," she said.

"How are you?" Hesitantly she sat on the edge of the bed and studied her friend. Overnight the color of Dara's eyes had darkened and against the pillow her matted hair showed no hint of the reddish highlights that, Abigail had once observed, made her look like Mary, Queen of Scots, in the famous portrait.

Dara shook her head. "I keep thinking about last summer, how we'd race home to be with each other and talk about our plans. When I graduated we were going to work for a year, travel for a year, then Kevin would go into politics and we'd have a baby. We both liked the name Emma. It's as if all that meant nothing."

A baby, thought Abigail in bewilderment. She began to say that Kevin was a rat, but Dara's lips quivered. "I brought you some books," she said hastily. "Ms. Wilson gave a terrific lecture today on Whitman and Ginsberg."

"I need to ask you a favor. Please don't tell Mum. She'd just worry and it wouldn't help anything."

"I won't," said Abigail, startled to realize that it hadn't occurred to her to tell Fiona. Despite all the time she'd spent in Dara's company, she still hadn't mastered the ways normal people behaved. "Promise, though, that you'll try to get better. Think of what you tell your clients: remember the people who do love you, the small things you enjoy. Remember how you rescued me that first Christmas. And that boy you helped to pass his exams last term? He'd have failed without you. And"—she was groping, trying to summon memories that wouldn't upset Dara—"that day we climbed Arthur's Seat with Fiona."

Dara gave the faintest of nods.

T HE FOLLOWING DAY SHE RETURNED TO HER ROOM AND STARTED going to classes again. Abigail tried to make sure she was home every evening; they studied, as they had when they first met, with their doors ajar. If she went out she persuaded Dara to come along. Neither of them mentioned Kevin.

A fortnight after the letter, Dara worked a shift at the counseling center. That evening, she told Abigail that her own despair had helped her to understand that of other people. "It doesn't matter how stupid the reasons are, if you're in the grip of a feeling it isn't stupid. You can't imagine it will ever change." The only thing that did help, she went on, was not being alone. "If you hadn't been here that night, I don't know what I'd have done."

A year ago, even six months, this acknowledgment of their intimacy would have made Abigail happy. Now she said, "What about your family? Your friends? Your work?"

"Everything was hidden by his letter."

"The doctor asked me if you'd taken pills." She felt embarrassed by the revelation but Dara seemed unmoved.

"We're taught to ask that at the first appropriate occasion," she said. "You need to know if you're dealing with a medical emergency as well as a psychiatric one." She did not, as Abigail had hoped, say that she would never do such a thing.

Later, when she was sure Dara was asleep, Abigail paced back and forth in her small room. For months, while Dara doted on Kevin, she had felt herself being relegated to a smaller and smaller place in her friend's thoughts, and that feeling had led her to do what would once have been unimaginable: without telling Dara, she had applied to study drama at several universities, including Yale University in America. Now Kevin was gone and Dara needed her again. But for how long? As soon as another man came along, she would be shoved aside. Yet if she hadn't met Dara in the laundry room she would probably have had to leave St. Andrews. Every turn of the room brought a different, contradictory thought.

A week later, in an overheated tea room, she finally confessed what she'd done. To her surprise Dara said Yale sounded perfect; they would be mad not to give her a scholarship.

"But what will you do?" said Abigail.

And then another surprise, another betrayal; Dara announced that the manager at the counseling center had suggested she apply for a course in counseling at Glasgow; she was thinking about it. Abigail was so upset that she finally brought up Christmas.

"I thought I'd better make my own plans," she said, "given—" She waved toward the steamy window of the tea room behind which lurked the unmentionable Kevin, and, unbeknownst to Dara, her even more unmentionable stepfather.

"I'm sorry," said Dara, blinking. "I wasn't paying attention. God, I feel terrible."

She went on and on until Abigail had to comfort her and say it was fine; the hotel was paying her well. Later, alone in her room, she tried to reimagine the conversation: Forget the hotel, said Dara. You have to come to Edinburgh. It won't be any fun without you. But she kept hearing the words Dara had actually said: "I suppose it's for the best. I need to catch up on all the work I missed."

F ROM THE MOMENT THE PLANE LANDED AT KENNEDY AIRPORT AND she stepped out into the sultry heat, Abigail was enthralled. Once again she was the outsider, but this time it was for comprehensible, even desirable reasons. People had no idea how different she really was. After three years at Yale, she moved to New York to share a house in Brooklyn with four other aspiring actors. Life in America stretched before her; she was sleeping with several men she liked, she was getting parts, she had a waitressing job where they let her off for auditions. When the postcard came from her father—*the doctor says four months, maybe six*—she was rehearsing a new play. She sent back a postcard of the Chrysler building: *So sorry, hope you feel better soon.* But the morning after the play opened she woke to an image of her father, sitting in the stern of a small boat, smiling as the wind filled the sails. Staring up at the cracked ceiling of her shabby room, Abigail knew she couldn't ignore what was happening three thousand miles away. This was her last chance to get revenge, before the tumor in her father's brain beat her to it.

"But I was planning to come over and see you do your stuff on Broadway," he said when she phoned to announce her visit.

"I'm not on Broadway, or even off it."

After all his wandering, he was living in the seaside town of Whitstable, not far from Chatham, when the headaches started. He had moved there after running into an old friend, an oyster fisherman. The two of them had a scheme for selling bivalves directly to London restaurants. But by the time she arrived in Whitstable, ten days after the phone call, it was clear that her father was no longer going anywhere. For the first time that she could remember, he was preoccupied not with the future but with the past. If she had wondered about getting a second opinion, his detailed account of how his parents left Germany in 1938 would have convinced her that there was no need.

That her grandparents were Jewish had always struck Abigail as a small oddity, like her grandmother's hatred of carrots, or her grandfather's tapping the barometer each time he passed. In every other way, with their tea drinking, their gardening, their churchgoing, they had seemed quintessentially English. But now her sojourn in America had made her more aware of Jewish history. She listened eagerly as her father described their heroic flight from Hamburg. They had walked, ridden in carts, hidden in the coal wagon of a train, and finally crossed the North Sea in a herring boat. Once they were settled in Chatham, his father had returned to Germany to fetch their parents.

"My earliest memory," her father said, "is of the night he came back, he and my mother in the kitchen, crying." His father's parents had been too frail to travel; they had both died of natural causes in 1940. As for his mother's parents, that was even sadder. Teachers in a small town, they didn't think of themselves as Jewish and refused to believe that anyone else would. In 1941 they boarded a train for Belsen.

"So why didn't I know any of this?" Abigail said. "I never heard of Hanukkah until I was twenty."

"Hanukkah," her father said dismissively. "When Mama and Papa got off that herring boat all they wanted was to forget this shameful thing that had happened to them, to be like everyone else. That's why they changed my name, mine and my sister's, to the most English names they could find: George and Mary. Remember how Mama used to praise your hair and complain if we cut so much as an inch? She believed when the next pogrom came your hair would save us." He pulled back his lips in the disturbing grimace that was now his smile. "You should put that in a play."

"I'm not writing a play." But even as she spoke she was thinking that wasn't a bad idea. Actors often wrote plays; it would be an occupation for the long days. "Did Mum know about this?"

"No. She wasn't interested in the past, her own or anyone else's. It was one of the things I liked about her. We probably weren't ideal parents"—he smiled again—"but we did have fun together."

"Ideal? You were a nightmare. I never knew where I'd be sleeping, where my next meal was coming from. You haven't a clue what it was like, being dragged from pillar to post, watching the two of you make a mess of everything."

"But look how well you've turned out." He patted his head, as if to quiet the tumor, and shut his eyes.

He had told her he didn't sleep anymore but that sometimes it was too much trouble to pay attention. All her efforts to make him acknowledge his wrongdoing foundered on the rocks of his insouciance. At least you got to see the world, he said. Remember the Channel Islands? The beautiful walk down to the sea?

She remembered the fields of dying daffodils, the empty rooms waiting for guests.

B UT SHE HAD ALSO FORGOTTEN THINGS, AND ONE WAS HER FATHER'S interest in other people, his enthusiasms on their behalf as well as his own. The nurses, who came daily, urged him not to talk so much. What am I saving myself for, he would say. I hope your mother-in-law liked her birthday cake. Did Eddy pass his French test? He read Abigail's handful of reviews and was full of questions. Might she make a film soon? Or a commercial? "You're much prettier than that trollop in the Bacardi ads at the cinema."

"It's awfully hard to get into films. Anyway I'm not sure I'd be any good."

"What about one of those long-running serials? Though you have to be careful they don't put you in a coma or"—he patted his head—"give you one of these."

W HEN SHE HAD FIRST ARRIVED FROM NEW YORK, WITH A RETURN ticket for three weeks later, she had had a talk with her father, using words like "tumor" and "terminal." He had joked, feinted, parried, and tried repeatedly to change the subject. "Okay," he had said at last. "I'm not in great shape. If I could I'd go to the racetrack and fling myself under the winning horse. Or set sail in a small boat for the Azores. Neither of these being feasible, I'd prefer to stay at home for as long as possible. Hospitals are all about rules and you know how bad I am at rules."

"So after leaving me to sink or swim for most of my life you want me to stay and fucking nurse you?"

"Yes. Stay and swear at me and in six months you'll feel better and I'll be dead." He had spread his hands, as if he were offering her an irresistible bargain.

Abigail had talked to herself, talked to Dara, argued with her father, and at last, for reasons she couldn't comprehend, agreed to stay. She took over the living room of his modest ground-floor flat and shopped and cooked and answered the occasional phone calls. Her father was a man with many friends, but the friendships depended on his being out and about. Only the nurses and Yoav, the oyster fisherman, visited. Soon after she arrived, Abigail had phoned her mother. Any thoughts she had had that her mother would rush to her first husband's bedside, or at least commend her daughter for being there, were at once dispelled.

"Jesus, Abby, if he's ill he ought to be in hospital. That's why we pay taxes."

"When did you ever pay taxes?" said Abigail and hung up. That her mother, following the divorce, had turned into the stable, law-abiding person she had long wanted her to be, was another cause for rage. When she told Dara about the conversation, Dara said, "You mustn't feel bad. Some people are afraid of illness." She was still in Glasgow, but their relationship, which had dwindled to occasional letters while Abigail was in the States, had revived. They talked on the phone several times a week.

GRADUALLY, ALMOST WITHOUT NOTICING, SHE STOPPED HOPING that her father would make reparation, or that she would achieve revenge. Once or twice she purposely forgot to buy the newspaper or to get a book he wanted from the library, but he was blithely forgiving—

he didn't need to do the crossword, he could read something else—and her small meannesses gave her no pleasure. He was going to die as he had lived: feckless and unrepentant.

Her conversations with his sister, Mary, in Vancouver, only served to confirm this. Mary had moved to Canada with her husband at the age of twenty-three and come back twice, for her parents' funerals. Abigail had a dim memory of a woman in a black dress bending over her on one of those terrible occasions, the sole person present who seemed to understand that Abigail was speechless with grief. Now, despite her own poor health, Mary phoned often. If George's eyes were closed, she and Abigail would talk.

"George never did have a handle on reality," she said. "Even at primary school he had these schemes. Once he told everyone in his class that if they gave him a penny a week he would provide all the sweets they wanted."

"What happened?"

"He was forced to declare bankruptcy and three of the boys beat him up. Now tell me, do you need money? I can't get on a plane but I can send a check."

Three days later Abigail's bank account had a balance of five thousand pounds, the most money she'd ever had.

I N A FUNNY WAY, AS SHE TOLD DARA, NURSING HER FATHER WAS almost like returning to her childhood summers with their quiet routines. She worked on her play, a fictionalized account of her grandparents' flight from Hamburg. She walked on the pebbly beaches, admiring the seascapes and the brightly colored beach huts. She started fucking one of her father's nurses, Robert, a large, good-looking man with an abundant supply of marijuana. Occasionally she had a drink with her father's friend Yoav. He was handsome in a dark, Israeli way, but he wore his shirt open a button too low and was right on the edge of being old.

It was Yoav who suggested that her grandparents' household, idyllic for her, had been less so for her father. "I know those immigrants and their sons," he said. "They were pressing him all the time to excel, and at the same time passing on their suffering. George is a remarkable man. He refused to excel and he kept his suffering to himself."

They were sitting in the back garden, drinking the sherry she had found under the sink. In the next-door garden the lilacs were in bloom. "Suffering?" said Abigail. "He's never suffered an hour in his life, until now. Did you ever meet my mother?"

"A few times in Cornwall. Anyone could see she was losing confidence in George. She wanted someone who could support her. And maybe"—he put his hand on Abigail's bare knee—"younger pastures suited her better."

"Greener," she said, looking down at his hand until he removed it.

FOR MONTHS HER FATHER'S DECLINE WAS SO SLOW AS TO BE ALMOST imperceptible. He apologized for taking so long. "It's not like me," he said. "I've always been good at moving on." Then, quite suddenly, he was hurtling toward the end. Week by week he ate less, talked less, shat less. Each day it was easier for Abigail to lift him. Soon she would be free to return to America. But one morning she woke on the living room sofa and, like that morning in Brooklyn when she had known she was coming here, knew that she would not go back there. She did not want to be an immigrant, a wanderer. She would make a life here, in London with its many theaters, growing out of a single root. She carried her tea into her father's room and told him. "It wasn't even a decision," she said. "I just knew."

"Did Robert change your mind?"

"I thought we were being so discreet."

He gave one of his grimace smiles. "Is it September yet? If it is what I'd like to do is eat oysters. That's why I moved here, to eat the maximum number of oysters."

It was the second day of September. After she had bathed and fed him, she walked into town and bought a bottle of good champagne and two dozen oysters. That evening she and Robert scrubbed and shucked them and carried them in a basin of ice to her father's bedside. She had arranged various sauces but George was a purist. "Just the sea," he said. "I want to eat the sea." He drank two glasses of champagne and discoursed on oysters and the previous occasions on which he had enjoyed them. He ate five, then patted his head, lay back, and closed his eyes, leaving her and Robert to experiment with the remainder. They screwed once before, and once after, eating them. Neither of them noticed a difference.

TWO DAYS LATER HER FATHER FAILED TO RECOGNIZE YOAV WHEN HE bent over his bed. "Dalmatians," he said, "bred to have no brains. Nothing but teeth and assholes."

Yoav stayed for half an hour, reading aloud from the newspaper. Afterward, in the kitchen, he and Abigail spoke in whispers. "Sometimes," said Yoav, "he's his old self. Sometimes he's someone totally different." They agreed it was time to call the hospice.

The people at the hospice didn't care who George was. To them death was a way station; they helped people to pass through. They tended his body and played him classical music, which he had never liked. Hearing is the last sense to go, they told Abigail. She visited him twice, three times a day. At night she stayed up late, smoking joints with

Robert. Every time she came, she wondered if her orgasm had carried her father over to the other side. It seemed plausible that as she rushed over, so might he. In fact she was sitting beside him on a hot September afternoon, reading "The Little Match Girl," a story her grandparents had read to her often, when something rattled in his throat and his fingers fluttered. She reached for his hand and felt him leave.

She sat in silence for five minutes. Then she told the nurse on duty and went to the phone.

"He's gone, hasn't he?" said Mary as soon as she heard Abigail's voice. "I usually sleep until eight but I woke up a few minutes ago."

Abigail told her how peaceful it had been and promised to call again soon. She left a message on Dara's phone and went out into the sunlit afternoon. She walked through the streets, down over the pebbly beach to the water's edge. She had long felt like an orphan, and now she almost was one. Like Little Nell and Oliver Twist and David Copperfield, she thought, and Pip and Estella. She stretched out her arms and twirled around until she was dizzy. Later that evening she sat down and wrote a postcard to her mother telling her that her first husband was dead.

A YEAR LATER ABIGAIL WAS LIVING IN A CROWDED FLAT IN THE East End of London when she answered the phone and a polite, nasal voice asked if this was Abigail Taylor. Mary had died of a heart attack and left her niece five hundred and eighty thousand dollars.

"Five hundred and eighty thousand? Are you sure?"

"Canadian," said the man.

As he explained the details by which the money would be transferred, Abigail stopped listening. Instead she pictured herself and her grandfather digging in the sands of the Medway. Without luck, he had said, they would never find anything. Now, once again, that mysterious, scary force had intervened in her life. But when she said that to Dara on the phone ten minutes later, her friend said, "Or alternatively your good deeds are being rewarded. Mary would never have got to know you if you hadn't nursed your father. What will you do with the money?"

"I'm going to buy a house," said Abigail, announcing the news to both of them.

The next day she went to an estate agent's and began asking friends about neighborhoods. Four months later she had the keys to a terraced house in Brixton. Built while Queen Victoria was still on the throne, it had been poorly modernized and then neglected, but it was near the tube, had a new roof, and was divided in two, which meant she would always have an income. What had persuaded her to buy the house, though, were none of these sensible reasons but the thought that sprang into her mind at the first sight of the address—41 Fortune Street—that her grandfather would have liked the name. "Straight out of Dickens," she could hear him say, straw hat rocking. The pleasure of that image more than outweighed her own faint twinge of superstition.

She moved in with her boyfriend, Ralph, a stage manager, and together they fixed up the garden flat. They were both out of work and Ralph was handy; within a month it was ready for occupation. A couple of friends were interested, but Abigail didn't trust them to pay rent. How many times had her parents flitted at midnight?

She consulted the estate agent and he told her to look for a tenant with a respectable job who couldn't suddenly disappear. He also recommended furnishing the flat, which made it easier to avoid the opposite problem: someone refusing to leave. She bought a bed, a chest of drawers, a table and chairs, a sofa, and an armchair, and rented the flat to a man who was training to be a surveyor, and agreed to pay cash on the first of each month. She and Ralph moved into the upstairs and Ralph started renovating that too. Abigail was working again. When she came home at night, he would show her what he had done that day. "This is fantastic," she would say. "You're amazing."

He had almost finished the second bathroom—the redecoration had slowed down since he too got a theater job—when one night Abigail went for a drink with another actress. Liz had split up with her boy-friend at Christmas; now he was suing her for half her flat. "At first I thought it was just a threat, another way to make me feel bad, but the papers came yesterday. I bought the flat the year before I met him."

"So how can he sue you?" said Abigail.

Bitterly Liz explained that if you lived with someone for long enough they could claim you had a common-law marriage. The next day Abi-gail phoned the only solicitor she knew to check whether this could possibly be true. Very occasionlly, said Alastair, in some circumstances, but it doesn't happen overnight.

"What if you very specifically aren't married?" said Abigail. "If you've both agreed that that's the last thing you want?"

"Even then, if a certain amount of time has passed, I'm not sure how long it is in England, a partner can sometimes make legal claims. The law is meant to protect people, usually women, who've been paying half the mortgage, sometimes the whole mortgage, for years and suddenly find themselves out on the street, with nothing."

She had been living with Ralph for barely two years; still Alastair's remarks made her blood boil. Who cared if she enjoyed Ralph's com-pany and found him attractive? The idea that he could one day turn around and take half of her beautiful house was enraging. That Sunday morning she asked him to move out.

Ralph looked up from the toast he was buttering. "What do you mean, move out?"

"You know." She handed him a cup of coffee. "Find somewhere else to live. I need my own space. We can still see each other." She should have thought this through, not just launched in over a late breakfast, after a morning of sex. Ralph suggested, as he had before, that she use the top bedroom as an office.

"No, you don't understand. I don't want you in the house anymore."

"Did I do something wrong?" He set down his half-eaten toast. "I love you."

She saw the faint scar near his eyebrow where he had fallen as a child, the bruise on the back of his hand from when they had moved a table last week, and she almost relented. But the house had to be hers, totally hers. "You may love me," she said, "but I don't love you." Hastily she invented reasons. "We always talk about the same things. We never do anything, except work and go to the pub. You don't care about my acting."

"Abigail, I've seen every show you've done. I've helped you go over your lines until I thought I'd weep with boredom. Then I've sat in the theater applauding wildly."

All of which was true. She changed tactics and, completely contradicting the activities of the last few hours, insulted their sex life.

Ralph began to grasp that she was in earnest. "After all the work I've done you're kicking me out? Christ, Abigail, you'd be living in a hovel if it wasn't for me."

Then he asked if she'd met someone else and she said no in a way that suggested the opposite. Better to be a slut than a miser. For several weeks they battled back and forth. Who was this other person, Ralph kept asking. They could work on their relationship. Finally she had refused to discuss the matter, refused to talk to him about anything, refused to touch him. Psychological warfare, he called it, but her chilly silence at last persuaded him of what her arguments had failed to do; he gathered his possessions and left. The next day Abigail changed all the locks, even those of her tenant. It had been a narrow escape but she had learned. So long as she didn't get married or allow anyone to live with her for more than six years, she was safe.

"Also if you charge them rent," Alastair had said, "you're less vulnerable. You're establishing a relationship of landlady and tenant, rather than husband and wife."

"Fine," Abigail had said. "From now on, they all pay rent."

S INCE HER MOVE TO LONDON, SHE AND DARA ONCE AGAIN SPOKE less often, so as soon as she heard Dara's voice, at midday on a Tuesday, she knew that something was afoot. "I got the job," Dara said, and before Abigail could ask what job, poured out the details: she'd applied to work at a women's center in Peckham; she didn't think she had a hope of getting it; Abigail had been away when she came down for the interview. I mustn't get upset, thought Abigail. Lots of things happen in my life that I don't tell Dara, but not things that immediately affect her. Doing her best to conceal that mixture of anger and hurt which only Dara could engender, she offered fervent congratulations.

"So we'll be neighbors again," said Dara. "You'll have to show me round."

"You'll stay here, won't you? I've got plenty of room."

"That would be wonderful." Then her voice changed to what Abigail called her counseling voice, calm and overly patient. "But we must have an arrangement."

"What sort of arrangement?"

"Conditions, so you don't feel like you're stuck with me forever. If I stay more than a fortnight I should pay rent and I promise not to stay more than, say, two months."

"How about three?"

By the time they hung up she was as delighted as Dara. The news that she was the first person Dara had phoned had gone a long way to assuage her hurt. They had not, she reminded herself, spent more than a few days together in nearly seven years. No wonder if communication was erratic. Now once again their lives would run parallel; they would be best friends.

T HREE WEEKS LATER, WHEN THE TAXI PULLED UP IN FRONT OF the house, Abigail had fastened a sign to the door—*Welcome, Dara*— and tied a red balloon to the doorknob. They embraced and carried in her suitcases and boxes.

"This is lovely," said Dara, looking around the high-ceilinged hall. "Show me everything." They went from room to room and she praised and questioned. Where had Abigail found that mirror? Did she choose the tiles in the bathroom? "Oh," she exclaimed, as they came into the living room, "you still have that painting of us on the beach."

"It's one of my prized possessions. Axel looked after it while I was in the States." As Dara studied the painting, Abigail studied her. She was more smartly dressed than she used to be, and her hair was becomingly shorter, but the shadows under her eyes were darker. She looked, Abigail thought, like a woman acquainted with disappointment. For a moment all she wanted was to turn Dara back into the hopeful girl in the painting.

In the kitchen she opened a bottle of wine, poured them each a glass, and began to peel potatoes. When she said she was making Fiona's sesame salmon with mashed potatoes and fennel, Dara said that her mother was the one person she minded leaving. She hadn't told her about the job in advance, and Fiona's tearful reaction had surprised her. "She didn't seem to understand how stuck I felt. Everything in my life—my job, my friends, even my paintings—had become so predictable. Of course I couldn't tell her that I wanted to be close to Dad."

Abigail looked up from the potatoes, surprised. After all these years

Dara still cherished hopes about her father? But now was not the time to ask. "Fiona will forgive you," she said. "We must invite her to visit." Her own relationship with Fiona had been whittled away by time and distance, but she still regarded her as one of the touchstones of her life. The prospect of her coming to stay was deeply pleasing.

By the time the food was ready, it was almost dark. Abigail lit candles, and the sage green wall Ralph had painted took on a silvery quality. As she opened a second bottle of wine, Dara said, "You drink more than you used to."

"I drank before I came to St. Andrews but then I was too scared. There was so much stuff—art, politics, international affairs—that I didn't have a clue about. I felt like a Martian trying to pass. Drinking made me more likely to slip up."

"We didn't think you were a Martian. We thought you were so sophisticated. I was always trading on your expertise at getting jobs. And your looks." Dara pushed back her hair, a comment, Abigail knew, on the massively unfair advantage of her own hair, which she still wore long enough to please her grandmother.

"I was good at getting jobs but really I owe everything to you, and Fiona. You taught me how to be friends, and took me to the theater. She taught me manners and"—she raised her fork—"how to cook. That summer when you were in London, I used to go round every week. It made such a difference, knowing that she believed in me."

As she spoke, she had a sudden memory of the evening she'd shown up in her summer dress and found herself alone with Alastair. What was it he had called her? A hot little thing. Surely, after all these years, there would be no harm in telling Dara, but Dara was asking if she still kept in touch with her mysterious benefactor.

"Mr. MacPherson. No, I should send him a letter. I remember at first I thought it was a miracle: him choosing me. Then I realized your mother was the one who saw what was happening to me—those dreary holiday jobs—and put my name forward."

Dara blinked. "I didn't know that," she said slowly. "I always envied you the flat. I was so fed up with living at home, having to do chores and phone if I was going to be late, and there you were coming and going as you pleased."

Abigail had been sure that Dara too had guessed the secret of her stipend. Now she saw that her friend was upset, either by the news, or by her ignorance. Any idea of describing her encounter with Alastair vanished. Instead she said she'd been passing Westminster last week and thought of Kevin. Did Dara know what had happened to him?

"He's married. Two children so far, according to his Mum's Christmas card."

"What about the politics? Did he get his job in the House of Commons?"

Dara shook her head. "Advertising." She speared a sliver of fennel. "Falling in love is so odd," she went on. "One day you can see that someone is perfectly ordinary and the next the same person is brilliant, unique, amazing. Then, if things don't work out, they go back to being ordinary and you can't even remember what made them so special." She looked at Abigail. "I did like his passion for politics. And he wasn't serious all the time. When we were alone, he could be quite playful."

"You were so distraught when he sent you that letter. I worried you might do something stupid."

Dara gave a little downturned smile. "I'm a great argument for not having poison or guns easily available. Of course later I understood that my reaction had as much to do with my father as with Kevin."

"But you wouldn't take poison, would you?"

"No, of course not." Her voice was firm, her gaze steady. "I may have the feelings, but I also have enough perspective to know they'll pass.

What about you? You still seem so"—she hesitated, and Abigail wondered what word she'd choose—"so resilient in romantic matters."

"Or such a slut. And I suppose you think that has to do with my father too?"

"The ultimate insult."

"Not insult exactly"—though if not why was she bristling?—"just irrelevant. My grandfather was a huge influence but my dad was someone I wanted to get away from, and I did, and then I finally made my peace with him. I'm not looking for anyone to replace him, and I'm not looking for a bank manager either."

"But maybe"—Dara leaned forward, hands clasped—"the reason you keep everyone at arm's length is because of him. You never want to be that out of control again. Which is no bad thing, if it doesn't leave you lonely."

She saw Abigail's pout and laughed. "It's only a theory, Abigail. As I tell my clients, if the connection works, use it. If not, ignore it. So tell me, what would you be doing this evening if I weren't here? Who's the person you're closest to in London? When can I see your current play?"

By the time she finished answering, Dara was struggling not to yawn. "You may have to repeat some of that tomorrow," she said. She kissed Abigail's cheek and headed off to bed.

In the empty kitchen Abigail cleared the table and thought about what Dara had said. She had always assumed that the reason the women she knew praised their boyfriends so excessively was that they needed an excuse to have sex, but if Dara was right—she put a baking dish to soak—it was more complicated than that. An almost physiological change occurred. And perhaps, it was remotely possible, the reason that she was immune to this change did have something to do with her father. She pictured him patting his tumor, eating his oysters. How amused he would be to think he still played a role in her life.

The nearby church clock was chiming midnight as she climbed the stairs. In the silence that followed the last stroke, she paused at the door of the spare room. If she held her own breath, she could just make out the soft sound of Dara's: her best friend here, in her home.

MOST NIGHTS FROM THEN ON Abigail listened at Dara's door. Dara was usually asleep when she got back from the theater, and gone before she got up in the morning, but they traded notes about food and phone calls, and at weekends went on expeditions. Abigail was fond of her adopted city and she enjoyed showing Dara the sights she hadn't seen when she lived there with Kevin. They went to Greenwich and Kew Gardens, took a walking tour around St. Paul's, and visited Southwark Market. And wherever they went, whatever they did, they talked, catching up on the people and events of their years apart. After a few weeks, however, Dara insisted on house hunting. In spite of Abigail's pleas she was resolute. Being alone in the house, night after night while Abigail worked, was not why she had come to London. I can't build my life around yours, she said. We're too different. She decided to look for a room in a shared house, in the hope of broadening her circle of friends. By which, Abigail knew, she meant meeting a man. In bits and pieces she had learned about Dara's last two relationships and how they had fallen apart. She herself, since Ralph, had returned to her old, casual ways.

The night Dara moved out, Abigail arrived home at her usual time. As soon as she let herself into the hall, she was aware that something was different. She stood there breathing in the chilly air, trying to figure out the source of the feeling. Had she been burgled? Had a window broken or a pipe burst? But no, what she was sensing was absence, not presence. Everything she could see, everything she could measure, was the same, and yet everything was profoundly altered. She felt, as she never had before, even after Ralph left, alone.

She was still pondering this feeling a fortnight later when she went to her friend Tyler's house for Sunday lunch. The tube was slow, and by the time she arrived half a dozen people were seated around the table. A dark-haired man was gesturing toward the thick green stalk of an amaryllis. "Every plant has this point," he was saying, "where it's immortal. If it was left on its own, it would grow forever."

When they were introduced, Abigail asked if he was a biologist. "Heavens, no," he said. "I was quoting my O level biology textbook."

"Sean's doing his Ph.D.," Tyler explained. "On Keats."

"With many interruptions. Tyler said you were an actor."

As he passed the bread, she saw his gold ring. "So why did you choose Keats?" she said.

She worried that the question sounded naive, but Sean responded as if the need for explanation were entirely natural. He had always liked Keats's poetry, and, of course, his amazing letters, but what changed everything was a visit to his house in Hampstead. "When I stepped into the room where he wrote, with its bookcases and its tall windows, I realized that this was what mattered to me, not insurance and making a living."

Before Abigail could say that that was exactly how she'd felt when Dara took her to the theater, general conversation claimed them both. As Sean turned away, she caught sight of the blue vein tracing his temple.

SEVERAL HOURS LATER SHE WALKED SEAN TO THE BUS STOP. THEY were almost there when the Oxford bus came into view. She expected him to hurry away, but he said he'd catch the next one and continued talking about the summer he was ten; a bear had escaped from a visiting circus and taken refuge in their garden. A moment later, it seemed, another bus appeared. Sean, in the middle of asking if she'd ever acted at the Globe, stepped back from the stop. Abigail said no, though she'd like to. At last—she'd lost count of how many buses had come and gone—he sighed and said he must be going. He held out his hand, the one without the ring.

"I hope our paths cross again," he said.

"I'm sure they will."

As the bus disappeared into the traffic, she looked at her watch and discovered that, while they stood talking beside the busy street, more than an hour had passed. When she got home, she phoned Dara. She mentioned a film she wanted to see, and then said she'd met an interesting man. "Interesting how?" said Dara, and Abigail refrained from saying that he made time disappear and instead described Sean's passion for Keats. As she spoke, she pictured the vein in his temple, the sense of life pulsing just beneath the skin. Surely no accident that the first words she'd heard him speak concerned immortality.

TEN DAYS LATER SHE HERSELF CAUGHT THE BUS TO OXFORD, ON the pretext of seeing a play, and invited Sean to have a drink. She knew he was married, but what harm could it do to check if that mysterious thing with time happened again? She dressed with studied casualness, her best jeans, boots, a black pullover that set off her hair. In the pub she insisted on buying the first round. She was full of questions about him, and about Keats. What did Sean's parents do? Did Keats make a living from his poetry? Sean answered enthusiastically. While discussing *Endymion*, he mentioned needing to see the Elgin Marbles and she said if he wanted company . . . It was Sean who pointed out that she was about to miss her play.

By the time they met at the British Museum, Abigail was thinking of writing a play about the Romantics. "It would be a good way to introduce school kids to a wider group of writers."

Sean agreed, and told her about his book with Valentine. In a shop on the Charing Cross Road, they found a copy. Abigail held it up beside him. "Ladies and gentlemen, I give you the author of—"

"Coauthor," Sean corrected.

So they moved from one cultural pretext to the next. She was careful to conceal her true motives, and how every time they parted she felt as if someone—Sean? fate?—had thrown a pail of cold water over her. She knew that, if he were forced to recognize where they were going, he would flee. Sometimes after he left, though, she would retreat to the bed they had not used and lie there, trying out the words, "I love you." Had other people been feeling this all along and still managed to go about the world, dressed and productive? But even the word "feeling" was wrong: too small, too common. Meanwhile she noticed that, besides stopping time, Sean had had another strange effect. When she came into a room she no longer noticed who was looking at her. She responded to compliments with an easy, absentminded politeness. Everything, everyone, besides Sean, was irrelevant.

In February his wife went to a conference. Abigail invited him to dinner. Gaily she made them each a gin and tonic, and lured him into the living room. On the sofa he turned toward her. For Abigail, kissing had always been a doorway to be passed through, often quite briskly, on the way to the main room. Now they explored a few square inches of flesh, and then a few more inches. She looked into Sean's eyes and said the words she had rehearsed and he said them back.

The next day after he left, she phoned Dara to announce that he had stayed the night.

"Is that a good thing?" Dara said. "Not everyone has your attitude to sex."

"This isn't sex," said Abigail, and just stopped herself from spouting clichés. Why was it impossible to say anything truthful about the change that had come over her? "People get divorced all the time," she went on. "Look at our parents."

"Four great role models. I wish you luck, but I hate to wish another person harm."

"It's not a question of luck. Sean's marriage has been over for years."

She had listened very, very carefully as he spoke about his wife and she knew this to be true. Everything he said was couched in terms of history and obligation, rather than love and desire. Nonetheless Sean was gone, her bed was empty, and ten interminable days passed before they met again. When he came he could stay only for an hour, and she began to understand that their passion, which she had assumed would immediately, painlessly rearrange their lives, was, for Sean, a source of anguish and confusion.

"Why doesn't he leave his wife?" she asked Dara.

"Maybe he doesn't want to," said Dara. In an obvious effort at distraction she described some of her clients at the homeless shelter attached to the center. One woman couldn't leave her house because of an aversion to doorknobs. Another had been a bank manager until two years ago; now she heard voices and owed thousands of pounds. You should write this down, said Abigail. And Dara said that she was the writer. The play Abigail had attempted about her grandparents had fizzled out, and her plan to write about the Romantics had yielded only the notes she'd typed to show Sean, but now she thought she might be able to make something of these curious and touching stories; after all, she knew about being homeless.

In the months that followed she interviewed the women, and shaped their answers into a one-woman show. She and Dara met often to discuss the play, and to talk about Sean. Abigail had finally asked him the question she'd asked Dara: why didn't he leave his wife? At first he had been dumbfounded. His love for Abigail, he said, had nothing to do with his marriage; it existed in an utterly separate sphere. Gradually, however, he seemed to be coming around.

"I know it's not much consolation," Dara said, "but you wouldn't want to be with someone who could walk away from his wife as if she were a one-night stand."

"I suppose," said Abigail, though in fact that was exactly what she wanted.

After nearly a year she delivered an ultimatum, and went to Paris. She came back resolved to stop asking Sean to make a choice he was incapable of making. She would settle for being the mistress, and perhaps eventually she'd be able to enjoy taking other lovers; her one attempt in Paris had been disastrous. The day after she returned, Sean showed up with his suitcases.

"I can't live without you," he said.

She had been hoping to hear him say these words since their third meeting, but for a fleeting moment she heard her younger self retort, with crisp accuracy, Of course you can. Later, in the middle of the night, she woke quite suddenly to feel Sean lying beside her. Somehow, without a word or a gesture, she knew that he was awake, and that what kept him awake was regret, but before she could say anything, stroke his thigh or kiss his shoulder, she was once again, just as suddenly, asleep. In the morning they made time stop, and she told herself she had merely been imagining his dark mood.

To celebrate Sean's decision they spent a weekend at Tyler's house in the country. Dara joined them, and a dark-haired Welshman fell at her feet. Abigail liked Edward immediately and did her best to make sure that he took Dara home from the pub. Back in London the relationship seemed to blossom, although she sensed that Dara was, once again, being overly enthusiastic and that Edward had some reservations. Then it emerged, not long after Dara moved into the downstairs flat, that he was living with his old girlfriend; even worse, they had a child.

Dara broke the news to Abigail one night while they were making dinner. She seemed to think that the situation was analogous to what Abigail had faced with Sean; to Abigail's mind, it was entirely different. Edward's mendacity changed everything, and she found Dara's response—I'd never have gone out with him if I'd known—bewildering. But the few objections she dared to raise only made Dara cross. Looking at her across the coffee table, Abigail understood that nothing she said could stop Dara, any more than Dara could have stopped her at the height of her feelings for Sean. And then, in the middle of talking about one of her clients, Dara's lips turned pale as paper.

Once she had got Dara safely into bed, and returned upstairs, Abigail had what she would later recognize as one of her few presentiments. She sat on the sofa, gazing out of the dark window, and worrying about her friend. Sean had expounded at length on the many military metaphors for love in poetry: the sieges and skirmishes, the swords and arrows, the victories and routs. Now, as she watched the tree moving in the streetlight, she feared that Dara was not strong enough for the battle that lay ahead.

Mostly, though, she didn't have time to worry about Dara, or about anyone else. After the success of her one-woman show she had decided to start a theater company, and suddenly this had gone from being a far-fetched fantasy to something that was actually going to happen. Once again she telephoned Alastair for legal advice. He began to explain tax exemption for nonprofit organizations and then broke off to say that he was coming down to London in a fortnight: could they have lunch?

"That would be great but I think Dara is working."

"Dara?" Then he said, given Abigail's questions, why not keep lunch just the two of them; he would see if Dara was free for an early supper.

The address he had given her, his club, turned out to be a tall, cream-colored house near Trafalgar Square. When she stepped into the hall, the first person she saw was Alastair seated in a chair, facing the door, his briefcase on the floor beside him. He was not reading the newspaper, or studying a file, or checking his phone; he was simply watching the door and, for a few seconds, he went on sitting there, watching her as if she were stepping onto a stage. Then he rose to his feet and kissed her on both cheeks.

"You look lovely. If you're not ravenous, let's have a drink before we go into the dining room. The place gets pleasantly quiet after two."

He led the way upstairs to a large, elegant room and over to two arm-chairs beside a window. A few other groups of chairs were occupied but the room seemed to absorb all conversation. "So tell me everything," said Alastair, after he had ordered them each a glass of wine. "I haven't seen you since we had supper in America."

He and Fiona had been over in New York and Abigail had taken the train down from New Haven to meet them. They had had dinner on the Upper East Side and afterward—it was a warm summer eve-ning—strolled through the city. Alastair had talked, she remembered, about his childhood in the Orkneys: the sea all around him, the beau-tiful light. Now she briefly summarized what had happened since she bought the house: her acting, the success of her one-woman show, her plan to start a theater.

"And rumor has it," said Alastair, "that you've come down from Mount Olympus and joined the rest of us with our earthly passions." His arched eyebrows signaled his meaning.

"Yes, I'm living with Sean." She gave a few vital statistics.

"And does he pay rent?" Alastair smiled.

"Not at the moment," said Abigail, taken aback. "He's a poor scholar."

"I used to wonder what kind of man would bring you low."

Before she could say that she didn't think of herself as brought low, a waiter was standing over them: their table was ready. As she rose to her feet, she was aware of the wine she had drunk. I must watch myself, she thought. But Alastair had different ideas. After studying the menu, he insisted they start with oysters and a bottle of Pouilly-Fuissé. She told him about her father and his dying feast.

"I can understand that," said Alastair. "I plan to ask for oysters on my deathbed. I have to say I was surprised you came back to take care of him."

"I didn't mean to. I was worried he'd die without my getting to tell him how badly he'd treated me. And then there was no one else."

"Did he apologize?" He handed her another oyster.

"Not exactly, but I finally understood that his behavior wasn't"—she savored the smooth saltiness—"malicious. He really did think he was giving me an exciting childhood. By the time he died, my anger was gone."

Over the main course they talked about her theater. Alastair was impressed by her organization, the funding she'd got so far, and had several suggestions. She reached for her notebook, but he said they shouldn't spoil their lunch. He would jot down the main points for her later.

For coffee they returned to the armchairs by the window. In the street outside dusk was falling and people were going about their normal lives: a man went by on a bicycle, a woman walked a dog. Watching them, Abigail was filled with a sense of how far she had traveled from the marshes of the Medway to this quiet, expensive room.

"I'm afraid I've asked a lot of impertinent questions," Alastair said, eyeing her over the rim of his cup.

"Yes."

"I'm not like this with anyone else, but I feel entitled with you."

"Because you've known me for so long," she suggested.

"No, or only partly. Because—it's a little private vanity—I see myself as one of your authors."

He too, she realized, was quite drunk. "You and Fiona were very kind to me. I don't know where I'd be without you." She spoke both sincerely and automatically.

"So you didn't guess?" He set down his cup. "You're so clever, I was sure you would."

"Guess what?" she asked, even as she knew she shouldn't. What she should do was get out of her chair, pretend to be going to the ladies', and never come back.

Alastair laughed softly. "That I was Mr. MacPherson, so to speak."

Oh, so that was all, she thought, and was amused at the force of her relief. "I know he didn't pick me for my stunning acting. You and Fiona made it happen. She saw how hard up I was, that I hated to spend the summer as a chambermaid."

"No, not Fiona. Me. She liked you but she worried about you becoming too dependent on us. You really had no idea?"

"There was the letter, the flat, the checks."

"The letter came from me, if you remember. So did the checks. There was a Mr. MacPherson, a colleague of mine, and he owned the flat where you stayed, but I paid the rent, and your little stipend. I always enjoyed your grateful letters at the end of the summer. I still have them in my files."

"So Fiona . . . ?" So Fiona hadn't sympathized with her, believed in her.

"Knew nothing about it. It was my secret. Ours," he amended.

"But why?"

"One," said Alastair, holding up his fingers. "I was curious to see what would happen if someone gave you a hand. Two, I was grateful to you for helping Dara to get on her feet. Having you as a friend made such a difference. Three, I fancied you something rotten. As you surely realized that day you came round and I nearly succumbed. Remember we were talking about Dickens, about which book was the key to your life?"

She picked up her handbag and stood up. At once Alastair was on his feet. Before she could move, he seized her shoulders and kissed her ardently, openmouthed. For a moment she kissed him back. And then she was out in Trafalgar Square among the hapless tourists and the scruffy pigeons.

A FEW WEEKS AFTER LUNCH WITH ALASTAIR, ABIGAIL WAS WALKING home from the pub with Sean one evening when she asked him to pay rent. And a few weeks after that, she noticed that she was no longer immune to the glances of other men. The one person to whom she could have confided these changes was the one person to whom she couldn't. Most weeks she ran into Dara but they seldom talked for long and, even during their brief conversations, she found Dara's endless optimism about Edward hard to bear. Her friend had joined a cult in which all dissent was forbidden. And then one afternoon, when she was sitting in her office, two pages slid out of the fax machine, the first a curt note from Sean, the second a letter.

Dear Mr. Writer,

How is it that you don't see what's right in front of your face? Abigail was hanging out with Mr. Cupid in the pub last week and

*again yesterday, for all the world to see. Ask her who was with her
in Manchester last March.*

*You deserve better, Sunshine. Open your bright blue eyes and
wake up.*

A well-wisher

Her first thought was that the author had guessed her secret long-ings. One night in Manchester she had flirted with a young actor and narrowly avoided going to his room. And last Monday, when she and Sean's friend Valentine had a drink—she loved the conceit of calling him Mr. Cupid—she had found herself flushed and laughing. Valen-tine flattered her outrageously and his confidence was attractive. As was his willingness to produce crisp twenty-pound notes to pay for their drinks. During their third round, in the midst of telling her about the latest row at the BBC, his hand had come to rest on her thigh; she had left it there.

She phoned Sean to complain about the letter, and went home to make dinner. She could tell that he did, and did not, believe her; in bed that night she had to coax him. His doubt and his lack of passion justified what happened when she ran into Valentine at the pub the following week. "So listen," she said. "Someone thinks we're screwing around." She told him about the letter.

"Wild," he said. "I wonder if they're watching us now."

"Who knows?" She glanced around the room where there were at least half a dozen people she knew, including the stage manager and the accountant. Then she leaned over and kissed Valentine.

When she drew back, he looked at her questioningly. "'The grave's a fine and private place,'" he offered.

It was an old line but she drained her glass and rose to her feet. His car was parked nearby and every light was green. They both knew, she thought, where they were going and why, but at his flat he seemed nonplussed when she began to pull off her clothes. "Abigail," he said, "are you sure you want to do this?" But she was already reaching for him. They fucked on the sofa and then, a second time, on the floor.

Afterward she carried her clothes to the bathroom where she peed and washed, avoiding the perfumed soap and her reflection. When she came out Valentine was sitting on the sofa, naked, smoking a cigarette. She sat down beside him, keeping her clothed self at a careful distance. "That was fun this evening," she said, "showing off in the pub, but I don't want to hurt Sean."

"Of course," said Valentine. "That goes without saying. I wouldn't hurt dear old Sean for the world."

So we're going to do this again, thought Abigail. The letter writer was right.

O FTEN ENOUGH IN THE PAST SHE HAD HAD MORE THAN ONE lover, but she had never before concealed the fact. Now she discovered that she enjoyed the scheming, and arranging. The company was touring, performing in various towns, most of them no more than a couple of hours from London. Valentine would meet her in dingy Indian restaurants after the show; they would eat quickly and then she would sneak him into the hotel. Sometimes he stayed for an hour; sometimes he stayed until dawn. Afterward, alone in bed, Abigail would imagine talking to Dara.

You persuaded Sean to leave his wife and now you're cheating on him?

He already betrayed me, by regretting his decision to leave her.

And you're doing this with his business partner?

Valentine is Sean's friend. We're careful not to hurt him.

Abigail, that's absurd. Of course you're hurting Sean. Even if he doesn't exactly know he must sense the change.

But it's a good change. I'm much easier to get on with these days. And he doesn't sense anything. If he still sensed things about me, I wouldn't be doing this.

Back and forth the exchange would go, Abigail deftly conjuring up Dara's criticisms, until the knowledge that her own behavior was indefensible, and that she had no plans to change it, would drive her out of bed and downstairs to whatever the hotel had to offer in the way of breakfast and newspapers.

S HE HAD ALSO NEVER BEFORE HAD SUCH A SIGNIFICANT SECRET from Dara. Added to her doubts about Edward, it made it even harder to get in touch, but when they ran into each other at the supermarket in early November—she was buying food as an alibi for meeting Valentine—she was so pleased to see her that she at once suggested a drink. As she waited at the bar of the Lord Nelson, she glanced over at Dara sitting on the banquette, and was struck by how elegant she looked in her gray pullover and black skirt. When she set their wine on the table, she saw that Dara's eyes were carefully outlined and her lashes dark. "How are you?" she said. "You look fabulous."

"I'm fine," said Dara emphatically. She mentioned a new support group at the center. Then she said she'd been longing to tell Abigail about the amazing conversation she had had with her father the day they went to Sissinghurst. All her life she had believed him to be an only child. Now it turned out that he had had a younger brother, Lionel, who died in a rugby scrum when he was fourteen.

"But what Dad has been carrying all these years," she said, "is the fear that he killed Lionel by moving his head. Suddenly everything made sense. Why he was so distant, why he left, it all had to do with Lionel, and his guilt. I'm so glad"—she blinked—"that he finally felt able to tell me."

Within the awkward confines of the table, Abigail reached to hug her. She meant to comfort Dara, but she herself was comforted by her friend's familiar warmth: a constant presence in her topsy-turvy life. "I'm sorry I've been so busy," she said when she was back in her seat. "I hardly have time to brush my teeth."

"Yes," said Dara in her counseling voice. "Sean's told me."

At once Abigail could imagine Sean's litany of complaints: so just, and so inaccurate. And what would Dara say if she revealed that she had left Valentine's bed an hour ago? "I know the touring is hard on him," she offered.

"And the new book is a lot of work. When I ran into him a few weeks ago, he couldn't stop talking about the interviews."

"I wish he'd kept going with his dissertation. I liked it when he came home from the library and told me stories about Keats and Fanny."

"But"—Dara set down her glass—"you started charging him rent."

Perhaps it was the pressure of her other secrets, the ones she could on no account divulge, that made Abigail say, "Your stepfather told me to." Of course Dara asked what she meant and she explained about common-law marriage. "That's why I broke up with Ralph. I couldn't risk him suing me for half the house."

"Abigail, that's insane. Why would Ralph sue you? And poor Sean. I remember your saying you wanted him to feel that the house was his home. How can he do that when you treat him like a tenant?" She leaned back in her seat as if this startling information required a fresh perspective. "So even at the beginning," she said, "you had your doubts about Sean. That's so sad when he gave up everything for you."

Finally, thought Abigail, they were having her imaginary conversation. "'Everything,'" she said. "You sound like we're in a Harlequin romance. He gave up a grubby flat in Oxford and a boring marriage." She was surprised to hear her voice shrill. She had thought she was long past caring about how matters had unraveled with Sean, but Dara could still make her feel terrible. Afraid of what Dara might say next, or she herself, she asked about Edward.

Her ruse worked. At the sound of his name Dara forgot to scold and gave a radiant smile. At last they had a plan. He would spend Christmas with Rachel and Cordelia and then, as soon as the kindergarten started again in January, he would move in with Dara. "I've been meaning to tell you," she said, "that I'll be giving notice. We need a place that's big enough for three."

"You mean Rachel?"

"A baby." Dara beamed. "We're going to have a baby."

"A baby?" echoed Abigail. "But does Edward want a baby?"

"Yes, yes, he does, very much." Edward wanted a baby with her, and she—she smiled again—would have one tomorrow if she could. "I used to think all this talk about biological urges was a male chauvinist conspiracy but now I see babies everywhere. Don't you and Sean ever think about having one?"

"No." Hadn't she and Dara talked about this dozens of times at university? Didn't she remember that it was Abigail who had made the comment about male chauvinists? Furious, she stared at the surface of the table which was marked with so many beer rings and cigarette burns that there was nothing left to spoil. "Let me know your plans," she said brusquely. "I need to figure out what to do about the flat."

She stopped, dismayed. One thing to charge Sean rent, quite another to treat her oldest friend as if their relationship were based on money, but—and this was worse than everything else—Dara didn't seem to notice.

"Of course," she said, reaching for her bags. "Maybe we should be getting home?"

BACK AT THE HOUSE SEAN WAS IN THE KITCHEN, KNEELING BESIDE his upside-down bicycle, wielding a spanner. He barely looked up when she came in. So much for her fear that he'd been waiting for her. She explained that she'd gone to the pub with Dara and, as she put away the groceries, told him the news about Edward.

"Oh," Sean said, his face lighting up, "great. I'm so glad."

His pleasure intensified her own jumbled reactions. "But what if he doesn't do it?" she said crossly. "He's been vacillating for so long. Dara will be crushed if this doesn't work out."

Clearly taken aback by her tone, Sean set aside the spanner and reached for the oil can. As he dropped oil into the gears, he said that not everyone was as decisive as she was. Of course he meant himself but as she listened to him, to his eloquence on her friend's behalf, her distress and confusion subsided. She did love him; nothing she did with Valentine changed that. He finished his speech, stood up, and in one dexterous move turned the bicycle over. She crossed the room to rest her hand on the handlebars.

"Would you like to come to Coventry?" she asked impulsively. "You could visit the cathedral, work at the library."

He smiled and, for a moment, she thought he was going to say yes. "I'd love to," he said, "but I'm afraid my chapters aren't very portable."

Was she disappointed that he wasn't coming? Or that there would be no need to rearrange Valentine's visit? To hide her uncertainty, she kissed him.

EVER SINCE THEIR FIRST CHRISTMAS TOGETHER SHE AND DARA had, when in the same city, gone out for a festive dinner in December. This year, however, Dara said they were both so busy, why not meet when she got back from Edinburgh, in the new year. Abigail had been mildly dreading the occasion but, in the face of Dara's reluctance, she discovered an attachment to their tradition. She suggested breakfast, lunch, a drink—until Dara agreed to a late supper on the Sunday before Christmas. They were both working that day and they made their separate ways to the dimly lit restaurant in Southwark.

For years afterward Abigail would think about that evening and her many failures of attention. If she had seen Dara across the room perhaps she might have noticed how thin she'd grown, might have been concerned that her sweater had a hole in one sleeve and her dark trousers were frayed, but close up she still saw her familiar friend. When Dara filled their glasses and a few drops of wine splashed on the table, she attributed it to clumsiness rather than to Dara's trembling hands; when their food came and Dara feigned eating, moving the food around her plate rather than to her mouth, Abigail carelessly assumed she was, once again, trying to lose weight. The truth was that she was preoccupied. Coventry had brought several unwelcome revelations. While she and Valentine were in bed, he had made a joke about Mr. Cupid. In an instant she had guessed what she should have known all along: he had written the anonymous letter. When she confronted him, he had laughed and said who else. She had laughed too; if she had any power left it lay in not letting him see how upset she was. Then she had fucked him, and asked him to leave. The following morning, when she tried to take refuge in the newspaper, there was more bad news.

Now she confided this last humiliation. "I got a terrible review in Coventry. Not just the play but me in particular. Everyone was very nice about it but I knew it was true. I've got sloppy recently. Please." She raised a hand to stop Dara interrupting. "More than anyone, you know how far I've come. But for the last year or two, I've stopped getting better. I've become one of the scores of second-rate actors who almost make a living in London. I always used to wish that my grandparents could see me act. Now I'm glad they can't."

Dara set aside her silverware. "I'm sorry about Coventry but you're not second-rate. You were fantastic in *The Three Sisters* and you were great in that Caryl Churchill play. Your grandparents would be very proud of you. I know they would." For the first time that evening she sounded like her old self.

Abigail was suddenly unable to speak. She cleared her throat, trying to pretend it was just a cough, knowing Dara would know it wasn't. When she trusted her voice again, she said she'd been remembering something her father's friend Yoav had said. "He had a theory that Dad's lack of ambition was a way of rebelling against his parents. I'm not sure if that's true, but I do know that I grew up believing that you went for walks by the river, had some nasty experiences with rats and factories, and became the world's most famous writer. If I went to school and worked hard, I was destined for greatness."

Abashed at her own naivete she fell silent, but Dara was nodding. One of the first things she'd learned in their friendship, she said, was that Abigail had this core of ambition that she lacked. "We both had our lives fall apart when we were ten, but that only made you more determined to succeed. Whereas I ended up with the illusion that paying my dues as a child meant I'd be rewarded as an adult. But the truth is," she was speaking faster and faster, "and I see this all the time at the center, most people who get a difficult start in life continue to reap those difficulties. Damage gets—"

Abruptly, as if some renegade thought had leaped across her synapses, she broke off. Before Abigail could question her—what happened to damage?—the people at the next table launched into "For she's a jolly good fellow." By the time the cheering died down, Dara was back in counseling mode. Maybe Abigail hadn't given her best performances in Coventry; perhaps she needed to cut down on administration, take some classes. Abigail allowed herself to be consoled. The idea of classes at once appealed.

Over Black Forest cake they exchanged gifts: a biography of a well-known actor for Abigail, a necklace for Dara. They exclaimed and Dara tried on the necklace. In the shop Abigail had pictured how it would suit her new elegance, but now the beads hung gaudy and askew. She was glad when Dara didn't go to the ladies' to look.

There was no part of the evening that Abigail could recall without dismay, but the taxi ride home was the worst. She talked blithely about plans for Christmas; she and Sean were going to Tyler's house in the country. "Maybe the four of us can go there in the new year," she said. "Revisit the spot where Edward fell at your feet."

From the other side of the dark taxi came a sound, at the time Abigail thought, of agreement. Later she realized that Dara must have been choking back a cry of grief, a howl of rage. How could her lighthearted remark have seemed like anything but the keenest cruelty?

In the hall they embraced. As her arms met around her friend, Abigail felt as if she were embracing layer upon layer of empty clothes. "You're so—"

But Dara was already pulling away. "Thanks for a lovely evening," she said. Before Abigail could say more, she had opened the door of her flat and stepped inside.

NINE MONTHS LATER ABIGAIL WAS IN THE LOBBY OF THE NATIONAL Theater, buying a cup of coffee, when a voice said her name. She turned to find Dara's father standing beside her. She had not laid eyes on Cameron since the awful day of the funeral and if she had seen him first she would have slipped away. Instead they kissed awkwardly, and when he asked if he could join her, she said yes.

They chose a table near the window, and for ten minutes they did an excellent job of making conversation. But even as Cameron described his summer in Italy, even as she described the company's new project, Abigail could feel their real subject inexorably drawing closer. Suddenly, mid-sentence, he fell silent. "I miss her every day," he said. "And every day I remind myself that, when she was alive, weeks passed without my seeing her."

Abigail clutched her coffee cup. She could have said almost the same thing.

"I tell myself," he went on, "that guilt is a kind of indulgence, another way of not thinking about her."

"Dara," said Abigail. One night a few weeks after Dara's death she had awoken to the thought that she would never again use her friend's name in the same way, to address or summon her. Her vocabulary was, forever, one word smaller.

"Dara," Cameron repeated. "She was lucky to have you as a friend."

Abigail raised her hands as if to ward off the words. "I wouldn't say that. At every turn these last couple of years I failed her. I kept her at a distance."

"I'm sure that's not true." Then he frowned. "I'm sorry. That's what Louise does: contradicts me, tries to cheer me up. It doesn't help. Why did you keep her at a distance? You were best friends; she lived in your flat."

"I know—I would never have finished university, let alone become an actor, without her—but after she moved to London things got complicated and her living downstairs only made them worse. Actually"—it seemed essential to be scrupulously honest—"they've been complicated for years." She began, as best she could without Dara's help, to describe the arc of their friendship: how her easy affairs had upset Dara, how she had suffered from the way Dara became so absorbed in her lovers. "She used to say that suffering makes you stupid. Maybe that's what happened to me with her."

She asked if Cameron remembered Kevin, and described their

breakup, how upset Dara had been. "The point is that I knew how frail she was, but I thought she'd changed. I thought she believed what she told her clients: you won't always feel this way, take pleasure in small things. The evening she arrived in London, we talked about suicide. She said she'd never do it and I believed her."

"I'm sure she believed herself. But why did things get worse when she moved in downstairs? I remember how excited she was about being your neighbor, decorating the flat. It seemed like the ideal arrangement."

From the next table came soft laughter. A man and a woman were reading a picture book to a small girl. In the midst of her grief Abigail was grateful for these oblivious bystanders. "You could say I was busy," she said, "that I couldn't stand Dara's devotion to Edward, that I found life with Sean harder than I expected, but the truth is I had a certain idea about myself, and someone—Dara's stepfather to be precise—took that idea away. And then"—it was a relief to say this aloud—"I started sleeping with Sean's friend. I didn't dare tell Dara. It wasn't just that she'd have disapproved but that it would have changed the whole way she saw me. I wasn't sure we would still be friends."

Did her answer make any sense? She couldn't tell, but Cameron was listening as if he had taken lessons from Dara, his face intent. "So I began avoiding her. I began not asking about Edward. I began shutting her out. And when I did see her, I was preoccupied with my own problems and with making sure she didn't guess my secret."

For one minute, nearly two, Cameron simply sat there. "I regret to say," he said at last, "that I know exactly what you mean."

Abigail could tell from the sound of his voice how dry his mouth was. She had thought when Dara died that she had nothing more to lose in their relationship, but now she felt the winds of danger blowing. What if Cameron were to reveal something that entirely changed her memories of her friend?

"It was like this," he said. He gazed over her shoulder at a scene far outside this room. "Soon after I first came to London I met a girl called Annabel. She was pretty, sweet-tempered, bright, and when she took my hand, I felt my life had finally begun. She was also eight years old. Her parents were friends of Fiona's and we used to go round to their house. I would play with her, help her with her homework. Nothing more. Then Fiona and I moved north, and I more or less forgot about Annabel. I was happy in my job, happy with my family.

"We'd been in Edinburgh for three years when my father died and—I don't know how else to say this—things started to shift." He described his mother's descent into Alzheimer's, how he'd gone to stay with her and, in his boyhood bedroom, come across a copy of *Alice in Wonderland* with an essay about Charles Dodgson. "For the first time I knew there was someone else like me, someone else whose desires didn't fit into any appropriate category. A few months later a family moved into our street, a single mother, Iris, and her two daughters."

Sentence by sentence he built the case against himself. Once or twice he turned from the distant horizon to look at Abigail, searching perhaps for judgment or condemnation, but she was too busy listening to do either. This was the story Dara had wanted to hear for more than twenty years; she was listening for both of them.

"Ingrid and Dara," he went on, "became best friends. Ingrid was in and out of our house all the time. I was always aware of her, tuned to her frequency, but I was careful not to show it. Or I thought I was. Then Iris invited us to go camping one half-term."

"Dara said that was the best holiday of her life, the last good time."

Now it was Cameron's turn to react as if he'd been slapped. He raised his hands to cover his face, and she noticed how small they were for a man of his size, and how clean.

"This must be more than you want to know," he said, lowering them.

"No," said Abigail. "I want to know everything."

"I'll try to spare you that. What I hadn't realized was that Ingrid's older sister, Carol, had an absent-father crush on me. During our first full day at the campsite two things happened: she fell for an Australian guy, and I took a photograph of Ingrid that I shouldn't have." He described how in the night Iris had discovered Carol missing and roused him to help look for her. They had found her with Mike on the beach. In the midst of the row, Carol had yelled something about him and Ingrid.

"Everything might still have been all right if I'd told Fiona what Carol had said, but when she heard about it from Iris, she got suspicious. She stole my film and developed it. For over a decade I'd been the best husband and father I knew how to be; all those days and hours counted for nothing. She threw me out for one moment, one hundred and twenty-fifth of a second, to be precise, the shutter speed I used to take that photograph. We made a deal. She wouldn't tell anyone and in exchange I'd leave town, let her divorce me, and pay as much alimony as I could afford. She didn't let me see the children for four years."

So Dara had everything back to front, thought Abigail. It was her mother who had sent her father away, kept him from being in her life.

"I think," Cameron said, "Dara could have accepted almost anything about me, I mean acceptance was her job. If I'd been gay, or a thief, or an addict, or a masochist, she'd have understood. But whatever I am, it was a step too far. A couple of years ago I took her to an exhibition of Dodgson's photographs. I thought"—he tugged his earlobe—"it might allow us to have a certain kind of conversation. It was a disaster. She couldn't stop talking about how even if Dodgson didn't lay a finger on the children, he was still hurting them. I don't think I hurt Ingrid but I certainly ended up hurting Dara."

"She never got over your leaving," said Abigail simply. "In one of our last conversations she told me about your brother. I forget his name.

She was so happy that you'd confided in her. She was sure she finally understood why you'd been so distant, why you'd left."

"Poor Lionel," said Cameron. For the first time in several minutes his eyes met Abigail's. "Of course I've wondered if his death was what changed me, what made me different. I honestly don't know. As for telling Dara, she was pressing me again about why I'd left Fiona. I couldn't tell her the truth and I suddenly had the idea that Lionel might help me one more time."

"And what about Fiona? Does she still blame you?"

"I don't know. I hope she's forgotten the whole business. Or, if she hasn't, that she believes Ingrid was a single aberration I put behind me when I married Louise."

"Did you?"

Involuntarily she glanced toward the small girl at the next table. Cameron followed her gaze. "I do my best," he said, "but, as Alice says, a cat may look at a king. My eyes still function in a certain way. I wish they didn't."

Abigail nodded. There was no question of them forgiving each other. "The one thing I can't understand," she said, "is Dara not leaving a note. It seems so unlike her."

"She did," he said confoundingly.

"She did?"

"She tore it up. Sean found it and thought we'd be too upset. He sent it to me a couple of weeks after the funeral."

Sean found a note and didn't tell her. For a moment the knowledge of how much he must hate her was overwhelming. Then it was eclipsed by Cameron's revelation. Over and over she had railed at her friend, never expecting an answer. Now it turned out Dara had spoken one last time. "What did it say?" she said.

Amazingly, astonishingly, Cameron reached into his pocket, took out his wallet, and produced a folded sheet of paper. "For months I couldn't bear to look at it but a few weeks ago I pieced it together and typed up copies for myself and Fiona. These were her last words, even if she didn't want us to have them. There are some blanks where the paper was shredded." He handed the sheet to Abigail.

Wednesday, 24th December

Dear Mum and Dad,

I realize I've never written a letter addressed to both of you before. By the time I was old enough to do so, it was no longer appropriate. I'm glad you're happy and I want you to know that what I'm doing has nothing to do with either of you. And it isn't because of a black   , or hormones, or Christmas. The only thing that's kept me going these last four weeks was knowing that there was an end in sight.

A month ago, on November   I woke up and it was such a gorgeous day that I decided to go and meet Edward. I thought we could walk   rehearsal. There was a pub at the end of his street with tables outside; I sat at one of them reading the paper. I'd been there for about fifteen minutes when I saw a woman and a small girl walking on the far side of the street. I wasn't sure which house they'd come out of but I was struck by how much alike they looked, the same curly brown hair and rosy cheeks. The little girl was skipping and they were   and laughing. The woman was five or six months' pregnant. I was thinking maybe she'd have another daughter who looked just like her when a voice called, "Wait for

I can't tell you what that moment was like. For two years I believed that Edward and I were   a life together. When I got impatient with how long he was taking, I reminded myself

that I could never be with a man who abandoned his daughter.
But a part of me was always afraid he was lying. Sometimes
when   alone in my flat I could feel the fear, stalking me. I
started avoiding Abigail; her doubts made mine worse.

What I saw that day was much worse than my worst imaginings.
That one glimpse of Cordelia and Rachel made a mockery of
every   I'd spent with Edward, made a mockery of my existence.
By the time I left the pub I knew what I was going to do. I promised
myself I'd wait for a month to make sure. Every day I thought
about whether there was any alternative. There isn't. This is the
only door I want to open.

All my love,
Dara

Outside, Cameron led Abigail to a bench facing the river and sat down beside her. Are you all right, he kept asking. When she had stopped shaking, she said no.

"I'm sorry," he said. "I shouldn't have sprung the letter on you. I've had time to get used to it. Well, not used to it, but the first shock has passed. I no longer want to smash Edward's life apart. Or smash my own. However guilty you feel, I suspect I feel worse. You were her friend but I"—he displayed his neat white hands—"held her when she was two minutes old, I comforted her when she had bad dreams and taught her to swim. I tried to explain why people tell lies. I helped her to practice her knots for the Brownies." He laid his hands gently in his lap, as if he were laying the memories there. "I'm afraid I have to go now. I'm meeting Louise for a concert."

He looked at her and, for a few seconds, Abigail saw her friend's high forehead, her straight dark eyebrows, but not her wide, appreciative eyes. Then Cameron kissed her cheek, and walked away.

The Thames was at low tide, the river flowing slow and murky toward the sea. In Dickens's day the mud rakers would have been out, digging for buried treasures, but now the shore, at least the part she could see, was empty save for a flock of gulls. Oh, Dara, she thought. A month wasn't long enough, not nearly, to know if you would feel this way forever. Edward might have gone back to being an ordinary person. You might even have stopped blaming your father.

She listened but she heard only the scream of the gulls, the endless sounds of the city. Since Dara's death she could no longer imagine her friend's side of their conversations, but she did not need her voice to picture what it must have been like that day, outside the pub, to see Edward with his family, the baby she longed for growing inside another woman. What wretched luck had brought her, one misty September morning, to the canal, and then, a little more than two years later, to the sunlit street? Staring at the muddy water, it occurred to Abigail that she and Dara had each, in her own way, tried to deny the power of luck: Dara by her belief that childhood influences shaped your psyche and your adult life; she by her ambition and her belief that if you worked hard you could control almost everything, including your feelings. But her grandfather had been right: without luck you could dig all day.

Years ago in St. Andrews they had sat, cross-legged, at opposite ends of Abigail's bed, and debated the two endings of *Great Expectations*. Dara had championed the original ending in which Pip and Estella meet briefly in a London street and go their separate ways. But Abigail had sided with the many readers who didn't want to read a love story where the lovers end up apart.

"Which would your grandfather have preferred?" said Dara.

"I don't know." Abigail could feel herself pout. "I think he'd have wanted to believe they were reunited but he might not have been able to."

"Like me," said Dara. Her eyes widened, and Abigail could tell that she was pleased with whatever she was about to say. "What Dickens should have done was print both endings side by side, and let us choose for ourselves."

Before Abigail could protest that that was cheating, that you couldn't have two endings, Dara had picked up the book and begun to read aloud the account of Pip's final meeting with Estella. She stumbled a couple of times—usually it was Abigail who read aloud—but by the last sentence her voice was warm and steady.

"'I was very glad afterwards to have had the interview; for in her face and in her voice, and in her touch, she gave me the assurance that suffering had been stronger than Miss Havisham's teaching, and had given her a heart to understand what my heart used to be.'"

Later that same day, Abigail recalled, they had made sandwiches, borrowed a thermos for tea, bought cakes and chocolate biscuits and gone down to picnic by the sea. It was Dara who had brought her camera and Abigail who had asked a man walking his dog to take their picture, which later Dara had turned into the painting that now hung in the living room of Abigail's empty house on Fortune Street. She could no longer bear to call it home; nor could she bear to have anyone, friend or lover, pay her rent.

ACKNOWLEDGMENTS

In addition to the works mentioned by my characters, I also made generous use of *John Keats* by Robert Gittings and *Keats* by Andrew Motion, *The Norton Critical Edition of Alice in Wonderland* and *Lewis Carroll* by Morton N. Cohen, *The Life of Charlotte Brontë* by Mrs. Gaskell, and *A Biography of Dickens* by Fred Kaplan.

Rich Sylvester and Chris Forrest introduced me to several of the key locations in the novel. The Roses and the Shorters contributed in many ways, large and small, to the writing of these pages. With them all, and with Eric Garnick, I share many days that I mark with a white stone.

Roger Sylvester, for more than four decades, has shared with me his love of reading and his encylopedic knowledge of Victorian authors. To him and to Merril Sylvester I owe an inexpressible debt.

Several dear friends read the novel at various stages and offered brilliant comments and advice. I am profoundly grateful to Andrea Barrett, Susan Brison, Richard Ford, and Camille Smith. Whatever shortcomings remain are entirely mine.

My gratitude, once again, to the wonderful Amanda Urban. And my deep thanks to Jennifer Barth for entering so fully into the lives of my characters, and for helping them to find a place in the world.

About the author

About the book

Read on

Insights,
Interviews
& More . . .

Meet Margot Livesey

© Rob Hann, Retna Ltd.

I GREW UP in the peculiar world of a boys' private school on the edge of the Scottish Highlands. My father taught there and my mother, Eva, was the school nurse. Trinity College, Glenalmond (as it was then called), was founded in 1847 by future British prime minister William Gladstone for the sons of clergymen, and situated in a remote place with the aim of keeping these young men free from vice. Even in my childhood, Gladstone's project seemed relatively successful.

Glenalmond was not only a remote institution but a very masculine one. My father was among the few married masters. I, and the half dozen other children, had to be driven ten miles over the hills to attend school in the town of Crieff. Last time I was there I noted that the girls still wore the same grim, grey, boxlike uniform that I had (though Ewan McGregor is a former pupil, so maybe it's getting more trendy).

Growing up in such a quiet place, we made our own entertainment: playing pirates and Robin Hood, building dams and forts, going to the farm to feed the pigs, reading. For most of my childhood I read a book a day. It's no wonder that I came to believe books are the key to life and seldom leave the house without one. Once or twice a year, we made an expedition to the city of Edinburgh, with its dark medieval buildings and its elegant Georgian New Town. My heart still leaps when I get off the train at Waverley Station and look up at Edinburgh Castle.

Despite my love of Edinburgh, when I applied to university I headed purposefully south to the University of York in England, where I took a degree in English and philosophy. Only years later did I notice that we studied no living authors—the curriculum stopped in 1941, when Virginia Woolf walked into the river. After graduating, I traveled for a year in Europe and North Africa with my boyfriend at the time. He was writing a book on the philosophy of science, and a month into our expedition I wearied of exploring cathedrals and castles on my own and sat down to write a novel. Over the next nine months, in campgrounds and cheap hotels, I wrote ardently, and I had filled several notebooks and reached an end by the time we returned to England. When I reread my novel, however, it turned out to be bad in almost every possible way. It didn't occur to me to study writing—I didn't know then that such a thing was possible—but I did know that I wanted to close the huge gap between my reading and my own efforts. I spent the next six years working mostly in restaurants, mostly in Toronto, and writing stories between lunch and dinner shifts.

Eventually these stories crept into print, ▶

❝ For most of my childhood I read a book a day. ❞

Meet Margot Livesey *(continued)*

and a friend told me about creative writing and suggested that I might, by virtue of my publications, be able to teach this mysterious subject. I applied for a job at Tufts University and was hired just before the school year began. I still recall the pleasure of entering a room to talk about Chekhov rather than to ask people how they wanted their steaks done. Since then I've taught in a number of American universities and writing programs; I am a writer in residence at Emerson College in Boston and at Bowdoin College in Maine.

I owe a great debt to my American friends and students, but I still spend as much time as I can in London and Scotland. The landscapes of *The House on Fortune Street* are places I love, and the characters, although largely imagined, practice professions with which I am familiar. I am lucky to number several therapists and social workers among my circle, and for several years I read scripts for a theatre company (though one very different from Abigail's). Two friends are wonderful photographers, and in my teaching I encounter many graduate students. Only Cameron's day job as a chemist was something that I had to actually research.

On my daily journeys back and forth to the school in Crieff, I passed a Roman fort overgrown with heather and bracken. I sometimes think of the ideas for my novels as being similar to that fort, buried in my memory, disguised as just another hill, until life sends me a reminder. My novel *Criminals* began when I was walking to teach at Emerson College one snowy evening and saw a poster of a baby beside a bus stop. What would it be like, I wondered, to find a baby in one of the bus stations of my youth. *The Missing World* grew out of an article in *People* magazine about a woman who had been in an accident and lost

66 I still recall the pleasure of entering a room to talk about Chekhov rather than to ask people how they wanted their steaks done. 99

all memory of her fiancé. His descriptions of their second courtship reminded me of the odd liabilities and liberties of living as an expatriate where there is often no one to correct your memories. More directly, in *Eva Moves the Furniture*, I turned back to the landscapes of my childhood and my mother's gift of second sight. *Banishing Verona* grew out of a long friendship with a boy with Asperger's syndrome: I wanted to show what it was like to navigate the world—especially the world of intimate relationships—from such a different angle.

The House on Fortune Street has two elements of autobiography that I can identify: my own relationship with fortune and my attitude to family history. My life has been profoundly shaped by two chance events: my mother's death from cancer when I was two and a half, and meeting the man who brought me to North America when I was seventeen. That relationship ended long ago but left me with the shape of my present life: living and working in Boston, flying back to Britain whenever I can. As for the legacy of my mother's death, the heartache of that was much deeper and longer lasting. After Eva died, my father married the new school nurse: a woman close to his own age who had no interest in children. Growing up with two adults who were always telling me that a good child should be seen and not heard, I was convinced that being an adult would solve all my problems. I was shocked to discover that early misfortune was no guarantee of later good luck, that it was harder to escape my childhood than I had thought. Yet some people do seem mysteriously lucky, or mysteriously unscathed. What would happen, I wondered, if two women, each with a difficult childhood, became friends, and how would that friendship accommodate the ups and downs of romantic love? ∾

> 66 *The House on Fortune Street* has two elements of autobiography that I can identify: my own relationship with fortune and my attitude to family history. 99

Writing *The House on Fortune Street*

Several significant events prompted me to write *The House on Fortune Street*, but the biggest single source—the climate as it were that allowed the book to come to fruition—was my childhood. Growing up in a small community in an isolated part of Scotland, I was always aware that the adults around me had many secrets. Some were simply things that shouldn't be spoken aloud, like the fact that my stepmother and the mother of my closest friend didn't like each other. But some were more complicated—the hidden desires of the many bachelor masters or what lay behind the decision of one of the married masters to adopt a child. One secret had a very sad ending. A young master had been reprimanded by the headmaster and then left in suspense as to whether he would lose his position. That evening the young man's car went off the road. There was, I learned years later, a note.

The "years later" of that last sentence is crucial. The nature of these secrets was seldom revealed by a single source, or at a single time, but usually unfurled gradually, over decades, in fragments, from multiple sources. The true story had to be pieced together, and sometimes the pieces contradicted one another, or my understanding of earlier events shifted in the light of new information. I wanted to write a novel that embodied this jigsaw puzzle process, hence my decision to tell the story through the eyes of four characters who think they know one another better than they do.

One other childhood source was my relationship at the age of twelve or thirteen with a married man who ran the local sailing club. George was surprisingly kind to me. I welcomed his generosity, and no line was ever crossed, but much later I realized that

> **Growing up in a small community in an isolated part of Scotland, I was always aware that the adults around me had many secrets.**

the adults around me had been concerned about his motives. In writing about Dara's father, Cameron, I drew on these events to ask a more universal question: What happens if you love the wrong person, as a friend, as a lover, as an object of desire, or even as a family member?

But none of these preoccupations would have found its way onto the page without the help of a young man who became my neighbor in London in the late nineties. A graduate student, he supported himself by working as a ghostwriter. His current project, he told me, was a handbook to euthanasia. Over the course of the next year, I ran into him periodically, and each time he seemed gloomier and more disheveled. Eventually he began to spend most of his time sitting on the pavement outside his house, until one afternoon a middle-aged couple appeared and took him away. Soon after his departure I began writing a novella about a young man, Sean, who is hired to work on a similar project and who doesn't notice that his neighbor Dara is sinking into despair.

The novella failed in a number of ways, not least because it didn't do justice to the suicide that was its central event. I put it aside to work on first *Eva Moves the Furniture* and then *Banishing Verona*, but the characters and the situation stayed with me; when, after an absence of nearly seven years, I returned to those pages, I found that I knew what I wanted to do. I began at once to write the second section, which is told by Cameron. How could I have imagined that a suicide didn't involve family history?

While the events of my childhood provided the essential climate of the book, I should also add that my adult life in America influenced *The House on Fortune Street*. Living in a country where people talk more freely about their deeper feelings, and where theories of the self are openly debated, has made me ▶

> 66 But none of these preoccupations would have found its way onto the page without the help of a young man who became my neighbor in London in the late nineties. 99

more conscious of how damage gets passed down in families and how, despite our adult freedoms, it can be painfully difficult to escape childhood legacies. A therapist friend introduced me to the theory of the wounded caregiver, the person who becomes a therapist not realizing the degree to which she's motivated by her own needs. I at once realized that this was exactly the model for Dara, a person whose pain is camouflaged by her solicitude towards others.

The other major decision that I made in returning to the material was to give each character what I call a "literary godparent." Sean, the graduate student/writer of the first section, was doing his dissertation on Keats, and so it had seemed natural to draw on Keats's letters, with their wonderful discussions of romantic love, art, passion, and ambition. I decided the other characters should also have a book or author who accompanies them throughout their section and who points to their deepest concerns. Charles Dodgson, better known as Lewis Carroll, the author of *Alice's Adventures in Wonderland*, seemed the perfect godparent for Cameron. I made Cameron, like Dodgson, an ardent amateur photographer who expresses his yearning for young girls through photography. Dara herself was accompanied by *Jane Eyre* and Charlotte Brontë. Of course Dara hopes that her life will turn out like Jane's—I had fun re-creating the famous first meeting between Jane and Rochester—but unfortunately she follows more closely in Brontë's own footsteps. And for Dara's best friend Abigail, the actress, Charles Dickens, with his love of theatre, his huge ambitions and insecurities, seemed the ideal godparent. Like Dickens, Abigail experiences the happiest years of her childhood around the town of Chatham,

❝ The other major decision that I made . . . was to give each character what I call a 'literary godparent.' ❞

8

southeast of London. Then she comes to the city to seek her fortune.

I've never written a novel that I thought was easy, but the structure of *The House on Fortune Street* made it a particularly complicated undertaking, and there were many moments of despair. It was only as I embarked on the last section, Abigail's section, that I began to really believe that the jigsaw puzzle would come together and that this way of telling a story could yield profound satisfactions. ～

Author's Picks
Favorite Books

The following list appears in "Meet the Writer," an exclusive interview with Margot Livesey conducted by BN.com. Reprinted by permission of Barnes & Noble.

• *Jane Eyre* by Charlotte Brontë
   I read this novel when I was twelve or thirteen and identified passionately with Jane. I was almost an orphan, I went to a school I detested, and I was still waiting for Rochester to fall off his horse at my feet.

• *Sunset Song* by Lewis Grassic Gibbon
   The Scottish journalist Lewis Grassic Gibbon wrote this novel after writing many books of nonfiction and shortly before his early death. The book is set on a small farm outside Aberdeen, where Grassic Gibbon grew up, and revolves around Chris Guthrie, the farmer's daughter, who is torn between her loyalty to the land and her love of education. The ending brings tears to my eyes every time.

• *Parade's End* by Ford Madox Ford
   Ford's novel *The Good Soldier* is frequently mentioned in literary circles for its wonderful depiction of jealousy and betrayal, but I'm even more interested in his stupendous novel *Parade's End* and his ruined hero Christopher Tietjens. Tietjens is a good man who almost always acts in his own worst interests. The scenes with his ex-wife are hair-raising and the account of the First World War, and the battles behind the battles, is remarkable.

• *The Fountain Overflows* by Rebecca West
   From the moment I read the opening sentence, "There was such a long pause that I wondered whether my Mamma and my Papa were ever going to speak to each other again,"

I was hooked on this gorgeous, eccentric novel about a family of musicians.

• *Invisible Cities* by Italo Calvino
Surely everyone who reads this book is captivated by Calvino's inspired account of the imaginary cities that the explorer Marco Polo describes to Kublai Khan. And surely we can't help inventing our own cities.

• *Memoirs of Hadrian* by Marguerite Yourcenar
At my detestable school (and later at one I quite liked) one of my great pleasures was studying Latin. I loved the smug feeling of suddenly understanding the origins of certain words. And I loved reading about gods and heroes and adventures. *Memoirs of Hadrian* is not an easy book, but if you can make it through the first twenty or thirty pages then you're in for an amazing experience. How often does a book make you feel that you're on intimate terms with a man who ruled the ancient world?

• *Lolita* by Vladimir Nabokov
I laughed, I cried, I sighed with readerly delight and writerly envy. Recently my pleasure in Nabokov's tour de force was deepened by reading *The Annotated Lolita*.

• "A Simple Heart" by Gustave Flaubert
My childhood was full of elderly aunts, women who'd lost their husbands or lovers or sons—or the possibility thereof—in two world wars, and all these women were devoted to housework. So I responded strongly to Flaubert's beautiful story of a housemaid who ends up giving most of her affection to a parrot.

• *The Collected Stories of Mavis Gallant*
This marvelous Canadian writer, who has spent most of her adult life in Paris, does more in a short story than many writers do in a

Author's Picks (*continued*)

novel. Her stories are beautifully crafted, sophisticated, engaging, and, in the best way, utterly surprising.

• *William Trevor: The Collected Stories*
    Over and over again this great Irish writer with his brilliant prose and his inexhaustible gift for empathy, shines a light on the secret, carefully hidden lives of his seemingly ordinary characters and in doing so shines a light on our lives.